Honora and Arthur - the

Honora and Arthur
- the Last Plantagenets

Love and loss in Tudor times

Based on a true story

Joanne McShane

YouCaxton Publications
Oxford & Shrewsbury

Copyright © Joanne McShane 2019

The Author asserts the moral right to
be identified as the author of this work.

ISBN 978-1-912419-83-8
Printed and bound in Great Britain.
Published by YouCaxton Publications 2019
YCBN: 01

All rights reserved. No part of this publication may be reproduced,
stored in a retrieval system, or transmitted in any form or by
any means, electronic, mechanical, photocopying, recording or
otherwise, without the prior permission of the author.

This book is sold subject to the condition that it shall not, by
way of trade or otherwise, be lent, resold, hired out or otherwise
circulated without the author's prior consent in any form of binding
or cover other than that in which it is published and without a
similar condition including this condition being imposed on the
subsequent purchaser.

YouCaxton Publications

enquiries@youcaxton.co.uk

To Frank, without whose encouragement and support I would have lost heart.

Contents

1. Stowe

Chapter One	1
Chapter Two	8
Chapter Three	21
Chapter Four	32

2. Umberleigh

Chapter Five	40
Chapter Six	51
Chapter Seven	57
Chapter Eight	69
Chapter Nine	73

3. Soberton

Chapter Ten	79
Chapter Eleven	99
Chapter Twelve	106
Chapter Thirteen	118

4. Calais

Chapter Fourteen	130
Chapter Fifteen	139
Chapter Sixteen	154
Chapter Seventeen	169
Chapter Eighteen	181
Chapter Nineteen	194
Chapter Twenty	201
Chapter Twenty One	210
Chapter Twenty Two	219
Chapter Twenty Three	225
Chapter Twenty Four	249
Chapter Twenty Five	260

Chapter Twenty Six　　　　　　　　　　273
Chapter Twenty Seven　　　　　　　　292

5. Return To Umberleigh

Chapter Twenty Eight　　　　　　　　303
Chapter Twenty Nine　　　　　　　　314
Chapter Thirty　　　　　　　　　　　327
Chapter Thirty One　　　　　　　　　340
Chapter Thirty Two　　　　　　　　　352
Chapter Thirty Three　　　　　　　　366
Chapter Thirty Four　　　　　　　　 379
Chapter Thirty Five　　　　　　　　　391
Chapter Thirty Six　　　　　　　　　　402

Epilogue　　　　　　　　　　　　　　412
Author's Note　　　　　　　　　　　　414

THE PLANTAGENET FAMILY TREE

Edward IV King of England ~ Elizabeth Wayte

Arthur Plantagenet = Elizabeth Dudley Grey (First Wife)

Elizabeth Plantagenet = Francis Jobson

Bridget Plantagenet = William Carden

Frances Plantagenet = John Basset

Honora Basset

Arthur Basset

THE BASSET FAMILY TREE

John Basset = Elizabeth Dennis (First Wife)

- Anne = James Courtenay
- Margery = William Marres
- Jane
- Thomasine

John Basset = **Honora Grenville** (Second Wife)

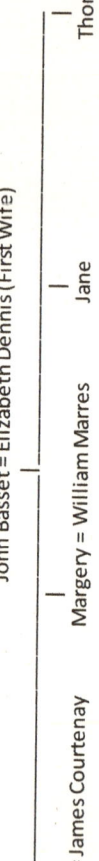
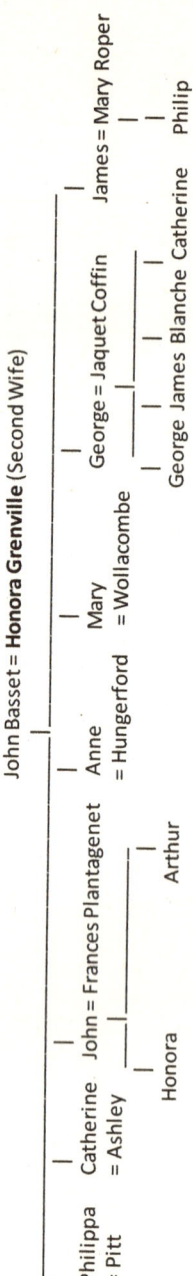

- Philippa = Pitt
- Catherine = Ashley
- John = Frances Plantagenet
  - Honora
- Arthur
- Anne = Hungerford
- Mary = Wollacombe
- George = Jaquet Coffin
  - George, James, Blanche, Catherine
- James = Mary Roper
- Philip

THE GRENVILLE FAMILY TREE

Thomas Grenville = Elizabeth Gilbert (First Wife)

Philippa	Catherine	Mary	Agnes	**Honora**
= Harris (1)	= Arundel	= Bluet (1)	= Roscarrock	= Basset (1)
= Arundel (2)		= St Aubyn (2)		= Plantagenet (2)
= Stennings (3)				

Jane
= Arundel (1)
= Chamond (2)

Roger = Margaret Whitleigh

Richard = Maud Bevil

Roger = Thomasine Cole

Richard

Thomas Grenville = Jane Hill (Second Wife)

Jane = Baton   John (Reverend)

1. STOWE

Chapter One

20th October 1562

A messenger arrived today with the news that the Queen is ill with the pox and is not expected to live. Indeed, in the time it has taken the news to reach us, the whore's daughter has probably breathed her last and finally, England can be rid of the curse of the Tudors and can slowly heal herself of the misery they have caused.

I have been on this earth over seventy years now, a great age and hearty with it. They say some thrive on trouble and it seems I must be one of that kind. For trouble has certainly been my bedfellow at times. But I have lived – Lord how I have lived! I, Honora Grenville of Stowe, daughter of a Cornish gentleman, achieved my dreams and in the end, after all the glory, found them sadly wanting.

But those days are long past and now I am to spend my time quietly at Tehidy with George's children about me, reminding me of the old days at Umberleigh and Soberton when my own children were small. It is so very easy to sit listening to their chatter, allowing my mind to drift back to the past, to how it all began …

I came into the world howling and screaming (if my brother Roger was to be believed) one summer night in 1491. I was my mother's seventh child and only a few hours after bringing me into the world she passed away. She was a Gilbert, from a long-established Devonshire family. My father's family, the Grenvilles, have been in Cornwall since the Conqueror's time.

Our Cornish manor and the place of my birth is situated on the wild north coast at Stowe. It is an area of barren hills, buffeted mercilessly by the wild Atlantic storms which blow in suddenly and violently, flattening all in their path and throwing unwary ships against the rocky and unforgiving cliffs. But it is also a place of haunting and addictive beauty. If one knows where to look there are hidden valleys between the hills where the wind does not blow so fiercely and where trees and wild animals abound. In these sheltered valleys small rivulets trickle their crystal-clear waters to the sea. Wildflowers and mosses grow there and the sun filters warmly through the trees. One such place very near our house is the Coombe valley, where I used to ride as a child and where I would sit on the mossy riverbank and dream of one day becoming a grand lady of the Court.

Our house at Stowe was and still is the grandest manor house in the whole of north Cornwall. The Grenvilles have long been one of the most influential families in the West Country and my father was one of King Henry the Seventh's leading advisors. The house is situated in a sheltered depression between three hills, quite close to the coast. If one climbs the rise next to the house up to the chapel, one can see the sea on a clear day. The high road approaches the house from the south-west and dips sharply

Chapter One

as it nears the entrance to the main courtyard. It is built of granite blocks and roofed with slate tiles.

To the right along the south wall as one enters the courtyard are the stables and farriers' workshop, then come the kitchen and buttery. The house itself is a long, two-story edifice at the far end of the enclosure. Most of the ground floor is occupied by the hall and a smaller family dining chamber. At the end of the hall is an oriel chamber from which my father's parlour was reached. Next to that are the stairs to the bedchambers above. It is a solid and comfortable house, well suited to withstand the savage climate of the north Cornish coast.

That same summer of my birth another baby came into the world in faraway London – a boy-child named Henry Tudor. This child was the second son born to King Henry the Seventh and his wife, Elizabeth of York, and so was not expected to feature greatly in the politics of the nation. If only some portent or soothsayer had been able to predict the misery which this baby would one day inflict on this country and its people, he would in all likelihood have been strangled at birth.

Just three months after my mother's death my father married again. His new wife, far from becoming anything like a mother to me, left the care of me to nursemaids and set about having babies of her own. She remains a shadowy and distant figure in my memory.

When I was two my oldest sister Jane left to get married. Years later she told me how it had broken her heart to leave me when she went off to marry John Arundel of Trerice. It was a good marriage and despite her protests my father would not let her stay. With six daughters to marry off and an offer like this from the son of one of the grandest old families in Cornwall, he was not about to let sentiment get in the way of good business.

My brother Roger also married about this time. His wife was Margaret Whitleigh, an heiress from Devonshire. I cannot recall the time before this. Margaret was a part of our household for as long as I can remember. She was a good and kind person and was the only mother-figure I ever knew.

Our house filled once more with children. Apart from my half siblings, I soon had a bevy of nephews and nieces surrounding me. My nephew Richard was born when I was three. From the start I took a dislike to him. He was a true Grenville, red-haired and aggressive. He screamed constantly for attention and, because he was her first baby, Margaret was able to give him all her time. He continued to expect this kind of veneration throughout his life and I often felt that what he really needed was a good sound thrashing. He was a clever little opportunist who manipulated people at every turn to do his bidding. He was a charming and fickle friend and a malicious enemy. We were thrown together as children and again as adults, but we never liked each other.

I was a contented but solitary child, much more of a Gilbert in appearance than a Grenville. My hair was dark, and my complexion pale. I never grew tall like the rest of my family but am short of stature and slight of figure. I spent my early days roaming both indoors and out, exploring every corner. There were always so many people about and so much going on that I was never short of someone to talk to. In fact, I spent a good deal of time looking for places where I could be alone.

Chapter One

One of my favourite places was the chapel – St Christina's. This was built on a rise just away from the house. It was a quiet and holy place furnished with an altar of oak, carved intricately, and smelling of age and oil. There were always candles burning in the chapel, which flickered in the semi-darkness and created an ethereal atmosphere of movement and stillness. Shadows danced on the altar where the body of Christ was kept. There were statues of Jesus and Mary, of which my favourite was Jesus. He had sad, kind eyes and I always felt as if I had to be good so as not to upset him and make those eyes even sadder. I whispered to him that I would do anything to make him happy and used to gaze up at him with devotion; he would nod and smile at me in the flickering candlelight. I spent hours in there with Jesus and the candles and was usually frozen when I came out, so my next stop would almost invariably be the kitchen.

This was so different from the chapel that I would experience a strange sensation of unreality when I first entered. In the kitchen all was bustle and warmth. Cook was a huge woman who ruled her domain uncontested. The maids scurried about, preparing monstrous amounts of food for our populous household and frequent guests. Despite the constant hurry and activity, it was a happy place, and Cook always gave me a biscuit or pastry and called me her 'little lamb'. The fireplace in the kitchen was huge and occupied the whole end wall. It was always filled with pots and pans which simmered and bubbled. As I grew older Cook allowed me to perform small tasks and over the years, I became quite a good cook myself. The feeling of happiness I experienced in the kitchen at Stowe is one of my most vivid memories. To this day, when I am distressed, I can find solace in a kitchen.

Another favourite place was a narrow seat under the bay window of the oriel chamber. There was a screen partially covering one side and I was just able to squeeze in behind it and sit hidden on the seat, savouring the warmth of the sun. From there I could see anybody who approached on the high road and at the same time could hear everything that took place in the hall and in the parlour, where my father spent much of his time and received his guests. As a result of this I overheard many conversations which I was undoubtedly not supposed to hear, and which meant nothing to me at the time. I can remember feeling very excited by these conversations but at the same time quite nervous because I knew I risked punishment if I was found.

My earliest clear memory occurred one summer's day when I was six years old. I was sitting in my window seat hidden by the screen when I saw horses approaching, then heard the sounds of men's voices entering the hall. My father greeted the men and brought them past where I sat and into his parlour. I can remember that they sounded hot and tired and their voices were strained and anxious. Quiet as a mouse, I sat and listened.

They were talking very seriously about someone called Perkin Warbeck and of a rebellion and more taxes and it was all terribly confusing but very exciting as well. I do not know how long I sat there listening, but it must have been quite a while and I had been sitting so still and quiet, straining to hear the voices behind the door, that my foot had gone to sleep. In trying to ease the pressure of it in my cramped space I knocked the screen, which fell with a crash

Chapter One

and in my shock, I fell off my perch and landed on top of it with my kirtle in disarray and my bonnet askew over one eye. The parlour door opened, and three brawny sets of stockinged legs appeared in my line of vision.

'Well, well,' I heard one of the men say, 'it seems my little sister-in-law has got herself in a bit of bother.' I looked up and recognised my sister Jane's husband, John Arundel.

My father was not so indulgent. 'Honora!' he boomed. 'What is the meaning of this?'

My shock turned to dismay and I dissolved into tears. The sobs were rapidly turning to hysteria when I felt a pair of strong arms beneath mine and I was lifted to my feet. I looked up and beheld a pair of sad, kind eyes exactly like those I prayed to daily in the chapel.

'Jesus?' I whispered, awestruck.

Then my cheeks flamed as my father began to laugh.

'Well, John Basset, I have long admired you but have never quite endowed you with divine qualities! Get along with you now, Honora, we have important matters to discuss.' And with that he slapped me smartly on the rump and I was sent packing.

That was how I first met John Basset of Umberleigh.

Chapter Two

My father seemed to forget the incident of the screen because he never mentioned it again. He was a very busy man and spent much time away in London as he rose in power and wealth under Henry VII. Our family escaped the burden of heavier taxes imposed on other families after Perkin Warbeck's rebellion because of his position at Court.

Only a week or two after that first meeting with John Basset I was playing in the stable yard with my half-brother, John. It was a warm summer morning and we were intent on a game we had invented which consisted mainly of rolling large round pebbles towards a circle drawn in the gravel, or so I remember. In any case we were thoroughly engrossed in our game when we heard the sound of a lone horse approaching. I recognised Mister Basset as soon as he drew rein.

'Good morning, Mistress Honora and Master John,' he said gravely as he passed us. Then without another word he entered the house.

My curiosity, as usual getting the better of me, I followed. My father met him in the hall, and they spoke there.

'John, I had not expected to see you again so soon,' I heard my father say. 'You are lucky to catch me; I was on the point of leaving for London.'

'I had not expected to return to Stowe so soon either if upon my return to Umberleigh last week I had not received the news that my house at Tehidy is no more.'

'How so?' my father asked in a shocked tone. 'Has it burnt?'

Chapter Two

'Not burnt, but dismantled by rebels,' answered Mister Basset. 'It seems I am unpopular with the masses for supporting the King and not the rebellion. So, they have removed my house for me and dispersed the materials throughout southern Cornwall.'

'Did they harm your servants?' enquired my father.

'No harm was done to man nor beast,' Mister Basset said. 'The intention was only to teach me a lesson as far as I can gather. I am on my way there now to inspect the damage and to begin rebuilding.' He gave a wry, mirthless laugh. 'There is more than one way to get yourself a new house I suppose. But I came this way to ask if you have one or two good stonemasons you can lend me for the work. The more skilled men I can gather, the sooner Tehidy can be rebuilt.'

'Certainly, John, take whichever of my men you can put to good use down there,' replied my father genially. 'There are far too many living off the fat of the land here at the moment anyway.'

And with that my father slapped him on the back and they moved away towards the parlour. Seeing me standing at the end of the hall, my father called to me.

'Honora, please ask the kitchen to send refreshments to my parlour.'

Mr Basset smiled at me and they were gone. I dealt with the errand for my father then returned to the stable yard and to my game with John. After a short time both men came out of the house. They went down to the stables and spoke to several of the men there who had tried unsuccessfully to look busy when they saw my father approaching. Then, after saying goodbye to Mister Basset my father shouted an order to his groom to have his horse ready in half an hour and went back inside. Mister Basset came over to us.

'What are you playing, children?' he enquired politely.

'It has not got a name,' replied John. 'We just play because we like playing.'

'You are a lucky boy to have a sister like Honora,' said Mister Basset to him. 'You will make sure you are always kind to her, will you not?'

'Oh yes, Sir,' John said sincerely. 'Honora is my best friend in the whole world.'

'I am glad to hear it, very glad to hear it,' said Mister Basset gently. I thought him the nicest man I had ever met, so unlike my own father who was always giving orders and shouting at people.

My sister-in-law, Margaret, continued having a baby every year or so and at some stage my stepmother died, but she had made such a small impression on my life that I hardly noticed her passing.

I became very fond of my brother John. He was a good, quiet boy and was viciously bullied by my nephew Richard even though he was older. I was always able to control Richard with my sharp tongue, so John came to regard me as his protector.

One blustery spring afternoon when I was about ten, I had been in the stables watching the farrier at work. He and his apprentice had been chatting amicably as they hammered the horseshoe into shape. I loved to listen to the talk of the men; it made me feel grown up and important.

'It is blowing up rough this afternoon, William,' said the farrier in a pause between blows. His strong arm glistened with sweat in the afternoon light and each time he raised it

Chapter Two

above his head tiny droplets ran along his skin then splashed away in the sunlight as he brought the hammer down and struck the iron.

'There will be a fierce storm tonight,' he said at the next raising of his arm. Then crash, down the hammer came again.

I was entranced with this talk, crash, talk, crash and with the shimmer of his perspiration as he worked. By the time I came away the wind had increased to such an extent that it blew me sideways as I turned towards the house. I moved over closer to one of the barns where the wall provided some little shelter from the buffeting.

As I passed the half open barn door a faint movement within caught my eye. Curious, I entered the gloomy interior. At first, I saw no-one, then Richard closely followed by John emerged from behind some old boxes. John's clothes were torn and dusty and his knees were scraped and bleeding. I could see that he had been crying.

'What has happened?' I asked.

The boys remained silent.

'Tell me, Richard!' I demanded angrily. 'What happened?'

'It was John,' Richard said, 'he knocked the nest down.' He ran out then and John slipped past me and quickly followed him.

I looked down to the floor where there was a mess of broken eggs and owl pellets. Above me the barn owl mother was flying about in distress. There was nothing I could do but I knew in my heart that my gentle brother would never have done such a thing unless goaded. Promising myself that I would get to the bottom of it, I closed the barn door and headed for the house. The wind was so strong now that

I had difficulty even walking that short distance as the gusts nearly blew me off my feet.

John and Richard were both very quiet at supper that night and at one stage I am sure I saw Richard kicking John under the table. By bedtime, the storm was raging. As we made our way upstairs, we could hear the slates being torn from the roof and flung away by the gale.

Sleep was very hard to come by with all the noise and several hours after I had retired, during a brief lull in the storm, I thought I heard faint sobbing coming from somewhere outside my chamber. I went to investigate and found John kneeling on the floor outside his own bedchamber. His hands were folded in prayer and he was crying as if his heart would break.

'John, my love, what is it?' I asked, putting my arm about his thin, cold shoulders.

'It is the storm, Honora. It is all my fault. God is angry with me because I destroyed the nest.'

'No, no,' I assured him, 'God is not doing that. We get these storms all the time.'

'But R-Richard said,' stammered John.

'What did Richard say?' I asked, suspicion flaring in my mind.

'H-he said that God was sending the storm to punish me and that if I died in the storm I would go to hell!' He cried more bitterly than ever.

'Why did you do it, John?' I asked gently.

'Richard told me to,' he answered. 'He said I was more like a girl than a boy and I could only prove to him that I was a real boy if I climbed up to the nest. I did not mean to knock it down, Honora, but when I got there the mother owl flew at me and tried to peck me and I almost fell. That is when I knocked the nest down.' His sobs increased in intensity.

'Then, if Richard told you to climb up there, God knows about it, and he knows that it is really Richard's fault that the eggs were broken, does he not?'

'I s-suppose so.' John sounded half reassured.

But he smiled sadly then and seemed comforted. I took him to his bedchamber, settled him back in bed beside the sleeping and angelic-looking Richard and returned to my own.

The next day I cornered Richard in the hall and gave him such a talking-to that he left John alone for a long time afterwards.

Another time when Richard was able to spoil John's and my peaceful existence occurred a year or two later when I was about twelve. John and I each had our own little pony and one of our favourite places to ride was down into the Coombe Valley. It was like another world in there and as we would leave the barren hill-top and descend further and further into the wooded depths we used to feel like adventurers, or travellers from another time. We had one special place at the foot of the valley where the stream curled in a semi-circle around some large rocks. There, between the rocks was a grassed area where there were few trees and the sun would reach in the middle of the day. We used to persuade Cook to pack us some food and retreat to our private hideaway as often as we could. There we would sit and eat our lunch and John would talk of God and of his dreams of serving Him all his life. It was easy to feel very close to God in that spot and I felt it too. But my dream of the religious life did not last as John's did and as he stared up at the clouds and made his plans, so I did also but mine were all of fine clothes and a handsome gentleman who came andwhisked me away on his white stallion to live in palaces far, far away.

One day as we lay side by side on the grass and shared our innermost thoughts, we were rudely interrupted.

'Ha! So, this is where you hide, is it?' It was Richard and he was sitting on one of the rocks looking down at us.

'Richard!' I exclaimed in dismay. 'How long have you been up there?'

'Long enough to listen to your stupid talk of grand gentlemen on white horses, and to John's silly idea of becoming a priest,' he said nastily.

We felt defiled, and our wonderful, secret place no longer held its magic. Slowly we picked up the remains of our lunch and left our spot in the Coombe Valley. I returned there a few more times after that but it was never the same again. I do believe John never went back. Richard was even nastier than usual that day because he was jealous that we had not invited him to join us. But he would not have fitted in anyway, for he was never a dreamer.

One benefit of my closeness with my half-brother was that unlike my sisters, who never learned to read or write, I gained an education. Once my father knew that John was interested in the religious life, he engaged a tutor for him. This worthy gentleman rode from the village of Shop three times a week. Because I was John's close companion, he was quite agreeable for me to join them. My father made no protest.

Chapter Two

As the years went by and I grew older one of my pleasures was to ride to the coast and watch the sea. I have an intense love of the sea. I enjoy the sight, sound, and smell of it. I love to watch the seabirds and the ships. I take pleasure in the feel of the salt spray and the sound of the thud as the waves crash below me. Sitting on a cliff-top at Stowe I would feel reassured by the unceasing movement and permanence of the sea. I would also be reminded of the fragility of life by the constant crumbling of the rock as the cliffs wore away piece by piece. The only time I do not love the sea is when I am on it. Sea-crossings induce in me such feelings of sickness and terror as cannot be imagined once I am again safely on dry land.

The years of my childhood passed, for the most part happily and peacefully. I became too big to sit in my window seat and had to give up eavesdropping on my father's conversations in the parlour. As he rose in importance our house seemed even more busy and full of people than before. Mister Basset was a frequent visitor and each time he called he seemed to seek me out. I continued to be in awe of his sad, kind eyes and gentle voice and I always looked forward to his visits.

Mistress Basset was quite different. I can only remember her visiting on two occasions, but she was one of the most unpleasant women I have ever met. She was also the only person I knew at that time who had her own silk-covered mounting stool. An extra horse was needed for the journey to transport this object and a groom would have to hurriedly dismount and place it in position before his mistress would deign to alight from her own horse. Her voice could be heard from the time she arrived and was still echoing back to us as their travelling party moved off again. It was constantly raised and resounded about the house at a pitch which caused one's head to ache. She was always carping and complaining. Poor Mister Basset and her servants were in a constant state of trying unsuccessfully to please her. I, on the contrary, did no such thing.

I was left in no doubt but that my feelings about Mistress Basset would be mutual after one evening at supper. There were several people staying at our house that night. Apart from the Bassets there were also my sister Jane, her husband John Arundel and Francis Harris who was courting my sister Philippa. Everybody was in high spirits as my father had recently returned from London with a new title and was now a very important man indeed. The conversation was flowing as was the wine and even Mistress Basset was having trouble being heard. She was sitting next to her husband and I was next to her. During a brief lull in the conversation her voice rose above the rest.

'So, John, unless you arrange immediately for another chamber for me, I refuse to spend even one night in this house.'

Mister Basset looked so sad and worried that I wanted to kill her.

There was a hushed silence as he spoke quietly to her. 'My dear, Sir Thomas has many guests tonight and I am sure his housekeeper has made the best arrangements she can to accommodate us all.'

She looked up and smiled toothily at my father. 'Surely, Sir Thomas, you can have no objection to my having the large chamber which faces the morning sun. I shall simply be unable to sleep in any other,' she simpered.

Chapter Two

I have no idea what my father's response would have been for at that stage I tipped my soup in her lap.

I missed the ensuing uproar as I was sent straight away to my chamber (which I shared with my sisters and which was the very one Mistress Basset had her eyes on). My sister Agnes was the first to join me in bed some time later. She was in such a state of merriment that I had difficulty getting her to tell me what had happened after I left.

'Oh, Honora, it was so funny!' she laughed. 'Mistress Basset's face was absurd. First, she went white as a sheet, then she turned red, and after that she became purple, so I thought she would burst. She actually forgot to breathe for some minutes, and I have never known her silent for so long. I do believe everyone admires you greatly.'

'But what of Mister Basset?' I asked. 'Surely he must think me a dreadful little demon now.'

'I do not know about that,' Agnes replied with a shrug of her shoulders. 'Naturally, he was very kind and solicitous to his wife, but everyone else felt she deserved it so what does it matter what he thinks?'

But I cared very much what he thought and was ashamed of what I had done because I knew that by making her look foolish in front of so many people all I had succeeded in doing was to make his life even more difficult than it already was.

Our guests all left early the next day and I kept to my room until they had departed, thus sparing myself the embarrassment of having to see any of them. Fortunately, my father also left early for London and I avoided punishment. Perhaps, he too, secretly admired my action!

Early in the new century it was arranged for my sister Philippa to marry Francis Harris of Lanrest. Philippa had been a wonderful older sister to me, and I was sad at the thought of her going, but Mister Harris seemed to be a good man and she was content. My sadness was tempered by the fact that I was considered old enough to attend the wedding and take part in the festivities.

Our house was a clamour of sewing, cleaning, and cooking and I was to have my first really formal gown. For weeks, my greatest interest was in my gown. The kirtle was of green damask and was open at the front exposing a gold underskirt. Above the square, low-cut neckline a little frilled partlet collar showed. The close-fitting sleeves were of the same green as the kirtle. I loved that gown and wore it until long after it was too small and worn through.

The wedding was celebrated in Kilkhampton Church and the guests were invited back to Stowe for the festivities afterwards. I had to agree with Philippa that the Harris family were good Cornish folk and was happy for her union. Our hall was full to brimming with people for the feast at midday. Perhaps the happiest moment for me was when I realised Mistress Basset was absent. Mister Basset spoke to me during the meal.

'My wife is unwell,' he said. 'She hopes you will forgive her for not being present at your sister's wedding.'

Mr Basset always seemed so sincere that I could not believe he was poking fun at me, but I also knew that he would realise Mistress Basset's absence could not be a disappointment to me.

'I fear you jest, Sir,' I replied. 'I have no reason to desire Mistress Basset's company, nor she to miss mine.'

Chapter Two

Mr Basset gave his sad, amused look which I was beginning to know so well. 'My apologies, Mistress Grenville, I am abusing that trait in you which I find the most appealing.'

I felt confused by this and requested an explanation.

'Honora,' he began, 'I am an old man in your eyes and have become, I fear, somewhat cynical and jaded. But you have such a directness and honesty about you that in your company I feel refreshed.'

My confusion was increasing when a messenger interrupted the celebrations. My father went to greet him and after a time returned to the hall looking thoughtful. He easily gained everyone's attention as we were all curious already.

'The Queen is dead,' he said. 'She died in childbed.'

There was silence for some time and then everybody seemed to start talking at once.

'Poor lady,' said Philippa pensively, perhaps thinking of the fact that now she was a married woman, she, too might be lying in childbed in the not too distant future.

'Now she is gone,' said my father, 'unless the King marries again his only male heir is young Henry. He seems hearty enough but there must be cause for concern with both his brothers dead so young.'

'It was such a shame that young Prince Arthur died last year,' said Francis Harris. 'He had the makings of a good and wise king like his father.'

'And what of the young Princess Catherine?' John Arundel asked. 'She is kept almost a prisoner I hear.'

'I cannot comment on that John. My position as a Knight of the Bath renders it unwise. But I do think the best thing would be for Catherine to be married to Prince Henry. They say that her marriage to Arthur was never consummated so there should be nothing to hinder the alliance. Henry is almost twelve now and, in a few years, could have an heir of his own to secure the throne.'

This seemed very uninteresting to me and to my mind none of these events at Court would ever affect my life, so I went off to join in the dancing.

My life continued peacefully for the next few years. I often think back to my life as a young girl growing up at Stowe and I truly believe I had the most fortunate upbringing possible. Of course, I did not realise it at the time. Year after year came and went with the pattern of life dictated by the seasons and not by the orders of men as happens in more sophisticated societies.

When I was sixteen, my sister Catherine married John Arundel of Lanherne and soon after that my sister Mary married Richard Bluett. Our household was again shrinking in size. When I was eighteen and beginning to think my marriage could not be far off my life changed forever.

Chapter Three

The first change in that momentous year 1509 was the death of the King and the accession to the throne of his son, Henry VIII. The young King was handsome and well-loved. One of his first acts as King was to marry his sister-in-law, Catherine of Aragon, widow of his brother Arthur. This endeared him very much to his people, as Catherine had been a popular and forlorn figure since her widowhood.

Soon after this, our family and all the other important families in Cornwall and Devon were invited to another grand marriage. Mister Basset's daughter Anne was to marry Sir James Courtenay, a younger son of Sir William Courtenay of Powderham Castle in Devon. Never before had I attended such a gathering and my excitement mounted as the day grew near for departure. I spent weeks over the perfecting of my gown, which was pale blue with a silver underskirt. The seamstresses at Stowe did most of the work but I attended to the decorating and sewing on of the beads and silk edging. I have a flair for fine work of all kinds and take great pleasure in the creation of beautiful things. I have always found that the act of concentrating on the detail of the work and of co-ordinating my hands for the tiny stitches keeps my mind from straying to less pleasant topics. But at that time, I had no need for such distractions and simply enjoyed the act of creating an object of beauty. Once completed, the dress needed to be packed carefully for the long journey but at last all was ready, and we set out.

The day my family and I left Stowe on the two-day journey to Exeter I was in a state of tingling anticipation. We were a large party. As well as my father and our entire family, with the exception of my younger nieces and nephews, there were about a dozen servants to care for us and the horses. The weather was high and clear. Even the birds and animals seemed joyous as we rode along.

We travelled south-east from Stowe towards the village of Hatherleigh, then south to Okehampton where we spent the night at a large inn of comfortable enough proportions. After a passable night's rest, we started early the next morning in bright sunlight to complete our journey eastwards to the large city of Exeter. We skirted the foothills of Dartmoor and as we rode through the dense forests one of the grooms, who was a native of the area, told frightening stories of the witches who lived on the moors and stole the village children for their evil spells. He told the tale of Bowerman the hunter who was in pursuit of a hare one day and ran through a coven of witches who were very angry that he had disturbed their devilry. The next time Bowerman went hunting one of the witches changed herself into a hare and led him on a chase all over Dartmoor until he was exhausted. They then turned Bowerman into a stone which can still be seen near Manaton. The garrulous groom then launched into the story of the evil sprite, Cutty Dyer, who accosts drunk people and throws them into the river at Ashburton. My father admonished him to be silent which was a disappointment as I had been enjoying his stories enormously. I did not believe a word of them of course and knew that they were just foolish tales, told for entertainment and doing no harm to anyone for the hearing

Chapter Three

of them. I was most upset by my father's rebuke and hoped that the groom would not be punished for his storytelling.

'When will you learn, Honora?' my father rode up close to me and spoke severely. 'There are boundaries in our society which must not be crossed. And one of those boundaries is that between a gentlewoman and a servant.'

'But Father,' I protested, 'I was only listening to him.'

'You were encouraging him to step beyond his station and were thus demeaning not only yourself but him as well,' my father replied.

'I am sorry Father, it will not happen again,' I said but beneath my breath I added, 'not in your hearing anyway.' For the remainder of the journey I maintained a sullen silence.

We reached Exeter at dusk of the second day and found our accommodation, which was much more lavish than that at Okehampton and suited us very well indeed. The wedding was not for another day, so we had a full day to rest from the journey and to prepare for the big day to follow. I could not believe my eyes the next morning when I awoke and beheld the city in which I found myself. My father had told us that nearly 10,000 people lived here which, he pointed out, was nothing compared to London with its 60,000 or even Norwich with 20,000 but I had never before been in such a metropolis and I was very impressed. However, any hopes I may have entertained of sightseeing were dashed when at mid-morning a heavy rain began and continued unabated for the whole day. Not until the evening did the sun reappear to bathe the city in a golden glow.

The next morning there was no sign of returning rain and we arose very early to travel the short distance to Kenton for the wedding. It seemed the whole world was there for the Nuptial Mass and I could see very little due to the large numbers of people and my own lack of height but at last the ceremony was over and we again mounted our horses and travelled to the Castle for the wedding banquet.

I will never forget my first sight of Powderham Castle. It stands on a rise overlooking the estuary of the River Exe and is a gigantic structure of square towers and imposing battlements. As we rode through the huge gateway, I thought of all the people who had travelled through those same portals for hundreds of years, some gladly like us, and some in all likelihood with extreme reluctance.

We entered the enormous banqueting hall and were immediately swallowed up by the crowd and the bustle. But everything had been organised very well and soon a liveried servant was ushering us politely to our seats at one of the guest tables. Once I was seated, I was able to look around me and I saw where Mister Basset was situated at the high table with the wedding party. I looked for his wife but was unable to see her. I later heard that she was present but was spending the entire time lying on a couch in another room. It seemed she was ailing.

I found myself sitting next to my sister Jane and it was such a joy to see her again. She was mother to four growing children now and very content, but her husband John was not well, and he had remained at home with the children, so Jane was to represent her family on this occasion. Despite the difference in our ages we had always loved each other dearly and I was so happy to be seated next to her, sharing memories of life at Stowe.

Soon after all the guests were seated an army of servants entered the hall with great mountains of food. Beef, mutton,

Chapter Three

veal, lamb, kid, pork, rabbit, capon, venison, and fish all appeared together. They placed huge platters of these meats on the tables and then retreated to stand by the sideboards leaving the guests to feast. We did not have a drinking vessel by our side during the meal as we did on less formal occasions but would need to motion to one of the servants to bring us a drink from the sideboard when we were thirsty. I was feeling very hungry after the morning's exertions and I leaned forward to help myself to a slice of veal.

That was when I saw him.

Even when seated he was almost a head taller than the others at his table and his hair was like burnished gold. His face was strong-featured and shone with good health and humour. He was the handsomest man I had ever seen and was talking and laughing animatedly with his neighbours as he ate. Many times, during the previous few years I had tried to imagine what my future husband would look like and had conjured up images of masculine splendour in my mind but never had I managed to conceive such perfection as this.

My mouth must have dropped open like a fish as I stared like one dumbstruck. Then I realised he had stopped talking and was looking at me too. He did not stare as I had been doing but simply looked and as he looked his face changed and became serious. Our eyes were locked together for an eternal moment and I do believe we exchanged our vows silently at that time. No other man would do for me from that moment on and I did not even know his name, nor he mine.

We tore our eyes from each other then and continued with the meal, but the food tasted like parchment in my mouth and I ate little. When I could trust myself to speak, I asked Jane who he was.

'That, Honora, is Sir Arthur Plantagenet,' she replied. 'He is the King's uncle.'

'Oh,' I said in a small voice, all my hopes and dreams turning to ashes.

'But not a legitimate one,' she continued. 'He is King Edward's son by a Hampshire woman. He has found favour with King Henry both by his good looks and manners and by the fact that he can have no possible claim to the throne.'

I was still not feeling very comforted for despite my dreams I felt that such as I would be no match for a grand gentleman of the Court, legitimate or otherwise. I was sitting there with my head spinning and my thoughts so confused when I heard a deep voice behind me.

'My Lady Honora, would you care to dance with me?'

I wheeled around to find Arthur Plantagenet standing close to my shoulder.

'You-you know my name?'

'I made it my business to find out,' he replied.

And so, we danced, or at least I think we did. I could not feel my feet and my chest was pounding in such an uncomfortable fashion I felt sure he must notice. Soon we found our way out into the garden where he found us a seat in a secluded corner out of view of the house.

For the rest of that long summer afternoon we stayed hidden on our garden seat away from the crowds, safe in a perfect world of our own.

'And so, Mistress Honora Grenville, here we are all alone and free to do exactly as we like.' He spoke as if this did not happen to him very often. My life was just the opposite, I

Chapter Three

did virtually nothing but exactly as I liked and always had done.

I became aware that he had spoken again. 'Would you care to tell me about yourself?'

As if in a dream I managed to find my voice. 'There is really not much to tell, Sir. I am the unimportant daughter of a quite important man. My father is a Knight of the realm and serves on the Commission of the Peace for Devon. My whole life has been spent at Stowe and has been very happy but very dull.'

He looked deep into my eyes. 'Wherever you are Mistress Grenville, life would never be dull; of that I am quite certain. Please may I call you Honora?'

I would have agreed to him calling me anything at all just as long as he stayed by my side. 'Oh, yes, of course,' I said breathlessly.

'And would it be an imposition if I asked you to call me Arthur?'

'Arthur …' I repeated his name and it came out like a sigh. 'Would you tell me about yourself, Arthur?' I suddenly felt strangely shy, as if the enormity of this situation had only just dawned upon me. Here I was sitting so close to King Henry's uncle that we were actually touching.

'I have lived almost all my life at Court, firstly when my father Edward IV was King and then during the reign of Henry VII. I find myself there still, now that Henry VIII is King. I have never been able to decide anything for myself. Every step of my life has been governed by the wishes of Kings. I eat rich food, wear fine clothes, have more servants than I can count, and I own nothing.'

I had known that I loved him the moment from our eyes first met but my heart went out to him then as I had not believed possible. I wanted to hold him, for him to hold me. I wanted, oh how I wanted …

As he kissed me the world stopped. The birds fell silent and the bees ceased their industry. There was no breeze and the rustling of the leaves was a memory. I could feel myself falling into a deep abyss of pleasure and I never wanted to emerge again. Time did not exist.

'Honora, Honora,' he was murmuring, 'I will never let you go; you are mine now. Do you promise to be there when I come for you?'

'Yes, oh yes.'

'For I will come for you. One day, as God is my witness, I will come for you my darling and I promise that for me there will be no other. My heart and body are yours now, Honora. We are as one forever. Promise me my dearest, oh promise me that you will be mine.'

I promised him everything he asked and would have promised more had he requested it such was my state of mind at that moment. I knew not why he had fallen for me as he had but only that I had reached a peak of ecstasy such as I had never imagined possible in this earthly life. It was not only his nobility of bearing and his handsome face but was much more due to the goodness and gentleness which radiated from somewhere deep within him that made me lose my heart and throw caution to the wind. He also seemed to me to be very alone, in spite of always being surrounded by people. Oh, how I longed to be the one to ease his loneliness.

Chapter Three

'What do you want to know about the Court?' he asked me.

'Everything,' I replied. 'Tell me about the clothes and the King and the beautiful women. No, do not tell me about the beautiful women.'

'There is only one beautiful woman in the world, Honora, and she is here, and she is mine. But about the clothes, I have to say that sometimes it is difficult to tell if it is a court of people or of birds, such is the abundance of feathers worn. The men wear doublets so slashed it is impossible to tell which is doublet and which is undershirt and some fellows cut such a dash of crimson and sarcenet it is hurtful to the eyes.'

'Then is not it difficult to see what the real person is like under all those clothes?' I asked.

'There are no real people at Court, my love. Everybody is there to please the King and to increase their own power and wealth. They do that by finding out the King's pleasure and helping him to achieve it. There are no rules apart from obeying the King and no-one is what they seem.'

'You sound as if you do not really like it,' I said.

'If I never had to go back to Court, Honora, it would make me a very happy man. Then I could remain hidden away with you and become a country gentleman like my mother's father. But I am bound to abide by the King's pleasure and so I must return to Court. No-one who is a member of the nobility is permitted to do as they wish. The King decides what we do, where we go and who we marry.'

This last thing he said caused a sudden feeling of dread, as if a cold hand was gripping my heart for, I realised that

Arthur would have to gain the King's permission in order to marry me. What if it was refused?

'Arthur, is it possible that the King might refuse your request for us to be married?'

'I hardly think so, my darling. I am of no importance really. My illegitimacy prevents me from having any official standing at Court. Let us not worry about that at present and stay happy in this moment.'

But all too soon the afternoon began to turn chill and the festivities came to an end. The guests started to leave, and Arthur and his party had to reach their lodgings before nightfall in order to begin the long journey back to London the following morning. My joy turned to despair as he made ready to part from me and as he was about to ride away, he leaned down from his horse, took my hand, and looked into my eyes.

'I will come for you,' were his last words before he rode away.

I staggered back into the Great Hall in a state of total confusion. Already the afternoon's events seemed unreal. Perhaps I had simply been asleep in the garden all by myself for the afternoon and had dreamed it all. I saw that my own family were making ready to leave and joined them. I noticed that my father was not with them and went to mount my horse next to where Agnes was already mounted and awaiting me.

'Father is most displeased with you, Honora,' she said. 'You are fortunate he has been recalled to Court or you would have been punished, I am sure.'

I was not interested but she continued.

Chapter Three

'He was hoping that both our marriages could have been arranged during this day. Mine, at least, has been. I am to marry Mister John Roscarrock. But you were so busy making a fool of yourself with the King's bastard uncle that no decent man could get near you even had he wished to do so.'

'How dare you speak so of Arthur?' I flashed at her. 'And my marriage is arranged anyway; Arthur and I are pledged to each other.'

'We shall see,' she said. 'Fine gentlemen are easy to look at and fine promises are easily made.'

What a strange combination of days they had been. First, I was chastised for stooping so low as to encourage a servant to speak to me and then for daring to look higher than my station for love.

Chapter Four

I received a letter from my father soon after I arrived back at Stowe. He was furious with me and wrote that I would never be allowed to leave Stowe again until it was to my own wedding. He added that provided a half decent man could be found who did not mind that his prospective wife had disgraced herself in public, I would be married off at the first opportunity. I tried not to mind about this missive because I was used to my father's rantings and also because I kept reassuring myself that Arthur would soon be coming for me.

The next months were interminable. I awoke each day in an agony of apprehension. Would Arthur come today, would he come at all? Agnes married her John Roscarrock and left us. I was now the only daughter of my father's first family who remained unmarried.

Father himself did not return home for some months but when he did, he showed his displeasure with me by shouting and fuming that I was a disgrace to the family and had shamed us all by my unseemly conduct at Anne Basset's wedding.

'No respectable man will want you now Honora,' he said. 'What on earth were you thinking of to carry on like a street girl with that known philanderer?'

'Wh-what do you mean 'known philanderer'?' I stammered.

'That man, Arthur Plantagenet, is well known over the length and breadth of England, young lady. He has broken

Chapter Four

more hearts than his own father, King Edward, and *he* was famous for it!' he shouted hurtfully.

'No, no, Arthur is not like that,' I said, fighting back tears. 'He meant what he said to me. He wishes to marry me, and he will come for me. He said …' I finished lamely.

'Then it might interest you to know,' continued my father with a cutting edge to his voice, 'that he is very soon to marry Lady Elizabeth Dudley and will thereby obtain not only vast wealth but also the title of Lord Lisle.'

I felt myself going weak and my head was spinning.

'No, no that is not true. He meant what he said. I do not believe you. I do not believe you!' I shouted and ran to my chamber.

For days I remained in my chamber. I refused to come out or to eat. I drank only enough to keep myself alive and knew not why I did that for death was my sole desire. When I did emerge from the room it was to go to the Chapel and spend hours on my knees gaining solace from prayer. I decided I would join a nunnery as I was finished with men forever. My heart had been broken. I had fallen in love with a philanderer! But still some part of me refused to believe it. Deep down I knew that Arthur had been sincere. Perhaps he had said it all to other women before, but I felt sure that with me he had meant what he said.

No more was said about my marriage prospects or lack thereof. As the oldest remaining daughter, I occupied myself about the house. My half-brother John provided great consolation to me at that time with his quiet, kind ways. I changed my mind about joining a nunnery as I still had very vivid memories of Arthur's kisses and decided they would be inappropriate memories to take into the cloistered life.

One day a messenger arrived. For once the message was for me and my heart was in turmoil as I read it. I still have that letter. It was the only document I managed to keep from the pillagers in later years.

'My dearest love,
I have refrained from writing to you because I so detested what I had to tell you and nurtured a vain hope that something would happen to prevent my having to write it. By now the worst has probably happened and you will have heard the news from someone else and your heart will have hardened against me. By the King's order I am to marry Edmund Dudley's widow. There is no easy way to say it. We are doomed, Honora. It seems our love is to be a brief and cherished moment in our lives, never to be fulfilled. But never doubt for a moment, my sweet, that I do love you, or that we are not meant for each other by heavenly destiny. It is our earthly destiny which eludes us. Never forget me, Honora. You are in my heart forever.
Your own loving
Arthur'

I cried again after that but this time my tears were not because I thought I had been betrayed. Somehow, they were easier to bear knowing that Arthur loved me. He was a courtier and was bound by the King's order. He could do nothing else.

Shortly after his letter arrived, we heard that Arthur had married Elizabeth Dudley and my life continued,

Chapter Four

unchanged, at Stowe. I was desperately unhappy, and I think I cut a somewhat tragic figure in those days. I wore dark colours and did not bother to make myself look attractive. I was rapidly turning into a bitter old spinster. My tongue was sharp and my temper uncertain. I was even spiteful to my dear brother John on the day he left to begin his education for the priesthood.

'Farewell, dear sister and may God be with you,' he said as he was securing the last of his belongings onto the packhorses.

'Oh yes, God, always God with you is it not, John? A great comfort He has been to me lately for all the time I have been spending on my knees. Where was He when King Henry ordered my only love to marry another?'

John spoke gently, as always. 'God has a plan, Honora. It is not always clear to us, but He always has a plan. Continue to pray, dear sister, as I will also be praying for you.'

Without even bidding him farewell I turned on my heel and marched back into the house. Dear companion of my childhood, how could I have treated him in such a manner? I was so overcome with remorse after he rode away that I immediately sat down and wrote a message of apology which I despatched with instructions to the messenger to ride hard and not to rest until he had caught up with my brother. I missed John dreadfully in the ensuing weeks and months. He had been my closest friend and now he had gone to fulfil his dreams, even as I would never fulfil mine.

Time went on and there were more weddings to attend. My nephew, Jane's son John Arundel, married Mary Bevil, the daughter of the Sheriff of Devon. She seemed like a nice girl and it was a happy wedding at which I tried to join in with a smiling face. My nephew Richard, with whom I still enjoyed a frosty relationship, spent a great deal of time that day with Mary's sister Maud, who was clearly prepared to give him all the admiration he craved. They were sure to get on well.

My sister Philippa's husband, Francis Harris, had died soon after their marriage and she also remarried at this time. Her new husband was Humphrey Arundel of Yewton in Devon. Mary's husband, Richard Bluet, had also died soon after her marriage and she remarried Thomas St Aubyn of Clowance. I attended these weddings but could take no joy in them, remaining by myself and repudiating any who attempted to make conversation with me.

Early in the year 1512 I went to stay with Jane at Trerice. Her husband, John Arundel, was very ill and she needed company or so she said. I think, with the benefit of hindsight, that she realised I needed to be taken away from Stowe and given something else with which to occupy my mind.

It really was a good change. With Jane I was able to speak about Arthur and my relationship with him, brief as it was. It was the first time I had spoken of my feelings since everything had happened and was a healing experience for me. Dear Jane was always so good and understanding. She listened to me until I was finished and then considered carefully.

'Love comes in many guises, Honora,' she said. 'There is more than one kind of love.'

'But my love for Arthur …' I interrupted.

'Your love for Arthur was something which few people experience,' she continued. 'It was, *is*, the strongest passion

Chapter Four

you think you are capable of feeling. But love can be experienced again.'

'I can never love another man,' I said.

'But you can marry,' Jane replied, 'and by marrying you will get children and you will feel such a love for your children that the pain of your love for Arthur will be eased. You may even begin to love your husband just a little.'

'Oh, Jane you are so wise, but father says no man will want me now because I have disgraced myself.'

'Time is a great healer, Honora, and memories are short. You will marry.'

After that I began to be more like my old self again. Jane's husband, John, needed caring for as his health grew worse and I became skilful at making medicines from plants to soothe his discomfort. I found I had quite a gift in this way and they were both very grateful for the willow bark beverage I brewed to ease his pain. He and Jane were a very close couple and it helped her to know his suffering was lessened. He died in July and I stayed on with Jane for some weeks afterwards. She soon had suitors knocking at her door and in September that same year was married to John Chamond.

I visited her a year later as she cradled her new-born son in her arms.

'You see, Honora, there is more than one kind of love,' she whispered to me.

I had learned my lesson.

My father, Thomas Grenville, died in 1513. I was saddened by his passing for although he had been a stern and authoritative figure, he was my father and as such I had loved and respected him. Roger was now the head of our family and was still filling Stowe manor with a new Grenville every year or so. I returned to Stowe and helped Margaret with her brood.

The new King, Henry VIII, was proving to be just as keen on war as his father had been opposed to it. His armies were winning battles both in Scotland and in France, but he was spending vast amounts of money to finance it all. He was rapidly emptying the vast coffers his father had filled with our taxes.

In 1514 my half-sister, Jane, married William Batton. I was now the only unmarried member of my family apart from John, who was in his final year of studying to be a priest. One day Mister Basset arrived and after exchanging brief but polite civilities with me he entered the parlour with Roger and the door closed behind them. They were in there for some time and then Roger came looking for me.

'Mr Basset has something to say to you Honora and I advise you to consider carefully what he has to say. It will be said with my full blessing.'

Puzzled, I entered the parlour where Mister Basset greeted me and shut the door.

'Honora,' he began, 'my wife has recently passed away after a very long illness. Were you aware of that?'

'No,' I replied. 'I am very sorry for your bereavement, Mister Basset.'

'Thank you, my dear,' he said softly. He seemed ill at ease and different from any other time. I wondered if it was due to his wife's death. Then he looked into my eyes and spoke in a stronger voice. 'Honora, I have come here today to ask you for your hand in marriage. Would you do me the honour of becoming my wife?'

Chapter Four

I was stunned. I had always looked upon Mister Basset as an old man, someone more like an uncle than a husband. I really liked him and respected him but had to think quickly to try and see him in this new role.

I realised he was speaking again.

'I am sorry if I have upset you Honora. If you refuse me, I will think no ill of you. I love you too much to hurt you.'

There was that word again. He 'loved' me. I suppose he had loved the previous Mistress Basset after a fashion too, though Heaven knows how. But could I ever love him? Certainly not in the way I loved Arthur but remembering what Jane had taught me I took his hand and said:

'Yes, John, I will marry you.'

2. UMBERLEIGH

Chapter Five

Early in the year 1515 I married John and became Honora Basset. The wedding was a huge affair with both our large families present. It was celebrated in Kilkhampton Church and presided over by my uncle Richard Gilbert. It was certainly not the wedding I would have chosen for myself, but I did my best to look on the positive side. Mister Basset was a good man and if my father was correct when he said all those years ago that no man would want me after I had disgraced myself at Anne Basset's wedding then I supposed I ought to be grateful.

My gown was amber coloured with a heavily embroidered overskirt and plain underskirt. The sleeves were ivory and tight-fitting with puffed shoulders. My headdress was of the same material as my overskirt and the whole outfit was edged with beaded brocade. I had spent many contented hours with the seamstresses at Stowe perfecting it, taking pleasure in the work, and trying to remain cheerful about the event at which it was to be worn.

It was difficult, however, not to dwell during those hours upon what could have been. As I sewed each bead into its designated place to form the intricate pattern my mind would drift away, and I would find myself imagining that

Chapter Five

it was my wedding to Arthur for which I was preparing. I pictured the scene in my mind, imagining his soft kisses and his strong arms, thinking of him laying me down and covering me with his beautiful body. Imagining his kisses becoming more urgent ... I would be brought back to reality by a comment from one of the seamstresses about some mundane matter to do with the weather or some snippet of gossip. It was difficult not to howl my sorrow to the four winds when that happened because the pain was so much worse to bear after I had allowed myself to detach from it for a while.

My outfit was immensely heavy, and its heaviness mirrored the leaden weight in my heart as I walked into Kilkhampton Church on a cold winter's morning supported by the arm of my brother Roger.

After the marriage ceremony we had a banquet at Stowe. I entered the Great Hall with my new husband to the cheers and congratulations of all present. I managed to fix a bright smile on my face although in my heart I felt as if all my dreams were turned to dust and my life was over.

We partook of venison, guineafowl, partridges, and puffins. These latter are found in great quantities nesting on the cliffs near Stowe. The main meal was followed by fruit, sweetmeats, cheeses and wine. I nibbled at the food but felt quite ill and had to force each mouthful down, so lost was I in my misery. I managed to hide my feelings, or so I hoped, and no-one seemed to notice.

Musicians played the lute and recorder throughout the meal and there was dancing to follow.

'My dear, I hope you will not mind if we leave the others to the dance,' whispered my new husband. 'I am not by nature a dancing man.'

Meekly I replied that I did not mind but I would have loved to dance. It would have helped in a small way to make the day endurable. In those days I only knew the basic country dances but had always enjoyed the pastime. However, I was now married to someone who was not a dancing man, so it seemed my dancing days were over.

Later that night John joined me in the bedroom which I used to share with my sisters, now all married and gone from home as I was about to do. They had explained to me what I was to expect on my wedding night, and it was with a feeling of utter dejection and humiliation that I steeled myself for the inevitable assault upon my person. He was very kind and gentle but afterwards, as my new husband lay snoring beside me, the tears fell unchecked down my face and pooled in the hollows of my neck as I wept bitterly and silently for what might have been. My wedding night ought to have been so very different to this.

It was with a profound feeling of sorrow and resignation the following morning that I, at the age of twenty-four, left Stowe with my fifty-two-year-old husband for the journey to Umberleigh. We had a long, tiring day's ride and it was late in the afternoon before we arrived. My first impression was of a large, white-washed house set in a spacious courtyard and surrounded by masses of outbuildings, also white-washed. There was a gentle feel about it, situated as it is on a sheltered plain near to the River Taw. Beyond the house is a large wooded hill, surmounting which can be seen the tall tower of Atherington Church. The whole place

Chapter Five

seemed a far cry from Stowe with its windswept hills and ocean gales. I was determined to be a good wife to John and to try and be happy in my new home, but my heart was frozen in time and in Arthur's image. I could not free myself from that prison of the soul into which our brief meeting had plunged me.

'Welcome to Umberleigh, Mistress Basset,' said John lovingly as he assisted me down from my horse upon our arrival.

He looked so expectant and almost young in his desire to shower me with kindness. I looked around me at the attractive, well-built house and out-buildings then my gaze lifted away over the hills towards Cornwall and the sea.

'Thank you, John,' I replied, 'but do you think I might lie down a while? The journey has tired me.' Very polite, very correct I was, never rude or unpleasant but how I must have disappointed him on this and so many other occasions in those early years of our marriage.

I did not lie down after all but remained standing in the bedchamber looking sadly out of the window. To the west was Stowe and all the happy memories there, to the east was London and Arthur. I observed servants passing backwards and forwards beneath my window, going busily about their work like ants in an ant hill. I realised with a start that they were now my servants. I was the mistress of this house. There was some little comfort to be had there, I supposed.

Arthur was never out of my mind and I hungered for news of him. I had heard that his wife had produced a daughter in London the previous year and that she was named Frances. But I had never heard from Arthur since that one terrible, wonderful letter and knew not whether he was happy or if he ever thought of me.

That year, 1515, was a year for marriages. John's daughter Margery left Umberleigh to marry a local yeoman farmer called William Marres. In the same year, my nephew Richard Grenville married Maud Bevil. She had adored him from the time of their first meeting at her sister Mary's wedding to John Arundel. Despite my own opinion of Richard, he did seem genuinely fond of Maud and it promised to be a good enough marriage.

I resolutely made the decision that I must make the best of my situation. With that in mind I forced myself to take an interest in my surroundings and would frequently venture out to watch the men working in the fields. I have to admit that I did enjoy this. To see the oxen pulling the heavy plough with the ploughman steering behind and a boy to whip them on up the hills always impressed me. I can still hear the sound of the swish, swish as the ploughshare cut cleanly through the rich Devon soil.

As I used to do at Stowe, I also found great comfort in the kitchen at Umberleigh. There was a huge fireplace taking up more than half of one side of the chamber. Over this hung the cauldrons and the roasting spits. To each side was a brick workbench beneath which were several smaller fires. There were holes in the bench over each of these fires and cooking pots were placed on each of them. Besides the cook there were several maids to help in this, the busiest spot at Umberleigh. At first Cook openly resented my presence.

'The previous Mistress Bassett never came down here,' she informed me bluntly when I first ventured into her territory dressed in my oldest, most worn gown. But I persisted and

Chapter Five

over time we became firm friends. She taught me the art of cooking and I have such vivid and wonderful memories of working together with her at the huge table, with the fires burning and our conversation so easy and relaxed. The kitchen is truly the heart of the home.

My husband John still had two daughters living at home, Jane, and Thomasine. Jane had inherited her mother's personality and never stopped complaining. She was eighteen years old when I came to Umberleigh, but it was apparent even then that she would never marry. No man would have willingly put himself in the way of that censorious tongue. Thomasine was sixteen and as timid as a mouse. She had never come to terms with her sister's carping and haranguing and I would often find her shaking from head to foot after a confrontation with Jane. They were not an easy pair to live with.

But outwardly my life was easy. My husband had provided every comfort possible to make my life happy and I lacked for nothing. John's and my bedchamber at Umberleigh was a huge, high-ceilinged room with windows on two sides. The sun entered the room when it first rose in the morning and did not leave it until mid-way through the afternoon. We had a large four-posted bed with a soft, comfortable mattress and luxurious coverings. He also gave me a parlour to myself into which no-one, not even he, entered without my permission.

Meanwhile, the first year went by in my marriage. John was a good, kind man and deserved better than he was getting from me. I cannot imagine that he was made happy by his first wife and I fear that he was not at first entirely happy with his second. I tried so hard to be a good wife -

perhaps too hard. But I could not give him the love and devotion he merited because I had already given that to Arthur. I was dutiful and fruitful and seemingly all the things a wife should be, but John deserved more.

We had been married just over three months when I discovered that I was with child. This came as no shock to me. It is the sole purpose of marriage. I had been well-schooled by my sister Jane about the entire business of pregnancy and childbirth and so was prepared for every stage of the whole unpleasant process. I had no difficulty at all carrying the child or any of the children to follow. Likewise, I found the business of childbirth, whilst extremely painful, not unbearable and forgotten about the minute it was over. In this I know I am very fortunate as so many women lose their health and indeed their lives in performing this duty.

A wet-nurse had already been found in Atherington and as soon as my first pains began, she was brought to the house. She was, therefore, settled in her chambers well before the baby was born and was able to take her (for my first born was a girl) away to be fed immediately afterwards. It is a known fact that breast-feeding delays the return of fertility, so it is not a good idea as the role of a wife is to produce as many babies as possible for her husband.

We named the baby Philippa. She was from the start a good, quiet little girl and was never a trouble. I was told that I was fortunate as first babies are often difficult. John must have been disappointed that he still had no son, but he did not show it. I insisted that the baby be brought to me during my period of confinement whenever she was not being attended to by the nurse and was contentedly holding her, marvelling at the perfection of her tiny hands and long

Chapter Five

eyelashes when John came to visit within a few hours of her birth.

'My wonderful girl has produced a girl of her own. Are you happy, Honora?'

'Of course I am happy, John,' I answered. 'How could I be otherwise? I have all a woman could wish for.'

His eyes were sad and kind, just as they always were and ever had been.

We saw a great deal of Anne and her husband, James Courtenay. Soon after Philippa's birth they came to stay and brought news of Arthur.

'His wife has produced a second daughter,' said Anne to me one day when John was out of earshot. 'I have heard that he treats her very badly and spends most of his time drinking and carousing with his friends. You had a lucky escape there Honora.'

I had had no such thing, to my way of thinking but refrained from saying so.

'He is in high favour with King Henry,' she continued. 'They seem to be two of a kind. The King is not treating Queen Catherine well despite his earlier promises. Since the birth of Princess Mary, he has shunned her and spends his leisure time with mistresses.'

If Anne was insinuating that Arthur had mistresses, I did not wish to hear it, so I changed the subject rapidly. But later when I was alone in bed before John joined me my heart ached for my lost love and for what we could have shared.

'Arthur, oh, Arthur,' I cried softly, 'you would have no need for drinking and carousing if we were together.' All the passion which I had known briefly for one summer afternoon came flooding back to me and I shed bitter tears which fell unchecked down the sides of my face and soaked my pillow. Oh, how I hated the King for what he had done to my life by ordering Arthur to marry another!

Then I heard John's footsteps approaching the bedchamber, so I dried my face, turned my sodden pillow over and steeled myself to again be a dutiful wife.

The next summer there was a bad outbreak of Sweating Sickness. That year it was very serious, and many people died. In Devon we were away from the worst of it but still lived in fear as death comes so suddenly to those affected. The illness begins with fever and headache, followed soon after by a violent sweat. Death occurs from three to eighteen hours after the first onset of the symptoms. London was the worst affected and I was in daily terror lest Arthur contracted it. Even though I believed I would never see him again, I could not bear the thought of him dying. The worst of the agony for me was not being able to confide my fears to anyone. I could hardly tell my husband or his daughters that I still thought daily of my lost love!

But the sickness passed with the onset of the winter and I could only hope that Arthur had been spared. Life continued as before, and I was again expecting a child. This time I hoped, for John's sake, that it would be a son.

On the political front there was some good news. French money had boosted England's rapidly emptying coffers. It seems we had captured the great French fortress of Tournai during the war and sold it back to them for 600,000 crowns! It was almost like a game.

Chapter Five

My second daughter was born in 1518 and we named her Catherine. Once again John showed no sign of disappointment.

'Another beautiful daughter, my dear,' he said and immediately enquired after my own health. 'You must rest now for as long as you need. I will not trouble you again until you feel completely recovered.'

Poor John, he must have known that the business of begetting a child was a 'trouble' to me. And it should not have been, for no man could have been a more gentle or considerate bedfellow. He was no longer a young man and even though he must have been very worried by this time about his property and lack of a son to inherit, he never showed it by any unkind word or act towards me.

It was with great joy on both of our parts when, the following year, our son John was born. John, my first-born son, my angel. Now I knew what Jane had meant about different kinds of love. For the first time since I had met Arthur, I was overwhelmed by a feeling so strong it surpassed the power of thought. I had not felt the same about Philippa and Catherine because motherhood had been tempered by a feeling of having somehow failed but this time, I had achieved all that was expected of me. John's Baptism in Atherington Church was a joyous affair at which my husband's eyes shone with a different light. Our eyes met as the water was poured over our son's head and I saw that the sadness had gone from his. I had never seen him look like this and I felt my heart swell with a love I had never thought I would be able to feel for him.

Later that night when he took me in his arms, I was surprised to find that at last I could give him some of the tenderness he deserved. It was as if something inside me had been unlocked. Our marriage changed for the better after that. We never reached great heights of passion and our coupling remained no more than a duty to me but at least I no longer dreaded the business as much as I had before.

In the same year as John's birth King Henry also had a son. Unfortunately, however, it was not his wife, Queen Catherine, who bore the child. A mistress by the name of Elizabeth Blount had the baby who was christened Henry Fitzroy. To the shame of all concerned both the baby and his mother were given all the honours which should have belonged to the Queen and Princess.

But in Devon our life continued peacefully and was unaffected by such events. I was busy with my children and John was happier than I had ever seen him. I continued to think of Arthur on almost a daily basis but was developing a kind of love for my husband now, just as Jane had prophesied. I was content.

Chapter Six

Early the following spring, John planned a visit to his estate of Tehidy in South Cornwall. It was an area rich in tin mines and every so often he needed to check on their progress. On this occasion he invited me to accompany him. I jumped at the chance. The children were all well, so I had no qualms about leaving them with their nurse. John was six months old now and thriving. I was not yet with child again, so the trip would pose no physical problems for me. We decided to go by way of Stowe. I had not seen my family there in the five years since my marriage. We also planned to visit my nephew John at Trerice. My sister Mary lived close to Tehidy and I hoped to get a chance to see her as well. The day we left I was in a state of high excitement.

It was a fine spring morning with a warm sun and a chill in the air. The horses pranced and quivered as if they shared my impatience to be away. At last we were off, accompanied by enough servants to tend to our needs on the journey. We headed west from Umberleigh through Atherington and passed by the small monastery of Frithelstock. We could see the monks working peacefully in their fields as we rode along. I slowed down as we passed and thought fleetingly of the monks and their age-old traditions of work, prayer, and silence. It gave me a comforting feeling to know that amidst the change and turmoil of the material world here was something good and holy that had not changed in hundreds of years and would in all likelihood go on forever. How rudely that illusion was to be shattered in the years to come and how disbelieving I would have been if I had been told then that I would play a role in their downfall!

We continued on our way over the sparsely populated hills and towards the coast to Stowe, arriving late in the evening. It had been a long, hard day's ride but it still remained to greet my family.

Roger came to meet us as we dismounted stiffly.

'Honora, dear little sister,' Roger clasped me to his breast, 'and John,' he turned to my husband, 'how are you both?'

'Somewhat tired after our journey but happy to see you well, Roger,' answered John, while I looked about me and murmured assent.

It was wonderful to see Stowe again and to appreciate how little it had changed. It seemed strangely quiet but then I remembered that it was quite late, and the children would be asleep.

'You will be wanting nothing but a little refreshment and a soft bed.' Roger interpreted our needs accurately.

And with no more ado we were provided with both. Less than an hour later saw us both sleeping soundly.

We spent the next day at Stowe. John and Roger went off to inspect the estate and talk of weighty matters. I remained at the house and spoke with Margaret. She was unchanged, still the same pleasant, motherly woman I remembered. Now that I had children of my own our relationship was different, and we spoke more as equals.

'You seem softer, Honora,' she said. 'Motherhood agrees with you.'

'You will remember me as I was five years ago, Margaret. I do not know how much you knew at the time, but I was loath to marry John because my heart had been given to another.'

'Of course, we knew,' she said kindly and patted my hand. Then with a small laugh she added, 'one would have to have been blind and deaf not to have known. You did not try and hide your feelings, Honora.'

'Oh dear, I am so sorry for my behaviour. How miserable I must have made you all but now that I have my girls and my darling little John, I am quite content.' But oh, how my heart ached as I spoke those words. I could never have explained to her that although I loved my children dearly and would willingly have given my own life rather than to allow any harm to befall them, there remained a gaping void in me and a deep sadness. If she thought that perhaps I protested my contentment a little too strongly or that my words lacked total conviction, she made no comment and changed the subject.

'You find me a little downcast, Honora,' she confided. 'My daughter Agnes has just left us to marry John Fitz and has moved to Devon. It happens to all mothers that they must be separated from their daughters, but it is a sad time nevertheless.'

'And where is Richard?' I asked.

'He and Maud are still living here with us, but Richard can never stay in one place for long and they are away much of the time. I believe Richard wants more from life than to be simply a West Country gentleman, but he does not know as yet what it could be.' She sounded indulgent. 'They have two delightful children and have named them Roger and Margaret. Is that not just wonderful?'

'Yes, wonderful,' I replied, wondering if marriage and fatherhood had softened Richard at all. I doubted it.

But although Margaret's older children were leaving home, she still had a large brood of younger ones to fulfil her motherly instincts. With the morning light Stowe had once again filled with the same childish laughter and prattle that I remembered from my own early years.

It was hard to leave the next day, but the horses were saddled early and John was anxious to be off. The morning had dawned overcast but warm and we set out after morning prayers and breakfast. As we rode south along the coast it began to rain softly but not enough to cause us to halt our journey. We rode through patches of thin mist and fog, during which the view was limited to a few hundred yards.

After we had been riding for some time, John said, 'I have a mind to break our journey at the next hamlet. There is a sight you may be interested to see, my dear.'

'Where are we, John?' I asked.

'The hamlet is called Tintagel and there is a castle there that is reputed to have been the birthplace of King Arthur,' he replied.

'King Arthur,' I repeated softly. He after whom my love had been named. Yes, I would very much like to see his birthplace. 'That would be very nice, John,' I said aloud. 'I could do with a rest anyway.'

And so, we came to Tintagel. We stopped for refreshments at the tiny inn, after which we mounted our horses again and rode the short distance to the coast. The sea was dark, and waves were crashing at the base of the cliffs. The mist had thickened to a fine drizzle. We halted at the place where the mainland stopped abruptly and the steep path

Chapter Six

descended to a narrow, perilous neck of land, over which one had to cross in order to reach Tintagel Head. There the castle stood, a ruin of ancient stone walls standing high on the rugged promontory. John and two manservants decided to cross over to the castle whilst I and my maids remained on the cliff top. We watched as they slid down the path to the neck and inched their way across. At any moment I expected to see them falling to their deaths in the churning waters below, but they reached the other side safely and once there they had an equally steep climb up to the castle ruins. As soon as I was assured of their safety, I left my maids, who were sheltering from the drenching mist and wandered further around the cliff top.

After I had gone a hundred yards or so I found myself looking across a narrow inlet towards a deep cave from which the mist swirled as if a great cauldron boiled within. I would not have been able to reach the cave as the entrance was covered by the tide but as I stared in awe, I was startled by a voice behind me.

'That be Merlin's Cave,' said the voice.

I spun around and found myself face to face with an old, gnarled man of the sea. His lank hair hung in damp strands over his weathered face and his skin was wrinkled and tanned from a lifetime of exposure to the elements.

'Do you mean Merlin the magician?' I asked.

'Aye, that be he,' answered the old man. 'That be where he created the spell on the night King Arthur was conceived.' He cackled gutturally. 'And that be where he hid Uther Pendragon before he smuggled him into the castle to lie with Gorlois' wife.' He cackled again and then the mist swallowed him and he was gone.

Curiously, I was not at all frightened by the sudden appearance and disappearance of the strange man. It was as if I had been transported out of my own body and into a world of spirits.

I could only just see the cave now because of the gathering fog and then from out of the mist which eddied from the dark opening I imagined I saw a figure emerge. Could it have been Merlin the magician himself? His robes swirled around him and he carried a staff which he pointed towards me through the fog. The surging waves were being sucked in and out of the cave entrance behind him and the pattern of the sound they made became his voice.

'Arthur will be yours,' he said hauntingly. 'Arthur will be yours; Arthur will be yours.' Three times in all I heard it.

As rapidly as the vision had appeared, it was gone. In that same moment, the fog and mist cleared away and the cliff-top was bathed in sunlight. Had I imagined it? Surely so. It had merely been a trick of the light, brought on by the strangeness of the place and my longing for Arthur. But still, it had served its purpose. From that moment on I knew with certainty that somewhere, somehow, my love and I would be reunited. Whether it be in this world or in the next I cared not. Quite simply, I believed, and the belief gave me strength.

Chapter Seven

After my strange experience at Tintagel, we journeyed onwards to Tehidy, making only a brief stop to refresh ourselves at my nephew John Arundel's house at Trerice. My husband was subdued on the journey, I think perhaps he had been more frightened by his rash decision to cross over to Tintagel Head than he was willing to admit. Lost as I was in my own thoughts; I did not press him for conversation.

My first impression of Tehidy was of elegance and grandeur. It was a new house built in the year following the uprising of 1497, when the old one had been dismantled by rebels. This was a massive structure of hewed granite, built to last. It stood there in solid defiance against those who had so wantonly destroyed its predecessor. It was set in a sheltered valley only a few miles inland from the sea. To the west between the house and the sea was a large, flat expanse of exposed moorland where the salt wind blew constantly, and nothing grew but heather and wild grasses but here in the valley of Tehidy Park there was dense forest and luxuriant growth of both plant and animal life. It was a place of repose and a welcome sight after the long journey.

We stayed at Tehidy for several weeks, during which John toured the estate and inspected his mines. He had many discussions with his senior workmen. I listened in on as many of these talks as possible. I had no other activities with which to occupy myself and besides I had an interest in how the business was run. It was pleasing to note that

I was even able to make useful suggestions at times which John, fortunately, did not seem to resent.

It has been both a useful attribute and a burden for me to bear during my life that I seem to have a better head for business matters and a better judge of character than many of those about me. It is difficult for a woman because we are supposed to be the weaker sex and not to think of such things at all, leaving them to the men. But if I can see something more clearly than a man, why should I not speak out? That has always been and continues to be, my opinion.

My sister Mary and her husband, Thomas St Aubyn, came to stay with us during that time. They had four small children whom they had left at home at Clowance with their nurse. I was so happy to see Mary as we had not met since her first marriage so many years ago. She was very happy with her second husband who was a merry, delightful character. We spent several hours together during which we joked and laughed about the old days and discussed our children. But I made no mention of my apparition at Tintagel. Mary had not a mystic bone in her body and would not have understood.

'Thomas, I have a business proposition to put to you,' John said one evening.

'Oh John, I am not much good at business, I am afraid,' answered Thomas.

'It is nothing too onerous,' said John, 'but I have long been worried about Tehidy. It is too far away for me to manage properly from Umberleigh and with the tinworks and timber it is too valuable an asset to let run down for want of a good overseer. What say you? Would you be willing to take on the task, for a suitable recompense, of course?'

'I suppose I could come up here every week or so to check on things,' said Thomas doubtfully, 'but I warn you, John, I am no businessman.'

Mary laughed indulgently. 'That is certainly true,' she said, 'and no good at chiding lazy workmen, either.'

I wondered then whether my husband had made such a good bargain, but the benefit lay in Thomas' nearness to Tehidy and for that reason alone it was an opportunity not to be missed. And so, it was arranged, and Thomas St Aubyn became our overseer at Tehidy, a situation that was to continue for many years.

But speaking of the children with Mary I had felt a pang of guilt at having abandoned them at Umberleigh and became anxious to return. So, when our time at Tehidy was over I was happy that John decided to take the more direct route home through Launceston because of some business he had to conduct there. I was relieved to return to Umberleigh and to my little family, who had all fared well in my absence and had already consigned the mysterious happenings at Tintagel to the back of my mind by the time I arrived home. Life returned to normal.

The following year my daughter Anne was born. Unlike Philippa and Catherine who were both plain girls, Anne was a beauty from the start. Now that we had our son, both John and I could take more pleasure in the birth of a daughter. Jane and Thomasine, despite their peculiar personalities, were basically kind women and helped me greatly in the house. Jane had taken on the role of housekeeper and kept the servants well under control. The house ran smoothly if not always harmoniously under her authoritarian rule. Thomasine was wonderful with the babies and they responded to her gentle ways.

Having those two to oversee the running of the house and family left me free to pursue an interest I had had since I was a very young woman and to experiment with herbs and wild plants which I found growing in the hedgerows and garden. I talked to as many of the local women as I could, gleaning knowledge from them as to the medicinal properties of plants. It only required a person to give a small cough or mention in passing that they had a headache for me to brew a potion for them and insist they drink it. It became quite a jesting matter for the members of our household, but they admitted to me on many occasions that my remedies had helped.

My next daughter, Mary, was born a year after Anne. Mary was another beautiful baby and soon became a favourite with everybody because of her lively personality and winning smile. I was becoming so involved with my family life that Arthur was not in my thoughts quite so often. When I did think of him, I no longer felt the same pangs of pain I had previously, although he remained like a glowing candle in my heart, my first true love.

Two years after the birth of Mary I produced my second son, George. I had never seen my husband so happy. Despite his sixty years he looked almost young again as all his worries about inheritance were lifted from his shoulders.

My happiness was compounded after George's birth by another trip back to my childhood home of Stowe. The occasion was my brother John's installation in the post of Rector of Kilkhampton Church - a position which he still holds today. My dear brother, companion of my childhood; it was a homecoming for him in every way.

The Church at Kilkhampton was very new at that time, having been built only a few years previously by my brother Roger. The only part which had been kept from the earlier Norman-built structure was the huge old carved stone doorway, through which the new Rector entered with a humble grace which endeared him immediately to his new flock and brought tears of love and admiration to my eyes.

Roger had recently been granted a Knighthood by the King and he and his family continued to be successful and prosperous. He had become known throughout Cornwall as 'The Great House-keeper'. I will always be grateful for that time together as Roger died suddenly one month later. My nephew Richard was now head of the Grenville family.

Thus, it happened that after only one month we again made the trip back to Cornwall for Roger's funeral and it was there that I overheard some strangers talking. They must have been representatives from Court.

'And how is Lord Lisle, the newest Knight of the Garter, performing?' asked one. 'Still astounding everyone with his amazing grip on foreign affairs?'

'Not exactly,' replied the other, with a nasty-sounding laugh, 'but I hear he has had a grip on his wife again.'

'Yes, I heard that the Lady Elizabeth is making another attempt to produce a Plantagenet heir to upset His Grace the King.'

At the sound of my first love's name I had pricked up my ears.

'If the Lisles produce a son this time it could be very dangerous for them given the King's current mood. The country is just as likely to accept the offspring of a bastard Plantagenet as a bastard Tudor and Henry knows it.'

I wandered away pensively, realizing with a start that it was the first time I had thought of Arthur for a long while. But once I began to think of him all the old feelings flooded back, and I remembered again the curious prophesy at Tintagel.

John and I returned to Umberleigh and our life together. He was no longer a young man and the two trips to Cornwall in such a short space of time had visibly tired him. He began to spend more time reading in his parlour and became quite breathless if he exerted himself too much.

Due to John's failing health, the following year was spent quietly at home. I did not complain as I had realised when we married that sooner or later the difference in our ages would lead to such a situation. Besides, I had the children to occupy my time. We had regular visits from friends and family and were kept abreast of all the happenings in London. Anne and James Courtenay were always a good source of news.

'Would you believe it!' Anne said to me one July day as we sat in the shade in the garden at Umberleigh. 'In the past two months young Henry Fitzroy has been created a Knight of the Garter, Duke of Richmond and now, Lord High Admiral. The child is only six years old for goodness' sake!'

'I suppose as he is the only son King Henry has, it is unavoidable,' I said.

'Yes, but he has been given official precedence over the Princess Mary,' she replied, 'and she is the legitimate heir after all.'

Chapter Seven

I agreed that this was not right. 'No, a bastard should have no precedence over legitimate children, of course. But surely the King would never put him before the Princess in the line of succession.'

'The talk is that it is just what he is considering doing,' she replied, 'or of getting himself a legitimate son.'

'I cannot see that happening,' I said. 'Queen Catherine has had so many miscarriages already. She can never bear a son now, I fear.'

Anne looked steadily at me. 'It is not with Catherine that he wants to get his son,' she said.

'But what do you mean?' I asked. 'He is married to Catherine. He can get no legitimate heir but through her.'

She looked sad. 'There is talk, only talk, mind you, that he wishes to divorce Catherine and marry another.'

I hastily dismissed such an idea. 'No, he cannot do that. He is married to Catherine and Church Law forbids divorce. Let us forget this and speak of other things.'

The Court news was startling and unsettling but as far as I was concerned only idle gossip and of no great consequence. However, my nephew Richard stopped by one day on his way back to Stowe from London with news which I found far more disturbing to my peace of mind than any about the King and Queen.

He alighted from his horse with his usual buoyancy and hugged me violently, as he always did unless he was out of humour. Richard loved to be the bearer of startling news and with his customary lack of tact and displaying a total disregard for the hurt he would cause he whispered to me as I escorted him inside. 'I have news for you, Aunt Honora, which I had better tell you away from your old husband's jealous ear.'

'Please do not speak so disrespectfully of my husband, Richard,' I said sharply, 'and what could you possibly tell me that John ought not to hear?'

He continued conspiratorially. 'Your casual acquaintance of many years ago is now a merry widower.'

I stopped dead in my tracks and turned to stare at him.

He stated officially, as if addressing a gallery of people, only in a hushed tone, 'Elizabeth Plantagenet Lady Lisle, wife of Lord Arthur Plantagenet, died recently following the birth of a daughter.'

As I said nothing, he continued: 'Lord Lisle is now a single, eligible gentleman with wealth, property, a title, a Knighthood, and the position of Vice Admiral of His Majesty's Fleets - recently granted him due to the extreme youth of the Admiral himself - to commend him. I cannot see him remaining single for long, can you?'

Somehow, I maintained my composure. 'Richard,' I stammered, holding back the tears which threatened to engulf me, 'you are the cruellest, most hateful person I know.'

His face took on an entirely false expression of ruefulness. 'But I thought you would want to know,' he said, feigning hurt feelings.

'Oh, you thought that, did you? I very much doubt you thought that at all, Richard. You know exactly how much your words have wounded me. He is single and I am married.' I turned from him, the tears pricking my eyelids. 'I am retiring to my chamber, Richard. You will find John in his parlour. Please do not upset him by telling him any of that which you have just told me.' I turned and walked with dignity away from him but once in my chamber I flung myself on the bed and howled with frustration and despair. Was Arthur at this very moment arranging his next marriage, or having it arranged for him by the King?

After my storm of tears had passed, I dried my face and sponged my eyes with cold water to hide the traces. Then, steeling myself and setting a fixed smile on my face, I made my way downstairs again to find John alone in his parlour.

'Where is Richard?' I asked.

'He did not stay,' John replied. 'All he needed was a drink to refresh himself before continuing his journey. Did you have a chance to speak to him at all, my dear?'

'Only briefly,' I replied lightly, 'but Richard and I never had very much to say to each other so that is of no consequence.'

He seemed satisfied with that and I was grateful that at least my nephew had restrained himself from inflicting pain on my husband.

The following year my son James was born. From an early age James was a showman. He soon had a large following of admirers and an equally strong band of those who found him difficult to tolerate. James always elicited strong feelings of some kind in those with whom he came in contact.

Of the other children, Philippa and Catherine were growing into young ladies. They would never be beautiful or clever, but both had a quality of goodness and honesty about them, much like their father, which ensured that they would always gain respect. John was quick-witted but unassuming and everybody loved him for his careful, studious nature and for his integrity. Although young, Anne and Mary were both rapidly developing into beauties. Anne was the more practical of the two whilst Mary loved to sing and dance and lived in her own carefree fantasy world. George, though only two, was already showing signs of the reserved, serious person he was to become.

John, my husband, was becoming frailer. There was no sudden deterioration in his condition. He simply weakened gradually month by month. We talked more now than we ever had before and developed a closeness which had eluded us until then.

One night as I slept beside him, I felt his hand gently touch mine.

'My own Honora,' he said gently.

'Yes John,' I replied, 'can I get you something, a drink perhaps?'

'No, my dear, I need nothing save your presence at my side. I am content.'

I held his hand more tightly as it dawned on me that I loved him more than I had ever realised. He was silent for a while, then I heard him give a faint chuckle.

'I have always been a careful man and have only ever done one impulsive thing in my life. Do you know what that was?'

I could remember not even one hasty act and said so.

'It happened one day in the year 1515, soon after the death of my first wife.' He stopped to draw breath, as even speaking now tired him. Still I could not think what he could possibly mean. Then he continued. 'Ever since a certain incident many years earlier when a little girl had mistaken me for her Saviour, I had watched her grow into a beautiful woman.' He stopped again and I felt his hand tighten around mine.

After a time, he continued. 'One day with no preparation and no forethought I rode to Stowe and requested that young lady's hand in marriage.'

I remembered with shame the early years of my marriage. 'There must have been many times,' I said, 'when you bitterly regretted that impulse.'

'Never, Honora, never did I regret for a moment. Our life together has been full and rich. You have made me the happiest man in England.'

I leaned over and kissed him then and soon he drifted off to sleep.

The news from Court worsened and it seemed certain that the King would pursue his divorce from Queen Catherine. He was infatuated with a woman named Anne Boleyn; with whose sister he had already carried on a protracted affair. The gossip was that Anne had refused to give him access to her person unless he married her.

I found it both sad and frightening that the future of our realm and of the established rules of right and wrong were now ordained by one man's unsatisfied lust for a cunning and ambitious woman.

But Court gossip paled into insignificance for me on the last day of January 1528 when my husband, John Basset of Umberleigh, died peacefully in his sleep early one frosty morning.

I was sleeping lightly by his bedside but still aware of his shallow breathing, until he gave one deep outward breath, like a gentle sigh, then breathed no more. As he had lived in peace and tranquillity, so his life ended. I folded his hands across his breast and closed his dear eyes and as I did so I shed bitter tears of shame for the wife I should have been and for the love he so richly deserved, that I was never able to give him.

We buried my husband at Atherington Church one bitterly cold early February afternoon. Many came to pay their respects to a man whom all had admired. John was, I think, the only man I have ever met who had no enemies. Of course, that was made easier for him by the fact that he lived his life during a time of relative political stability. But I feel that even had he lived later, during our time of unrest and strife, he would have managed to avoid becoming involved in the trouble.

My tears seemed unstoppable during the service. All John's children were there, including his two married daughters and every one of them was as grief-stricken as I was. They, however, had nothing to repent and mistakenly construed that the cause of my sadness was no different to their own.

After the funeral I returned to Umberleigh with my children and Jane and Thomasine. Life continued much as it had before. We were well off and had no worries, John having left us very well provided for. The children were all healthy and we were living the life of prosperous country gentlefolk. When I thought of Arthur it was only fleetingly as something wonderful and beautiful – a memory to be treasured from my youth.

Chapter Eight

One morning in late February I was in the kitchen with Cook, several maids, Jane, Thomasine and my four daughters preparing pies for dinner. John was in the library with his tutor and the two little boys were in the nursery. I remember the weather as being still, cold, and frosty and it was good to be in the kitchen where it was warm. We were all covered in flour, some from hands to elbows and some all over their persons. It must have been because of the children's prattle and the general din of our activities that we failed to hear the sounds of an approaching horse. It was as I was placing a tray in the oven that I realised the girls had fallen silent and turned curiously to see what was amiss.

'I told you I would come for you,' he said.

He was standing in the doorway, a tall figure with his back to the light, his head haloed by the pale winter sun. I could not see his face, but the voice had remained unchanged in nineteen years. Feeling myself going weak, I gripped the table for support. In one fluid movement he entered the room and took me in his arms. Then the sweet softness of his lips met mine.

I was eighteen again, I was sinking into an abyss of pleasure, time did not exist.

How can I describe my feelings? Whatever I write would sound trite and insufficient to the magnitude of the passion which overpowered me. I was in the arms of my beloved and it felt like a thousand years or only one second had passed since I was last held in his embrace. The only certainty was that we had both come home. As we kissed, we murmured each other's names over and over. His strong arms encircled me. His love encompassed me. Oh, what a memory to carry in my heart for the rest of my days! Even now, so many years later, when I recall that moment, I feel such a surge of love and longing that it feels as if my heart will burst.

When, at last our lips managed to part, I looked behind me and became aware of four shocked young faces and two scandalized older ones staring at us, each one of them standing completely motionless as if rooted in stone. Cook and the maids were nowhere to be seen. Jane was the first to regain some of her composure and hastily herded the girls from the kitchen, Thomasine following in their wake with a nervous, uncomprehending glance behind her.

After they had gone, we stood and looked at each other, just as we had looked all those years before and the same silent promises were made. Then we were in each other's arms once more and all the passion of that long-ago day returned. Some part of me still could not believe this was happening and for a moment I imagined that I had lost my wits all together, until I heard his voice again.

'Oh darling, my one and only darling,' he was saying as he covered my face and neck with kisses, 'how have I lived all these years without you?'

'Oh Arthur,' I sighed, 'I thought you had forgotten me. Arthur, darling Arthur, please, am I dreaming again or is this real?' I had dreamed this dream so often but surely my mind would not play such a cruel trick as this.

His voice came muffled as he spoke with his face pressed against my neck. 'Yes, my darling this is real. Oh, Honora, never for a moment did I forget you. My marriage was a sham, an arranged affair ordered by the King.'

He stood a little back from me then and looked deep into my eyes. 'Will you have me now, Honora, after all the sadness I have caused you?'

Willingly and without reservation I gave him his answer. It took a good while, but he seemed satisfied with it.

I told him about the day at Tintagel and about the prophecy. 'I always knew in my heart that you would return to me, my darling but I feared that it may not be until the next life.'

'I am not a spiritual man, Honora, but I do believe that it is our destiny to be together and that your vision was in some way assuring you of that. As for our reunion being in the next life,' he laughed, 'far better for it to be in this one, at least initially, eh?'

When we emerged from the kitchen it was to find four very curious girls, one uncertain boy and two disapproving women waiting for us. It then dawned upon me for the first time that what had just occurred, whilst as natural as breathing as it had been for Arthur and me must have been shocking and upsetting in the extreme for the others, as well as breaking all the rules of propriety.

'My dear family,' I began, 'I know this morning has been a strange and surprising one for you all and for that I am sorry. But the circumstances of Lord Lisle's and my reunion today are exceptional, and we crave your forgiveness.'

I looked to Arthur for assistance and he continued for us.

'Your mother and I first met many years ago. Due to circumstances out of our control we were forced to part.' At this stage, his voice began to falter, and I had to continue.

'Now we have both been widowed, we are free to marry,' I finished lamely.

It all sounded so cold and practical when said like this. But those who had seen us earlier in the kitchen must have guessed at what lay beneath our calm exteriors. John, who had not witnessed that dramatic scene, looked unsure and overwhelmed. George and James, being so young, would be unaware of the significance of the day. Philippa and Catherine were both polite but were obviously distressed by the sudden arrival of this stranger who was to take their father's place so soon after his death. Anne and Mary were more agreeable and smiled coyly at him, much taken with his fine clothes and handsome visage no doubt. Jane and Thomasine had nothing to say but did not look entirely displeased. Arthur was, after all a grand gentleman and their stepmother was rising considerably in the world by marrying him.

Chapter Nine

It seemed that no sooner had we been reunited than we parted again. Arthur needed to return to London whilst I remained at Umberleigh and began preparing for our wedding. There was much to be done, not least finding somewhere to live. We would need to be much closer to London as Arthur was still part of the King's Court and had duties there. He asked his cousin John Wayte if there was anywhere in Hampshire that could be found for us. Mister Wayte agreed that indeed there was and began proceedings to lease us his manor of Soberton, south east of Winchester. I would not see it until after we were married but Arthur assured me that it was one of the most beautiful spots in the country and I relied on his judgement. He had spent some time there during his childhood and had a great love for it.

Umberleigh would have to be left to a caretaker and we decided on John Bonde, Vicar of Yarnscombe. He lived close by and promised to attend to the running of the estate according to my wishes.

Arthur and I planned to have some weeks alone at Soberton before Jane and Thomasine brought the children down to join us. Arthur's own girls would also be coming to live with us as soon as we were settled.

I missed him so terribly during the ensuing months, as the practicalities of everyday life took over and the heady excitement of our reunion became a memory. I needed to decide what to take with us and what to leave, which servants wished to undertake the journey and relocate to such distant parts?

At least once a day I had to pinch myself to make sure it was not all a dream and each morning when I awoke it took a few moments before I adapted to this new reality. For so long I had imagined a life with Arthur, my moods undergoing a range of changing states from youthful ecstasy on the day we had first met nineteen years earlier, which had turned so soon after to utter despair. Then resignation as the wife of John Basset, flickering hope after the apparition at Tintagel, despair again after Arthur's first wife died and now to overwhelming joy in the knowledge that we were finally to be married. Sometimes it was almost too much, and my mind would rebel and cease to function all together.

And if it was too much for me, spare a thought for my children. They had lost the father they loved and now he was to be replaced by another. No-one had asked their opinion or sought their approval. When I think about it now, they were remarkably brave and loyal to me in that they never once showed any displeasure or hostility towards me. Indeed, they outwardly seemed quite excited about this new life they were to lead.

'Where is Hampshire?' asked Mary. 'Is it near London?'

Trust Mary to be the one who wanted to know about London. At six years of age she already had stars in her eyes.

I told them what I could about Hampshire. I knew almost as little as they did but passed on the bit of information Arthur had furnished me with, telling them that it was nearer to London than Devon but still quite a distance from it. Mary looked disappointed to hear this, bless her.

Jane and Thomasine were invaluable to me during that time. Once they had become used to the idea of my

Chapter Nine

remarriage and had put my unseemly conduct behind them, they were very enthusiastic indeed.

Then, during the summer, it seemed that happiness could be snatched from me after such a brief glimpse. There was another outbreak of Sweating Sickness. As before it hardly touched us in Devon, but London was, as always with plagues of any kind, badly affected. I was in a fever of anxiety and sent messenger after messenger begging Arthur to leave the city while the danger persisted. He also sent messengers every few days assuring me that he was well but not able to leave.

It seemed fate would at least step in to solve one worsening problem. The King's fancy lady, Anne Boleyn, who had been given chambers at Greenwich rivalling those of the Queen herself, contracted the sickness. But fate is fickle, and Mistress Boleyn survived.

But my prayers were answered in relation to Arthur and the danger passed with him remaining untouched by the sickness. In October, our wedding took place.

We were married quietly by Reverend John Clappe early one overcast morning at Atherington Church with no pomp or lavish ceremony. We did not even have a wedding banquet. It was our day, a day of reparation for us for all the years we had missed, and we wished to share it with as few people as possible. As Reverend Clappe said the final words which bound us together as husband and wife forever in the sight of God and we turned to each other for the sealing kiss, I felt cocooned and protected by our all-conquering love. As we left the church, the sun, which had been veiled by a thin covering of grey clouds, burst forth and bathed us with its golden rays.

'Lady Lisle,' he said lovingly and placed his hand gently under my chin, tilting my face upwards towards him and the sunshine.

'My Lord,' I replied, just before he kissed me for a long time.

At last he released me and gestured to his groom to bring our horses.

'We had best be off if we are to reach Witheridge by nightfall,' he said, helping me to mount my horse and paying much more attention to fondling my person than to actually assisting me at all.

Arthur had promised me that we would take the journey in easy stages, covering no more than 20 miles in one day. We travelled eastwards and spent that first night at Witheridge. He also made sure that a few hours short of each destination he sent a servant on ahead to ensure that our accommodation arrangements were satisfactory. We travelled at no more than a walk, talking and laughing the whole way, making up for all the years of togetherness we had lost and arrived at Witheridge in the late afternoon.

'And now, Honora, let us to bed,' whispered my shameless husband of less than one day, as he helped me dismount from my horse.

I will not write of our lovemaking, for it is no-one's business but our own. I will simply say that from that first time in my new husband's bed I was transported to such heights of pleasure and passion as I had never known existed. All the years of wanting and yearning were repaid in full every time we lay together.

We slept until late the next morning and I was the first to awaken. As I opened my eyes, I was initially unsure of where I was, then becoming aware of gentle sounds next to me I looked across to where he lay. The morning light shone softly upon his sleeping face, with its clean-cut features and high forehead framed by the golden hair which had so attracted me all those years ago. He was so beautiful and oh, how I loved him. Recalling with pleasure his gentle handling of me the night before and the feelings he had awoken in me, I leant over to kiss his sleeping lips. As I kissed him, he awoke and took me in his arms again. My joy was complete.

'We had best be leaving, had we not?' I asked, after some considerable time had elapsed.

'We have only been married one day,' he sleepily replied, 'and already you are seeking to kill me, Honora. A man needs his rest, you know.' The smile on his face suggested that rest was the last thing on his mind.

But soon we were ready to continue our journey. We travelled as far as Whitnage that second day. And after another night much as the first had been we set out again on the third day to continue travelling eastward. After four more days riding, we arrived at Salisbury

'You seem tired, my dearest,' Arthur said when we arrived in that ancient town.

'Yes, I am,' I admitted. 'All these days in the saddle have sapped my strength somewhat.'

'Not to mention the nights, eh?' He gave me a conspiratorial wink.

'I would sooner have the nights without the hours of riding in between and that is certain,' was my reply to that.

'Well, our journey is almost over and another couple of day's travelling will see us home,' he said.

The following day we set out early in fine clear weather and covered the last miles through Romsey and Bishop's Waltham to Soberton in two days.

My first view of my new home was in the honeyed glow of that late October day. The autumn had been a kind one and the harvest was well in. Soberton was bathed in warm afternoon sunshine and welcomed us with Hampshire gentleness. The house is long and low and nestles comfortably in the small valley of the Meon Brook. It seemed to beckon us that day with outstretched arms as we approached.

As he helped me down from my horse in the wide stable yard I was reminded of another homecoming, that of a new bride to Umberleigh many years before. The bride was the same but, oh, how different she felt!

'Our new home,' he said and kissed me gently, then again with more urgency.

The grooms had hastened to take the horses from us once we had dismounted and as we entered the house, the servants bowed and curtsied and I remembered that I was now a grand lady - Lady Lisle. And together with my Lord I ascended to our chamber.

3. SOBERTON

Chapter Ten

We did not have long to enjoy married life in our new home before it became necessary to undergo another journey. As the new Lady Lisle, I needed to be formally presented at Court and so, after only a few days of bliss with Arthur at Soberton, we left for London. We approached the city along the river on the south side. As we neared Richmond my first sight was of the new palace built only thirty years earlier by Henry VII. I had never before seen anything like it with its tall slender brick towers rising gracefully above the Thames. It was a magical and beautiful sight, my first impression of the big city.

After Richmond we travelled through some open countryside before the city of Westminster loomed, grand and imposing from across the river. There I saw buildings of supreme architectural splendour. Furthest from the river was the great Abbey, to the northeast was Westminster Hall which was the seat of government. There was also Cardinal Wolsey's Palace which had been greatly improved and added to since belonging to that powerful gentleman.

Along the river from Westminster and as far as the city of London, was a row of great houses with gardens running down from the Strand to the river's edge. Then came London itself. This was where the merchants lived and apart from its churches the city had few impressive buildings. Where we were on the south side was the town of Southwark with its tenements and inns. It was a place of entertainment, where the bear gardens and theatres were to be found. We passed them by and then reached London Bridge and the Tower. I saw that imposing structure with the whole width of the river between and still a shiver ran down my spine. How many poor souls had been incarcerated there, never again to see the light of day or to smell the fresh air of freedom?

'A grand sight, is it not, my love?' Arthur sounded proud. It was, after all, his royal ancestors who had built it.

'But a sorry one for many who have entered its portals, I fear,' I replied with a shudder.

'Those days are past,' said my love blithely. 'With King Henry on the throne a new age of enlightenment has arrived. The Tower of London will be a barren and empty place from now on for lack of guests.'

How secure we felt back in those halcyon days before the terror began.

But the Tower was not our destination on that day at least. We passed it by and continued on to Greenwich Palace where my presentation was to take place.

We arrived the day before the presentation and I attended my first Court Banquet that evening. I had attended grand events before, or so I thought, but nothing prepared me for this. After refreshing ourselves in our lavishly decorated chamber at the Palace, Arthur escorted me to the Banquet Hall. There were musicians playing and the sound of their lutes, sackbuts, citterns, and other instruments, combined with the vibrant colours of the hangings and clothes almost

Chapter Ten

overwhelmed me as I entered. Arthur, of course, was used to all this so was able to guide me steadily to my place at the high table very near the King's empty seat. We sat for quite a while before the King arrived but after a time the trumpets announced that we all should stand, and he entered accompanied by an extravagantly dressed but extremely plain-looking woman.

'That is Anne Boleyn,' hissed Arthur in my ear. 'Do not make the mistake of calling her 'Your Grace' if she speaks to you.'

I was outraged that this woman should be taking the place of the rightful Queen and was grateful that Arthur had warned me who she was. Otherwise I would have naturally assumed that she was the Queen and made a dreadful mistake on my very first visit to the Court.

My first sight of the King was a total surprise. From everything I had heard of him I had pictured a man with a much more virile presence. But apart from his vast height and bulk he created no great impression of masculinity at all. Indeed, his skin was soft and fair, almost like a woman's and his hair was a reddish, sandy colour. His mouth was small with full, pink lips. But it was his voice which most surprised me - it was thin and high-pitched and had a feminine quality about it which I found most unsettling. I had to suppress an almost irresistible urge to break out in a fit of nervous giggles until I felt Arthur squeeze my arm reassuringly and knew he had sensed my discomfort.

Then the food arrived, great platters of it. First was the meat - venison, wild boar, mutton, beef, pork, and rabbits. After that came the poultry - dotterel, quail, partridge, crane, puffins, magpie, pheasant, blackbirds, wildfowl, goose, duck, turkey, swans, capons, pigeons, storks, egrets, guineafowl, herons, snipe, and peewits. It seemed every kind of winged and four-footed creature was lying dead before me. Once the vegetables and fruit arrived, I feared the tables would collapse under the immense weight. My senses, already reeling from the music and finery were so assailed by the sight of so much food that I was barely able to eat at all. Servants circulated constantly amongst the guests, replenishing our cups with wine.

From the moment of our arrival we had been constantly entertained. I loved the musicians, particularly the lute players but found the other performances overwhelming. The mummers, jugglers and jesters were exhausting to watch but when a fire-eater appeared, I lost my appetite completely and longed for it to be over.

As a rule, I love to dance but by the time the dancing began I was craving the comfort of my bed and found myself constantly stifling yawns. At last it was finished and once the King and Anne Boleyn had left, we were free to do likewise. With relief, we retired to our chamber.

'Oh Arthur, is it always like that?' I asked, once we were in the privacy of our room.

'I am afraid so, my dear,' he replied, 'but we will make sure that we attend only those banquets which we are forced to. Be assured that I have no more liking for these occasions than you.'

The next day I was to be presented to King Henry. Despite my exhaustion, I spent a restless night and awoke the following morning with a throbbing head and dark circles under my eyes. It was the most important meeting of

Chapter Ten

my life and I was terrified that my bucolic manners might offend His Grace.

Arthur reassured me with a twinkle in his eye. 'Darling girl, even though you are a country-bred lass you will outshine all the fine ladies of the court with your natural charm and beauty.'

I wished I could believe him. King Henry would not be blinded by love for me as was my sweet husband.

Now that I was such a fine lady, I had maids to dress me and prepare me for the presentation. I also possessed far grander clothes than I had ever owned before. My gown had the usual square, low-cut neckline, the border of which was embroidered with gold thread and my over sleeves were sewn with pearls and precious stones. My hood, which I am ashamed to say followed the fashion set by Anne Boleyn and was named a 'French Hood', was heavily embroidered and decorated. Unlike our traditional pointed English gable hood, it was round in shape and displayed the front of my hair. It had only a small veil at the back instead of large side lappets like the gable hood. My voluminous over-gown was extremely heavy, and I felt most uncomfortable. For the first, but certainly not the last time in my life, I wished to return to more simple pleasures. How long ago it was since I had lain on our rock in the Coombe Valley with my brother, dappled sunlight filtering through the trees and our heads full of dreams. Well, here I was living my dream and already I was tiring of it. Not of Arthur, of course, but of this ridiculous stage which was King Henry VIII's Court.

But there I was, Honora Grenville of Stowe, at the ripe old age of thirty-seven, in the Grand Hall of Greenwich Palace being formally presented to the King. My nephew

Richard was there, beaming with pleasure and pride at my rise in social stature, due far more to a hoped-for furtherance of his own prospects than for any fond cousinly feelings, I suspected. For everyone else in the chamber it was just another day, as newcomers to the Court had always to be formally presented although I did detect some curiosity towards me. I heard their whispers as I passed between them. Was this the woman who would beget a male Plantagenet heir to infuriate the King? I had to admit that this thought had not thus far occurred to me. With an unpleasant shock I realised that from now on my life was not going to be straight forward but lived as if on a tightrope. Nothing I did was going to be private anymore but would, of necessity, become a matter of state.

As I entered the Great Hall my legs threatened to give way under me, so exhausted was I from lack of sleep, so overwhelming was my nervousness and so great the weight of my gown. However, I managed to curtsey gracefully enough, as I had been taught to do and was relieved to see that the King was alone. Neither his wife nor his would-be wife, were present.

The King graciously took my hand as I stood from the curtsey. 'So,' he said in his curious little voice, 'this is the woman for whom my uncle was prepared to defy his King all those years ago.' He looked at me with a puzzled expression as if quite unable to see the attraction.

If I had been nervous before this utterance by King Henry, his words removed what little composure I had so far been able to maintain. I had no idea that Arthur had endeavoured to defy the King in order to marry me in 1509, having simply assumed that he had given in meekly to the

Chapter Ten

King's order. My heart bounded and leapt anew with love for this man I had married but for now I needed to regain my senses and show respect to my sovereign.

'Y-your Grace,' I stammered. I was barely able to stand by this time, my mind in disarray and my legs like jelly. Not only was I still in shock over what the King had said about Arthur almost refusing to marry Elizabeth Dudley, but I was still feeling completely over-awed by the magnitude of the occasion and at the same time under-awed by this strange man, the King.

I became aware that the King was speaking again. 'A pity,' he said curiously and then added, 'still, all's well. You have my favour, Lady Lisle. Take that care you keep it.'

And with that he turned away. My presentation was over.

I was left feeling totally nonplussed. What had he meant by those words? Was it a pity that I had not married Arthur 'all those years ago' or was it a pity that I had married him now? There was also the underlying threat in his words 'take care that you keep it.' Almost fainting with the stress of it all, I watched him walk away. Arthur was immediately by my side and assisted me gently from the hall. Never was I more relieved to be by my husband's side as we exited that place.

We returned hastily to Soberton unsure of whether I had been a success or not. One could never tell with Henry.

We spent several blissful, love-filled weeks alone before sending word to Jane and Thomasine for the children to be brought to us. It was with such a joyous outpouring of maternal love that I hugged my little ones as they dismounted in the stable yard at Soberton after their journey. The younger children's nurse and several other servants who had chosen to make the journey had accompanied them and they were to remain with us as well.

Little James was only two and had no idea of what was happening but ran into my arms when he was handed down from the pillion in front of Thomasine. The others looked about them with approval for Soberton is a very beautiful place.

'Oh, my children, we are all to be so very happy here,' I said eagerly. And we were. I know now that those first years of my marriage to Arthur were the happiest of my life. At the time, of course, we thought they would go on forever.

Arthur and I spent as little time as possible in London, retreating to Hampshire whenever we could. He loathed his duties at Court and saw no need for them at all.

'I really think that the King only wants me in London so that he can keep an eye on me,' he said as we walked together in the garden out of earshot of the servants. That was another thing I needed to learn very quickly in my new life. Never speak ill of the King and if you do, make sure that you are not overheard.

'Why do you imagine he wishes to keep an eye on you, my dearest?'

'Because he seems to think that either I, or my adherents have designs on the throne.' He gave a great bellow of laughter. 'I am not even aware that I have adherents but apparently Henry thinks I do!'

I felt the first prickle of fear.

Between the two of us we had a large family. Jane and Thomasine remained with us. Jane was very much an old maid now but despite her sharp tongue was a good organiser and a thrifty housekeeper. Thomasine was becoming more timid and mouse-like with each passing day and the boys teased her unmercifully but without malice. She tended the flower garden and added pretty touches to the interior of the house.

Philippa and Catherine both loved to help in the house and followed Thomasine's example. John was becoming scholarly and had a good head on his shoulders. He had a tutor, under whose watchful eye he learned fast. He was never robust like his brothers but grew well enough. Anne and Mary increased in beauty and charm with every passing day.

'They will marry early,' said Arthur one day as we watched them at play. 'In another few years the suitors will be beating a path to our door for those two.'

How easily we make such light predictions and how fickle is the hand of fate that blows us like thistle-down, first one way and then the other!

George and James were both strong, healthy boys. They played happily enough together despite their contrasting personalities and were able to run free in the gentle surrounds of Soberton. I was fortunate in all my children.

Soon after my own family had arrived, Arthur's daughters were bought down to join us. Frances, the eldest, was fourteen when we moved to Hampshire. She was a fine, attractive girl and despite the difference in their ages she and John developed a fondness for each other from the start. Elizabeth was two years younger than Frances and was a very aloof and cold sort of girl. Of course, I had never met her mother, but I always fancied that she must have been quite like her. Bridget, the youngest, was only three at the time. She came to regard me as her mother, and I looked upon her as my daughter. Her position in our large household was much as mine had been as a child at Stowe and I felt close to her because of this.

At Court there was much unrest. The King was still pursuing Anne Boleyn and had all but abandoned his wife, Queen Catherine. Divorce proceedings were now talked of openly. King Henry was attempting, it seemed, to prove that his marriage to Catherine had always been unlawful because of her previous marriage to his brother, Prince Arthur. The Pope was having none of it, but Henry was like a caged lion, prowling about his prison in an attempt to escape. Meanwhile Anne preened herself and paraded around the Palace as if she were already Queen.

'I cannot understand this hold she has on the King,' Arthur said one day. 'You have seen her, my dear - what do you think of her beauty?'

I replied that I thought her plain and common-looking. 'But I assumed that she has something which men desire, which is not apparent to women,' I added.

'Not that I can see,' replied my worldly husband, 'and I have been known to have an eye for such things.'

I chose to end the conversation at this point as I had no wish to know anything of Arthur's past life and indiscretions. Whatever had happened in his youth and during those unhappy years when he was married to Elizabeth Dudley was of no concern to me. From now on I knew with certainty that he was as devoted to me as I was to him and with that, I was content.

We made a good friend at this time, one of the very few true friends we made at Court. His name was Stephen Gardiner and Arthur invited him to visit us at Soberton.

Chapter Ten

'I know you will like him, Honora,' said my love. 'He is the only really honest person I have met at the King's Court in many a long year.'

The day he arrived to visit us, he alighted from his horse and looked around him for some moments, breathing deeply as if savouring the air. 'Oh, this is truly beautiful,' he said. 'I was born and raised at Bury St Edmunds and I miss the countryside so much at times, it is like a physical pain. It is so wonderful to breath fresh air.' I knew what he meant as the stench in the city is almost too much for one to bear who has not been born to it. Is it a feature of us all that we desire finery and riches only to yearn for the simple pleasures of childhood?

Bishop Stephen Gardiner had been appointed the King's Secretary at about the same time as I was presented. He had previously been secretary to the Chancellor, Cardinal Wolsey. Wolsey had once been the most powerful man in the kingdom after the King and had hoped to become the new Pope. His power had been on the wane since he had been unable to procure the King's divorce. The Pope was ailing at that time and Wolsey had his eyes set upon Rome. He thought that if he could be elected as the next Pope, he could grant the divorce and retain his place in the King's affections. But the Pope lived on and Wolsey's position became ever more uncertain.

As for our new friend Stephen, he was a chubby man, fond of a good, peaceful existence. He had brown hair and eyes, a soft mouth, and a fine, light moustache. Upon his new appointment he was immediately sent to Rome to try and procure the divorce but like Wolsey, he also failed. On his return, a Legatine Court was opened at Black Friars to rule on the validity of the King's marriage. Wolsey was deprived of his post of Chancellor and Thomas More was appointed. Meanwhile, Wolsey left London in disgrace, a fallen man, whose only crime was that he had been unable to grant the King that which he desired. It was a lesson to us all.

We always felt at ease with Stephen and he with us. We discussed topics and said things which would certainly have had us arrested if said in any other company but the trust between us was immediate and well-founded.

'Poor old Wolsey has been dispatched unceremoniously with never a thank you for all the hard work and dedication he has put in for the last thirty years. It serves as a warning to all of us,' he said as we walked in the garden after supper. All such discussions took place in the garden, never ever indoors.

'What of his replacement, Thomas More?' I asked.

Stephen laughed merrily. 'If Henry thinks he will achieve his goal with this new Chancellor then I am certain he is to be sorely disappointed. More is a staunch supporter of the Queen. I am at a loss to understand why he has been given the position.'

'Perhaps Henry thinks he can be bought,' said Arthur quietly.

'Then methinks Henry is going to learn that there are some people who cannot be bought,' answered our friend.

Also, in that year, 1529, the Reformation Parliament met for the first time. We were not alarmed at first. There were abuses in the Church which no-one could deny, and this Parliament was, we thought, designed to stamp out abuses and make the Church better able to serve God as it was designed to do. We all felt that it could be a good thing. How easily we were duped as our most holy institution was torn apart piece by piece from this mild beginning.

The following year, Cardinal Wolsey was arrested at Cawood near York. It took us all by surprise as he had committed no crime that anyone could see. Of course, he was only the first of many, but we did not know that then. He died a broken man, on the way back to London for his trial.

'I am saddened by Wolsey's fate,' said Arthur when we heard. 'He was a greedy, selfish man, but only in so far as many men are greedy and selfish. He had gained for himself the opportunity to satisfy his greed and had made good use of it. But none of that is a treasonable offence that I can see.'

'What was his offence?' I asked.

'The crime for which he was arrested was treason,' answered my husband. 'I really do not know if any details had been worked out. Henry seemed afraid that he was going to try and regain his power. Our King, Honora, is not always rational when he feels threatened.' I found that a very frightening statement.

Oh, how we treasured the times we could escape from London and seek refuge at Soberton where we were well away from such fears and dangers and where our days were filled with the happy chatter of children and with peace and love.

In the year, 1531, the storm-clouds continued gathering force about the Court. That same year also saw the beginning of the rapid rise of one who was to become our nemesis. A man called Thomas Cromwell, who had succeeded Stephen as Wolsey's secretary, wormed his way into the King's affections with a new suggestion - that England should break completely with the Pope in Rome and that Henry should become the head of the Church of England. This was an astounding proposal and not taken seriously by anyone, except the King. Cromwell's reign of terror had begun.

'The fellow makes my flesh creep,' Arthur said with a shudder. We were closeted in the privacy of our bedchamber in the palace, lying close together but still whispering, such was the necessity for caution. We hoped everyone in our retinue was trustworthy but even for the most loyal servant, coins slipped into a hand have a great tendency to loosen the tongue.

'I met cousin Pole today and we spoke of the man. Pole refers to him as 'The Messenger of Satan'.'

'Who is cousin Pole, Arthur?'

'Reginald Pole. He is the son of my cousin Margaret Pole and is a favourite of the King. I saw him briefly on his return from Padua where he has been studying for the Priesthood. He has already left again and is currently in France. Henry offered him the Archbishopric of York if he would support the divorce, but he refused and has considered it wise to absent himself from England for the time being.'

'Would it really be unsafe for him to remain? Surely if he is a favourite of the King ...'

'The King's favourites only remain favourites as long as they do his bidding, my dear, and that is how Master Cromwell has ingratiated himself. He has no principles and his only loyalty is to himself. Therefore, he will do and say whatever Henry wants. He is the son of a labouring man from Putney and was by all accounts a ruffian and a bully in his youth. Although he has covered these characteristics with a veneer of courtly manners, he remains a ruffian and a bully.'

'People do not change,' I murmured. He kissed me then and pulled me closer.

'Thank Heaven for that, my dear, steadfast darling.'

He went on to say more about Thomas Cromwell. 'One of his ploys is to always hedge his bets. He displayed his devious double-dealing ways during the time of Wolsey's fall by openly defending him but at the same time completely detaching himself from him. Anyway, let us hope that he is only a flash-in-the-pan. He is, after all, nothing but a low-born upstart and surely the King will never tolerate him for long,' stated my husband with hopeful optimism.

I was not so sure. A labourer's son from Putney does not crawl out of the gutter and rise to prominence at Court without being exceptionally clever and conniving. He was not likely to make a mistake now.

However, we ceased talking then as Arthur had discovered far more important and pleasurable matters to attend to.

I was able to form my own opinion of Thomas Cromwell a short time later. I was forced to attend a lavish banquet given in honour of Anne Boleyn's birthday. How I rebelled and ranted against having to go. Once the maid had left the room after assisting me into my glittering gown and head dress I was still fuming. 'For goodness sake, Henry is making a state occasion out of the whore's birthday! Whatever next? Will we have to celebrate the day her linnet begins to sing?'

'Hush, my dear, please do not vent your spleen quite so loudly,' Arthur chastised me gently, with a quick check over his shoulder to ensure that the door was closed but still was unable to refrain from laughing at my words. 'Anyway, I do not think she is quite the whore yet. Word has it that she has still not agreed to become the King's bedfellow.' He was whispering now, very quietly.

'Then that explains the hold she has on him. It is the anticipation of delights to come. Let us hope for her sake that she proves worthy of the wait.'

We left the relative safety our chambers then and proceeded to the Great Hall, so any further private conversation was impossible. Upon finding my allocated spot at the table I was dismayed to find myself seated next to Thomas Cromwell.

'Oh, joy of joys,' I thought to myself, 'this evening is going to prove even more of a torture than I had imagined.'

One look at his small, piggy eyes and coarse features was enough for me to take an instant dislike to the man, even if his reputation had not already done the job. He was very shrewd, and I am sure he read the expression on my face and knew immediately that I had his measure. Perhaps he marked me down even at that early stage as somebody to be watched closely.

'So, Lady Lisle, you are newly arrived at Court,' he said in a sly, silken voice as we commenced serving ourselves from the huge platters of meat in the centre of the table.

'As you are yourself, Master Cromwell,' I replied haughtily and turned dismissively away from him, focusing my attention on the repast, and sneaking a look at Anne Boleyn, who was seated at the King's side and acting as if she were Queen already. She was gaudily dressed in an excessively low-cut gown, immodestly displaying her bosom. Her chest was adorned with glittering jewels, undoubtedly given to her by Henry.

Chapter Ten

My rebuff had unsettled Cromwell. He obviously expected far more deference than I was prepared to give him. In hindsight it was a rash and foolish way for me to behave but how was I to know then how powerful this man was to become?

'It would seem that we both have a lot to learn then,' he said quietly, still with the same smooth tone but with an edge to his voice which clearly implied that it was I who had much to learn and not he.

He spoke no more to me after that and devoted the rest of the evening to conversing with the person on the other side of him.

From that moment on, my skin prickled whenever Thomas Cromwell was near. Arthur, more in hope than anything else, still chose to believe that the man's days were numbered. It was not to be, however, and Cromwell was made a privy councillor early in 1531, which gave him open access to the King's confidence whenever he desired it.

It was at about this time that our good friend John Wallop had a violent quarrel with Cromwell. Wallop was a neighbour from Hampshire who had achieved fortune and prominence as a soldier and was also a member of the Privy Chamber. Along with Stephen Gardiner, he was the only real friend we made at Court. I never enquired as to what the quarrel was about, but Cromwell was not a man to be trifled with and I do not think he ever forgave John for that day but he, too, was blind to the threat.

'He is nothing but a fat, limping pig,' said our handsome, sun-bronzed soldier friend, referring to Cromwell's club foot which gave him a strangely uneven gait.

'Yes,' I replied, 'but a fat, limping pig with the King's trust.'

'Every dog has his day,' he replied blithely, 'and his will be short. Do not worry your pretty head about it, Honora. Come, let us make merry whilst we are still young and beautiful.'

'Young and beautiful,' I mused, 'those days are well and truly gone, if indeed they ever existed.' Still, our friend had succeeded in lightening the moment, which he was always able to do. 'Really, John,' I laughed, 'I do not know why we bother with you.'

But, of course, I did know. He was one of the most delightful and refreshing people I have ever met. A few minutes in his company could remove cares and restore a smile to one's face, no matter how evil the day.

In March of that year another shock went through the religious community. Parliament used the Statute of Praemunire to pronounce all the clergy automatically guilty of abuses. This statute was an old one, over 100 years old but due to its at once comprehensive and vague language the Parliament was able to use it to suit its own ends. The King showed his 'mercy', however, and granted the clergy a general pardon provided they pay a ransom of 100,000 pounds. He also at this time took Cromwell's advice and required an acknowledgement from the clergy that he was the 'sole protector and Supreme Head of the Church and clergy of England'. He also stipulated that they would be prosecuted for any further offences.

I became very concerned for my brother John when I heard about these 'reforms' and immediately wrote to him. I received a reply, very carefully worded, saying that he

Chapter Ten

agreed with everything in the Statute and was happy to comply with all the stipulations contained within it. This uncharacteristically formal letter from my beloved brother was the first warning I had that my own letters in future would need to be just as cautiously phrased. How insidiously we were all lured into the net.

Later that year the situation of the Queen and Princess, already uncertain, became terrifying. They were forced to leave the Court. The Queen was to take up residence at Moor in Hertfordshire. Princess Mary was forced to separate from her mother and move to Richmond. Frightening as this was for them, it would have been infinitely worse if they had known that they were never to see the King again and worse still if they had foreseen that mother and daughter were only destined to meet once again, briefly, in this life. The witch, Anne Boleyn, must have been crowing with glee by this time.

Not for the first time, I rued the fact that we were forced to spend so much time at Court. As a mother, my heart bled for the poor Queen. She must have been out of her mind with worry, not only about her own fate but infinitely worse, not knowing the fate of her daughter. The storm clouds were gathering, and it was a frightening and uncertain time.

Without our haven at Soberton I do not know how we would have coped at all. The children were growing and gave us nothing but joy. My estates in the west were doing well and if I sometimes thought with a pang of a wild Cornish storm, my life with Arthur more than compensated for any homesickness. We remained wonderfully happy together and each time we returned to Soberton it was, for us, like the first time we entered its portals, a joyous homecoming for two lovers. All the years of waiting and fearing we would never meet again were receding into memory.

How I grew to love that cluster of buildings on the Meon Brook. During the spring and summer Arthur and I would take the children and walk along the riverbank and the quiet lanes. I would gather herbs and flowers whilst the children would run on ahead, laughing and shouting. There was, and perhaps still is, a large orchard filled with every kind of fruit tree. I particularly loved the autumn when we would gather the fruit. I used to spend many pleasurable hours in the kitchen with cook learning the art of preserving and jam-making. The winters were just as wonderful. We would settle ourselves in the house with roaring fires and sing merry songs together, nibbling on roasted chestnuts. Arthur would have me practise the Court dances, which I was needing to learn. This always caused much merriment amongst the children, who were far from flattering about my lack of grace.

'Pay them no heed, my darling. There is more to life than dancing.' Arthur was ever supportive but also unfailingly honest. It did not escape my attention that he refrained from insisting on my swan-like grace or the butterfly-like lightness of my feet.

Chapter Eleven

Late in 1531 we had the great pleasure of seeing Stephen Gardiner created Bishop of Winchester. It was one of the most moving experiences of my life, to be in that ancient and beautiful Cathedral surrounded by the tombs of Monarchs and Bishops long dead, to hear the glorious sounds of the choir echoing like the voices of angels in the lofty nave above us, to see the centuries-old wall paintings and the carved choir stalls and misericords. And in the midst of all this beauty and history we viewed the ascension of our good friend to his elevated and holy position. I am not sure how many of the other people there felt as I did. Most of them, I think, were only there to curry favour with Stephen and cared not a whit for the sacredness of the occasion.

Once the ceremony was over, the newly created Bishop was still surrounded by a large group of admirers, some long-standing and some very new, clamouring now for recognition. If I knew Stephen Gardiner, he would have no difficulty in telling the two groups apart.

'Look at them all,' he whispered to us. He had left the throng and moved over to where we stood, a little apart from the crowd. 'They are like buzzards around a carcass. I despise the lot of them, but I do happen to quite enjoy the benefits which this life is granting me and so my dear friends, stand back and watch the play, for today I am the main character.'

He walked over to the nearest group with outstretched arms and a dazzling smile. He maintained the smile whilst they kissed his ecclesiastical ring and sang his praises. To a casual observer it would have seemed as if he was completely taken in by the falsehood of it all, but we knew better.

Stephen was an unusual character. He was at once austere and sensuous, a man of principle and one who trod the middle ground. Perhaps that was the secret of his success during the tumultuous years of Henry VIII's reign; he could show whatever quality was necessary to the moment when it mattered. But whatever his faults and contradictions, he was always our friend.

During the following year, 1532, more people came to see what I had already seen - that Cromwell was not just a fly-by-night but was here to stay. Almost every day saw him assume a little more power and worm his way further and further into the King's confidence. Even Arthur finally realised what was happening.

'Well, now Henry had better take an inventory of all his belongings,' he announced in a savage whisper one day in April as he joined me in our chambers at Greenwich. 'That thief and rogue Thomas Cromwell has just been appointed Master of the Jewels.'

I laughed for once, when that name was mentioned.

'He has been Master of the King for some time now, so I suppose he might as well have control over his diamonds and pearls too,' I replied in jocular fashion.

'Hush, my dear,' said my husband quietly, his voice taking on a worried tone. 'It is one matter to speak carelessly of Cromwell but never be heard to say a slighting word against the King, for both our sakes.'

I lowered my voice but was not ready to let the matter drop yet. 'For goodness' sake, Arthur, is Henry really so blind that he is unable to see through this man? I know that I have said Cromwell is clever, but neither is Henry stupid. What prompts him to hand over so much power to one man?'

Arthur's reply was said so quietly that I had to strain my ears to hear it. 'Because, my dear, our King is so blinded by lust and by his need for a male heir that reason has deserted him. Cromwell has promised to get Anne Boleyn into his bed as his legal wife. It is as simple as that.'

'Then may God help England,' was all I said.

But I needed to remind myself that I really must take heed of Arthur's warning and be more cautious in my speech. I was rapidly coming to realise that in the palace the walls had ears and there were spies at the ready to report back to their mentors any ill-considered words. Prominent positions at Court were few and there were many who felt, perhaps rightly, that Arthur's position was only maintained because of his kinship with the King and not due to any outstanding abilities on his part.

However, at Court we were, and obliged to join in the activities and entertainments so lavishly provided. One of those activities was bear-baiting. On the south side of the Thames at Southwark were the bear gardens. These were circular enclosures with high sides in which seats were built for the spectators. In the centre of the enclosed area there was a sturdy pole and a thick chain to which the bear would be secured by a stout collar.

I only went to one baiting and was horrified as soon as we arrived to see the poor creature thus tethered and terrified. As we watched it was further tormented by having pepper blown in its nostrils and by other, coarser brutalities, before the hounds were let loose on it.

At first, they only nipped into the creature's skin, backing away as the bear managed for a short time to keep them at bay but they had the strength of numbers combined with the fact that their prey was tethered and stood no chance at all against them. Their bites became deeper and more savage as they tore at its flesh, exposing the muscles and bone as the bear's strength failed and it soon reached the point where my nausea was threatening to make me ill and I felt myself about to scream with the horror of it.

'Oh, Arthur, please my dear, can we leave now?'

'Not before the King,' he answered. I closed my eyes and placed my hands over my ears in a vain attempt to block out the terrified screeches of agony from the poor beast as the hounds continued their evil work, but Arthur reached up and took my hands in his own.

'I am afraid that with so many eyes upon us just waiting for some show of disloyalty to His Majesty even showing your distaste for this, one of Henry's favourite spectacles, will make us a target for the spies, my dearest love. I will do all I can to prevent you ever having to go through such as this again but for today, for both our sakes, please try and remain strong.'

'I will try, Arthur,' I promised, and somehow, I was able to keep my promise but that was only because I knew that beside me sat the love of my life who understood just what I was going through.

'This is no sport,' I heard him say through gritted teeth, as the bear drew its last agonised breaths through blood-filled nostrils.

But not all the entertainments were so bloodthirsty. There was one leisure activity which I did enjoy and that was

Chapter Eleven

the jousting. These were tournaments between horsemen and were daring demonstrations of strength and skill. A large, open area would be fenced off and gaily decorated barricades erected to protect the onlookers from the hooves of the horses. Elevated seats were provided for us to better see the sport. Severe injuries were rare, but the contests were fast and exciting to watch as the huge beasts and their riders thundered towards each other across the turf. As they drew closer to each other my heart would be in my mouth in anticipation of the clash of the lances and invariably, totally against my will, I would close my eyes just at the moment they met so that I never saw which rider fell and who was the victor until a split second later. Try as I might, I could never train myself to keep my eyes open for that defining moment.

For Arthur, this annoying habit of mine was just as entertaining as the tournament.

'Ha!' he would shout jubilantly. 'You did it again, I saw you!'

'I did not, I did not!' My denial had a childlike ring to it, as if I had been caught in some act of mischief.

'Oh yes you did, my sweetness, and you may as well cease your lies,' Arthur's voice would be both stern and loving. 'I was watching you the whole time.'

'Then,' I would primly reply, 'if you were so busy spying on me you missed seeing the climax of the joust as well.'

'I would far rather look at my love's beautiful face than at any sweating horseman anyway,' and he would kiss both my eyelids for good measure.

Even the days spent at Court had a few such happy moments.

One evening in May 1532, Arthur entered our chambers looking tired and haggard.

'Thomas More has resigned his office as Chancellor,' he told me. 'Henry seemed to think that because of More's gratitude and friendship to him he would stand mildly by whilst the Queen was divorced and replaced by Anne Boleyn. Stephen was right in his prediction. More has steadfastly refused to sanction a divorce and has taken the only course open to him and resigned.'

'Will that be an end to it?' I asked. 'For More, I mean. Do you think Henry will allow him to go quietly or will he have to pay for what the King will regard as disloyalty?'

Arthur thought about that for a while and then said sadly. 'The latter, I am afraid. We at Court are beginning to see that when Henry's friendship is lost it is replaced by a cold hatred and the desire for vengeance.'

My heart felt as if it had been gripped by an icy hand at those words.

I remembered then that a small package had been slipped into my hand as I had stood in the Great Hall that day amongst the other ladies of the Court. We did a lot of standing around, doing nothing and being of no earthly use to anyone. I found it ridiculous and tedious in the extreme. Anyway, as the package was handed to me, I heard a soft whisper. 'For your Lord. Burn it as soon as he has read it.' I turned to see who had given it to me but saw nothing apart from the blank, impassive faces of the Court ladies.

I gave it to Arthur and watched as he read it. 'Who is it from, Arthur?'

'Reginald Pole, to inform us that he will not be returning to England as it is too dangerous. He warns us to be ever

Chapter Eleven

watchful and to absent ourselves from Court as soon as we are able. The times are changing too fast,' he said in a bewildered tone as we placed the missive in the fire and watched it slowly crinkle up and burn away to ash.

As the last of the fragments glowed and went out, I tried to ease his mind a little. 'I have heard, my love, that the King is already becoming tired of the whole matter,' I said.

'I do not think that is the case at all,' replied Arthur with a sad shake of his head. 'Henry is tired of being opposed but remains determined to get his divorce by any means.'

'Perhaps if we return to Soberton for a while, things will settle down.'

Arthur readily agreed and pleading illness, we once more escaped from London to spend the summer at our beloved Soberton.

Chapter Twelve

That summer features in my memory as the zenith of my life. Some of the children had been placed with local families whilst we were at Court. We brought them all home and were a family again. I return to that summer time and time again in my mind when the blackness descends upon me. Often in the night when I am wakeful from despair and loss, I am able to will my spirit away to that summer of '32 and I am again at Soberton ...

The first voice I hear is Jane's.

'Baxter left the milk out again, Mother, and it has gone off. What am I to do? The maid will never learn to dust the stairs properly, they are a disgrace. Master James and Mistress Bridget have come in all covered in some unmentionable filth from the stables. I really do not know how you expect me to cope with all this ...' On and on she goes in my mind, never ceasing. What a comfort it is to me now!

Then I see Thomasine like a shadow moving silently about the house, arranging the flowers, and setting things right. She is followed by my two oldest girls, homely Philippa, and Catherine. What a good example of diligent housekeeping they had from her.

And John, dear John, my first-born son, my angel. I see him as a boy growing into manhood, honest and serious, so like his father. I see him reading in the parlour and I see Frances by his side, she older in years but both so perfectly matched by their gentle natures and devotion to each other.

Chapter Twelve

Anne and Mary appear. Two girls on the verge of womanhood, both becoming aware of their growing beauty but not spoilt by it. Anne, the more practical of the two, so thoughtful of the needs of others, wearing her beauty like a mantle. Mary, gay and carefree, with never a practical thought in her head. When I see Mary, it is with her lute, playing the happy little tunes she so loved.

Then George plods into view, quiet and reserved, seemingly always content, never a trouble. I cannot ever remember having to chastise George. He was an adult even at eight.

But James was completely different, bright and precocious, charming and handsome. James had high opinions of himself and his abilities even then at age six. Life was never dull around James. I see him hand in hand with Bridget, leading her into mischief every day. I see their two little faces, upturned and glowing as they return from yet another adventure

That was our last summer at Soberton. Even the weather treated us well. I think perhaps God gave us that summer to strengthen us for the trials that lay ahead. Arthur and I were still young lovers in our hearts, even though we were no longer young in years. And it was this awareness of the passage of time which gave a sense of urgency to every day for us. Each day was a gift to be enjoyed to the full and each night was even more precious as we lay together in the quiet of our chamber.

'My love, my beautiful Honora,' he would say as we lay entwined, 'how did I live all those years without you?'

'Or I without you,' I would reply.

As the years went by, we had frequently wondered why I never became with child. After all we had both proved ourselves fertile and although I was approaching the age where my courses would cease this had not happened as yet. I was by that time over forty and we both wanted so desperately to have a child together.

Still, we did not allow our concern over this lack of a child to mar our happiness. During those long summer days, we would walk or ride through the forests and fields and along the Meon Brook. Sometimes we went alone and sometimes one or more of the children would accompany us. Occasionally Arthur would hunt with his cousins, the Waytes. I have never been overly fond of the hunt so never joined them. And as we hated to be parted from each other, Arthur only went when good manners prevented him declining the offer.

As the warm summer days began to shorten and the fruit ripened on the trees our contentment increased and the Court and politics were forgotten. Soberton was our life.

We were all in the orchard one warm, late August afternoon picking plums for preserving. James and Bridget were shouting and laughing as usual, our baskets were full, our clothes and mouths stained red and our hearts were high. Then in the distance we spotted dust from a lone horseman. As he drew closer, I recognised the livery of a King's messenger. My heart sank and I knew instinctively that our idyll was over.

Later as we lay in our chamber, we spoke of what the message had meant.

'I suppose we ought really to feel honoured,' I ventured.

Chapter Twelve

'Yes, I suppose we ought,' replied Arthur with absolutely no conviction in his voice.

'And it will only be for a few weeks,' I tried to sound reassuring.

'Yes, it will only be for a few weeks,' replied Arthur in a dismal tone.

Then he held me close and tight.

'But I do not wish to leave, even for a few weeks, Honora. I do not want to change what we have here, it is so perfect. I am afraid that once we go, we will never be able to recapture what we have now, at this moment.'

How tragically right he was to prove to be.

But I continued resignedly. 'Well, my dearest love, as you once told me, we have no choice but to obey the King's command.'

'And I remember what it cost us then,' he said with defiance in his voice.

'It cannot cost us so dearly this time, my only love,' I said and looked into his eyes. 'Now we are together, and so shall we remain. All we are ordered to do is accompany the Court to Calais to meet the French King. It might even be fun,' I ended without conviction.

And so, our final summer at Soberton ended. We rejoined the Court and after preparations, which included my acquiring a whole new wardrobe of fine gowns, we went over the rough waters to Calais.

From the moment I set foot on the ship and felt it rising and falling beneath my feet, I felt cold beads of sweat break out on my face and the beginnings of nausea in my stomach. I made a dash for the side where I clung on to the railings taking deep gulps of air, desperately fighting the urge to disgorge my breakfast into the waters below. And this was before we had even left the dock. From the moment the ropes were untied, and we moved away from the shore into the turbulent, relentlessly rough waters of the Channel I thought I was dying and indeed, felt that death would have been preferable to the misery I was suffering. Once I had completely emptied the contents of my stomach into the sea, Arthur assisted me to stagger to our cramped, airless cabin where I remained for the next ten hours, alternating between sleep and pathetic moaning.

Arthur remained by my side for most of that miserable journey, occasionally venturing up to the deck for some air. Poor man, it cannot have been much fun for him either.

'It is only the sickness which afflicts many first-time sailors, my darling. It will pass as soon as your legs are once again on firm land and your next voyage ought to be much better. We will make a sailor of you in no time.' I managed to turn my head slowly on the pillow and shot him a look of pure venom.

'Sorry, not one of my better jests,' he said contritely and gently wiped my forehead with a cool, damp cloth.

We docked early in the morning, just as dawn had broken. I was barely able to stagger off the ship, only managing to make it down the gangplank because I was supported by my husband's strong arms. It was not a good start to our visit to Calais. Arthur's prediction that I would feel better once we left the ship was not born out in fact. I continued to feel wretched, most likely because I was almost fainting with hunger by that time. Despite my weakness, I can still remember my first impression of Calais. It is a walled town, so all I saw from the dock was a massive stone fortification and two great wooden doors which opened straight on to the wharf area. We were taken through these doors which closed behind us with a loud clang. I thought the sound was quite terrifying. To our surprise we were greeted personally by Lord Berners, the Governor. He was a thin, frail old man who did not appear to have a very strong hold on life.

'Welcome to Calais, Lord and Lady Lisle,' he bowed low, almost obsequiously. 'I sincerely hope that you find Calais to your liking. I have done my best here in the many years it has been my humble duty to serve His Majesty. As you can see, the defences are very sound. If there is anything you wish to see during your stay, I will be only too happy to escort you.'

Arthur thanked him most courteously but confided in me later when we were settled into our chambers at Lord Berner's house that he was completely baffled as to why Berners assumed that he would wish to take a tour of Calais.

'It is hardly a beautiful sight,' he said, with a wry expression.

I agreed. 'A bleak, ugly town indeed. Thank Heaven our stay is to be a short one.'

The accommodation was far from luxurious, but I cared not. I have never been happier to lie down on a bed that did not move and after a short period of time, to partake of some food and drink. After that I did begin to feel well again, thank goodness, and was able to take a better look at my surroundings. From the window of our chamber I could see out over the town and observed that it was built in a square shape, surrounded entirely by the town wall. It was, in fact, a fortress. The buildings were clustered tightly together, and the lanes and alleyways appeared narrow and even from this distance I could see that they were full of filth. Fortunately, we were left to ourselves that first evening and Arthur sent for our supper to be brought to our chamber where we ate in peace.

There was a banquet the following evening at which our presence was required. I chose to wear the most lavish of my gowns, a silly, jewel-bedecked thing with the fashionable square-cut bodice and embroidered underskirt. I rebelled slightly on that occasion in that I wore the traditional English gable hood and not the French Hood so favoured by Anne Boleyn. I have heard it said that we ought to be careful what we wish for. As a child I wished for such trappings. Now I wished to be wearing comfortable, plain garments with my sleeves rolled up, safely back in the warmth and comfort of the kitchen at Stowe, or Umberleigh, or Soberton. Anywhere but in that great hall at Calais, surrounded by the King's minions and with his fancy lady taking pride of place by his side.

For of course, Anne Boleyn was there, and rumour had it that she had now admitted the King to her bed. What I found most strange was that the King paid her very little attention. It was almost as if, once having achieved his goal of bedding her, he had completely lost interest. I actually caught him looking at her at one stage during the feast with a look almost of distaste. Still, she appeared not to notice and acted as if she were already the Queen.

There she sat preening herself and looking like the cat which got at the cream. Her dress was of the finest silk, embroidered all over with the most delicate stitchery I had ever seen. It must have taken hundreds of hours toil by the best seamstresses in the country to have worked such fine detail. She was dripping with jewels which hung low right into the cleavage of her bosom, so brazenly displayed due to the low cut of her gown. Her sleeves were voluminous and made the act of eating her food look difficult in the extreme but as she appeared to eat almost nothing this apparently posed no problem. Her hood was, as always, of the rounded French style.

We had been told that the reason for our being there was to meet the French King, Francis, and we were quite unable to understand the reason for this. We were also surprised at how much attention King Henry seemed to be paying to us. Halfway through the meal he requested that Arthur and I move to join him at the head table, replacing Lord Berners and his wife who exchanged places with us. Lord and Lady Berners seemed to find nothing unusual about this. It was all very strange. Once we were seated by his side, Henry began quizzing Arthur about his impressions of Calais.

'So, Uncle, how goes it with you? Have you a liking for this place?'

'I have not been here long enough to form an opinion yet, Your Majesty,' replied my husband, still not understanding why we were there or why his opinion should count for anything.

Henry continued to probe. 'Lord Berners has been a very good governor here. His work has pleased me greatly. He has done much work on the defences. Do you think they could be improved in any way?'

Once again poor Arthur was forced to admit that whilst he thought the walls appeared sufficient to withstand an armed force of attackers, he had not really given the matter any thought. He was looking so miserable and out of his depth that I was tempted to say something to ease his discomfort but was completely unable to think of what it should be. Fortunately, King Henry's attention was diverted from us at that moment because the French King stood up and made ready to begin the dancing.

When King Francis danced, no-one had eyes for any but him. He was an exceptionally good-looking man, almost the same age as King Henry but not quite so large. He had an athletic build and elegant manners. He danced first with Anne Boleyn, as was expected. She, who had been educated in France, performed the intricate steps gracefully and perfectly which obviously pleased both the French King and her own. With a practised skill which, against my will, I was forced to grudgingly admire, she performed the Galliard, Almain, Gavotte and other new dances so recently brought to England from France. To my complete bafflement, the next lady he favoured with his invitation to dance was me. I had no wish to exhibit my rural dancing skills in front of the noblest peers of two realms but, as always with the wishes of Kings, there was no choice but to obey. The steps had been so recently learned and so rigorously practised that I was at least able to perform them correctly if not with the same amount of grace as the Lady Anne had done. I was still quivering with nervousness when I returned to my seat by Arthur's side.

'You were wonderful, Lady Lisle,' he whispered in my ear.

'Oh, Arthur, I was so nervous,' I replied, speaking in a hushed tone so as not to be overheard by the King, seated next to Arthur. 'Why on earth did he ask me?'

'Because you are the most beautiful woman here, of course,' he replied without hesitation.

Chapter Twelve

'Do not be so silly.' I giggled and slapped him lightly on the arm. 'Answer me truthfully if you can.' The King had decided to speak with Anne Boleyn at that moment so we could converse quietly without him overhearing.

'Then I really do not know,' he said thoughtfully. 'The whole evening has been strange, almost as if we are being tested for something. I suppose in time we will find out what.'

'Yes, first to be moved to sit by the King and then to be asked those questions about Calais.' I was thoughtful. 'Why on earth does His Majesty want to know what I think about Calais? It is nothing to do with me. And then for Francis to dance with you in precedence over all others excepting Mistress Boleyn. It makes no sense.'

'Well, thank you,' I said feigning hurt pride.

'You know what I mean, my darling,' he said. 'Important as you are to me, in terms of hierarchy he ought to have asked Mistress Berners before you, at the very least. Mind you she looks so ancient it is doubtful she would have survived the experience.'

We both laughed then and spoke no more of the matter.

Once the official part of the evening was over, we were free to mix with whoever we liked. Arthur and I spent a delightful hour with our old friend Stephen Gardiner. Besides his new duties as Bishop of Winchester, he was still the King's Secretary and was finding the job to his liking.

'But how do you fare on the subject of the divorce?' Arthur asked.

'You know me,' he replied with a twinkle in his eye, 'I can state my opinion for a good ten minutes, after which no-one is yet quite sure what it is.'

'An admirable quality, I am sure, Stephen,' I said sharply, 'but how does that satisfy the King?'

'I am in a fortunate position as Secretary,' he replied in a more serious tone. 'I am employed to record what others say and not to form judgements of my own.'

'But does Henry not wish to know where you stand in this matter of the divorce?' Arthur asked.

'Not really, he simply assumes that as a loyal subject I support him fully in all that he wishes to do - *and*,' he continued quickly as I began to protest, 'you would both do well to follow my lead and keep silent where it is expedient to do so.' He gave us both a long, meaningful stare.

We were quiet for a few seconds after this, then he said as if by way of explanation, 'We are not all made to be martyrs, Honora and we are not all like King Canute to try and command the tide to turn before it is ready. Our lives are ruled by destiny and chance. Whether I agree or not with what the King wishes to do is irrelevant as I cannot change it.'

We were silent again for a while.

Then Arthur said. 'Thank you, Stephen, for your wise counsel. Honora and I will both benefit from your prudent advice.'

I was still not convinced that they were right. Surely there comes a time when one must do and say what one knows to be right, I thought. But then I thought of Reginald Pole, exiled from his country and of Thomas More, forced to leave his post as Chancellor and I said nothing.

We were not to be enlightened any further as to the reason for our strange experiences at the banquet and the following day were free to return to England. Much as I dreaded crossing the Channel again, I stepped almost gaily on board the ship, glad to be leaving Calais and happy in the belief that I would never have to make the journey again.

Chapter Thirteen

After we returned to England we were obliged to remain at Court as the King seemed anxious to keep Arthur by his side. The Parliament was still passing law after law, curbing the power of the Pope over the Church in England. It was stated that all annates or tithes which formerly had been paid to Rome were from now on to be paid directly to the Crown. They also passed the Act of Appeals which prevented any appeals to Rome, thus ensuring that the only law to be obeyed by Englishmen was English law.

Then at the end of January in the year 1533 we heard some news which, though long expected, we found shocking, nevertheless. The King and Anne Boleyn had been secretly married and Anne was expecting a child. We were amongst the few who heard the news at this time. Support for poor Queen Catherine was still strong amongst the general population and the King wished to have the law firmly on his side before making an open announcement. The Archbishopric of Canterbury was vacant and despite our friend Gardiner's expectation that he might receive the post it was to be granted to a new power in Court circles, Thomas Cranmer. Unlike Gardiner, Cranmer was openly and actively supporting the King in his divorce proceedings.

We were coming out of the chapel following morning prayers one day in early February when a page presented Arthur with a summons for us both to attend the King immediately. This was most unusual as Arthur saw the King most days anyway and I was never expected to be present, spending the long, boring days in idleness and gossip with

Chapter Thirteen

the other ladies of the court. Full of consternation and utterly perplexed, we hurried to the King's chambers.

To our relief, the King's face was benign and full of good humour.

'Hah, Uncle, you made good time!' As I arose from my curtsey, he addressed me as well. 'My dear Lady Lisle, I see you have quite recovered from your dance with King Francis.' He seemed to find this quite amusing, so we were forced to do likewise.

'You cannot help but to have noticed on your visit to Calais that Lord Berners was not long for this world,' he went on and we waited, nodding slightly which was, apparently, all that was expected. 'He has now gone to meet his maker and so Calais is ready to receive its new Governor.' He stopped speaking and clearly expected some response this time but we both looked blankly at him, not knowing what our reply should be.

'Well, Uncle, what have you to say?' Henry began to look impatient.

Poor Arthur, he looked so miserable in his confusion and I was unable to be of any help to him as I was no less perplexed than he.

The King was by this time clearly tired of toying with us and spelt the matter out. 'For goodness' sake, Uncle, have you been blind as well as deaf these past weeks? The position is yours, man. You are to begin your preparations immediately.'

We were rendered speechless with shock and were unable to make any response, but it was obvious that none was expected as Henry, once having delivered his command to us, turned on his heel and left. And so, it had been decided, we were to leave Soberton and England and move to that vile outpost on the coast of France.

The shock and horror we felt was profound. These feelings totally overrode any sense of honour or excitement. Now the King's strange behaviour on our visit to Calais was explained, as was the whole reason for our being taken there in the first place. It also explained why the French King had danced with me before any other Court ladies apart from Anne Boleyn. We felt like puppets at a masque, our strings being pulled hither and thither by our puppet-master, the King.

Night after night, as we lay in bed and talked about this latest order from the King, we sought in vain for a way of escape.

'We could return to the west country,' I said, grasping at straws. 'We could say to the King that our estates are being run down by managers and we are needed there.'

This was, in fact, true. Umberleigh did not seem to be returning the profits it had previously and we had received no news from Tehidy for many months.

'The King cares not a trifle for our estates,' said Arthur with brutal frankness. 'I think that having cousin Pole out of the country has planted the idea in his head that it would be expedient to have all his relations removed from England.'

'Why?' I asked.

'I do not know,' Arthur said wearily. 'It is just that I must be the last man in England to be suited for the post of Governor of Calais, so there has to be another reason.'

'I am certain that Cromwell is behind this, Arthur,' I said angrily. 'The King does nothing these days without his say-so. He knows that we have his measure and wishes us removed from Court so that he can move more of his own lackeys in.'

But it was worse than either of us realised, as Cromwell manoeuvred us into his net like pawns on a chess board. Oh, foolish Honora, to have made an enemy of the man with your thoughtless jibe!

Arthur had been quite correct in saying that he was not suited for the position. He had neither experience in, nor talent for, diplomacy and Calais was in such a sensitive area that it needed a Governor with both qualities. France was still loyal to the Pope, but it was also becoming a hiding place for heretics, both of which were against Henry's policies. Calais, because of its proximity to France was bound to become caught up in any conspiracies or plots formed by either camp. We only partly realised at the time what a dangerous mission it was to be.

Lord Berners was fortunate in the timing of his demise. During his time as Governor, Calais had been relatively quiet. The troubles there, as in England, were only just beginning. Whether he would have proved to be any better at dealing with them than we did is a matter of conjecture.

But our reluctance was futile. The decision had been made by the King and we were to go to Calais. There was no room for negotiation and no possibility of appeal. We returned to Soberton to organise our departure.

A few days later while we were still too shocked to have made any progress in our plans for our family and belongings, we received a visitor. We greeted the newcomer in the parlour and were faced with a stocky, compact man of middle height. He brought with him a document of introduction from Stephen Gardiner which told us that he was named John Husee and was the son of a Hampshire gentleman of the same name. He was to be our secretary and servant. Gardiner assured us that he was sending us the best there was. Husee, he wrote, was both trustworthy and shrewd and knew 'how the system worked'. The implication was that we did not and in this he was frighteningly correct. We had gained a treasure.

Husee waited whilst Arthur read Gardiner's letter and passed it to me. He thus knew from the outset that I was of equal importance.

'We bid you a warm welcome, Master Husee,' said Arthur, extending his hand, 'and words cannot express our gratitude to Bishop Gardiner for sending you to us. We have no knowledge of the task which lies before us and know not where to start.'

'I understand that this whole business has come as quite a shock to you, Lord and Lady Lisle. My hope is that I am able to ease your passage into this new position and am willing to do anything within my power to make the process simpler for you.'

'Oh, Master Husee, it is such a relief to have you here!' I was so relieved at the sight of this capable-looking man that I became quite tearful.

Husee immediately took control and helped us to clear our heads for the daunting task of placing the children and organising our move. He very quickly became so embroiled in the day-to-day existence of our household that it seemed he had been with us forever. The children, almost without exception, took a liking to him and he to them.

The exception was James.

Chapter Thirteen

'Mother, Mister Husee has been ordering me about again,' complained my youngest one afternoon as I was frantically sewing some lettice bonnets for Bridget. 'He says I am to go to the Abbey of Reading next month and I feel I would be much better suited to go to Calais with you.'

'Well, James, Mister Husee is quite right as you know. I have already explained to you that you are going to Reading to begin your education.'

'Yes, Mother, but I was going to talk to you about that. I think I would be far better advised to go to France and attend college in Paris,' continued my seven-year-old.

I almost weakened then as I looked into his pleading eyes. He was, after all, my baby and I was going to miss him so terribly. But just as I was about to change my mind, John Husee entered the room. He looked first at James with a glowering expression and then turned to me enquiringly.

'John,' I said, 'James and I have been discussing his future.'

Husee had already taken stock of the situation and stepped in boldly.

'Yes, My Lady, I have just this moment finished drafting a letter to the Abbot at Reading. James has been accepted there already and this letter is to confirm his placement. It is a very good institution for a young boy to begin his education. I have heard that the French Colleges are not nearly so suitable,' said Husee with another savage look at my son.

And so it was decided that James was to remain in England under the guidance of the Abbot of Reading. I regret that Husee never became fond of James. I think he always felt him to be a 'mother's darling', which perhaps was correct. How I wish he had lived to see the kind of man my James became.

My worries about Umberleigh were to be settled, I hoped, by the offers of both Jane and Thomasine to return to their childhood home as caretakers. They were still hopelessly incompatible, but I hoped that it would work out. Neither of them wished to go to Calais and, unlike Arthur and myself, they were fortunate enough to have a choice in the matter. John Bonde was still in charge of Umberleigh, but I was beginning to have suspicions as to his suitability for the post and was grateful for family members to be once again taking up residence there.

Thomas St Aubyn had offered to continue as caretaker of Tehidy for us. His estate at Clowance was only a few miles distant so it would be no hardship for him. This was a load off my mind as Tehidy was a rich source of income from the tin-mines and needed someone close by to oversee the workings. I did feel that he was not much use as an overseer but was better than nothing and he was family.

John was also to stay in England. He was to live for the moment with our neighbours the Nortons at East Tisted near Soberton. Richard Norton and John had become firm friends, so it was a good plan. As soon as he was old enough, it was arranged for John to commence his study of law at Lincoln's Inn.

The Abbey of Hyde at Winchester was George's destination, so he had not far to go either. We had made the acquaintance of the Prior at Hyde and he was more than happy to undertake the education of my model second son. George, as usual, made no demur and seemed content to do as he was told.

Chapter Thirteen

Arthur's second daughter, Elizabeth, with whom I had never formed a cordial relationship, chose to go to her half-brother, John Dudley. Dudley was Arthur's stepson and the few times I had met him I had found him to be an unpleasant, arrogant man. Stephen had warned us that he was not only fiercely ambitious but also ruthless and dishonest. He had recently been appointed Master of the Tower Armory and was a man on the rise. Elizabeth was welcome to him.

Little Bridget, she of the piquant face and gurgling laughter, was also to stay close to Soberton. She was to go to the Abbess of St Mary's at Winchester. Of this lady, Elizabeth Shelley, I had formed a very good opinion and would not have been happy to send Bridget to any other. The Abbess assured me that we would receive frequent correspondence concerning her young charge.

The other girls were all to cross the Channel with us. Philippa, Catherine and Frances were to remain in Calais whilst Anne and Mary were to be placed with noble French families. Anne would be residing with the family of Thibault de Riou at Pont de Remy. Arthur had met Sieur de Riou back in 1527 when he had taken part in an embassy to the French court. He had kept in touch with this gentleman and had come to regard him as a good friend.

'I have heard back from Thibault,' Arthur entered our bedchamber waving a document as I was packing clothes with one of the maids. 'He is only too glad to have Anne and suggests his sister Anne de Bours for Mary. She is married to the Seigneur de Montmorency.' Both girls were ecstatic with this plan. Mary's eyes, in particular, shone delightedly at the prospect of living with the French nobility.

At that time relations between England and France were cordial. It seemed a very good plan for the girls in all respects. They would be close to us and would gain much refinement from their time in these households.

All our plans were made by Arthur and me and facilitated by John Husee. One by one, the children left and apart from one, I shed bitter tears at each parting. None of this was what we had planned for our marriage. We had envisioned many years together with our combined families at Soberton. We had even thought that perhaps as time went on, we would be able to spend less and less time at Court until our presence there was not required at all. Now the exact opposite was happening.

Husee became an indispensable member of our household in those few months leading up to our departure from Soberton. I suppose it was fortunate that we were so busy for we had no time to continue feeling sorry for ourselves. Once the organising began it took over our lives.

There had been more political developments during these months as well. Cromwell was made Chancellor, so at last Henry had found his man. There could not have been two more different men than More and Cromwell to fill the same position.

The day after Cromwell's investiture we learned that Henry and Anne's marriage, which had been a badly kept secret, was to be divulged openly.

In May 1533, our presence was required at Court. This was to hear the Royal Decree which declared the marriage of Anne Boleyn and Henry to be legal and valid due to the fact that he was never legally married to Queen Catherine.

Chapter Thirteen

'So now the whole country is to know about the marriage,' Arthur said in a resigned tone after we had listened to the reading of the document and were closeted in the relative privacy of our chambers.

'About the bigamy, you mean,' I answered scornfully.

'No,' replied Arthur, 'as you heard, Henry has got around his inability to procure a divorce by having his marriage to Catherine declared null and void from the beginning. He was, in fact, never married to her.'

'Never married to her!' I exclaimed angrily, forgetting to keep my voice low. 'Next they will be saying the Princess Mary is illegitimate. Is there no end to the tricks this King will perform to satisfy his lust?' I raged. 'And what happens when he tires of the whore, as I have heard he is beginning to already? Will this marriage be declared null as well?'

'Hush, my dear. For mercy's sake, hush. You will have us both clapped in the Tower if you do not take care. Now,' he continued, 'if you will stop your ranting and listen quietly, I will tell you something else I heard today.'

He sat back down and opened his arms for me to settle inside them. This I did gladly and with my head resting against his chest I soon relaxed and was able to listen to the rest of the news.

'The King's son is now a Lieutenant of the Order of the Garter. It is rumoured he is to be married before the year is out.'

'But he is only fourteen,' I could not help interrupting.

'Too young to be married or too young to be a Lieutenant?' asked Arthur with a laugh.

'Do not mock me Arthur,' I said primly. 'It is too young to be anything but a boy.' I thought longingly of my own childhood at Stowe and of the boys there, my own brothers and nephews, running free and wild at the same age this poor little King's bastard was now. As I thought of him in his gilt-edged prison, I felt sorrow for him.

'Honora, my love, you must learn to accept what happens,' Arthur pleaded, 'especially when it does not affect you and cannot be changed. Do not take everything to heart so much. You cannot solve all the problems of the realm, so try not to worry about them.' He held me close and I knew he spoke sense, but we were two different people and I could not stop worrying about things which I knew were wrong.

'On that note,' he continued, and his voice became sad, the words coming slowly and reluctantly, 'I will tell you of the news that does concern us. The new Queen is to be crowned on the first of June and you and I are to be there. Immediately following that we are to set sail for Calais.'

My heart sank. I think that for all this time, during all the preparations, I had still clung to the hope that something would happen to prevent us having to go. But it was not to be. In a few weeks' time we would be in Calais and our time at Soberton would be over. The children were already gone, and when we returned to Hampshire two days later, the house had a cold, empty feel about it, so different from the welcoming warmth of the day of our arrival. I felt Arthur's gentle hand on my face and realised that he was brushing away my tears. We clung to each other for a while and then I said:

'Take me to bed, Arthur. Comfort me there.'

Thus, ended the happiest period of my life. Oh, if only time could be reversed, and I could find myself back at

Chapter Thirteen

Soberton again with Arthur and the children. If only, if only...

4. CALAIS

Chapter Fourteen

'I do not wish to go, I am unwell.' I was being dressed in a sumptuous new gown for the coronation of the King's whore as Queen of England. Nothing would persuade me that she was his legal wife or his wife in the eyes of God and nothing would persuade me that she was my rightful Queen. That position was held by poor Queen Catherine, who was being kept a prisoner.

Arthur looked beseechingly at me and begged me with his eyes to show tact and restraint in front of the ladies-in-waiting. Out of love for him and for that reason only, I held my tongue and stood like a statue whilst the women fussed around me. We were to have an official position both at the coronation ceremony and at the banquet afterwards. I felt like such a hypocrite and wondered how I was expected to live with my conscience. As I stood there, I prayed that I would be forgiven for my human weakness in not remaining true to my principles. Perhaps, as Stephen Gardiner had said, we were not all meant to be martyrs.

The coronation and banquet are not clear in my memory. I know I smiled and curtsied in all the right places and spoke politely to Anne Boleyn at the presentation. I know I danced, ate, and conversed but as to what was said or what

Chapter Fourteen

we ate I have no recollection. Afterwards, my husband was relieved.

'Thank you, my dear, for today,' he said. He had dismissed my ladies-in-waiting and was helping me out of my heavy jewelled gown. 'I know how hard it must have been for you.'

'You know, Arthur, I have just thought of one good reason for looking forward to Calais.' I smiled at him.

'And what is that?' he asked.

'We will be spared having to see Anne Boleyn every day and calling her 'Your Grace'. I really do not think I could keep it up for long.'

Arthur laughed, but quietly. 'Even in Calais, Honora, there will be spies. We must guard our tongues there even as we must here. Please remember that.'

Once again, I promised him I would be careful.

A few days after the coronation we set sail for Calais. As before, I spent the entire voyage lying on my bunk groaning and holding my stomach. I missed the sight of the white cliffs and the sparkling water and I swayed and swooned as I set foot on land at the other end. As the Grenvilles of the next generation are becoming a family of seafarers, I definitely am only suited to life on solid land.

I arrived feeling sick, dejected and afraid. Arthur had no more an idea of how to be a governor than I did. We had been given no instructions and no funds. It seemed we had been exiled and yet had committed no crime.

Calais was just as I remembered it from the previous year's visit - a dull, odorous cluster of houses surrounded by a frighteningly imposing rectangular wall. It is neither a pretty town nor a welcoming one.

The house was our first problem. How on earth Lord Berners had managed in it was quite beyond our understanding. The kitchen was cramped and primitive, the bed chambers damp and musty. The servants had to sleep on palliasses in the attic, women in one room and men in the other or else find accommodation elsewhere. The only decent chambers were the Great Hall where we had attended the banquet on our previous visit and the state chambers which we had for our own use and to sleep important guests.

Arthur was sworn in as Governor on the Tenth of June. Our new life had begun. One of the first surprises we had on assuming our new position of importance was how many really good friends we had of whom we had previously been unaware. Gifts and warm letters of appreciation began to flood in immediately, accompanied by good wishes and full of praise for our goodness and kindness. The fact that these letters were from people we hardly knew or knew not at all and usually contained a paragraph requesting a favour for the writer or for one of his kin tempered my appreciation of them somewhat. Arthur, on the other hand, never believed in looking too deeply into people's motives and revelled in his new-found popularity.

'Arthur, do we really need another dog?' The latest letter was from an acquaintance of a friend of one of Arthur's cousins in Hampshire. He professed life-long devotion and sent a gift of a young hunting dog. After two paragraphs praising my husband's honourable nature and generosity he asked if there was a place to be had in our household for his son who he described as a paragon of virtue and just as devoted to us as he, the writer was. Given that the lad was

Chapter Fourteen

fourteen years of age and, like his father, had never set eyes on us, this was perhaps exaggerating the situation slightly, which I pointed out to Arthur.

But my darling was not to be deterred. 'I do seem to remember the family,' he mused. 'I believe them to be of good sound yeoman stock. Perhaps the boy needs a hand up in life, and we can always give the dog to someone else.'

This last was true, gifts of animals and birds were passed around from one to the other, barely having time to settle in one place before they were again packed up to be sent to another. If we were confused by the turn our lives had taken, one wonders how these poor creatures felt about theirs!

'As you wish, dearest,' I sighed with resignation. I was learning to choose my battles, and this was of small importance.

The other surprise, which was immediately apparent, was that the town had been badly run-down and ill-provisioned. Poor old Lord Berners had been failing badly, it seemed. The staff were lazy and ill-trained. Nothing had been maintained and the whole place was in disrepair. Arthur sent urgent letters to the King requesting the necessities to keep Calais functioning.

As the months went by and his letters had not been answered he began to get very worried.

'What is happening here, I wonder?' he said to me. 'I have done all I can. I have written letter after letter detailing what is needed. Nothing has arrived and no word has been received. I cannot keep Calais functioning on fresh air alone.'

This unhappy state of affairs persisted throughout the summer. We were thoroughly miserable and apart from brief letters from Husee, had received little news about our children to set our minds at rest. It was as if we had entered a void and the world had forgotten us. Then, in early September, we had a visit from our friend Stephen Gardiner. He was passing through on his way to Paris on ambassadorial duties.

'What a joy it is to see you, Stephen!' I greeted him with relief. Here at last was tangible proof that England had not forgotten us.

'Honora, Arthur, my dear friends,' he embraced us both.

As we led him into our house, which was more like a merchant's home than a Governor's mansion, he was looking at us searchingly.

'The last months have not been kind to either of you, I can see,' he said unflatteringly as we entered the parlour.

'Oh, Stephen, we feel so trapped here. The place is so awful, and we have no idea how we are supposed to proceed with neither instructions nor funds and I miss my children so very much.' My voice broke then, and tears began to fall.

'Perhaps these will help,' he said kindly and produced a packet of documents from his pouch.

Arthur took the packet quickly, almost rudely from Gardiner's grasp. Then, with an apology for his bad manners he began to read.

Whilst he read, Stephen and I spoke of the need for us to have a place to where we could escape when Calais became too much for us.

'A little country house, close enough to here so it can be easily reached but far enough away that we can be completely alone,' I said dreamily. I then asked Stephen if he had any news of the children.

Chapter Fourteen

'John is happy and well,' he told me. 'Richard Norton speaks nothing but good of him, which is only as I would expect, knowing John as I do.'

'My dear, good John,' I said with a catch on my voice. 'What of the others?'

'George is progressing quietly and is causing no bother and the Lady Bridget is losing her bonnets faster than they can be replaced!' He sounded indulgent as everybody did when recounting Bridget's mishaps.

I laughed, relieved that the children were well and acting true to their natures.

'What of James?' I asked.

'James is settling in,' Stephen replied evasively, then continued after careful thought. 'He is not like the others, that one. He has immense ability and an adventurous nature. It would be a shame to try and curb him too much.'

'Do you think we should remove him from Reading?' I asked, sensitive to the concern in my friend's voice.

'For the moment, no, I think it is all right. He is learning fast and is not yet bored. Do not worry, Honora, I will keep a close eye on Master James for you,' he assured me.

At that moment we were interrupted by a howl of rage from my usually placid husband. Never before had I heard such a sound from him, and both Stephen and I stared at him in horror.

'What is it?' I gasped. 'Arthur, what has happened?'

'I will tell you what has happened!' he roared. 'That upstart Cromwell has sent this, this *rag*!' He waved the letter about violently. 'He dares to criticise my request for provisions and writes to me as if he were the Lord and I the shop-keeper's son.' I had never heard Arthur so upset.

'What else does he write?' I ventured.

'He pretends that His Highness is also displeased with me. I will wager anything you like to name that my letters never even reached the King.'

Stephen said quietly. 'Between the three of us, I must warn you to be ever-watchful of Cromwell. He is as devious as a snake and cunning. I also feel that your letters did not reach the King. As the King's Secretary I would have known, and no such letters have been sighted by me. Write another letter and I will deliver it into the King's own hands for you.'

Later when the house was quiet, Arthur told me of some more of the contents of the letter.

'I have not told you all of Cromwell's poison yet, my love,' he said as we lay together. 'He had the gall to mention you.'

I stiffened. 'How so?'

'He seems to think that I listen too much to your counsel and advises me against the practice.'

I lay pensively for a while. I had known since our first meeting that Cromwell knew I had his measure. So, he warned Arthur against taking my advice, did he? Well, we would see about that. If it was war he wanted, it was war he would get.

'And do you intend heeding his advice?' I asked, bristling with indignation.

Arthur squeezed me tight. 'No, I do not. We are partners and if I wish to discuss anything with you, I will continue to do so. You so often seem to see things more clearly than I do, anyway.'

That was true and I was grateful that Arthur realised it. He had no head for business and intrigue. He would

Chapter Fourteen

have been like a babe lost in the woods without me to guide him. In fact, since our appointment I had spent my mornings in Arthur's office with him. Together we read all the documents which arrived and decided between us on what action to take. Frequently I wrote the replies myself, handing them to him for signing.

Stephen left the next day on his mission to Paris, carrying a letter from Arthur to be handed personally to the King when he returned to England. A few days after he left, we received a message from London. Anne Boleyn had been delivered of a baby girl at Greenwich Palace on the Seventh of September. The child had been named Elizabeth. The King was reported to be extremely out of humour since the birth as he had placed all his hopes on Anne producing a son. He had shown such displeasure to her that she had been seized by despair. For once I almost felt sorry for the whore. Unless she could produce a son, she was of no more use than the real Queen and could be just as easily discarded.

Just over a week later, Stephen returned on his way back from Paris. His business for the King had not proceeded satisfactorily and he was not looking forward to reporting back to his sovereign, but he had good news for us.

'I have found you a country house,' he said happily.

'Oh, Stephen, where is it?' I gasped. I had forgotten all about our brief discussion before he went to Paris.

'It is at Landretun, only three miles hence,' he replied. 'It is only small but as soon as I set eyes upon it, I knew it was just the place for you two. Come now with me and see it for yourselves.'

We immediately had horses saddled and away we rode, three carefree people, off to view a house in the country.

That one of them was the Bishop of Winchester and the King's Secretary and another the King's Deputy in Calais was of no consequence. For that afternoon we could be ordinary gentlefolk without a worry in the world.

Landretun was just as lovely as Stephen had said. It was nestled next to a forest, a little cottage, snug and cosy. It was surrounded by a sturdy dry-stone wall and had an orchard of fruit trees. It seemed a world away from the drabness of Calais, even though it was only three miles. We could be here in no time at all and at the same time, right away from our daily cares. We entered the front door like children exploring a new wonderland. The cottage consisted only of a hall, a parlour, kitchen and two bedrooms. All the rooms were simply but comfortably furnished.

'Oh, Stephen!' I exclaimed. 'It is just wonderful! How did you ever find it?' I actually ran in and out of the rooms in my excitement.

Arthur looked at me with a glow in his eyes that had been absent ever since we had come to Calais. Landretun promised to be good for us in more ways than one. For a moment I almost wished Stephen was not there.

'It matters not how I found it,' he replied. 'The important thing is that it is here, it is vacant, and it is yours if you want it.'

Arthur and I exchanged joyful glances.

'Oh yes, we want it!' we shouted as one.

Chapter Fifteen

As the autumn progressed, we gradually became used to our new life at Calais. It seemed that Stephen Gardiner had either failed to have the promised audience with the King regarding our provisions or that his requests had fallen on deaf ears because none of our requisites arrived.

In October Arthur had another letter from Cromwell. This time Cromwell actually had the gall to berate him for not adequately provisioning the town! Referring to the previous administration he stated that:

'*...before this time, the town and marches of Calais have been well maintained and prospered ... the King's Highness is not a little displeased.*' He also had another jibe at me. '*For although My Lady be right honourable and wise ... her advice and discretion can little prevail.*' He ended the denunciation with a warning not to try and get further messages directly to the King. '*...importune the King's Highness with none other matters...*'

'I cannot believe Stephen gave my letter to Cromwell, I simply cannot believe it,' Arthur threw down the letter and sank his head into his hands.

'No Arthur, Stephen would never betray us. It is my belief that he did give your letter to the King, but that Henry simply passed it straight to Cromwell to deal with. In all likelihood he did not even read it.'

Arthur was furious and I saw a side of him that I had never seen before and rarely did see in our private life together. Arthur was a slow man to rouse to anger but once roused he did not hold back his venom.

He wrote back to Cromwell, again taking no pains to hide his disgust and in the most sarcastic terms requested to know how he was supposed to provision the town with no provisions. He stressed the number of times he had written and asked pointedly if the King had even seen the letters. He took issue with Cromwell's claim that the King was displeased with him and asked why the King did not write to him of this in person if it be true. Finally, just before Christmas the authorization arrived, and the town could be provisioned. It had been a long time coming and was to my mind just a little game of Cromwell's to indicate to us how much we were in his power. We were left in no doubt but that we had made an enemy of the most powerful man in the kingdom.

So great was our distress and worry that we escaped to Landretun for a few days. It was the first time we had gone there since purchasing it. We sent some servants to clean it and make it ready, stocking the pantry with enough food to last us and then went there alone, as became our habit. Entering the door of that little cottage, we felt its peace descend on us like a soothing tonic.

'It has been a long hard day's ride,' said my husband. 'Come, wife, let us to bed.'

'Arthur, it is three miles!' I laughed robustly as he led me towards the bedroom.

The following day I was resting in the garden of that little piece of paradise. It was a warm, still afternoon, rare

Chapter Fifteen

for the time of year, and I was at peace. As I slumbered in the sunshine, I noticed a man walking up the path towards the house. He looked to be a local farmer and I saw he had a little basket under his arm. My French was only slightly better than his English, so we communicated by gestures and occasional words. He placed the basket on the table next to me and opened it. Inside was the dearest, tiniest, loveliest little dog I had ever seen. He looked out over the rim of the basket with one eye hidden by an ear and the other looking inquisitively at me. I loved him at once.

'For me?' I asked. '*Pour moi?*' I gestured from the basket to myself.

'*Oui, Madame,*' replied the farmer, smiling broadly.

I reached in and took the little dog from the basket. First, I held him close then away from myself for a better look. He had the sweetest face imaginable and a permanently puzzled expression due to his habit of holding his head on one side and to the ear that fell half over his face.

The farmer began to laugh. '*Pourquoi?*' he said. '*Pourquoi?*'

I had no idea what he meant and repeated perplexedly. 'Purkoy?'

The farmer doffed his cap and walked away convulsed with laughter. It was not until my knowledge of French had improved that I realised we had most likely named the little dog after his air of always appearing confused.

Anyway, Purkoy became my constant companion and after several protests, Arthur even agreed to let him sleep on our bed.

Court news which reached us in December reported that young Henry Fitzroy, the King's illegitimate son, had been married to Mary Howard, daughter of Thomas Howard

Duke of Norfolk. How either of the young people felt about this arrangement was not mentioned.

Other information about the King's offspring was that the two Princesses, Mary and baby Elizabeth, had been sent to live in the same household at Hatfield. But Elizabeth was the acknowledged legitimate heir and Mary was in a subordinate position.

The requisition authorization, which we received just before Christmas, was brought in person by our newly appointed High Marshall of Calais, my own nephew Richard. Even though I had never been fond of Richard he was family and where possible I owed it to him to help him to advance in the world. His arrival was accompanied by the usual noise and bluster.

'Hello, Aunt!' he bellowed as he swung from his horse. He let go of the reigns which were hastily collected by a groom as his startled horse prepared to run off. Grabbing me around the waist, he picked me up bodily and spun me in the air, almost crushing poor little Purkoy, who I was holding in my arms.

'Richard!' I gasped as my feet touched back down. 'That is no way to treat the grandest Lady in Calais.'

'Is not it?' he asked innocently. 'Then please accept my apologies, Lady Lisle. And also, please accept my congratulations on your new station and, might I say, a hearty thanks for appointing me your Marshall.'

I never knew with Richard when he was speaking sincerely, if indeed he ever was, or when his words were edged with sarcasm. He always had a cynical tone to his voice which I found most unsettling.

Chapter Fifteen

Arthur had arrived to see what all the hubbub was about and was greeted in similar jocular fashion. That was when I realised that Richard had been drinking.

'Greetings, Uncle, how goes it?' were his first words to the highest official in the town.

Arthur was never at a loss with drunks and he summed up the situation much faster than I had done on this occasion.

'It goes mighty well, Richard, mighty well,' he said soothingly and taking Richard firmly by the arm led him smartly indoors.

That was how our new High Marshall arrived and how he continued right through Christmas and into the New Year. Richard appeared to regard his appointment as a grand cause for celebration. By New Year he was so sick that 1534 was several days old before he was in control of himself again.

Maud and the children joined us in the middle of January. She always had a settling effect on Richard and there was no repeat of this behaviour. For all his faults, Richard proved himself a capable official from that time on.

It was wonderful to have Maud living nearby. I spent many happy hours with her and the children. Philippa, Catherine, Frances, Purkoy and I would take the short walk to their lodgings, where the children would frolic with my little treasure whilst we women exchanged pleasant conversation.

'Oh, I have missed days such as this,' I sighed one dark day in late January as we sat together sipping delightful French wine. 'Calais has been nothing short of hell on earth until you came, Maud.'

'I can see that it is not a pleasant place,' agreed Maud. 'The air here is barely fit to breathe. I do hope the children remain well.'

With Maud every thought was for her children. She was a wonderful mother and a good wife to Richard, not that he deserved it.

John Husee wrote to us every few weeks with news and advice. He was reminding us constantly of the need to send presents to people such as Cromwell and Anne Boleyn in order to keep their favour. It irked me very much to have to send presents to the whore and I complied as little as possible with this unwritten law.

Whenever I did send her a present, I tried to make sure it was nothing I valued highly. One such item was a linnet which had hung in our bedchamber ever since we arrived in Calais. I have no love of caged birds, preferring to see them happy and free in their natural world. This little fellow used to sing loudly and constantly, whether from joy or frustration I never knew. What I did know was that the noise it made was very annoying as was the mess. So, I sent it to the Queen and received a message back that she loved it!

Then Richard had to go and spoil everything. On one of his trips to Court he told a lady-in-waiting about Purkoy and she told the Queen. The first I knew of it was a letter from Husee to say that the Queen spoke of nothing but my little dog and must have it. I had no choice but to let him go. My dislike of Anne Boleyn turned to hatred on that day.

But my hatred became even more bitter a few months later when I heard that little Purkoy had died, falling from an upstairs window and the Queen had not even missed him until several days later. My most treasured pet had been nothing but another dispensable acquisition to her. I shed bitter tears and not even Arthur was able to console me.

'Oh Arthur, I do wonder whether Richard is simply thoughtless or whether his every action is tinged with malice. Why on earth would he go and speak of Purkoy at all?' Arthur held me close.

'Darling, I am sure Richard meant no harm.' Oh, Arthur, you dear unsuspecting man.

'I will never forgive him, and I will never forgive that witch who killed my baby.' I burst into a fresh torrent of sobbing and all he could do was to soothe me as best he could and wait until the storm had abated.

But life continues and we must move on with it and make the best of every situation. Arthur was slowly learning how to run Calais and now he had Richard, who for all his faults, was proving to be a great help in this respect. But, oh, how I missed the days when I could roam free as I did as a child and no-one knew where I was. That was why we enjoyed Landretun. We always went there completely alone, Arthur and I, without even a cook. Once there we could simply be ourselves. The only times in those Calais years when we were completely happy were the days we spent at Landretun.

We went there in early February 1534. Two grooms made the journey with us carrying enough cooked food and provisions to last us. After they had unpacked the boxes, we sent them home with instructions to return in three days' time. It was freezing cold, but we had enough firewood to keep the fire in the parlour burning all day. We spent most of the time sitting or lying in front of the fire talking, eating, loving and sleeping. We even brought the bedding out of the bedchamber and spent the nights there. Once or twice each day we rugged up and ventured into the winter garden. The fruit trees were bare, of course, and covered in the most beautiful hoar frost. The surrounding stone wall had icicles hanging in the crevices between the rocks. We looked over the barren ground and made plans for where we would have the vegetables and flowers planted in the spring, just as if we were a regular couple of country folk. It was such a bitter-sweet time for us and over all too soon.

Immediately after those joyous few days at Landretun, Arthur had to go to London on business. We parted sorrowfully. It was to be the first time since we had married that we would be apart. Like a small child, my tears fell in torrents as he prepared to leave.

'It will only be for a short while, my darling,' he said bravely but I could see how the parting was hurting him as well. 'I leave Calais in capable hands.'

'I hope you tell Cromwell that,' I replied through the tears. 'I am sure he would be relieved to hear it.'

It broke my heart to be parted from Arthur. I waited on the dock until his ship was a speck on the horizon, then turned sorrowfully back towards the town. I suppose I could have gone with him, but London held no more attraction for me than did Calais and when I thought of the odious sea journey it took in order to get there, I made the difficult decision to remain where I was.

Whilst he was away, I made sure I kept myself busy. I spent every morning as usual, in the office, attending to correspondence. I carefully read through each document, dealing with those I was able to and putting the others in

Chapter Fifteen

a pile for Arthur to read when he returned. Another pile contained letters I had written for him to sign.

It was also an opportunity for me to spend more time with the girls. It is a fact that my love for Arthur, because it took precedence over everything else, did take me away from them. It was Philippa's idea that I should learn archery. King Henry was actively promoting the general population to become proficient in this sport, even women. Philippa, Catherine and Frances had been practising for weeks and Philippa had taken to it like a duck to water. Against my better judgement I agreed to join them one day. Oh dear, I was hopeless! I have never been strong in my arms and I am afraid that my feeble efforts only succeeded in sending arrows everywhere but towards the target. They frequently fell at my feet or landed only a short distance in front of me. It was a great source of merriment to the girls. I will say that Frances was the kindest, perhaps because her efforts were not much better than mine. Philippa had always been a strongly built girl and became very competent.

We spent many enjoyable hours in the kitchen as well. Once the cooks had recovered from their amazement that we wished to join them in their labours, they put their confusion aside and very soon we were all quite comfortable together.

'I do admire the way you cope in this bleak place,' I said to them as we squeezed tightly past each other in the confined space of the basement kitchen. 'Lord Lisle and I are looking out for better accommodation and I can assure you that a suitable kitchen is high on my list of priorities.'

The cooks exchanged gleeful smiles. 'Oh, My Lady, that sounds wonderful,' said the head cook, gratitude causing her already warm and rosy cheeks to glow afresh.

Even Calais has some pleasant memories.

The business for which Arthur was recalled to England was to witness the sitting of Parliament. He returned in late March looking tired and careworn. After I had overseen him rested and fed, we sat together and talked until late into the night. As I looked into his dear, beloved face, I tried to compare it in my mind with the handsome, carefree visage I had first seen back in 1509, and with which I had fallen so hopelessly in love. The same features were still there but now they were marred by lines of worry and bewilderment, as if he found the turn of events too much to understand. My gentle, good man deserved better than to be plunged into the dirty business of Kings. He was made for laughter and merriment, not for plotting and intrigue.

'Now we have the Succession Act,' he said wearily. 'The marriage of the King and Catherine has been annulled and his marriage with Anne Boleyn confirmed. As you predicted, Princess Mary has been declared illegitimate. Queen Catherine is now to be known as the Queen Dowager, which she is entitled to be as Prince Arthur's widow. All her lands are given to Anne Boleyn.'

'That is all terrible,' I said, 'but hardly news. These matters have been brewing for years now.'

'Yes, but now it has been made treason to say anything derogatory about Anne Boleyn or her marriage to the King.'

'Well,' I replied, 'we shall just have to be careful that we only speak of her in private, will we not.' I was trying to speak lightly to ease some of the worried look from his dear face. I could not understand why he did look so worried. After all, none of this was surprising or new. It was just the existing situation ratified by Henry's puppet parliament.

'There is also another act called the Submission of the Clergy which states that all clergymen must submit to the King and not to the Pope, or the Bishop of Rome as they are now calling him,' he continued.

'Yes,' I said, 'that is also terrible but not unexpected. It only sanctions that which is already in effect.'

He continued to sit glumly staring into space.

I crossed over to him and sat on the floor against his legs. 'Arthur, my dearest love, what is it? None of these Acts of Parliament can have upset you so.' I looked up into his haggard face and my heart ached to see him.

'I saw Husee,' he said.

'That is good, I hoped you would,' I replied eagerly. 'How is he?'

'He was able to say much to me that he is unable to write in his letters,' Arthur continued. 'He is a very worried man and concerned for our future and for that of the realm.'

I waited for him to continue.

'The man Cromwell is becoming drunk with power and it does not look like ending. The King is more under his influence than ever. Husee senses that Cromwell has us in his sights and feels that evil times are coming.' He stopped speaking and gripped my shoulder tightly, almost painfully. Then he gave a great groan as if Cromwell's torturers were already at work on him. When he spoke again it was in a voice taut with anguish.

'Honora, oh my dearest love, why did this have to happen to us? Why could we not remain safely on our estates in

Hampshire?' His voice began to break. 'Did we not deserve a little more happiness after all our years of waiting?'

For the first time since I had known him, Arthur cried. His body was wracked by immense sobs and I was powerless to stop them. It went on for long minutes until I felt sure my own heart would break from my inability to help him. It is a terrible and frightening thing to see a grown man cry. At last the storm was over and I eased him down to the floor with me. As I cradled him in my arms, I was afraid to move lest he begin to cry again. So, we sat there holding each other the whole night through, until the early dawn light began to filter into the room.

For hours neither of us had spoken. Perhaps we had slept a little. As the room brightened, we stirred and looked at each other. It seemed neither of us was willing to speak after the events of the previous night. What could we say?

'Who shall try to move first?' Arthur said at last, smiling wanly.

Then we began to laugh. Once we started, we could not stop. It was as if a madness possessed us. We were filled with an insane joy which acted as a foil to the despair of the night before. We were together and together we would face whatever evil times awaited us. Together we would beat Cromwell and be happy.

I had not had my courses during the time Arthur had been away and had been going to tell him as soon as he returned that our longed-for child may at last be on its way. But because of his distress and need to unburden himself I decided to wait until the following day. However, as we stood up shakily from our night on the floor, I felt a cramping pain in my belly and the tell-tale warmth which spelt the beginning of my bleeding.

We heard shortly afterwards that Anne Boleyn had again been with child but had miscarried. As a woman, I felt immediate sympathy for her, but this was tempered straight away by other, unkind feelings and the thought that it might possibly hasten the King's decision to separate from her and perhaps even return to his rightful wife.

And it was true that the King was not pleased at all and was now openly ignoring Anne for other, more attractive ladies of the Court. Her position became ever more desperate, but it was still in our best interest to send her gifts and I had the perfect one presented to me.

The Lord High Admiral of France had acquired two marmosets from the forests of Brazil. They were malodorous, chattering creatures and I had no hesitation in sending one of them straight to the Queen with my very best wishes and kindest regards. I did not hear anything about how my present was received for some weeks until we had a visit from Stephen Gardiner in May.

The three of us found a secluded corner in the garden where we could talk privately.

'Your gift to the Queen was not well received,' said Stephen with a twinkle in his eye. 'She has no liking for such creatures.'

'I am very sorry to hear that,' I replied insincerely. 'It cost me much heartbreak to part with it. I do hope she cares for it and does not allow it to fall,' I added, tears springing to my eyes as I again recalled in anger her treatment of Purkoy.

But it seemed that Stephen had far more weighty matter to discuss with us. We had heard little from London for the past month and what we had heard had been brief and vague.

'I suppose you know that I am no longer the King's Secretary,' he said after a moment of silence.

'It was a matter of some mystery to us that Cromwell addressed himself as Secretary in his latest correspondence,' I replied.

'Well, it is true. He is now Secretary and controls everything which the King reads or writes. Whereas before it was still just possible to get a message to the King without his knowledge, now it simply cannot be done,' Stephen sounded aggrieved. 'The 'Queen Dowager' has been sent to Kimbolton Castle in Cambridgeshire. It is as secure a prison as any,' he continued. 'Thomas More has been sent to the Tower for continually speaking out against the divorce. If he does not change his tune, his head will roll.'

'Is it true that a nun has been executed?' asked Arthur.

'Oh yes, that is true,' replied Stephen sadly. It took an obvious effort for him to tell us about it. 'She, together with a group of monks, has been martyred for refusing to accept the changes.' He sounded resigned and also, perhaps, somewhat impatient with such stubborn resolve in the face of death.

'I wonder how John is managing?' I said more to myself than to my companions.

'John?' asked Arthur, clearly thinking I referred to my son.

'My brother John, the Rector at Kilkhampton,' I replied. 'He is such a good holy man; I wonder how he is coping with all this.'

Chapter Fifteen

Stephen looked thoughtful. 'So far most of the priests have been all right. As long as they keep quiet and get on with their priestly duties no harm befalls them. It is the monks and nuns who are threatened. The King is starting to cast greedy eyes at their monasteries and if he can execute a few for treason along the way he has a good reason for persecuting them later on.'

A shiver of foreboding passed up and down my spine. I was not sure how much more bad news we could take. Little did I know that this was only the beginning.

Chapter Sixteen

As the summer of 1534 turned to autumn, we had a letter from Francis Lovell, a wealthy Norfolkshire landowner. He wished to ally his family with ours and proposed doing this by the marriage of his son Thomas to Arthur's daughter Elizabeth. We had no dispute with this and wrote back accordingly. However, only a few weeks later we received notification that the Lovells had changed their minds.

'Perhaps young Thomas has had a meeting with her,' I said spitefully to her elder sister Frances. 'Elizabeth would be far better advised to keep herself hidden from prospective bridegrooms until the wedding day unless she wishes to remain a maid.'

'Mother, you really should not speak so of Elizabeth,' Frances replied admonishingly. 'She has *some* good points,' she added with a little smile.

Frances and I enjoy a cordial and relaxed friendship. It was one of my dearest hopes that the friendship between her and John would blossom into something more when John grew older. The years were passing, and it was becoming more apparent that Arthur and I were to be denied a child of our own. If John and Frances were to marry, we might still have grandchildren between us. It was a secret and private dream. I did not confide it even to Arthur.

I had received some letters from James and his tutors. He still wished to be educated in France and his teachers felt that he had progressed so well that it would be possible the following year. I had accordingly made enquiries at Paris

Chapter Sixteen

and he was accepted to join the College of Calvy the next August. It was something to look forward to, the thought of James being close to us in the near future.

Meanwhile, the year was drawing to a close. Calais was proving a depressing and laborious place for both of us. Arthur was not the right man to administer such a volatile outpost. He had the education and presence but not the requisite nature for such a task. He was too open and honest and totally incapable of subterfuge, which was one of the most necessary attributes for a politician in those days, and perhaps in all days. His gentle, easy-going nature was too easily swayed and duped by scoundrels and tricksters.

The young lad from Hampshire had turned out to be nothing but a wastrel and a miscreant. It transpired that his father had sent him to us because he was at his wits end as to how to deal with him. After several weeks spent putting up with this unpleasant boy, we had packed him off home.

'Do you mind, dearest, if we decide together from now on when we receive such a request for help?'

'I certainly do not mind at all, Honora. I never wish to have the likes of such a terror under my roof again.' Poor Arthur, he had only accepted the boy out of the kindness of his dear heart.

Almost daily we were approached by one or the other seeking advancement and citing plausible reasons for their case, be it family connections, a debt owed or a reference from some other worthy. From that time on Arthur passed them all straight to me. Most of them ended up in the fire.

I have to admit that in business matters he was also hopeless. I am the one with the head for business but between us we managed to get through each day and to sort out the many problems that came and went. What neither of us realised was that there were far greater problems hidden from us which even I failed to recognise.

Christmas 1534 was almost upon us. We had sent the obligatory gifts to the King, Cromwell, Anne Boleyn and all others of importance at Court. We had received gifts from the sycophants beneath us in the pecking order and were preparing to relax, at least for a few days, during the Holy Season.

I was in a deep depression. The weather was foggy and low, and we had not seen the sun for weeks. Arthur and I both hated Calais with a passion and missed our younger children terribly. It was only our love for each other which gave us the strength to face each day.

The morning of December fifteenth began like all the others in that miserable Advent and I was sitting passively whilst my maid dressed my hair when I heard a clatter in the courtyard followed by a cacophony of voices. Then my maternal ear picked out one voice amongst the others.

'James!' I shrieked and jumped to my feet, upending my stool and spilling hairpins all over the floor. The maid sprang backwards, astounded, as I tried to disentangle my skirts from the legs of the overturned stool. And just as I freed myself and was making for the door it burst open and my youngest child ran into my arms.

'James, oh, James,' was all I could say as I held him tight against me. Tears of joy coursed down my face. I had my baby home for Christmas.

It is amazing how one's mood can change and with it the mood of a whole household. Suddenly the world was a brighter place and Christmas took on a festive air more in keeping with its traditional role. The house was filled with James' happy prattle and even the servants became more cheerful. To complete our happiness, we had Stephen Gardiner with us for a day. True to his word, he had been keeping an eye on James and had been instrumental in organising his departure from Reading.

The morning was relatively mild for the time of year, so we went into the garden for some air – and some privacy. James clung to my hand, smiling up at me with candour and love. I felt my heart overflowing with joy.

'James is one of the brightest pupils the Abbot can remember ever having,' Stephen told us with an indulgent look at his protégé. 'Although he is only eight, the Abbot feels he is quite ready now to continue his education in France.'

'It is arranged that he commences at Calvy in August,' Arthur replied. 'We had not expected him to leave Reading until that time.'

'I fear I must take full responsibility for that,' Stephen replied sheepishly, 'but I felt that as he had done so well at Reading it might be good for him to spend some time with his mother before travelling to Paris.'

He twinkled at me, no need for him to put into words that the mother needed the child equally if not more than the child needed the mother.

Arthur stood quietly, his eyes shining with love. He may have been slow when it came to political subterfuge, but he understood the workings of the human heart very well indeed.

'It was an inspired move, Stephen,' he said, smiling benignly.

James soon rushed off to explore his new surroundings and we moved further into the garden away from the house. We sat on a bench in the secluded corner where Arthur and I often went for private talks and the conversation turned to weightier matters. 'Stephen, we have been starved of news from Court apart from official letters. Tell us what has been happening if you will,' Arthur began.

Stephen heaved a great sigh and began.

'Thomas Cromwell is now Master of the Rolls. It is an empty title and adds not a whit to his power which is almost absolute already but puts one more string to his bow.'

He had a hatred of Cromwell which was equal to our own and we sat in silence for a while considering where it might all be leading.

Stephen continued. 'There is a new Act of Parliament, the Act of Supremacy. It merely formalises the existing situation. The King is the Supreme Head of all persons and causes within the realm of England. This includes the Church and gives Henry the authority to reform and redress all heresies and abuses within the Church.'

'Does that mean it is ruled that the Pope has no power at all in England?' I asked.

'That is so,' he answered.

'But,' I continued, thinking deeply, 'as the Pope already has the power and as the English King cannot over-rule the Pope, he has no authority to make such an act of parliament.'

'That is the opinion of many, but not said aloud by those who have no wish to part company with their heads,' said Stephen pointedly. He continued in a patient and resigned tone. 'As I have said to you before, dear friends,' he looked fondly at us both, 'there are times when a sensible man who enjoys this earthly life and wishes to die a natural death must keep silent. I am such a man. Each of us must make his own decision about which path he, or she, will follow.' He looked pointedly at me.

Another new act about which Stephen told us was the Treasons Act. It was now formally and legally a treasonable offense to wish, will or desire by writing, words or even thought, any kind of harm to the King, Queen or their heirs apparent.

'This is almost comical if it were not so dangerous a law,' Arthur commented.

'Yes, my friend. This act abandons any logical legal principle. It converts treason into a crime which has no character except heinousness,' said Stephen sadly.

'Even our thoughts can be punished by death,' I mused. 'England will be a vastly empty place if this law is ever able to be put into practice.'

We were again silent, plunged into morose and despairing thoughts of our own, when James reappeared.

'It is starting to snow!' he exclaimed. 'Oh, how wonderful, snow for Christmas! Come on you three, you look so glum. Come inside and let us be merry together, please do.'

We had failed to notice until then but the first few flakes were falling and by the time we walked the short distance back to the house it was snowing heavily.

'Young James is right,' said our friend, placing his arm protectively around the boy's shoulders. 'Be of good cheer, my dear ones. You have your son, it is snowing, and we are about to celebrate the birth of our Saviour.'

Stephen left us again by the night sailing. We parted fondly and comfortably as friends do. He promised to visit as often as possible, especially now that James was in Calais. He still retained a special spot in his heart for James. I think that was because, unlike many, Stephen was able to see past the façade and into the soul of a person. I never knew him to be wrong in his summing up of a character. James was never one to hide his feelings, blurting out his opinions loudly and forcefully, without thought. This trait indicates total honesty in those who possess it but because it frequently offends the listener it tends to make as many enemies as it does friends.

Christmas passed happily and peacefully. It made all the difference to us, having James present. Philippa and Catherine were overjoyed to be with their little brother again. Frances also made a fuss of him, but I felt that secretly she wished it had been his older brother who had been spending Christmas with us. James had the ability to bring people out of whatever depression they had sunk into and to take pleasure from each moment of the day, whatever the circumstances. This quality did not pass with his childhood but stayed with him throughout his life.

Our poor cooks were still struggling to cope in the pitiful conditions of our kitchen and in preparing the Christmas feast that day, they had been unable to manage the extra work involved. Several of the dishes were overcooked and the beef was so underdone that it was oozing blood and quite inedible. Arthur, having no knowledge of the art of cooking or of the particular difficulties faced by our own cooks, was all for complaining in the strongest terms. I was more understanding but was still upset that our meal was ruined.

Chapter Sixteen

My boy cared not a whit. 'What does it matter? We have plenty to eat without the beef. There will still be food left over.' He placed his hand behind his ear, with an intent look upon his face. 'Can you not hear it?'

'Hear what?' asked Catherine.

'The beast is still mooing!' He burst out laughing and we all joined in until the tears were streaming down our faces.

In February, my son John left his friends the Nortons and went to London to commence his study of Law at Lincoln's Inn. He was now sixteen years old and I had not seen him for nearly two years. I missed him terribly and resented that I was missing out on seeing him turn from a boy into a man. How I hated Calais.

It was also at this time that we had an example of how my husband's innocent nature could be duped by charlatans. His very own stepson, John Dudley, arrived bearing a wordy document concerning our lands in Devon and some in Somerset which Arthur had gained through his marriage to Elizabeth Dudley. It was written by a clever clerk in the employ of Dudley and his cohort Edward Seymour. It pertained to the rents from our lands and according to Dudley would vastly simplify the collecting of these rents for us. Like a child Arthur happily signed this document and before I had a chance to study it for myself, Dudley was gone. This one signature of Arthur's set us up for months of legal wrangle and lost rents from our properties, which ended up in Dudley's own coffers. It was not settled until a lengthy court battle months later.

Early in May we had a letter from Husee telling of the execution of several of the monks of the Charterhouses. They had been given the horrible traitor's death.

'I know you will be in a piteous state to hear this news,' he wrote, thus putting not only himself but us as well, at risk of arrest for treason. Such were the times in which we were living.

But life still had some few light moments. We continued to escape to Landretun as often as possible, and I was acquiring quite an herbarium there. I not only grew and cultivated herbs but spent hours searching the fields and hedgerows for new plants with which to experiment in my kitchen.

Arthur teased me about it. 'You will be hanged for a witch,' he jested.

'Better that than to be drawn and quartered for a traitor,' I replied.

I picked and dried my herbs, grinding them to powder and mixing potions which the local people used gladly as remedies for their minor ailments. I also gave them to our friends and acquaintances, most of who were satisfied with the results. One such customer whose remedy was effective if not a little dramatic was Edmund Howard. Edmund was the youngest brother of Thomas Howard the Duke of Norfolk. He had a large family of ten children and was always in debt. He was a light-hearted, shallow fellow but never wittingly caused anyone any harm. One of his daughters was named Catherine and would one day make his family famous but none of us knew that in 1535. Anyway, at the time, Edmund was Comptroller of Calais and was plagued by kidney stones. I gave him a potion made from the root of the Saxifrage and he wrote to me the following day to plead his absence from supper that night.

It seemed that my remedy did indeed cure his stones, causing them to break into small pieces which he then needed to pass. Unfortunately, this induced much discomfort and urinary incontinence. So much so that his wife gave him a beating and banished him from her bed! Poor Edmund was in such a state that he dared not leave his house for fear of disgracing himself.

How we laughed when we read that letter and for some time afterwards Edmund was the butt of our jokes, but he took it all in good heart and was able to laugh with us. Laughter was hard to come by during those years in Calais, so we made the most of what there was.

As the summer of 1535 advanced the news from London became ever worse. Thomas More, we heard, had steadfastly refused to recant his opposition to the King's marriage and at nine o'clock on the morning of the fifth of July he was beheaded for treason on Tower Hill. I wonder how the King felt knowing that his long-time and valued friend had lost his life for refusing to acknowledge the wife of whom he was already weary. We heard that More went to his death bravely and even made a light-hearted jest to the executioner.

In August James left us. We had a servant sent over from England, a man called John Worth and he accompanied my youngest to Paris where he entered the College of Calvy to continue his studies. I was saddened by his going, the last eight months had rejuvenated me so much, just having him close. But James was happy, as he had dreamt of Paris for years now and was at last achieving his desires.

Later that same month when we were still getting used to the silent space which James' leaving had left in our house, we received a document notifying us that there was to be a Royal Commission of Enquiry into the state of Calais.

'Royal Commission! What is the meaning of this? HONORA?' I was in the solar together with our daughters attending to some embroidery on several new bonnets when we heard Arthur shouting. The distress in his voice was almost palpable. Dropping my work to the floor, I shot the others a wide-eyed look and fled to his side.

Silently he handed me the document. It seemed that the King had at last got wind of some of the problems we faced but as he had never received the true facts about our difficulties, he felt that the blame must rest with Arthur's management. Accordingly, no doubt with advice from Cromwell, he had set up an enquiry into the state of affairs in Calais. It was a stunning blow and one which came as a complete surprise to us. For although we were still desperately short of money and unable to carry out all the work necessary, we had done our best and had been unaware that our achievements were under scrutiny.

'Oh, my darling,' I put the document down and reached out to him, 'my darling, darling man, perhaps this will be for the best. For surely now the truth will come out that we have been denied the funds we need and thwarted every time we tried to speak to King Henry about our troubles.'

Sadly, Arthur nodded. 'Perhaps so.' He sounded so very tired and, oh, how my heart ached for him.

Fortunately for us our friend Stephen Gardiner was a member of the commission. We had a chance to speak to him in private before the enquiry took place. He told us, before

Chapter Sixteen

we had even opened our mouths, that he was completely unable to talk about the enquiry. With great difficulty we obeyed him and discussed other subjects including More's execution.

'After the execution of More the King had a lot of bridge-building to do. There were many who felt that a great man had been sacrificed for ...' He searched for a suitable word.

'For the King's waning passion for a whore,' I interspersed.

'As you will,' said Stephen with pursed lips. 'You have a talent for stating things plainly, Honora. But what's done is done and More is dead.'

'Was he not your friend, Stephen?' I asked gently.

'Yes, he was a good friend and a great man, far greater than I. We both aspired to the same beliefs and adhered to the same principles but where he stood firm and unwavering, I continue to hold back.'

I had never heard Stephen speak like this. It seemed as if his friend's death had caused him to examine his conscience more critically than before. He must have read my thoughts.

'There may come a time when even I can no longer remain silent, my friends but for now,' he gathered his robes of office comfortably about him, 'I am an officer on the King's business and had better be about it.'

Just before he left us, he handed Arthur a document bearing the Royal Seal.

'I am very sorry, Arthur, I almost forgot about this.'

He gave us both a reassuring pat on the shoulder and went off to sit at the enquiry which was to decide our future. We half hoped that the enquiry would find against us because if Arthur was found wanting as Governor there was every chance we might be sent quietly back to England and that would be an end of it. But there was also the possibility that some charge could be trumped up against him, so it was an uneasy wait for us. At least we knew that we had one friend on the board of enquiry.

As soon as we were alone Arthur opened the sealed document. It was from Thomas Audley, the Lord Chancellor. He had investigated the case of Dudley and Seymour concerning Arthur's and my lands, stemming from the false agreement Dudley had coerced Arthur into signing some months previously. He had found in favour of Arthur, so we would once again be receiving the rent from the lands. It was a pittance compared to the amount we needed to keep Calais running but was better than nothing. It was also a good feeling to gain a victory over John Dudley.

The commissioners were closeted in the Great Hall of our house for several days poring over documents and interviewing witnesses. By night they took over the state chambers and Arthur and I had to move to the smaller, damp chambers at the other end of the house. Fortunately, it was summer, so they were not as bad as they could have been During this time the wait seemed interminable for us. We barely slept. During the days Arthur did a lot of pacing and I tried to do needlework, but my hands were shaking, and my palms were so moist that it was impossible to hold the needles. Every once in a while, we would reassure each other that all would be well. At last, on the fourth day, our wait was over, and we were called to hear the verdict.

We entered a room full of faces, some we knew, and some were strange to us, but Stephen Gardiner was the head of the enquiry and he spoke for them all.

Chapter Sixteen

'Lord Lisle,' he began, 'you have been called before this commission to hear our verdict on your administration of this town and on certain charges which have been levelled against you regarding that administration.' How unlike our kind friend he sounded as he spoke so coldly and formally!

He continued. 'I will not go into the details of what has passed during the course of this commission but will merely state our findings.' He looked more cold and severe than ever and I felt the damp sweat of fear pricking my limbs. This was not the Stephen I knew. He was still speaking.

'Lord Lisle, you are hereby cleared of all the charges brought against you, including those of taking bribes and of selling places in your retinue.'

I was numbed, I had not even realised that such charges had been made. I had thought the commission was only investigating Arthur's competence as Governor, not any crimes he was supposed to have committed.

'The commission has found,' continued this Stephen who was not Stephen, 'that you have performed your duties correctly and as well as could have been expected under the circumstances in which you have been operating. We will recommend to His Majesty the King that your powers are increased, and you will have more freedom to authorise the provisioning and supplying of this town and garrison. That is all.'

The members of the commission stood and filed out of the room leaving us stunned and rooted to the spot. In a few minutes we had been accused, acquitted, praised and empowered.

For some time, we both said nothing, such was our shock and disbelief at what had just transpired.

Finally, I found my voice. 'What just happened, Arthur?'

'It would seem that our situation has been more perilous than we ever knew,' he said pensively. 'It would also seem that now it is going to improve,'

'So, our troubles are at an end?' I suggested naively.

'We will see,' was all he answered.

But we had not reckoned on Cromwell's reaction. As the commission had been set up by the King, it reported directly back to him. For once King Henry had the true story of what had been happening in Calais. Cromwell would have been furious and must have decided then that he had not finished with Lord and Lady Lisle, not by a long shot.

Chapter Seventeen

Stephen stayed on at Calais for a few days after the commission. On the first occasion that the three of us were alone together I told him of my surprise and amazement at the bribery allegations.

'Stephen, you know that we do not take bribes,' I said still feeling hurt and betrayed by the allegations. 'Naturally, we send expensive presents to those in high places. It is expected. And conversely those who owe their situations to us give us presents. How can we be accused of wrong-doing when we are merely following the accepted system?'

'That is one of the many dangers of your situation, Honora,' he replied sadly. 'It is much like the position religion holds these days. One can be accused of criminal activity by simply adhering to what one believes to be the accepted belief or practice of the moment. It was only by carefully explaining your situation to my fellow judges on the commission that I was able to secure a verdict of innocence for you - this time.'

'How do you mean 'this time'?' asked Arthur.

Stephen lifted his hands expressively. 'The really frightening thing is that Thomas Cromwell is capable of twisting any facts to suit his purpose and as no-one yet quite knows what his purpose is, it is as if we are all playing at 'blind-man's buff', fending off assailants at every turn but unable to see where the next blow is coming from.'

'Then if you were all along so sympathetic to our cause why were you so stern and severe?' I asked, sounding I am sure, much aggrieved. 'You were like a stranger to us.'

'It was necessary so that the rest of the bench were assured of my impartiality. It would hardly have done if I had stood and embraced you both, would it?'

'But you need not have been quite so cold and imposing,' I said in a piqued tone.

'It was better that I overdid it than underdid it, my dear,' he replied and then he lifted his voice and said abruptly. 'Now, the commission is over, you are both in a far better situation than before, so why do you not put all this behind you and take a rest at your country cottage for a while?'

'Yes, why do we not?' Arthur put his arm around me in encouragement and I readily agreed.

We escaped to Landretun for ten glorious days. Once again, we took no servants at all and I did all our cooking and Arthur split sticks for the fires. The weather was closing in for the winter and much of our time was spent in front of a huge log fire, sipping mulled wine. When it was warm enough, we ventured outside and rode or walked at a leisurely pace along the country tracks, which meandered by creeks and hedgerows. But the evenings were best when it grew dark outside and we could bolt ourselves inside our little cottage and pretend that nothing else existed, not Calais, not the commission, just the two of us cocooned in our love, safe and secure forever.

When we arrived back at Calais there were two letters waiting for us. One was from John Husee. The plague had struck in London and he had taken it upon himself to have John removed from Lincoln's Inn and sent back to Hampshire until the fear of disease had passed. Such was Husee's goodness and care for my children in England.

Chapter Seventeen

The second letter was from Jane at Umberleigh. On and on she went about all the problems she was encountering, some real and some self-inflicted. She had complained ever since returning to Umberleigh that the caretaker there, John Bonde, was defrauding us. I had tended to take no notice as John was an old and trusted family friend and a vicar. We had also received several letters from Bonde himself full of complaints about Jane, so I had imagined that, true to her character, Jane had fallen out with him and it was nothing more than a petty quarrel. But this letter introduced a more serious matter. According to Jane, Bonde had installed a woman of low morals at Umberleigh and was using the house as a bawdy house. I could sympathise with Jane that this situation was intolerable. It seemed that Thomasine, being made of less steadfast material than Jane, had run away from Umberleigh and was living with her sister Margery Marres. Jane had stayed out of loyalty but was very unhappy. I immediately wrote to John Bonde, dismissing him from his post and instructing him to give all the household keys to Jane.

We received another letter from Jane just after Christmas. Our weir on the river Taw had been removed by order of the Crown. Private weirs had long been a bone of contention between landholders and the authorities. They were a good way for landholders to control the level of the river for fishing but because they prevented boats from freely using the waterways, they were unpopular. It was a disappointment to me but came as no surprise when it was removed.

The main effect Jane's letters had on me at this time was to remind me that back in Devon life was continuing just as it always had done. Whatever calamities befell us in Calais and whatever disasters happened in the King's Court, Umberleigh was still there, waiting for me. The great dramas and tragedies of Jane's everyday life acted as a balm to my frayed nerves.

But the loss of the weir was a worry, nevertheless. Ever since John Dudley had tricked Arthur into signing the false agreement our financial position had been getting steadily worse. The fishing from the River Taw had provided a secure, if small, source of income which was now not forthcoming. The promised payment for Arthur's work in Calais had not arrived. It was expensive to keep the children at their various boarding establishments and to pay caretakers and servants in all our households. We had to maintain the lifestyle of a grand Lord and Lady whether we could afford it or not and were living far beyond our means.

But despite our straightened circumstances, when the opportunity arose for us to move into a larger and more expensive residence we did not hesitate. Since we had first arrived in Calais it had been a sore point with us that whilst we were expected to live in the manner of a great Lord and his Lady our accommodation was far from suitable for this purpose. So, it was with relief when, early in 1536, we moved into new accommodation at the Staple Inn.

This is a large complex of buildings situated right in the heart of the town and is much more suitable as the Governor's residence. The house itself has three wings built as an open-sided square. The stables and workshops occupy the other side so that all the buildings face the cobbled central yard. There is a gated entry point at the furthest end from the house, next to the forge.

One wing was for ourselves and our family, with sunny, well-appointed chambers. The central section contains the Great Hall and reception chambers. The other wing was to be accommodation for guests and these rooms are as fine or even finer than those in which we were to live. In view of the promise I had made to the cooks I was more than pleased with the kitchen. It is situated behind the Great Hall and is vast and spacious. The cooking fires occupy the whole length of the longest wall and the work bench extends the full length of the room. The cooks were already moving their equipment in when Arthur and I arrived to take up residence and the looks of pure glee on their faces was all I needed to see.

Leaving them to their pleasant work I tugged on Arthur's hand and like a child, rushed off with him to find the garden. There are two gardens! One is reached through the kitchen and was already planted out with herbs and vegetables. The other is surrounded by a high wall and is reached through a side door. It is completely secluded, with trees, shrubs and flowers growing in abundance. A perfect place to rest in solitude or to speak privately.

For one of the few times during our time in Calais our hearts were light that day.

Early in the new year of 1536 we had some sad news from England. The rightful Queen and only legal wife to His Majesty King Henry had died. Queen Catherine entered eternal life at Kimbolton Castle Cambridgeshire, on the seventh of January. Princess Mary had been refused permission to see her mother even as she lay dying. It was a pathetic and terrible end to a tragic and saintly life.

Early in February, Stephen Gardiner, our trusted and trusty friend at Court paid us another visit. We greeted him eagerly and proudly showed off our new residence, ending with the private garden where we were able to speak to our hearts content without fear of being overheard. He was, as usual, full of news.

'The King was thrown from his horse in a jousting tournament on the twenty-fourth of last month,' said Stephen. 'The whole court was in a panic as he lost consciousness and was in that state for a full two hours.'

'Is he recovered now?' I asked.

'Oh yes, fully recovered but he will never joust again,' replied our friend. 'There was, however, another result of his fall. The Queen had again been expecting a child. Many felt that it was her last chance to regain the King's favour, by producing a son. It seems she fell into hysterics upon hearing of the King's accident. She was gripped by pains in her belly and five days later her child was born dead. It was a male child.'

As on the occasion of her previous miscarriage, even though I had a personal loathing for Anne Boleyn and hoped that this would put an end to her reign as Queen, I again felt an instinctive pang of sympathy for her. As a woman, I could not help but do so. My own attempts to have a child had been no more successful than those of Anne Boleyn. The only benefit I had over that lady was that my husband was kind and understanding with regard to my failure.

Stephen also brought us the latest news from parliament. There had been a new act passed which called for the dissolution of the smaller monasteries. These houses were to be examined by men called 'Visitors' who would report back to Cromwell of any abuses they encountered.

'But it is obvious that Cromwell will choose men he knows will give him the reports he desires,' said Arthur, aghast.

'Naturally,' replied Stephen, 'they will well understand the nature of the information they are to deliver to their master. They will report on vicious and carnal sins, exactly as the Act describes. They will wax lyrical on unthrifty and abominable living and Cromwell will have no option but to close the houses and divide the spoils.'

'Even so,' Arthur said more to reassure himself than anyone else, 'some of the smaller monasteries have a bad reputation for vice and they are the only ones being investigated.'

'At the moment,' was all Stephen said.

After Stephen returned to England, Arthur and I spent many hours discussing the news of the monasteries. I was worried about Bridget at St Mary's. It was only a small house and was sure to be visited.

'I am sure Bridget will be all right. Even if they decide to close the house it will take some time and we can decide then what is best for her,' Arthur reassured me. 'There is plenty of time.'

Then I said something for which I am still doing penance.

'Arthur, there is a small monastery quite close to Umberleigh.'

Arthur pricked up his ears. Gardiner had told us that the spoils of the monasteries would not all go to the crown. Submissions were already being placed by people such as us for the proceeds of suitable houses. Provided our case was found acceptable we stood a good chance of gaining at least some of the proceeds from Frithelstock if it should be dissolved.

'We cannot afford to ignore the possibility, Honora,' he said. 'I will apply immediately.'

For some unknown reason I had no qualms of conscience at the time. That was to come later.

My daughter Anne returned to us in March 1536. She had grown into a beautiful and accomplished young woman. Her time at Pont de Remy had clearly been of great benefit.

'Have you been happy?' I asked her as soon as she dismounted, and we were entering the house.

'Oh Mother, how I do love you! For that to be your first question shows me that you have not changed.' She gave me a warm hug and I smelt her expensive French scent, having already noted the new gown in the latest French style. 'Yes, I have been blissfully happy. Madame de Riou is a delightful person and Thibault is a darling. They made me feel like their own daughter and no daughter has ever been so well treated I am sure. Oh Mother, I have learned all the latest dances and have met the highest nobles of the French Court. The protocol there is quite different from that in England, much more dignified.' She was lavish in her praise of everything French. I was very glad to hear all this but also slightly concerned that life in the straightened circumstances under which Arthur and I were forced to live might be a disappointment to her.

She was keen to continue her advance in the world and eagerly wished for a place at King Henry's Court. Even though every fibre of my being warned me that her dream of life at Court was a dangerous one, I had to accept that there was no other way she could ever hope to meet a suitable prospective husband, so I immediately began to make enquiries for her. However, events at Court put a stop to all that soon after.

Early in May, John Husee paid us a hurried visit. As he entered the parlour at the Staple Inn, we both knew by the look on his face that something momentous had happened.

'My Lord and Lady,' he began breathlessly, 'I come in haste and in distress to inform you of the happenings in London. I could not trust my news to writing.'

'John do sit down,' I said by way of greeting and called a servant to bring him some refreshment. 'What is your news?'

He began bluntly. 'On the night before May Day, Mark Smeaton, a musician of the Queen's chamber, was arrested. It is rumoured that he was grievously tortured before confessing to adultery with the Queen.'

'Oh, no,' I gasped, 'not that, no, not that.'

Even hating Anne Boleyn as I did, I could not believe that she would be foolish enough, given her uncertain situation, as to have an adulterous relationship right under the King's nose.

'That is only the start of it,' John continued. 'The following day, at the May Day celebrations, the King attended with the Queen who obviously knew nothing of Smeaton's arrest. Suddenly in the midst of the jousting, the King stood up and left the Queen's side. She stood in surprise, not knowing what was afoot. Henry Norris, who was one of the jousters, was arrested in front of her and taken away. Still the Queen stood there, frantically looking all about her, not understanding any of it. For the first time ever, I felt pity for her.'

This was terrible news. Only six months previously, Husee had formed a close working relationship with Norris, who was a good friend of the King and Keeper of the Privy Purse. Norris had proved to be a kind-hearted and clever young man who had done much to further our interests at Court. His downfall would not be good for us in more ways than one.

Husee continued. 'It appears that the Queen was kept in ignorance of the reason for Norris's arrest and that she returned to her chamber in a state of confusion. There she remained until the next day when she and her brother were both arrested. This is where the accusations against her leave the realm of fantasy and enter that of the ridiculous. She is accused of not only carrying on an affair with Smeaton and Norris and with two others named Weston and Brereton but also with her own brother, Lord Rochford.'

I was aghast. 'That is completely abominable!' I exclaimed. 'I cannot believe it. She was a whore for the King to get a crown for herself but not a whore by nature, of that I am sure. She is too clever to perform such folly.'

Husee continued. 'Three days later Thomas Wyatt was arrested. He is a poet of some repute at Court and is said to have been the Queen's lover before ever she became the King's. They are accused of continuing the affair after her marriage to the King.'

Arthur had so far remained silent. Now he spoke in a quiet voice.

Chapter Seventeen

'It is too much. How do her accusers think they can prove so much adultery? Surely it would have been easier to have claimed only one lover for her.'

'They will not worry about proving anything,' replied Husee. 'On some of the dates when she is accused of consorting with Smeaton at Greenwich and Weston at Westminster she was with the King at Richmond.'

I was struck by the unfairness of it all and despite my fervent loathing of Anne Boleyn I was stunned that her end should be brought about in such a manner. If one such as she, for whom the King had defied the Pope and beheaded his best friend, could be dealt with in such a manner, what hope was there for the rest of us?

What happened next, we heard piecemeal from various sources. No-one was willing to write down the events of the ensuing three weeks for fear that they, too, would be drawn into the net that was closing around the Queen and her party.

The first executions were of Norris, Weston, Brereton and Smeaton. They were given the traitor's death of hanging, drawing and quartering. Two days after their deaths, Thomas Wyatt was released. No case had been proven against him. Given that no case had been proved against any of the others either, this was a mystery, but no doubt Master Wyatt did not wait around to ask questions.

The next day the Queen was tried and found guilty of high treason and her marriage to the King was ruled invalid. What a lot of trouble would have been saved if it had been accepted as invalid three years earlier and never taken place at all. Her brother, Lord Rochford, was the next to be executed and three days after his death, on the nineteenth of May, a day of glorious spring sunshine, Anne Boleyn was beheaded on Tower Green.

Arthur had been ordered to provide the executioner as she chose to be beheaded in the French manner, with a sword, not with an axe as is customary in England. How pitiable that this woman who had taken such pains during her life to effect French mannerisms and fashions should carry that trait right to her death. I took no pleasure in our small role in her death. Much as I had prayed for her removal, this was not the way I had wanted it, not for her, not for anybody.

On the day following the execution of Anne Boleyn, the King announced his betrothal. His new wife was to be Jane Seymour, sister to Edward Seymour who had joined with John Dudley in robbing us the previous year. It seemed the King was wasting no time in getting himself a new wife and that she would bring us no more joy than the previous one. After a ten-day betrothal, King Henry was married to Jane Seymour at Whitehall Palace. Anne Boleyn was hardly cold in her grave and a new era had begun.

Chapter Eighteen

The news of the King's marriage was told to us by Stephen Gardiner during a short day visit early in June of 1536. He had come to Calais with some more news for us which affected us far more directly.

I remember the day as high and cloudless. The bees were frantically busy about their business amongst the roses in the gardens of the Staple Inn and even Calais seemed to be in a light-hearted summer mood. We walked, the three of us, Stephen, Arthur and me along the formal paths of the garden until we found our usual seat, well out of earshot of the servants.

'I am afraid Cromwell's commissioners have visited St Mary's,' Stephen began abruptly as soon as we sat down.

'Oh Lord!' I gasped. 'What have they done?'

'We have been very fortunate in Hampshire that our commissioners are much fairer than those in some other counties. One of the four is William Berners, kinsman to your predecessor here in Calais. Their report was highly favourable. They found the house to be clean and the nuns virtuous and honest.'

'And on the strength of that they are not closing it?' Arthur was incredulous.

'On the strength of that and of the payment of the sum of 333 pounds,' said Stephen acidly.

'But that must be twice the annual revenue of the convent,' I said in astonishment. 'How are they expected to live once they have parted with that kind of money?'

'Especially,' continued Stephen, 'when you take into consideration that their manors of Urchfront and All Cannings have been taken from them and granted to the Queen's brother, Edward Seymour.'

So, our old foe Edward Seymour Lord Beauchamp, was on the rise now that he was brother-in-law to the King. More than ever, we were powerless and excluded.

'They have taken their money and their main source of income. The end is near for St Mary's I fear and that scoundrel, Seymour, is the beneficiary,' Arthur said with anger in his voice.

Suddenly, the day which had begun so bright and sunny clouded over and I felt a shiver run down my spine. We sat in silence for a while then walked slowly back to the house for the midday repast. During our meal Stephen gave Arthur a sealed letter from Cromwell which stated that he had been granted an audience with the King at Dover in July. Arthur had sent numerous letters to Cromwell requesting the proceeds of Frithelstock Priory and it was to be hoped that this meeting with the King would seal the matter.

'I am coming too,' I said spontaneously.

I had not been back to England since coming to Calais three years earlier and despite my dread of sea journeys I wanted desperately to get away from Calais and back onto English soil even if only for a while and even if it was only to be as far as Dover.

On the 21st of July, Arthur and I set sail over the Channel for Dover. It was a smooth crossing and I remained tolerably well, even managing a glimpse of the wonderful cliffs as we approached the shore. We arrived in the evening and were met by John Husee who had obtained modest accommodation for us in the town. We spent a comfortable night and the next morning travelled to the castle, where the King and his new Queen were shortly due to arrive.

As we waited in the huge hall of Dover castle, I felt curiously afraid and uncomfortable. As this feeling grew within me, I had a sudden and unaccustomed moment of panic. I gripped Arthur's arm.

'Arthur, get me out of here, quickly,' I whispered to him as I felt myself swooning.

He looked at me in shock, then holding me firmly by the elbow he smiled his way past the gathered crowds of fellow supplicants and steered me out through a side door. We found ourselves in a small courtyard. Finding a seat near a wall and out of sight of curious onlookers we sat down.

'What is it, my love? What ails you?'

I looked at him in distress, as the enormity of what we were about to do suddenly dawned on me. 'Arthur, here we are in Dover Castle, waiting to meet the King and hoping fervently that we may get the spoils from a Priory of innocent, holy monks.' I had to stop and get my breath before continuing.

'What has happened to me, to us?' I sobbed. 'This is not what we dreamed of.'

'No, it is not,' he agreed. 'None of what is happening is what we dreamed of, my dearest darling. But it is happening and if we are not granted Frithelstock we will be paupers.'

I stared blankly at the high wall in front of us. 'Many years ago, when I was a young wife, I travelled close by Frithelstock. I remember watching the monks working their fields in holy contentment. I remember seeing the walled cloister and the beautiful church. I felt such a sense of peace and continuity as I passed by. Arthur, I cannot be a party to their destruction.' I stared hopelessly into his eyes and panic gripped my heart.

He took my face in his hands. 'Honora, my dear sweet wife, we are not a party to it any more than we caused Anne Boleyn's death by providing the sword. What is happening will happen whatever we feel about it. The spoils of the monasteries will go to someone and due to the position in which we find ourselves through no fault of our own we must take the chance to gain what we can.'

As I began to protest, he spoke more emphatically. 'Honora, we cannot afford to pass up this opportunity.'

At that moment we heard a fanfare of trumpets. The King and Queen had arrived. Arthur helped me to my feet and tenderly straightened my gable hood before kissing me softly on the mouth. Arm in arm we re-entered the hall.

The result of that day at Dover was that we were granted Frithelstock. All the supplicants, and there were several of us, were called individually to stand before the King. He greeted each of us formally and took a rolled manuscript from a scribe which he then presented to us. In the privacy of our chamber later that night we read the document together. We had been granted:

'... *the site, church and demesne of Frithelstock Priory, the manor, rectory and advowson of the vicarage of Frithelstock and the manor of Broadwoodwidger.*'

The property was valued at 92 pounds and contained one thousand acres. It seemed that for a short time at least our money troubles were to be eased. It was the pangs of conscience which would continue to haunt me and still do to this day.

After the presentation of the documents the King left the hall and there was a break in the proceedings during which time, we all stood about wondering what to do next. After about half an hour there was another massive fanfare of trumpets and Henry re-entered with his new Queen on his arm. We were then presented to Queen Jane, whom I immediately felt to be not as soft and kind as everyone, including the King, imagined her to be. I saw something in her eyes which stated plainly to me that she knew very well what she was about. As I rose from my curtsey, I made sure that I smiled humbly and warmly at her.

The King seemed well pleased with his new wife and was in a jovial mood.

'Well met, Uncle. I see you have brought your bedfellow with you on this journey. A little comfort goes a long way, does it not?' He squeezed his new wife's waist in a most suggestive and non-regal manner.

He invited us to join the Court for the next week and this, of course, we did. An invitation from the King was not really an invitation but an order. We travelled back to London and attended banquets and masques every day. I never enjoyed Court banquets because of the extravagance and waste. The sight of tables groaning under huge amounts of food, most of which would not be eaten, sickened me. At least in our poverty-stricken life at that time there was no wastage. We needed to use every scrap of food there was. There is some good in everything or so I have heard, difficult though it is to see at times.

But I did love the masques. These short theatrical performances of stories from Greek mythology or the Bible fascinated me every time. On fine days they were often performed outside in the form of pageants. I had a great admiration for the actors and their skills, and I loved the ornate and colourful costumes they wore.

This time in London was a blessed relief from our miserable lives in Calais but my hopes of seeing the younger children were to be dashed, as there was no way I could escape from Court long enough to travel to Hampshire. However, I did manage to see John for an hour one afternoon. He was granted leave from his studies at Lincoln's Inn and we met at Westminster.

I could not believe my eyes. My oldest son had become a man in the years since I had last seen him. He was now seventeen years old and was barely recognisable from the fourteen-year-old I had last set eyes on.

He took my hand and bowed over it. 'Mother, it is such a pleasure to see you,' he said and then, seeing my look of disappointment, with one quick glance around him to see that there was no-one watching, bent down and gathered me in his arms. He had grown so tall that I barely reached his shoulder and he had to stoop to hold me.

'My John, oh, my dearly beloved son,' I murmured contentedly against his chest.

He released me and we walked together. As we walked, he told me of his studies and how they went. It seemed he would be finished in another year's time. We made tentative plans that he would then join us in Calais.

'I would enjoy seeing you all over there,' he said. 'How is Frances?' Almost as an afterthought but said quickly and shyly and I felt it had been the foremost question in his mind all along.

'She is very well, John and will be happy to see you when you come to Calais, of that I am sure,' I replied. My heart quickened in my breast. How I longed for those two to marry, but how afraid I was to say anything lest I somehow spoiled it. They were both proud people who would hate to think they had been coerced into marriage.

All too soon our time was over, and he returned to Lincoln's Inn, but I was content. He had grown tall and handsome and still retained the nobility and gentleness of manner which had been his since childhood

The following day just before we were due to return to Calais the King's son, Henry Fitzroy, died. He had never been strong and despite having the best doctors in the Kingdom, it had not been enough. The King did not arrive at the final banquet before our sailing and was reported to be in despair. The only effect it had on our lives was that since the Admiral of His Majesty's Fleets was now dead, Arthur lost his position as Vice Admiral. As it had been no more than a token position and had never returned any money he did not mind in the slightest.

We returned to Calais and life went on as before, except that we were no longer destitute. Our letters from Cromwell were no longer from My Lord Secretary but from Lord Privy Seal. The position had been held by Anne Boleyn's father but as he had lost it after the disgrace and death of his daughter it passed - automatically it seemed - to Cromwell.

The summer ended all too soon and autumn was once more upon us. Then in early October an unforeseen crisis occurred. Since the monasteries had first started to be suppressed it had seemed that as a whole the country tolerated, if not actively supported the changes but that was only in the southern counties for elsewhere widespread discontent had been simmering. Quite suddenly and without warning an uprising began at Louth in Lincolnshire. The rebels, under the leadership of a man called Robert Aske, demanded that the dissolved monasteries be restored and that many other grievances be remedied. They gathered their forces and soon 30,000 men were marching towards London. Just when it seemed that civil war could ensue, they hesitated and seizing the moment, the King's forces intercepted them, and they dispersed.

We only heard this news in fragments as Husee, our usual supplier of information, shut up like a clam and wrote nothing to us of the rebellion. We knew of no reason for this. Had Husee been 'got at'? Was he all right? He had, after all, been an associate of Henry Norris.

'Oh Arthur, you do not think Husee has been arrested do you?' We were in the garden, soaking up the last rays of the setting autumn sun. I was repairing the hem of one of my day gowns and Arthur was staring into space, thinking of I know not what.

He looked at me ruefully, as if he had been wrenched back from some far off, much more pleasant place. His voice sounded so tired and world-weary as he answered my somewhat rhetorical question. 'God knows, Honora, God knows.' He gave a deep sigh and returned to his dream.

But my mind was unfortunately still rooted firmly in the present. Why were we being so shut out? Where was

Chapter Eighteen

Husee? And Stephen? Was Cromwell behind it still pulling the strings as we, his puppets, danced our unhappy dance?

Once again, we felt as if we were in Limbo, cast out and forgotten but slowly and piece by piece the news filtered in. As the Lincolnshire uprising petered out a stronger and more fervent band of rebels gathered in Yorkshire. We only heard the full extent of the rebellion when our good friends Stephen Gardiner and John Wallop visited us late in November.

I breathed such a sigh of relief when they arrived. At least we had not been entirely forgotten.

'Thank Heaven for the King's business,' said John upon arrival at the Staple Inn. 'If it were not for politics and intrigue, we should never see each other.'

As always, I found myself smiling when John was around. He was so refreshingly unspoilt by his position. He and Stephen had been acting as ambassadors for England at the marriage negotiations of the Scottish King and the daughter of the King of France and had a few days' respite from the negotiations.

John, as usual, feigned no respect for royalty.

'The King of the Scots will shortly be assured of the hand of Madame Magdalene,' he said with a grin. 'I have never met a man of so few words. I was present at an interview he had with the ambassador of Venice and I swear to you that after the ambassador had spoken a long while with him and waited for a reply, he answered not a word. We had very few out of him either. His wife ought to suit him very well for she can speak, oh yes. She can speak not only enough for the two of them but for the whole of France as well!' At this he erupted into loud and infectious laughter in which we all joined.

After we had all settled down, Stephen Gardiner told us about the rebellion.

'It could go on for some time,' he said. 'The rebels have the strength of their beliefs to sustain them. And the King's forces are divided under three leaders. The Dukes of Norfolk and Suffolk and the Marquis of Exeter are all seeking to establish their own positions rather than uniting to defeat the rebels. They are only succeeding in tying each other in knots, ordering and revoking orders for men and money.'

I could not help but feel sympathy for the rebels. After all, I had heard they were fighting for the upholding of their traditional religious institutions and values. I put this suggestion to our friends.

'That is partly correct,' said John Wallop, 'but some of the rebels, particularly the Cumberland men, have risen less from anger at the dissolution of the monasteries than in protest against their landlords. They have refused to pay rent, pulled down enclosures and are assembling under the leadership of a man who calls himself Captain Poverty.'

'Oh, I cannot condone that,' I replied firmly. 'There is a set order about the way people live and no peasant can expect to change the way of these things. Where would our society be if that kind of behaviour was allowed to go on?' Immediately, the sympathy I had previously felt for the rebels was dissipated.

John looked at me with an annoying little smile on his face and his head cocked rakishly to one side.

'How right you always are, Honora,' he said, and I knew not whether he mocked me or not. 'We must at all costs protect our privileges.'

Stephen Gardiner took up the story. 'The whole north is a hotbed of rumour and hearsay.' He laughed merrily. 'It is said that the King intends to seize all Church jewels, that no church will be allowed to stand within five miles of another, that all men will have to hand their gold over to the exchequer and that no man will be allowed to eat white bread or capons without paying a fine!'

John Wallop joined in. 'There is another rumour which is just as far-fetched. The Yorkshire men fear that the dissolutions will drain money away from the north towards London. Have you ever heard anything so absurd?' In the silence which ensued he once again gave us that curious, searching look of his which I found so disconcerting.

I felt the need to change the subject at once. 'Have either of you heard anything of Husee? It is a long while since we heard from him and I am very worried as he was friends with Henry Norris.'

Stephen answered. 'I have heard nothing, which means he must be all right. If he had been arrested, I would know. I suspect he is simply lying low for the time being and taking care to put nothing in writing. Be assured my friends that he will still be working hard on your behalf and on behalf of your children.'

Gardiner and Wallop left us soon after and returned to Valence. Almost overnight the autumn turned to winter, the coldest in living memory. By Christmas all the rivers in England and France had frozen over. The King's soldiers in the North would have been having a hard time of it.

We had a letter from John Wallop just before Christmas. He wrote from Paris where he was staying now that his work in Valence was done. It seemed that his opinion of the Scottish King had not improved upon further acquaintance and he wrote humorously of the King's rough Northern manners and lack of polish. John could be unkind at times but very funny.

He also sent with his letter some bottles of Avignon water to help with my pregnancy and lying-in. For since November I had been sure I was pregnant. It still causes me anguish when I remember the joy we both felt at that time. We were neither of us young, indeed I was well past normal child-bearing age at 45 but we rejoiced that God had granted us this one last chance to beget our own child. John Wallop was one of the first to share our joy and in his letter, he wrote that one of the bottles would greatly relax me for the delivery if I took it in the days leading up to that event. The other, he wrote, would restore the shape of my breasts should they sag. He hastened to point out that whereas I would very likely not be needing such assistance, certain of our neighbours would benefit greatly from such treatment! He was such a naughty, merry fellow and we loved him dearly.

I will write no more of our longed-for child, save that it did not eventuate. It seems that my pregnancy was no more than the figment of an aging woman's imagination and the onset of middle age. As the weeks went by and my belly steadfastly refused to swell, we finally had to admit that all hope was gone. We would never have a child of our own. It would not have been so terrible for us if we had not, for a few brief weeks, been filled with hope and joy. It only made the disappointment so much harder to bear.

But life went on. James was still enjoying his college in Paris. John Wallop visited him there and reported back to us that he was well but that his study of the French language was not progressing as fast as could be expected. He therefore suggested that if he moved out of the College and into a private residence he would be forced to speak and understand the language more. We accepted his advice and James moved into the home of Guillaume le Gras, a wealthy merchant. John reported that my youngest son was not totally pleased with the arrangement. I imagine that a merchant's house did not offer the prospect of such a giddy rise in social standing as my youngest desired. However, we decided that for the present at least, that is where James could stay.

Meanwhile Christmas came and went, and the winter became ever colder. It seemed we had been plunged into a world without warmth. Day after day went by with no sun and no easing of the black frost without. No sooner had the snow fallen than it was frozen as solid as rock. In the countryside the wild animals died in their hundreds, incapable of sustaining life during that bleak January. We remained huddled in front of the fires in our huge house in Calais, unable to get even as far as Landretun. No news arrived from England and we knew not whether the rebellion was over. We had heard no more from Winchester and whether Bridget's convent still stood. We were marooned in a sea of ice.

Chapter Nineteen

The winter wore on with no end in sight and still we remained trapped in our frozen prison of Calais. We were heartily sick of the weather and of the place and not a moment passed when we did not wish ourselves safely back in England, preferably in the West, as far away from the Court and all its intrigues as possible. But wishes are not often granted on this earth or so I have come to believe and at Calais we remained.

The thaw set in slowly and it was not until February that we had notification from England that the rebellion had finally been put down.

'Now let the executions begin,' said Arthur upon hearing the news. 'Friend Cromwell will have a grand time deciding whose promising career to put to an end after this.'

'But was it not mainly a rebellion of the lower classes?' I asked.

'Yes,' he agreed, 'but they are not worth executing as they have nothing to steal. I should not be surprised if a few more of the clergy do not lose their heads, however.' It is a measure of how low my spirits had sunk that even these words had not the power to shock me.

The Seymour family continued to rise in prominence and power and as Edward Seymour's star ascended so did that of his cohort, Arthur's stepson, John Dudley. During the spring we heard that Dudley had been created Chief of the King's Henchmen.

'Those two rascals will fall out given time,' I said to Arthur as we brooded one day over the tide of their escalating fortunes. 'There is not enough room in the Kingdom for both of them to have the power they crave.'

'I suppose you are right,' he replied, 'and when that happens it just might be a spectacle worth watching.'

As the winter turned to spring the reprisals began over the Pilgrimage of Grace, as the rebellion was being named. Firstly, as a signal to us all that no-one, dead or alive, may defy a King the shrine of Thomas Becket in Canterbury Cathedral was desecrated. He was pronounced a traitor and his bones were dug up and publicly burned.

Then the present-day martyrdoms began. Ten monks of the London Charterhouse who had openly supported the rebellion were chained to pillars without food or water. Cromwell and his cronies were reported to have watched in turn as they died slowly and cruelly in the dungeons beneath the Tower. A woman called Margaret Bulmer was burned for treason for supporting her husband, one of the rebels.

Our revulsion and sadness over these vile murders was eased by the arrivals, first of George, then of John, in Calais. They had both completed their years of study and were to remain with us while the next steps in their careers were planned.

George arrived in April. He had thoroughly enjoyed his time at Hyde Abbey. As one of the larger establishments, it had so far escaped the interest of Cromwell's commissioners. He was by this time thirteen years old and had not begun the rapid growth which characterises the development of boys. He remained largely unchanged from the child with whom I had parted four years earlier. He was the same unsmiling, humourless boy I remembered. I wondered as I hugged him if he could tell that there was no spontaneous outpouring of maternal love, such as I felt for my other boys.

'Dear George,' I said as we embraced, 'how wonderful it is to see you.'

'I also am glad to see you, Mother,' he replied correctly.

After that, George greeted his sisters in like manner and proceeded to blend in with our household as if he had never been parted from it. He has never been any trouble to anyone, my George.

When John arrived in early June, I held him close to me and this time my welcome embrace was returned more warmly. He held me tightly and I knew he was glad to be with us again.

Then, abruptly I could sense that his attention was diverted. I released him just as Frances entered the hall and as he looked at her, I was transported back to 1509 and Anne Basset's wedding feast. Arthur's eyes had held the same expression on that day when he had first looked at me as I now saw in my son's eyes as he beheld his beloved.

They moved towards each other in one fluid movement and I saw then that all my years of hoping had not been in vain. As they took each other's hands I knew that I was no longer wanted or even noticed. I left them alone, understanding exactly how they felt. Had I not experienced that same perfect joy at Powderham Castle all those years ago?

As the summer progressed and the executions in England ceased, we all felt that the period of religious turmoil might at last be over, but we were to be proved perilously wrong. It had only just begun.

Chapter Nineteen

The first we knew of the next trouble was a letter from Cromwell accusing us of harbouring two seditious priests in Calais. These priests, William Minstrelsey and William Richardson, had long been favourites of mine. I knew that they still adhered to the belief that the Pope was the head of the Church, as I did and still do, but apart from that they had done no wrong that I was aware of.

However, that in itself was a crime and the Archbishop of Canterbury, Thomas Cranmer, had spies everywhere and one of them, a certain John Butler, had reported back to his master that they were traitors. We had no choice but to arrest them and send them to London for trial.

'I will have to write to Cromwell and protest their innocence,' I said as they were taken away.

'No, Honora, I can allow you to do no such thing.' Arthur had never forbidden me to do anything before.

'But my darling, they are accused of treachery and face the death penalty,' I protested.

'As we may just as easily do if we say anything in their defence,' said Arthur angrily. 'Do you not understand, Honora, this is a dangerous business and we are already in it up to our necks just by allowing them to preach here?' He stormed out of the room.

I had never seen him so angry, at least not at me. The only other times I had seen him in such a fury were when the malicious documents had arrived from Cromwell. He had never spoken to me in such tones in all our years together. This lack of support from my husband upset me more than the loss of the priests and I sat down in shock.

After only a few minutes, Arthur came back into the room and sat beside me.

'I am sorry, my love,' he said taking my hands in his. 'I did not mean to speak so harshly to you. But you must understand that dangerous times are coming, and we must be more than ever on our guard. My cousin Pole has been created a Cardinal by the Pope. When the King heard recently that the newly created Cardinal Pole was to be sent to England as Papal Legate he flew into a rage and announced that if Pole ever set foot in England he would be arrested as a traitor.'

I was taken aback. 'But Arthur, I never knew of this. When did you hear it?'

'Only this very morning,' said Arthur. 'One of the Court officials who came for the priests told me. He also said that there is a movement afoot in Europe to kidnap Pole and send him back to England in chains.'

I understood then why Arthur had been so upset as to speak harshly to me. Reginald Pole was his dearly loved cousin and also the King's. If Henry could go so far as to order Pole's arrest, then our own lives were cheap indeed. Once again, I promised to be on my guard.

Arthur had been told one more speck of news that day. 'They also told me that Cromwell has been made a Knight of the Garter. It would seem that there is never to be an end to his rise. He is a tradesman's son, a tradesman's son, for goodness' sake!'

For all his common touch, Arthur still retained the idea that there were some titles which should be reserved solely for the nobility. He went away shaking his head.

We began to receive letters from Husee again early in the summer. Of course, he wrote nothing about the reason for his prolonged silence but assured us that all was well.

Chapter Nineteen

As the summer progressed, he kept us informed about his endeavours on behalf of Anne and Catherine. At our request he was trying to obtain positions at Court for both of them. His efforts had been very much hindered by the recent troubles but as events settled down again, they came to fruition.

'Anne is to be the most honoured,' wrote Husee in late July. *'She is to be a maid of honour to Queen Jane. Catherine will be lady in waiting to Lady Rutland. The Queen is expecting a child in October so it will be an exciting time for Anne.'*

Despite my own distaste for the Court life, both my girls seemed to desire it. The fact was that we were now so poor there was no other way they could hope to advance or to find good husbands unless they took this chance. And even though I felt no warmth for the new Queen or her power-hungry family, my personal feelings played no part in this success of Anne's. Over the next weeks the Staple Inn was plunged into a flurry of activity. Both my daughters needed a whole new wardrobe of gowns suitable for their new positions in society. Anne's, of course, needed to be far grander than Catherine's but they both would be attired much more finely than they had been at Calais. The seamstresses needed to work long hours to have all in readiness for the great day of their departure.

Husee arrived in early September to escort both girls back to London and the Court. On the seventeenth of September 1537, a bright, cool, early autumn day, I bade farewell to my daughters. It was an exciting and nervous parting for us all but a happy one as we kissed on the waterfront. The sun sparkled on the rippling waves which looked for all the world like diamonds and the gulls circled noisily overhead. My only regret on that day was that Arthur and I were to remain in Calais.

Chapter Twenty

After Anne and Catherine's departure the house seemed empty for a while, but the hollow feeling left by their going was soon filled with more plans. The seamstresses were recalled and once again the Staple Inn was a hive of activity. John and Frances were planning to marry early in 1538 and everyone joined with them in joy and anticipation.

Our minds were temporarily distracted from the wedding plans in late October when we heard that Queen Jane had been brought to bed of a son earlier in the month but had sickened after the birth and not recovered. She had died at Hampton Court Palace twelve days later.

The King was reportedly torn between his joy at having a son and his sadness at the Queen's death, but I was becoming increasingly aware that the King was a stranger to normal human feelings, and I felt that he would not mourn her demise for long.

My own worry was for Anne's future. She had been employed as Queen Jane's maid of honour and now that her mistress was dead, what might her future hold? But on that subject, we were soon reassured, if that be the correct term. For the King announced a very short time later that he liked very much to have pretty girls about him and would not be dispensing with Anne's presence at Court. Indeed, the rumours began almost immediately that he was seriously considering her as his next wife! My mind was in turmoil. There was no way I could correspond directly with Anne to gauge her own feelings about the situation so all I could do was to wait and pray that all would be well.

'Arthur,' I whispered to him late at night in the privacy of our bedchamber, 'what do you think about this new infatuation of the King's for my daughter?'

'I can remember saying years ago that she would marry well,' he replied sleepily.

I was far from reassured by that statement and sat up in bed. 'But so far, the King has had three wives and none of them have prospered for long.'

He resigned himself to waking from his slumber and spoke patiently. 'Yes, but they have all been unfortunate cases, have they not? The first Queen, Catherine of Aragon, was divorced on proper religious grounds - the marriage was never valid.'

I snorted in derision. 'That is a falsehood and you know it.'

'Falsehood or not, it was still an unusual and singular situation,' he continued. 'The second Queen, Anne Boleyn, was executed for adultery, again, not likely to be repeated.'

'But she was accused on fraudulent charges, Arthur. We both know that, so it could easily happen again if he tired of another wife.'

'Even if the charges were fraudulent,' he continued resignedly despite my protests, 'he is hardly likely to do it again, is he?'

I was not so sure about that.

'This last Queen, Jane Seymour, died following childbirth, a common enough occurrence,' he said. 'The blame for that cannot be laid at the King's door... well it can, I suppose,' he added, laughing. 'And now, my troublesome wench, as you have succeeded in disturbing my rest, I demand compensation.' He leaned over me menacingly and his lips met mine. He had found a way to take my mind from my worries, at least for the present.

After the shock of the news of Queen Jane's death had passed, John and Frances' wedding plans were resumed at full speed and progressed well. Before the wedding, however, there was one more expense which we had to cover, and this was James' move from Paris to the College of Navarre. This was one of the best colleges in France and the sons of the highest nobility were counted amongst its pupils. James wrote that he was most excited about the move as he was not at all happy in the house of Monsieur le Gras or at the College of Calvy.

The tailors and seamstresses were put back to work, this time to improve James' apparel and make it more suitable for such company. Apart from the regulation scholar's cassock of frieze cloth, he needed a new jacket of camlet. He had his velvet bonnets trimmed with gold buttons. His violet camlet gown needed to be furred with marten and he had two new doublets made, one of grey satin and one of black velvet. He had a new black velvet coat and many new pairs of hose with pullings-out of black and violet taffeta. He needed a dozen new shirts, cloth slippers and leather shoes. All these clothes necessitated a new trussing coffer in which to keep them. The total cost was immense. We found ourselves rapidly running back into just as bad a debt as we had been in before the acquisition of Frithelstock.

However, it was a necessary expense in order that James would be suitably attired for the college, just one more in a long list of necessary expenses for us. John Worth travelled from Paris to collect the coffer and returned immediately to escort James to Navarre. Feeling satisfied that my youngest son would now be well settled, we once again concentrated on the wedding preparations. Everyone was in high spirits as the day of the wedding drew near. Frances and I became particularly close in those weeks.

'It seems strange,' she said to me one chilly afternoon in early February as we sat in front of the fire in my parlour. We were sipping mulled wine and had each been silent, thinking thoughts of our own. 'John and I have known each other for so long now,' she continued thoughtfully. 'We grew up as brother and sister and yet not as such. Our union has always seemed somehow inevitable, as if God had planned it from the beginning.'

'Frances,' I replied sincerely, 'I feel the same. You have been like a daughter for ten years and yet not my daughter. Nothing pleases me more than the step you are both about to take together.'

Frances looked into my eyes and hers had a terrified look about them. 'And yet, sometimes I am engulfed by a terrible fear, as if our happiness is not ordained by God and is not to be,' she said with a trembling voice.

'That is a natural nervousness for a bride to feel,' I soothed her. 'I certainly felt it before my weddings and both my marriages have been happy. So never fear,' I said and patted her hand.

But I was disturbed by what she had said, and I had not spoken the truth in reassuring her. I had never felt as she described. Before my marriage to John I had been resigned but not fearful. Before I married Arthur, I had been completely and unconditionally blissful.

However, the marriage went ahead and on the nineteenth of February, John and Frances married in Calais. Soon after the wedding they returned to England. They intended to settle at Tehidy, which pleased Arthur and me greatly. My brother-in-law, Thomas St Aubyn, was still caretaking for us but Tehidy should have been returning much greater profits than it was, and it was good that John was to be on the spot for us.

The day of their leave-taking was a sad one. Frances and I had been together almost constantly since Arthur and I married and had developed a loving fondness for each other, and it had been so wonderful to have John with us for those few months. John and Frances were glad to be leaving Calais and returning to English soil and I was happy for them but as I held my first-born son in my arms, I felt a wrench almost as if something inside me was tearing apart.

You will have to let me go, Mother,' he said gently, as he disengaged my arms from about him. 'The ship is waiting to depart.'

'Yes, yes, I know,' I sobbed, 'but, my son, when will I see you again?'

How much more terrible the parting would have been if I had known the answer to that question.

We stood, Philippa, George, Arthur and me, in the bleak February sunlight and watched until the ship was out of sight and over the horizon. Philippa and George were now the only two of our children remaining with us in Calais. We turned and mounted our horses for the short ride back to the Staple Inn. We all felt drained and exhausted as we dismounted in the courtyard.

'How I wish we had been on that ship,' Arthur said as we sat a while later in the parlour. 'To leave this cursed place and never return is my greatest wish and ever has been.' I agreed totally with him and after saying so we sat in gloomy silence.

A few weeks after John and Frances' departure Mary came back unexpectedly from her time at Abbeville looking subdued and frail. She retained her beauty and flawless skin but unlike Anne who had arrived back glowing with health and happiness, this clearly was not the same Mary we had sent away. I accompanied her to her bedchamber on her first night back with us.

'It is so good to have you back Mary,' I said as I smoothed her long shining hair, 'but are you sure you are entirely well? You seem somehow different.'

'Yes, Mother, I am well,' she replied. 'I really loved the de Bours family. Madame de Bours is such a fine lady and she gave me many jewels and gowns. She taught me to play French dances and tunes on the lute. Oh, Mother,' she turned to me with pain in her eyes, 'why did I have to leave? Why did Madame de Bours suddenly decide that I must return to Calais?'

'I do not know, my darling,' I answered her, 'but it may have had something to do with the trouble we were having in paying for your upkeep.'

It was true, I had also been surprised when Madame de Bours had written that she was no longer able to keep Mary in her household. She had hinted at some health problem, but she did not actually give a reason for her decision. We had found difficulty paying her ever since Mary went to Abbeville, but it had not seemed to matter before.

Before long, mysterious packages and letters began to be delivered to our house. The messenger was always the same, a man in the de Bours livery, who disappeared rapidly once his errand was done. Mary hovered constantly about the courtyard and always managed to be present when he arrived and gave him something equally mysterious to take away again. One day, as she tripped lightly inside with one of her packages, I was waiting for her.

'What do you have there?' I asked.

'Oh, Mother!' She was startled. 'It is nothing, nothing at all.' She tried to push past me to go upstairs to her chamber, but I stood in her way.

'You will tell me, Mary.' I was firm.

She broke down then and told me all about it. Right there in the front hall she blurted out for all to hear about how she had fallen in love with Gabriel de Bours, the son of the household. They had been secretly exchanging gifts and letters ever since she had left Abbeville.

It was clear to me now why Madame de Bours had sent her away. The stepdaughter of an illegitimate, impoverished English gentleman, Lord or otherwise, was no match for Gabriel de Bours Seigneur de Montmorency. At the tender age of sixteen Mary had made her first conquest and a grand one at that.

'Do not be angry, Mother, please,' she begged me tearfully.

'Oh, Mary,' I said gently, 'how can I be angry? Do not imagine that I cannot remember how it is to be in love.'

She looked very dubious about that but elected to say nothing. I realised I must have seemed so old to her and far removed from romance and passion. How could I tell her that her dreams would in all likelihood come to nothing? Gabriel was soon to go to the French Court where he would almost certainly find himself - or be found - a grand match which would dash all her hopes. I had seen it all before and suffered its consequences. No, I chose not to tell her of such things but to let her cherish her happiness for as long as she could.

Accordingly, I promised to turn a blind eye to her secret messenger, which I did for the next two years. For, to my surprise, Gabriel did not stop writing as I had feared but continued to send a steady stream of letters and small parcels for Mary's eyes alone.

Soon after Mary's return, we had a visit from Sir Francis Bryan, who was probably the closest friend King Henry had and who had managed to retain this doubtful honour throughout the King's entire reign. I did not much like Bryan, who I felt was a dissolute and dishonest character. However, it was certainly not in our best interest to broadcast such privately held opinions and we welcomed him heartily to Calais.

'I have a proposal to make to you,' he said one evening after supper. 'It concerns your son George.'

Arthur and I pricked up our ears. George was becoming a bit of a concern to us as he was now fourteen and still not placed in any form of employment. He was growing into a heavily built, somewhat pompous young man and I was finding his constant presence about the house quite a burden.

'I have a vacancy at Woburn for a young man of George's attributes to serve me and at the same time to gain valuable experience for himself in the Public Service,' continued Bryan after a pause, during which he must have observed our rapid exchange of glances.

Chapter Twenty

'We thank you very much, Sir Francis,' replied Arthur. 'My wife and I are both very grateful for this opportunity you are offering our son.'

Thus, it was arranged. In no time at all George was acquainted with his good fortune and packed off to England to join the household of Sir Francis Bryan. As always, George himself made no demur about his fate nor expressed an opinion of any kind. He merely did as he was told just as he always did, dutifully and obediently.

Of all our children, only Philippa and Mary now remained with us at Calais. We were a sorry little band of people, trapped in a gilded cage and yearning for the day when we would be free.

Chapter Twenty One

That same month, March 1538, an event occurred which marked the beginning of the end for us. Of course, we did not know it at the time. It is only in retrospect that things become clear.

The event I speak of was the appearance in our lives of Gregory Botolf. He arrived on the fifteenth of the month, bearing a letter of introduction from our good friend and servant John Husee. What better recommendation could he have had than a letter from our most trusted advisor? I do not think Husee had ever failed us before, so how was I to know how tragically wrong he was to prove on this occasion? My usual discerning character judgement abandoned me and I, also, was entirely duped by Gregory Botolf for the entire two years of his service in Calais. He was well-spoken and well educated and had considerable charm. It is only now, with the benefit of hindsight, that I can see the enormity of his duplicity.

What I know now and did not know then, is that Botolf was a thoroughly corrupt character. He was the black sheep of an otherwise respectable Suffolk family. He soon became known amongst the soldiers and officials of Calais as 'Gregory Sweet-lips', apparently because of his plausible tongue, which he used to good advantage to gain and keep our favour.

One of the other chaplains in our household, a man called Oliver Browne, once came to me with a complaint about Botolf.

Chapter Twenty One

'My Lady, why can you not see that he is deceiving you with his polished manners and charming ways? To my mind he is the most mischievous knave that ever was born,' he said hotly, when I dismissed his complaint as false.

'Master Browne,' I replied in my most lofty and haughty manner, 'I fear you over-reach yourself, Sir. Pray do not forget to whom you speak.'

'Please accept my apology, Lady Lisle but make no bones about it, the knave will one day be hanged,' he prophesied as I turned from him.

Another, who was as badly deceived by Botolf as I, was young Clement Philpot. Philpot was another of Husee's recommended servants and although of far greater merit than Botolf was to prove just as poor a selection. He entered our service the same spring as Botolf and the two of them quickly became friends. According to Husee's letter of introduction Philpot was;

'...Sir Peter Philpot's son and heir. He is neither the first nor second son but the third and wisest of them and seems to be of a gentle disposition.'

The Philpots are a Hampshire family and had been our neighbours there. I had no memory of young Clement but had a great liking for Sir Peter and his wife. The future did indeed look promising that spring as our new servants settled into their posts.

After Philpot had been in Calais for about two months, Arthur and I discussed with Philippa a possible match with him. She was now twenty-two and no beauty. It was our opinion that she could not afford to hesitate much longer.

But in this matter, Philippa showed surprising perception and also great strength of character.

'I have no liking for him,' she said quietly and firmly in response to our suggestion.

'How so?' enquired Arthur. 'He seems personable enough to me.'

'Personable he may be,' stated Philippa, 'but he has no backbone. He is weak and can be too easily influenced by smooth talk and charming manners.'

She showed great skill and tact in expressing herself this way. What she was probably trying to say was that she and everyone else in Calais, excepting Arthur and myself, could see how much under Botolf's influence he was but knowing our blindness in that area, she refrained from saying it.

'Well, Philippa,' said Arthur, showing only mild disappointment, 'it is neither your mother's nor my way to force unwanted marriages upon our children, so I will say no more. Only remember that the chance is here now and may not come again.' With that he said no more on the subject and it was closed forever.

This refusal of Philippa's to marry Clement Philpot was probably the only fortunate aspect of the entire drama which was to unfold.

Meanwhile our financial situation was again becoming steadily worse. We were having trouble paying even the tradesmen who provided the necessities of life and the luxurious clothes and lifestyle which were expected of us were becoming impossible to maintain.

It was during the month of June that the head cook knocked on the door of my parlour. This was a most unusual occurrence; in fact, it had never happened before. I stopped writing the letter to James which I had been working on.

'Lady Lisle, please forgive me for this interruption but we are to have no milk.'

'No milk, how so?' I was still composing the letter in my mind and she had not yet gained my full attention.

'My Lady, the milkman says he has not been paid for two months and that we are to get no more milk until he is.' She looked as if she was about to burst into tears.

My thoughts left James at that moment. 'My God, have we sunk to this?' I said quietly. She either did not hear me or pretended not to as she waited for my next utterance. I reached for my purse and gave her a sum of money. 'I am truly sorry that you have been placed in such a position, Cook. Will this cover the expense do you think?'

'Yes, My Lady, this will do for the moment.' She beat a hasty retreat then, leaving me to my humiliation.

Arthur had been trying for months to get an audience with the King to plead for more money and at last in late August of that year he had a positive answer. Husee wrote that the King would be in Dover in early September and would be pleased to see him there.

At the end of August, Arthur sailed to Dover. I accompanied him to the harbour to say farewell and clung to him until the last moment before had to board the ship.

'Take care, my darling,' my voice was muffled by his shirt front.

'That I will do, my love,' he replied. 'You will be on my mind and in my heart every moment until I return.'

Our kiss was more like that of two young lovers than of an aging married couple and out of the corner of my eye I saw the sailors who were waiting for him to board the ship smirking at each other. But I did not care and kissed him all the more fervently. Then he left my side and boarded the craft. Before long he was out of sight.

When I arrived back at the Staple Inn it was in time to see several finely liveried horses in the process of being stabled. Surprised and curious, I entered the house. The housekeeper hurried towards me as I entered the hall.

'The Bishop of Ely is here, My Lady,' she told me as she took my riding cloak. 'He awaits you in your parlour.'

Feeling more than a little alarmed, I proceeded down the hall. I had heard much about Thomas Thirlby, Bishop of Ely and none of it had been to my liking. It was said that he was very friendly with Archbishop Cranmer who was leading the march towards heresy in the Church of England. He had played a prominent part in all the so-called religious reforms that had taken place and was, therefore, not someone with whom I wished to spend very much time. My mood was frosty as I entered my parlour.

'Bishop Thirlby,' I extended my hand to him as he stood upon my entry. 'Welcome to Calais. Unfortunately, you find my husband away from home. He has just this hour left for a meeting with the King at Dover.'

He smiled sweetly and I found myself looking into a pair of gentle, friendly eyes. This unexpected warmth surprised me, and I rapidly snatched back my hand which he was still holding.

As he spoke to me, I noticed that even his voice had a pleasant quality about it. 'I am pleased in any case to make your acquaintance, Lady Lisle and my visit is more in the way of a break from official duties than an extension of them.'

I summoned a servant and requested refreshments to be brought to us. He explained to me what he had been doing.

'The King had hoped to procure a marriage between the Princess Mary and the Duke of Orleans. I have been in France these past weeks trying to settle the arrangements.'

'And how did the arrangements proceed?' I asked, not much interested but needing to make polite conversation.

'Not well,' he replied and then added somewhat injudiciously, given his position and the fact that he knew me not at all, 'the French King was not at all interested, I am afraid. King Henry seems to have forgotten that he has declared Princess Mary to be illegitimate. Francis has not.'

I thought to myself that it served the King right. He had created this complication himself. While I was musing over these matters the refreshments arrived and as we ate our talk turned to less weighty topics. Against my will I found myself liking him very much. He was not the heretical ogre of my imagination but a soft-hearted man of simple tastes and much more catholic in his beliefs than I had thought.

'I passed by a wonderful orchard on my way here,' he said during our discussion. 'It was by a stone cottage near the village of Landretun.'

'That may well be our cottage,' I said with a smile. 'Arthur and I bought it soon after we came here but have never had the time to make use of the fruit from the orchard, I am afraid. It must be ripening now.'

'It is definitely ripening,' he replied enthusiastically. 'It is already starting to fall from the trees. Do you think we might go out there tomorrow and gather some for bottling?'

Thus, suggested the Bishop of Ely and King's ambassador to the French Court.

'What, you and I?' I asked, open-mouthed in astonishment.

'A few servants to help us might make the job more quickly done,' he replied with a laugh. 'Come on, Lady Lisle or may I call you Honora, what do you say?'

I was too astounded to say much at all but carried away by his boyish enthusiasm I agreed and the next day saw us heading out to Landretun with a handful of servants and enough baskets to fit a very large amount of fruit. It was a wonderfully warm and mellow autumn day. The fruit was indeed ready for picking and we all set to work. I was unused to such manual labour and spent a great deal of time sitting under the shade of a quince tree. From this vantage point I was surprised and amused to see Thomas Thirlby working energetically alongside the servants, laughing and joking with them as if there was no vast gulf of wealth and importance between them at all. It was late in the evening when we returned, tired and dirty from our day's work, to Calais.

During supper my industrious houseguest said. 'We must make sure we get a good rest tonight for tomorrow the real work begins. Tomorrow,' he announced, 'we must attend to the bottling.'

Once again, my visitor had rendered me speechless. As I prepared for bed that night my mind was in such a confused state that I knew not what to think. I realised that I had not thought of my absent husband all day and that was most unusual but then the whole day had been unusual, and the morrow promised to be even more so. I eventually drifted off to sleep, fatigued from the day's toil.

Chapter Twenty One

Early the next morning, after prayers and breakfast, I entered the kitchen of the Staple Inn with the Bishop of Ely. I can still remember the expressions on the faces of the cook and kitchen-maids as we conscripted them to assist us and commenced our work!

'Good morning everybody,' I said blithely as if it was a routine occurrence that the Lady of the house and a Bishop wandered into the kitchen with their sleeves rolled up. 'How many girls can you spare to assist us, Cook? You have no doubt seen the baskets of fruit in the cool room. We need to get busy bottling.'

Cook managed to close her mouth, which had dropped open and remained so during my little speech. 'Oh, um, I expect that I can spare Peggy and Martha, My Lady. Perhaps, Susan as well if we do without venison pie.'

'I think we can safely do without venison pie for today, Lady Lisle,' said Thirlby. 'Do you not think so?'

'I think that perhaps just for today, it would be possible,' I said, enjoying our small private jest, which was entirely lost on the servants.

There followed one of the most extraordinary days of my life. It was spent bottling fruit with one of the King's most important ministers, who also happened to be a consecrated Bishop. We preserved quinces and barberries, damsons and plums. He taught me several recipes which I still have today. I experienced the same perfect contentment which I always feel in a kitchen, absorbed in the companionable task of food preparation and feeling completely happy. All the troubles and worries of Calais slipped for a few blissful hours to the back of my mind. When it was done, we stood back and surveyed our handiwork.

'Well, Honora, I think we have done a fine day's work here,' he announced with satisfaction.

I laughed. 'It still feels unreal,' I said. 'Who will ever believe this?'

'Only those who are fortunate enough to taste our finished product, I expect,' he replied with a chuckle.

Due to our taking over the kitchen and staff for the whole day, our evening meal consisted largely of our own freshly cooked fruit and whatever cold provisions could be found in the pantry. It was one of the most enjoyable meals of my life.

The next day, Bishop Thirlby left Calais to return to England. As I parted from him he held my hand as he had done at our meeting, only this time I did not pull it away.

'I will never forget this time,' he said sincerely. 'It has been the first real thing I have done in a long time and I am grateful to you for it.'

'But it was all your idea,' I stated.

'Perhaps,' he replied, 'but do you think I would have suggested such an idea to any of the other grand ladies of my acquaintance? Honora, I saw in you the need to spend some days like this just as I also had the need of it. Let us hope that the memory of it gives us the strength to face the days ahead.'

He left then, and I never saw him again. His brief entry into my life provided a breath of fresh air and just as he had hoped, gave me the strength to carry on.

Chapter Twenty Two

I had two letters from my Lord whilst he was away in Canterbury, where he had needed to travel in order to meet the King. Thanks to my diversions with Thomas Thirlby it seemed, for once, that Arthur was missing me more that I, him. But at least the trip seemed to be going well and the King was receptive to his requests. He had been granted an annual pension from the King for the rest of his life which we hoped would be enough to keep us from penury at least.

Arthur returned home on the tenth of September and had been home for less than two weeks when he received a letter from Sir Anthony Windsor. Windsor was a good friend of ours in Hampshire and had been keeping a close eye on Bridget and her security at St Mary's ever since the scare of the first visit by Cromwell's commissioners in 1536. The letter conveyed nothing to us of the impending destruction of St Mary's, but he must have had prior knowledge which he chose not to divulge in writing.

What he did write was that he had thought it time to remove Bridget from St Mary's and that she was now living in his household under the care and tuition of his wife. He promised that she would lack for nothing.

That letter was dated the sixteenth of September and within a few days we heard that the commissioners had again descended upon St Mary's and had proceeded to destroy the holy relics there. How grateful we were to Sir Anthony for his timely removal of our daughter and what terror she must have avoided seeing, as Cromwell's ruffians laid waste to what had been her home for five years.

The times were certainly confusing and dangerous for us all. It was so difficult for the ordinary person to know what was the accepted doctrine and what was heresy. Although the King had swept away the Pope and his authority, he still kept to the orthodox doctrines of the established Church. This was not enough for some who wished for more of what they termed reforms. I remained firmly of the belief that we had already gone too far and wished for a return to the way things had been before. There were so many different opinions and schools of thought and spies abounded ready to report back to their various masters twisted accounts of what they had heard.

We received frequent accounts of the burning of heretics and these unfortunates were often simply people who had gone just a little bit further in what they preached than the official religious doctrine of the moment. Whilst I could not agree with their beliefs, I remained uneasy as all too often it seemed they had simply been caught saying the wrong thing at the wrong time. The heresy of today could just as easily be the established doctrine of tomorrow.

Late in September that year we had a visit from another of the King's ministers, who we also knew by repute rather than by personal acquaintance. His name was Sir Thomas Wriothesley, and, like Thomas Thirlby, I was prepared to dislike him from his reputation alone but unlike Thirlby he lived up to my pre-formed opinion of him.

'My Lord, My Lady,' was all he said, upon dismounting, extending his hand to each of us in turn.

Chapter Twenty Two

The hand that held mine briefly in its grasp was cold and moist like a fish and the eyes that looked for a moment into mine were steely grey and flickered with a harsh and cruel light. This was no Thomas Thirlby to be bottling fruit with.

Arthur escorted our unwelcome guest indoors and I trailed behind, not wanting to join them but not wanting poor Arthur to have to deal with him alone either. Reluctantly I followed them into the parlour after sending to the kitchen for refreshments.

Wriothesley looked about him with a curl to his lip. 'I see you have acquired more lavish accommodation since my last visit to Calais in Lord Berners' time.' I was not deaf to his insinuation that the previous house was not considered good enough by such noble people as us but had been quite suitable for the previous governor.

I rose to the bait. 'That house was in a bad state of disrepair and was not suitable for lodging state guests,' I said. 'If we had only ourselves to consider it would not have mattered.'

'Indeed,' he said quietly, 'I was under the impression that Lord Berners housed many state guests there. I must have been mistaken.'

We were saved at that moment by the entry of a footman with a tray of food and drink. Wriothesley's attention was immediately diverted to the consumption of every morsel placed before him. We sat in extreme discomfort as he noisily chomped his way through the bread and cheese and swilled our ale, oblivious, it seemed, to our presence. It was almost as if the previous exercise in putting us in a defensive position had merely been his usual way of passing the time.

Fortunately for us his visit was brief, merely undertaken to refresh his men and horses before the long ride ahead of them. Soon, but not soon enough, he mounted his horse and together with his vast army of servants continued on his way to Flanders. He was at that time, in 1538, the King's ambassador to the Netherlands and was on his way there to arrange a marriage for King Henry and also one for his daughter, Princess Mary.

I shuddered as he rode away. 'That is one person I would not like to cross.'

'Nor I,' said Arthur, 'I hear he takes great pleasure in torturing prisoners before their execution, even women.'

We both hoped we would never meet Thomas Wriothesley again.

We were still standing in the courtyard thinking dark thoughts about our departing guest when there was another commotion without and a thundering of hooves and in a great flurry of dust our friend, Stephen Gardiner, rode in.

'Ha!' he shouted playfully, 'a welcoming committee!' He dismounted as lightly as he could due to his increasing bulk and stood before us, such a contrast to the one whose dust had barely settled.

'Stephen!' we both shouted together. 'What a pleasure and a surprise!' We were both talking and fussing at the same time, so relieved were we to see him.

'Well, well, why so very pleased?' he asked.

'We have just this moment bidden farewell to another guest, Thomas Wriothesley,' I said.

Stephen laughed. 'That explains all. It is not so much my arrival you celebrate as the departure of another. Master Wriothesley has that effect on many people.'

Chapter Twenty Two

We were still laughing when we entered the house and soon afterwards, we sat down to dinner. It was some time since we had seen Stephen and it was such a relief to us that he had remained unchanged and was still our dear, good friend.

'What brings you to Calais, Stephen?' Arthur asked during the meal.

'Personal rather than official business this time, I am glad to say,' he answered. 'I am here to enquire after young James Basset.'

'James?' I queried with surprise. 'He is at the College of Navarre but from the tone of his last letter it has not been the enjoyable or socially elevating experience he had hoped for, I fear.'

This was indeed true. James had been most miserable at the college. We had received a letter only two weeks earlier in which he had written that the education was poor, the conditions harsh and the food terrible. He also wrote that most of his letters were dictated and that this was the first one he had been able to write and smuggle out of his own accord. In a panic I had written to John Worth, who assured me that all was well, and that James was exaggerating the situation. I was not reassured by the tone of Master Worth's missive and wondered if he was another who had not warmed to my son.

Stephen continued speaking about James. 'I have long taken an interest in that young man,' he said. 'If you were agreeable, I would like to take him back to England with me as a member of my household.'

We were most certainly not averse to that proposal and said so with alacrity.

'Then,' said Bishop Gardiner, 'on the morrow let us send to the College of Navarre and have James brought back to Calais in preparation for his departure.'

To have James back in England and under the wing of Stephen Gardiner was more than we had dared to hope for. Without further ado he was brought to Calais and his delight at not only leaving the College but also in his new prospects was apparent. Within days, my youngest child left to begin his new life with our dearest friend as his protector. John Worth travelled back to England with them but was no longer to be in our service.

Once again, it seemed, our fortunes were on the rise.

Chapter Twenty Three

One day in late October, I was sitting peacefully in the garden. It was one of those special October days, with a soft light filtering through the thinning golden leaves which were falling gently about me. Each slight puff of wind brought a few more floating down to land at my feet. It was very quiet in the garden, the birds resting now after a busy summer raising their young. All was peace. I was enjoying working on a particularly fine piece of embroidery which was taking my full attention and successfully distracting me from everything else when I heard Arthur calling me.

'Honora, Honora, where are you?' His voice came to me from inside the house, strained and taut.

'I am out here,' I answered, gathering up my work, 'in the garden.'

He appeared in the doorway looking pale and distraught.

'Arthur, my love, what ails you?' Something was obviously badly amiss.

'They have arrested Margaret Pole,' he gasped. 'My cousin is in the Tower.'

I moved over on the wooden bench and he sat down beside me. His whole body was trembling. This was terrible news. Margaret Pole, Countess Salisbury was Arthur's cousin, daughter of Edward IV's brother Clarence. She was the mother of the exiled Reginald Pole and together with Arthur, they were among the last remaining Plantagenets. Margaret was not a young woman. She was sixty-eight years old. Incarceration would be no light matter for her, regardless of what the finding of her inquisitors should be.

'What possible reason can there be for arresting a frail old woman like that?' His voice was small and defeated.

I moved closer to him on the bench and took his hands, rubbing them between my own as if to warm them but I had no answers for him and remained silent. How could I tell him of the terrible fear which assailed me and of the sense of helplessness which was increasing with every passing day? The only solace I could offer was from the comfort my physical presence could provide. I stood and held out my hands to him and together we went indoors.

It is one of my only consolations now, at the end of my life, that of all our troubles none were ever between us. Left to ourselves, my love and I would have lived to ripe old age in peace and tranquillity. But that was not to be.

To make matters worse, we soon realised that the pension which the King had promised Arthur a short time before was not going to be nearly enough to secure us financially. We needed to act quickly before our creditors descended upon us like a pack of ravening wolves. Since Arthur had pressing duties in Calais it was necessary for me to take the trip to England to see what could be done.

'Arthur, what if I am unable to secure more funding? What on earth are we to do?'

'There is only one thing which can be done, my dearest. We will have to part with Soberton. Do you remember Walter Bonham?'

I nodded, having a vague recollection of such a person living a few miles from Soberton.

'Well, he sent me a letter some time ago to say he was interested in buying the lease from us if we ever wished to sell it. I did not mention it to you at the time because I did not wish to upset you and because I was clinging to the hope that it would not become necessary.'

'My darling, I will do everything within my power to see that it does not come to that,' I assured him.

On the night before my departure in early November we were as tender and loving with each other as we ever had been.

'Oh, how I detest to be parted from you,' he said as he nuzzled my hair and caressed me gently.

'And I from you, my dearest,' I replied, 'but let us not speak of tomorrow. Tonight, we are together.'

The night passed all too quickly, however, and dawn saw us once more at the docks. This time it was I who stepped onto the ship and Arthur who remained on the shore, to become an ever-diminishing speck on the dock as I sailed for England.

It was a calm enough crossing but, as usual, I began to feel ill the moment I stepped off firm land. I parted with my breakfast before Calais was out of sight and spent the remainder of the crossing lying miserably on the hard, wooden bunk in my cabin.

I arrived in Dover on the sixth of November and after collapsing on the soft bed in my lodgings, sank into a deep sleep and awoke the next morning feeling weak but no longer so ill. After eating a hearty breakfast, I was almost recovered and travelled as far as Canterbury where Husee met me.

'My Lady,' he greeted me warmly, 'it gladdens my heart to see you again.'

'I am also glad to see you, John,' I replied, 'and grateful to you for the services you provide us in our absence.'

'There is much I cannot tell you in my letters Madam,' he said, with a sideways glance to ensure that we were not overheard. 'There have been more arrests.'

'Do you mean more since that of the Countess of Salisbury?' I was shocked but not surprised.

'Yes, it seems the entire Pole family is to be prosecuted as well as Sir Edward Neville and the Marquis of Exeter.'

'John,' I thought quickly, 'you must send a dependable messenger straight to Calais to inform Arthur of this news. It must be someone who can be trusted with a verbal message.' My skin pricked with fear. 'He must tell my husband to be ever on his guard.'

Husee found his messenger and did as I asked. There was no more to be done for now and the next day we set out for London. I wrote to Arthur every day and he to me, loving letters to reassure each other of the one constant good thing we had but carefully avoiding any mention of the latest arrests.

I set to work immediately. My audience with the King was on the fourteenth of November. He had put on weight since I last saw him. There was a florid, unhealthy colour to his fleshy cheeks and his girth had expanded to monstrous proportions. He seemed to have trouble walking and limped quite noticeably as he entered the chamber into which I had been sent to await his presence.

He greeted me warmly, going so far as to assist me to stand from my curtsey. It was the first time I had seen him without a lady by his side and he looked quite alone. For the first and only time, I felt a small jolt of sympathy for him.

'It pleases me to welcome you back to England's shores, Aunt,' he said, and I thought I detected a note of sincerity in his voice. He hobbled to his chair and beckoned me to sit as well. It was the first time he had called me 'aunt' and I felt a surge of optimism. So far, I had said nothing and was about to begin when he spoke again. 'You find me here, a lonely widower, bereft of companionship and alone in my bed at night.' He sighed and then said something which made my heart lurch uncomfortably. 'If it were not for the presence of your daughter, Mistress Anne Basset, I should be desolate indeed.'

'Your Grace finds my daughter pleasant company?'

'Pleasant indeed, we take a walk together daily, as far as my poor sick leg will allow in any case,' he pointed in frustration at his leg, which, I had not failed to notice, was bandaged heavily.'

I was determined to see Anne during my visit and resolved at that moment to caution her. Much as I wished for her to further herself in the world, I was very afraid for her if this meant becoming mistress or wife to King Henry. But for the present I needed to attend to the business for which I had made the journey.

'Your Grace, I have travelled here to seek your help in the matter of funds for the administration of Calais. Our coffers are quite empty, and it has reached the point where we are no longer able to pay our bills.'

But he only brushed my request aside with an imperious wave of his hand. It was plain that with me he desired only to speak of social matters and instructed me to speak of financial and business affairs with Thomas Cromwell. However, he spoke fondly of Arthur and his affection seemed genuine still. It appeared he did not associate us in any way with the treasons, imagined or otherwise, of the Pole family.

I lodged that night at Westminster Palace and attended a lavish banquet at which I was seated at the high table very near the King. It appeared that he wished me, and the whole Court, to know that Arthur and I were still in high favour.

The only enjoyable episode during that visit to Court was seeing Anne again. She looked radiant and beautiful as she greeted me.

'Mother, what a delight it is to have you here,' she said, presenting her cheek to me for a kiss. She seemed genuinely pleased to see me, but her greeting was formal, as befitted her position and I loathed it.

Still, many eyes were upon us, so I had to restrain myself from throwing my arms about her. 'Dear daughter, how do you fare here amidst all this glitter?'

'I find it very much to my taste,' answered Anne. Then, as we moved away from the ever-present crowds of courtiers she relaxed and with a little giggle she whispered. 'The King gave me a new horse and saddle last week. He insists I accompany him whenever he rides out.'

I knew not whether to be happy or afraid. We continued walking to an empty spot in the garden and I broached the subject tentatively.

'Anne, how close are you to the King?'

'Oh,' she gave a small tinkling laugh, 'I am aware of what the gossips are saying but there is nothing in it. The King is lonely at present and enjoys my company. There is no more to it than that, I can assure you Mother.' Then she put on a pompous and affected voice. 'Master Cromwell would never

Chapter Twenty Three

approve of such a lowly match for the King. He is looking towards one of the Royal Houses of Europe for the next Queen.'

I looked rapidly over my shoulder. 'Mind yourself daughter, is it safe to speak thus of Cromwell?'

'Oh yes,' she laughed again, 'the King does not really like him you know. He tolerates him for his undoubted abilities but when we are together, we have a merry time mocking him behind his back.'

I did not know quite what to make of this very close relationship of my daughter and the King but since Anne was obviously quite happy about it and seemed to be under no illusions as to its future direction, I said no more, only adding a caution.

'Just be careful, Anne. Master Cromwell may be mistaken as to his standing in the King's affections, but he remains the most powerful man in this country after the King and is very much to be feared.'

Two days later and still unable to obtain an audience with Thomas Cromwell, I attended a public debate at York Place at which a clerk called Lambert, who had been a chaplain at Antwerp, was brought to defend his heretical beliefs before the King. There were also present bishops, doctors, judges and sergeants of law. Lambert was unable to sustain any logic to his arguments when faced with such a bench of learned men but refusing also to forsake his opinions, was taken away for trial.

After that was done the King issued a proclamation stressing his orthodox opinion forbidding the marriage of the clergy and approving several Catholic practices which the Reformers wanted abolished. It was a diversion for me from the distasteful but very urgent business for which I had travelled to London.

Another event to take place a few days later was a meeting with Bridget. I had sent a message to Sir Anthony Windsor and he brought her to London.

She was thirteen now but was hardly changed in appearance from the little girl I had left years before. She was slightly taller than she had been but was still no higher than me, unlike her sisters who had inherited the Plantagenet length of limb, but she remained so thin and slight that I wondered if she were well.

'Oh, yes, mother, I am quite well,' she said in answer to my concern. 'I was very happy at St Mary's and Sir Anthony is like a father to me. How is my father?' She added this quickly as if she were embarrassed by what she had said.

'He is very well, my dear,' I told her, my own heart aching for a sight of his face. 'He bids you be of good cheer and hopes to see you soon.' I have no idea why I said that. There was no hope of Arthur seeing her soon but trite talk rolls easily off the tongue.

We spent a passable hour together but so much had happened in the preceding five years and she was no longer the little girl I had mothered and loved. She was now a young lady and I must have seemed like a stranger to her. I think we were both grateful when Sir Anthony came to take her away, back to the family she now regarded as her own. It was only after she had gone that I realised she had not once asked after James. I remembered with a pang what inseparable playmates they had been during those years at Soberton. Such is the way with the passage of time and the manner in which fate shapes our lives that now she barely remembered him, if indeed she remembered him at all.

The days were passing, and I was finally granted the long-awaited audience with Thomas Cromwell. I had put on my most austere and simple gown for the dreaded meeting and as I entered the room, I had a sinking feeling in my breast, as if I already knew what the outcome would be. Cromwell was alone in the room, which was sparsely furnished with a huge desk situated on a raised platform, behind which he was seated. He thus had the advantage of looking down upon whoever had the misfortune to be addressing him. The only other item of furniture was a low, hard chair placed directly in front of the desk, towards which he gestured.

'Lady Lisle, please sit down,' he himself remained seated. I took the message in that. He regarded himself as well above the accepted rules of propriety and need not stand when a lady entered the room. The King was the only other man I had ever met who had no need to observe that formality.

He said no more but sat still and silent waiting for me to begin. Once again there was an unspoken message. 'You are here to see me, not I to see you, so get on with it.'

I felt a lump in my throat as I took my seat, as if a tight band were constricting my neck. Taking a deep breath, I began nervously.

'My Lord, as you know, Lord Lisle and I have been in Calais now for over five years. During that time, Arthur has performed his duties honourably and efficiently.'

'That is a matter of opinion,' interjected Cromwell with a bored look on his face.

Already sensing that this interview was going to prove a waste of time and feeling hot, damp and uncomfortable, I blundered on.

'Sir, we are in desperate financial straits. We have received little money from you to carry out our duties or maintain our household. We are expected to provide lodgings and entertainment for every dignitary who passes through the town. My estates here in England are neglected and run down in our absence. We have creditors knocking at our doors daily, demanding payment for even the most basic of necessities and no way of paying them.'

'Stop, stop!' He put up a hand and cried out imperiously. 'Lady Lisle, it is no fault of mine if you and your husband are living beyond your means. And if you wish to imply that the blame lies with the King ...' his voice trailed off menacingly.

I felt myself close to tears of humiliation and frustration and was determined to deny him the pleasure of witnessing such a show.

'No, my Lord, of course I am implying no such thing. I was wrong to bring our personal troubles here to you. You have much more pressing matters with which to deal. Please, accept my humble apologies.'

Hastily I stood, accepted his inclined head by way of dismissal and took my departure. I maintained my composure until I was well away from his presence and from the eyes of his servants. Walking erect and proud, I left the building, not allowing myself to cry until I was safely back in my own rented lodgings. Once there, I gave vent to tears of frustration and misery, but I could not afford the luxury

Chapter Twenty Three

of wallowing too long in despair. I needed to get us some money, and fast.

It was now the end of November and I had been away over three weeks. So far, my trip had gained us nothing. The trials of the men arrested with Margaret Pole took place at this time and all but one, Geoffrey Pole, were found guilty. It seemed in each of these purges there was always one who escaped, as if that could in some way vindicate the executions which were to follow. Arthur's cousin, Margaret Pole, remained in prison but so far untried.

I sat down that night and wrote another letter to Arthur, a loving missive which conveyed my profound loneliness and deep longing to be with him.

The next day I steeled myself to do that which we had spoken of but had kept as a last resort to only do if the situation could not be remedied in any other way. I would sell our lease of Soberton. How can I describe the sadness which that decision created? We would be selling that of which our happiest memories were made, our marriage home, our haven, the one place where we had lived as a real family together.

I sent a message to Walter Bonham to join me in my lodgings and to bring a notary with him. Of course, being a shrewd businessman and aware of our desperate situation, he quibbled about the price. I held out for as long as I could but knowing full well that beggars cannot be choosers, I had no option but to agree to his demands. When it came time to sign the agreement, I had to force my hand to perform the task. I felt like a traitor to our happiness and to our memories. But all too soon the deed was done, and the papers signed. Soberton belonged to Walter Bonham and our life there was over, never to be recaptured.

That was the third of December, a cold bleak day when the very air seemed to be sighing. 'It is over, it is over,' moaned the wind as it swirled around the corners of the house and blew down the chimneys.

I remained in London for nine more days, hoping against hope that I could obtain another audience with the King and that he would agree to help us, but it was not to be and on the fifteenth of December, after notifying Arthur of my impending arrival, I returned to Calais.

The tears over which I had kept so tight a reign in London began to flow as soon as I caught sight of my husband waiting on the shore before my ship docked. By the time I staggered into his arms, green from sickness and red-eyed from misery, I must have given the watching sailors something to talk about over supper.

'Oh, my love, my love, it has been the most horrible time of my life,' I wept as he held me in his arms.

'Come, let us away,' he soothed and petted me. 'Say no more until we are alone.'

He took me straight to our private chambers and between storms of weeping I told him all about my trip from beginning to end, keeping the most depressing detail until last.

'And Arthur, I have sold Soberton.' I ended on a sob and more tears. I had reached such a state of exhaustion and sadness that I felt I would never stop crying.

'Hush now, my sweetheart,' he held me and stroked my hair. 'It was the only course of action left open to us. You did what was best. You always do.'

Chapter Twenty Three

He helped me over to our bed and lay me down. Covering me gently with the bedclothes he sat down next to me and continued to soothe and caress me until I fell asleep. I slept all the rest of that day and night and when I awoke the following morning, he was with me, lying by my side in our bed, just like on any other morning.

'Good morning, my dearest girl, are you feeling better now you are rested?'

'So much better, Arthur, now I am home with you.' I feasted my eyes on him. 'Oh, my darling, how I detest it when we are apart.'

Just after Christmas we received a message from Reginald Pole. The courier came in secret and wore no livery as even receiving a message from one accused of treason was in itself a treasonable offence. He delivered the message verbally. It seems Pole had visited the Court of the Holy Roman Emperor to seek his assistance in re-establishing Papal authority in England. He wished to know whether we would be willing to support him should his plans come to fruition. Having knowledge of such a plot placed us in a perilous situation. We were, in fact, duty bound to report knowledge of it to the King but since doing so would implicate us and lay us open to charges, we chose to say nothing. We hastily sent the messenger away with no reply.

'I cannot believe that my cousin was so uncaring of our welfare as to place us in such danger,' said Arthur after the man had gone.

'He is bound to be distraught about his mother's arrest,' I said. 'He may feel that the only way now is to try and ignite some kind of Holy War against England.' I shivered. 'Let us hope that he does not try to contact us again.'

Early in the new year my nephew Richard Grenville resigned his post as Marshall of Calais and returned to Stowe with his family. I was not sorry to see him go, although to be fair, he had performed his duties well enough. Maud and I parted kindly, though.

'Farewell, Honora,' she said, kissing me briefly. 'I am not sad to leave this place, as I am sure you would understand.'

'I truly wish we were leaving with you,' I answered sincerely.

'I know that Richard is not always easy to put up with,' she said sadly, with a furtive look to make sure Richard was not within earshot, 'but believe me when I say that deep down he has a great affection for you and although he often acts rashly and causes hurt, I am certain he would never intentionally do you harm.'

I was not so sure. As a child I used to make the same excuses for Richard but now he was no longer a child. Still, I reserved that opinion for Richard, not for his wife with whom I had no quarrel.

'Do not fret, Maud,' I reassured her, 'I am happy for you that you are returning to English soil and I wish to God that we were accompanying you. I will be praying that you have a safe journey back to Stowe.' My voice caught as I said the name of my first home. How far away it seemed, and how long since I had last smelt the fresh Cornish air and ridden my horse over the barren hills to Coombe Valley. I gave her a letter for my brother John in Kilkhampton just before they rode away to meet their ship.

Soon after their departure we received news which cheered us immeasurably. John and Frances had been blessed by the safe arrival of a daughter. To make the occasion even more special for me, they had named her Honora. How we wished they were not so far away and that we could see our granddaughter. John penned the letter himself and he also told us that Tehidy was returning better profits since he had taken up the running of it. It seems Thomas St Aubyn had not been keeping such a close eye on things there as he had promised to do, and the miners had been cheating us in our absence. It was not likely that we would be seeing much of the money for a while as most of it was going towards repairs and maintenance, but it was a start.

'So, you are an old grandmother,' teased Arthur that night after we heard the news.

'And you, my Lord, are a grandfather, let us not forget that,' I replied flicking him playfully with the long ends of my gable-hood as I removed it for the night.

He grabbed me around the middle and turned me towards him. 'Such a trim waist does not belong to a grandmother.' He kissed my mouth. 'Nor such soft lips,' he murmured and as he continued to praise my body parts in turn, I quickly finished my toilette and changed for bed.

In February 1539, another Act of Parliament was passed in England which completed the dissolution of all the monasteries, great and small. It was called the Act for the Dissolution of the Greater Monasteries and spelled the end for those few remaining houses which had still held out against Cromwell's bullies. Any monks who continued to defy them from that time on were accused of treason. To prove this point, the Abbots of Reading, Glastonbury and Colchester were all hanged. I had met the Abbot of Reading once, in 1533, just before James went there and I remembered him as a kindly, intelligent man of noble bearing. He became just one more martyr in that year of 1539.

Following soon after that Act another was passed which was called the Statute of Six Articles. This Act abolished diversity of opinions in matters of religious doctrine and gave a positive definition of heresy. A special procedure was set up for the prosecution of heretics, with commissioners to be appointed in every diocese. The commissioners were empowered to compel the attendance of accused persons before them and to try them with a jury. The cause of the reformists had received a set-back. This was all well and good but people like us were caught in the middle. We were certainly not heretics but due to my adherence to the old ways we still risked prosecution. There was no easy way out and few safe paths to tread.

Just when it seemed that Cromwell's power might be on the wane, as he was well-known to be sympathetic to the reformists, we heard that he had been made Lord Great Chamberlain of England.

'Ugh, now he wears every robe of office bar those of the King,' said Arthur in disgust. 'He had better be wary lest he can no longer carry the weight.'

Early one dismal morning in March, just as we were completing our breakfast there was a great noise in the yard of horses and shouting. We hurried out to see what the commotion was about and were met by the sight of ten or twelve horsemen, wet and bedraggled, dismounting in the rain. Seeking to know who they were and what their business was, we spied one who seemed to be their leader, as he was shouting orders to the others. He had a hooded cape which hid his face, so we had no idea who he was. Arthur went over to the man and they spoke for a few seconds before they both walked rapidly towards the house.

As they came in and the stranger removed his soaked outer garments, I realized that our visitor was Thomas Wriothesley. I recognised him with difficulty, however. He was so changed from the arrogant, frosty, superior man of his last visit so short a time ago.

On that occasion he had done his best to discomfort us by insinuating that we had only acquired the Staple Inn because we had felt Lord Berner's house was beneath us. Well, now the boot was on the other foot and we were going to make the most of it. Arthur and I both acted rashly that day. In our defence I can only say that so great had been our suffering in the last years that our minds had become unhinged. Caution and wisdom deserted us.

Wriothesley was soaked to the skin. His head covering hung in a sodden mass over his ears and eyes. His boots squelched as he walked, and he was shaking with cold.

'I am so sorry, Sir Thomas, that you have been in danger,' Arthur was saying as they entered the porch. 'Please, join us in the breakfast room and tell us what has befallen you.'

Arthur stood back and gestured to Wriothesley to move ahead of us. As he did so he caught my eye and gave me such a look of delight that I almost laughed out loud, only just restraining myself in time.

We returned to the breakfast table and encouraged our guest to eat what was left of the food. It gave me great pleasure to see that man devouring our scraps with such relish. He shivered as he ate and I feared or rather, hoped, that he had caught a chill.

'I have been in the Netherlands, as you know,' he said between mouthfuls. 'I was there to negotiate a marriage between King Henry and the Duchess of Milan and to arrange another between the Princess Mary and Don Luis of Portugal. Both these proposals came to nothing.' He sounded quite disgusted, not, I felt certain, at his own failed powers of negotiation but at the stupidity of the other parties in refusing.

'I also endeavoured, whilst I had the chance, to apprehend English criminals who are taking refuge in the Low Countries. Those places are full of both heretics and Papists from England who are living comfortably there and plotting against our Sovereign.' He was still stuffing food into his mouth at a great rate and I wondered how long it had been since he last ate.

'And did you manage to capture any of these villains?' Arthur was all concern, but I recognised the ironic inflection in his voice.

Wriothesley appeared too engrossed in his food to notice any such subtle cadences and continued speaking in the same affronted tone.

'No, I did not.' He stopped eating and looked directly at us. 'But I was very nearly captured myself.' His voice had the hurt and persecuted tone of a little boy who feels he has been chastised undeservedly. I could restrain myself no longer and choked loudly, trying to hold back my laughter. Arthur spoke quickly.

'Honora, my dear, if you are about to have one of your unfortunate attacks, I suggest you go to another room. Sir Thomas has troubles enough of his own and will not wish to witness your sad affliction.'

Chapter Twenty Three

To the best of my knowledge, I have only ever made two enemies in my life. I freely admit that it is down to my own stupidity and folly that these two happened to be the most powerful and dangerous men in the land at the time. The first was Thomas Cromwell, when I made a thoughtless jibe at the banquet where we met for the first time. The second was Thomas Wriothesley at Calais that day. Oh foolish, foolish woman.

Mumbling incoherently and holding my hand to my mouth, I left as suggested. Once safely out of earshot in our own bedchamber, I succumbed to my 'sad affliction' and laughed as if my sides would burst. I was still in a state of complete helplessness when Arthur entered.

'Sir Thomas has been taken to our most comfortable guest chamber and is changing out of his wet clothes,' he said, joining me in laughter. 'It seems he has ridden both day and night since leaving the Netherlands, stopping only to change horses. He has been followed all the way by messengers from the Regent of that country who had orders to arrest him.'

'Why?' I asked, pleased but bemused.

'Because,' Arthur became suddenly serious, 'King Francis and the Emperor have formed a coalition against our King and war is imminent. Wriothesley would have made a handy hostage.'

'Oh!' Suddenly it did not seem so funny anymore. 'Then we in Calais are surrounded by enemies,' I said quietly. It appeared Reginald Pole had had some success in stirring up trouble for Henry after all.

'So it would seem,' answered Arthur. 'Now, more than ever, we must mind what we say and to whom we say it. There are enemies within as well as without.'

Wriothesley stayed only long enough for our servants to dry his clothes and make them fit for him to wear again. In a few hours he and his party set sail for England. He barely spoke to us again before leaving but his parting words sent shivers down my spine and made me realise that I had done an evil morning's work that day.

'The times are changing, Lord Lisle,' he addressed Arthur, completely ignoring me and sneering unpleasantly as he spoke. 'There are many who are about to discover that their positions are not as secure as they had thought. I would advise you in future to guard your tongue – and for your wife to do likewise.'

'Oh Arthur, what have we done – what have *I* done?' I said as he sailed away.

My love was silent but, dear man that he was, he did not reproach me. Instead he held my hand tightly as we returned to our chambers at the Staple Inn to await the next blow, for we felt certain by this time that the only news we were ever to hear was to be bad news. And so it was.

The following month, we heard that Margaret Pole had been attainted for treason. This came as no surprise as she had been held all this time a prisoner.

'But there is no way they would execute a woman of her age and nobility,' said Arthur when the message came.

'No, surely not,' I agreed.

Late in May we had a visitor whom it always gave us pleasure to see and that was John Wallop. Our friend John seemed to constantly roam from place to place doing a

Chapter Twenty Three

minimum of work and enjoying life enormously, whilst at the same time convincing his masters that he was doing a thoroughly good job indeed. He had become very rich upon the death of an uncle and had also been granted the proceeds of Barlinch monastery in Somerset. John had no children, but I felt that he was not really suited to fatherhood as he enjoyed the roving life too much. On this occasion he had no official reason to visit but came simply to see us.

He looked at us both in turn and spoke bluntly. 'You two need a holiday.'

'Do we look so very terrible?' I laughed.

In usual forthright fashion, he told us that our faces were lined, and we looked older than our years. I replied that his face bore as many lines, if not more, than ours.

'Ah,' he answered, 'but they are the marks of sunshine and laughter. Yours are from worry and too much sitting indoors.'

'Life has not been a bed of roses for us lately, you know, John,' I said feeling a bit put out and hurt by what he said. 'We cannot all travel about the countryside without a care in the world you know.'

He apologised immediately. 'Oh Honora, I am so sorry. I say the stupidest things at times. What I really meant was that you should try and get away more. How long is it since you were at Landretun?'

With a shock I realised that I had not been since I went there with Thomas Thirlby the previous autumn. I could not remember when Arthur went last.

'Arthur?' I looked at him.

'It must be at least eighteen months, perhaps more,' answered my husband. 'We never seem to have the time anymore.'

'Well make time,' suggested John. 'You never know what the future might bring. Make the most of the present.'

'What about it?' Arthur said that night when we were alone.

'What about what?' I asked.

'About going to Landretun,' he said. 'It could be just the two of us, like we used to do.'

I felt a surge of longing sweep over me. Going to Landretun seemed like the best idea in the world and I wondered why it had taken John to alert us to it.

'Oh yes, Arthur, let us go as soon as possible,' I said and threw my arms around him.

It only took us a few days to prepare and once John had returned to England, we sent some servants to clean and freshen the house for us as it had been closed up for so long. Then, after having the kitchen pack and deliver enough food to last us for two weeks, we set out, just the two of us, on the short ride to Landretun.

It was a fresh, warm morning in early June. We rode in sunshine past flowering hedgerows and lushly growing fields. Birds and bees flew about us in profusion and the world was a joyful place. It struck me then, as it has so often during my life, that no matter what a mess we humans make of our lives and of the world in which we live, the plants and animals just get on with doing what they do.

Within an hour we arrived. Arthur alighted from his horse and helped me down from mine. Then, picking me up like a newly married bride, he carried me into the cottage.

Chapter Twenty Three

How can I write of those two weeks we spent at Landretun? Even now, so many years later, my tears fall silently when I recall those wonderful, beautiful, romantic days of our last summer together.

'Dearest love, how happy was the day when I first set eyes on you,' said my husband as we lay like two young children in the long, concealing grass of a field. He was playing with my hair which I was wearing undressed and uncovered like a country maid.

'Do you remember how I stared?' I asked him.

'I remember nothing but the wonder of you and the beauty of your eyes,' he said, looking deeply into those same eyes as he spoke.

'And I remember the most handsome man I had ever seen,' I replied. I then told him one of my secrets. 'When I was a small child my brother and I used to ride to our magic place and dream dreams. His were holy and religious dreams. Mine were of you.'

'How do you know they were of me?' He asked.

'We were destined for each other, Arthur. Do you not remember what you wrote in your letter?' I leant over to the basket which lay on the grass beside us.

I had kept that letter close by me all those years and had brought it with me to Landretun. Together we read it, the letter Arthur had written to me more than thirty years earlier when he feared we would never meet again. Together we cried over its contents and then we loved. There under the sun in a French field, more like young peasants than an ageing noble couple, we loved hungrily and desperately as if we knew even then that our time was running out.

On our last day in Landretun, without even telling Arthur, I took the letter and placed it in a jar which I sealed with wax. Then I went outside and carefully selecting the spot, I buried it next to the fence at the bottom of the orchard, marking the spot with a stone.

Chapter Twenty Four

After we returned to Calais we felt somehow strengthened, as if our brief time at Landretun had empowered us to face our troubles and anything which the future might bring. Our love was like a protective barrier, which grew stronger every day and shielded us from the onslaughts of the harsh reality in which we found ourselves.

In August we had a letter from Anne that at first alarmed us but at the same time eased one nagging worry which had been plaguing me for some time. Together with several other young ladies from the Palace, Anne had travelled down to Portsmouth to view the King's Fleet. They had very much enjoyed their outing and had been in high spirits but shortly after the trip Anne had fallen ill and had needed to leave Court temporarily and stay with her friend, Joan Denny, until she recovered.

Once I was assured that Anne's illness was not severe or life-threatening, I came to regard it as a blessing. King Henry was famous for two things where his pursuance of young women was concerned. He could not abide illness of any kind and he never wasted time hankering after one who was not present.

'I must admit I am not entirely upset by this illness of Anne's,' I confided to Arthur in the privacy of our chamber.

'That is a most unnatural sentiment in a mother,' chided Arthur but he smiled as he said it and I knew that he understood.

'I have been very worried by her closeness to the King. I am aware that there is talk of a Cleves marriage but knowing

King Henry as we do, you have to agree that Anne is better off away from Court until the treaty is signed.'

'Yes, my dear, I know exactly what you mean,' he agreed. 'The sooner this marriage with Anne of Cleves is negotiated, the better for all of us.'

Early in September we had a visit from Stephen Gardiner. He was on his way to Cleves to finalise the negotiations and get the treaty signed. He was jovial and in good spirits.

'Well, here I am off to play match-maker for His Grace,' he said with a smile. 'Let us hope I have more success with my negotiations than our dear friend Wriothesley did with his!'

We burst out laughing, hastily looking around us to check that the doors and windows were shut.

'Oh Stephen, you should have seen him that day he came here on his way home from the Low Countries!' I laughed afresh at the memory. 'The mighty Wriothesley, torturer of women and burner of heretics, looked more like a drowned rat.'

'And a hungry one,' chipped in Arthur. We both laughed merrily, trying to put away the fear which his parting words had instilled in us.

'Well now he is trying desperately to dissuade Henry from this marriage with Cleves,' said Stephen, 'which is presumably why I am the ambassador this time and not he.'

Arthur was surprised. 'For what reason does Wriothesley not wish for the marriage?'

'A political one, I think.' Stephen sounded thoughtful. 'This marriage is of Cromwell's orchestration. Wriothesley is most likely opposing it for that reason, gambling on the chance that it may prove unsuccessful, which would lower

Cromwell's standing as a promoter of it and advance his own as one who opposed it. It may even be that during his time in the Low Countries, Wriothesley may have heard or seen something which has alarmed him about Cleves or even about the Lady Anne herself.'

I was becoming tired of this discussion and had a far more pressing matter about which to ask Stephen.

'Enough of Anne of Cleves,' I interrupted. 'How is my boy?'

Stephen also sounded content to leave the subject of the King's marriages. 'Your boy is a credit to himself and to you. I would have brought him with me on this journey, in fact I desired his presence very much, for my sake as well as yours. But he is advancing so well and so rapidly in his studies at present that I was loath to interrupt them.'

I was immensely happy to hear that. I had always held a high opinion of James' abilities, second only to James himself, but others had been less ready to believe in him. Stephen, alone, had shared my faith where James was concerned and to my relief we were being proven right.

Stephen went on his way after only a day's rest, but his brief visit had brought more than news of the Court and our son. He had brought with him a letter from Cromwell, which stated that Arthur had been granted an audience with both him and the King if he left immediately for England. We straight away set about preparing.

Since Thirlby's visit the previous year I had been keen to put my newly acquired preserving skills to the test so once again that autumn I had been actively bottling fruit and making marmalade and I am sure, making myself very unpopular with the cook and her kitchen hands in the process. Amongst Arthur's other provisions for that trip were some bottles of my very own quince marmalade as a gift to the King.

Our parting in early October was, as always, prolonged and tender. 'Good, dear Sweetheart never fear but that I will be back by your side in a week or two,' he said, as he held me to his breast.

I clung on to him, loath to let him go but let him go I must and shortly afterwards I once more watched as his ship faded into the mist on the horizon.

I used the time whilst he was away collecting and drying the last of the herbs from my garden and labelling them in airtight jars. Philippa was trying to finish embroidering an altar cloth for our chapel, so I helped her with that. Mary was far too busy pining for Gabriel to be of much use with anything. I had never repeated my failed attempt to learn archery since my one and only lesson several years earlier so, encouraged by Philippa, I spent some time one day when the weather was fine, in practising that art. It only served to reinforce what I already knew, that I have not a talent for it, so have not done it since. Still, my miserable efforts did give my daughters the opportunity for a good laugh, just as they had on the first occasion.

By keeping myself busy in these ways, as well as attending to Arthur's administrative tasks for him, the time passed relatively quickly and within a few weeks my love had returned.

'Most successful, most successful,' he answered in reply to my urgent queries as I welcomed him home. 'I had more money out of Cromwell this time than from all of my previous entreaties combined.'

Chapter Twenty Four

'I suppose the threat of hostilities has finally awakened him to the fact that Calais is impoverished and vulnerable.'

'Well, it has taken him six years to get my message, but it is gratifying that he has it at last, I suppose.' My husband was too relieved to be overly cynical.

'And did you see the King?' I asked.

'Oh yes, and he was full of praise for all that I have done here. And,' he looked tenderly at me, 'he asked very kindly after you and sent his grateful thanks for the marmalade, accompanied by a demand for more!'

'And that he may gladly have!' I laughed. 'Perhaps his guests will eat it at his wedding feast.'

For the King's wedding plans were now well under way, with the treaty being signed at the end of September. Calais was put into a state of intense preparation, since the new bride was expected to be lavishly entertained as she passed through on her way to England in December, only one month hence.

All the chambers in the guest wing needed to be renovated with fresh furnishings and carpets. The Great Hall underwent a complete redecoration with new tapestries depicting the coats of arms of Tudor and Cleves. Dozens of seamstresses needed to be employed for that task alone. Copious amounts of food would be needed, so our suppliers were all given advance notice to have it in readiness. Entertainers were brought over from England, mummers, jesters, singers and musicians, jugglers and acrobats. Every inn and lodging house throughout the town needed to be cleaned and prepared for the many guests, for whom there would be no room at the Staple Inn. The cost was immense and rapidly used up the funds which Cromwell had given us. There was no time for anything but thinking of and working towards the ceremonies of welcome to come. I hardly saw Arthur during those few weeks, except in our chamber at night and then we were too exhausted to do more than exchange a few tired words before sleep.

It was during these preparations that we heard of the fall of St Mary's at Winchester on the fifteenth of November. That noble old house, Bridget's home for several years, had at last succumbed to the pressures of Cromwell's commissioners and had been forced to close its doors. The nuns of St Mary's had fared better than many of their counterparts in other monasteries, being granted pensions which would keep them in moderate, if not luxurious, comfort. But we only heard of these matters briefly and they were not enough to interrupt the hustle and bustle of activity as we readied ourselves for the grandest event we had so far hosted at Calais.

As the day for the arrival of the party from Cleves drew near, our preparations increased in intensity. Huge amounts of food were brought in from around Calais and from England.

On the second of December, Sir William Fitzwilliam Earl of Southampton, the Lord High Admiral, arrived with a large escort to await the bride. They also needed lodging and entertaining and our coffers were once again empty.

'What are we supposed to do?' The strain and exhaustion of the last weeks was showing on my love's face and in his voice. 'It seems that we no sooner fancy ourselves in a slightly better situation than the rug is pulled from under our feet once more.'

Chapter Twenty Four

On the eleventh of December, Anne of Cleves, with her escort of 263 attendants and 228 horses arrived from Dusseldorf, having travelled no more than five miles a day since their departure. What a sight they made!

The Earl of Southampton rode to meet them, cutting a fine figure as the King's representative. He was wearing a coat of purple velvet cut on cloth of gold, trimmed with aglets and trefoils of gold and a gold chain upon which hung his Admiral's badge of office. With him, all attired in cloth of gold and purple velvet, were Lord William Howard, Sir Francis Bryan and Lord Grey of Wilton with the other four hundred Lords and gentlemen who had been enjoying our hospitality for over a week and two hundred yeomen in the King's colours of red and blue.

I waited at the Lantern Gate with the other ladies and gentlewomen and after their arrival we went down to the docks and viewed the two ships which were to take the party to England. They were called the Lion and the Sweepstake and were decked with 100 banners of silk and gold. As we all turned and re-entered Calais, the 200 gunners on board the ships let off such a volley of gunfire that the air was filled with smoke.

At the banquet that night we entertained the Princess and her retinue with no expense spared. Along with the traditional English table loaded with meats of all kinds, there were German dishes in her honour. These included fried beans with bacon, cheese soup and stewed turnips. I noticed several of our English guests surreptitiously turning up their noses at these strange new dishes. I personally enjoyed trying them. We also provided a selection of German wines to compliment the English beer and ale.

The Princess had brought her own Meistersinger as part of her entourage and this gentleman entertained us beautifully with his wonderful voice and music, even though we understood none of the lyrics.

After the extravagant banquet, we were exhausted both in body and mind and retired gratefully to our chamber.

'I will certainly be happy after tomorrow when we can say goodbye to these hundreds of guests,' Arthur said wearily as he prepared for bed.

But in that we were to be sorely disappointed. The next morning when we awoke it was to find that the weather had changed overnight from a very mild December to a violent winter storm. The wind blew so strongly that it reminded me of a good Cornish gale. The rain fell sideways in great lashing streams thrashing heavily into the windowpanes and blowing in under the roof tiles. There was no way the ships could sail and no way of telling when it might be possible. Our guests would be with us for some considerable time yet.

There was nothing to do but make the most of a situation over which we had no control and that was what we set about doing. At least it gave us the chance to get to know Anne of Cleves, which we had been unable to do from our brief meeting of the evening before. We found her very different, both in manners and dress from our English ladies but refreshingly so. There was none of the strict protocol and hierarchy about her or her courtiers, who had a much more relaxed and natural way about them than Englishmen of the same social standing. Anne was not unpleasing to look at but was no beauty either, being far broader in her features than our King was wont to appreciate in his women. However, in a political marriage such as this, beauty is a rare commodity and is not usually considered to be of consequence.

'Please, do tell me,' she asked me in her thickly accented and barely intelligible English, 'my English is not good I think?'

I searched for a suitable answer. 'I am sure you will learn very quickly, Princess.'

'Please, will you be teaching me how to play with the cards?' she begged. 'I am hearing that the King is liking that very much.' It took her a good minute to get that one sentence out with many hesitations and ponderings over which word to use. I wondered how the King would tolerate such laborious conversation.

I gladly taught her a few simple card games in order to please her, but I had an ominous feeling that she would be needing more than a scant knowledge of cards in order to please King Henry. At last after fifteen long days, the weather finally cleared enough for the ships to set sail and as we bade farewell to Anne of Cleves, I realised that I had grown to like her very much and feared for what kind of reception she might have when she met her future husband.

We heard nothing until early in the new year, when John Wallop brought news.

'The Lady Anne has met with the King,' were his opening words.

'I like not the tone of your voice, John,' Arthur leaned towards him for more information.

'After continuing her slow progress towards London from Dover she reached Rochester on New Year's Eve,' said John. 'She was by this time accompanied by the Duke of Norfolk and a great company of Lords, Knights and

Esquires.' He sighed at this point as if he found the rest of the story wearisome.

'Where did she meet the King, John?' I asked, anxious to hear more.

'At Rochester,' he answered and then continued with a cynical tone to his voice. 'It seems Henry had a wish to meet her privately to nourish love between them prior to the marriage.'

He stopped again and once more I had to prod him to continue with his story. I had never seen John so subdued and unable to find a funny side to a situation.

'As I heard it, the King entered her chamber incognito, wishing to see her first before she knew who he was,' he continued at last. 'He found her looking out of her window at a bull-baiting and she was so enthralled by the spectacle that she barely paid him any attention, turning only briefly to acknowledge his presence.'

'Well, that was hardly fair,' said Arthur. 'If he expected her to greet him properly as her future King and husband then he ought to have had himself announced.'

'Quite,' John replied with a sigh. 'Anyway, after telling her who he was and spending the evening in her company, Henry left her side, outwardly not displeased but inwardly seething with anger at those who had trapped him into this situation. He told his ministers the next morning that he had no wish to marry one who pleased him neither by her looks nor her manners and sent Cromwell to investigate a way in which the contract could be broken.'

'Oh, dear God,' I was saddened not only by the possible political implications of such an act but by my feelings of pity for the poor Princess and her failure to impress the King at this, her first and only chance to do so.

Arthur was the next to speak. 'But the treaty cannot be broken, can it?'

'No,' answered John, 'it appears not. Henry was hoping that a contract once made between the Princess and the Marquis of Lorraine might be used as grounds but as that contract has long been annulled it is clear that it cannot stand in the way of this marriage.'

He laughed then, albeit a little sadly, the first time he had done so on this occasion.

'And so, the victim has resigned himself to his fate, with fortunately, little outward sign of his extreme mortification.'

A few days later, on the sixth of January, King Henry was married to Anne of Cleves at Greenwich Palace. He had reportedly said to Cromwell on the morning of his wedding: 'If it were not to satisfy the world and my realm, I would not do that which I must do this day for none earthly thing.'

It seemed that Wriothesley had guessed correctly and as this marriage was to spell the beginning of the end for Cromwell, so it saw the rise of Thomas Wriothesley.

However, the King had his new wife, and nothing occurred to show the world at large that Henry was already setting moves afoot to have his marriage annulled. But the matter of the King's marriage paled into insignificance for us during the next four months as events in Calais rapidly spiralled out of our control.

Chapter Twenty Five

On the thirteenth of March 1540, just after our midday meal, we were on the point of leaving the dining room when the chief guard from the Lantern Gate was announced. He looked very proud of himself as he imparted his startling news.

'Lord Lisle, I have brought you a hostage!'

Arthur and I were taken completely by surprise by this pronouncement and Arthur requested more information.

'A young French nobleman has arrived at the Lantern Gate, together with a small retinue. We cannot intercept those scoundrels because they remain on French soil, but the nobleman has insisted on entering our territory and I have brought him here under heavy guard. What do you wish me to do with him, My Lord?' The guardsman looked so pleased with himself and I could see that in performing this one act he was certain of his own personal advancement.

My heart lurched uncomfortably. I greatly feared that I already knew who this foolhardy French nobleman was sure to be. I looked at Arthur in despair. He, like me, had long been aware of Mary's youthful passion for Gabriel de Montmorency and had been of the opinion that the affair would probably run its course and die a natural death. Hoping against hope that another name would be spoken I asked the guard who it was.

'He gives his name as Gabriel de Montmorency Seigneur de Bours,' answered the soldier, deliberately mispronouncing and saying the name with contempt in his voice.

'Oh, Gabriel!' Mary squealed and to the utter amazement of the guard she darted past us and out into the hall where I heard the excited sounds of her voice, coupled with the low murmur of a man's.

We were at a total loss as to how to deal with this situation. Of course, what we *ought* to have done was to have him arrested and sent in chains to London as a handy hostage. How could we? Mary fancied herself in love with him and apparently, since he was prepared to risk his freedom, he also loved her. Asking the guard and his men to wait in the stable yard for further instruction, we had Montmorency sent in to meet us.

He was certainly a good-looking young man and was dressed in all the finery for which the French Court is famed. Feathers and lace swirled about him in such profusion that even when he stood still he seemed to remain in motion. Mary, after her first delight at seeing him, blanched as she realised what a contrast her simple garments were to his gaudy apparel and babbling excuses, scurried away to change. We were left facing Montmorency across the room, with absolutely no notion of how to deal with him. At last he broke the uncomfortable silence.

'My Lord and Lady Lisle,' he began in faultless but heavily accented English, 'please do forgive my rudeness in arriving unannounced but I have a very good reason for calling today.'

Arthur had collected himself by this time and remembered his manners.

'Come this way, Seigneur de Bours, let us be seated,' and he ushered our guest into the parlour.

Clearing his throat, Montmorency spoke again.

'My Lord, My Lady,' he nodded to each of us in turn, 'I will come straight to the point. Having recently achieved my majority I am now free to select a wife of my own choosing. Having known your daughter Mary for many years now, even though I have not seen her for a long time, I have no hesitation in wishing for her to be my wife. I have come to seek your agreement to this.'

Arthur and I stared at each other. Glad as we were for Mary's good fortune in capturing the heart of one of the wealthiest gentlemen in France, we could see only too well the danger such an alliance would place us in.

'Seigneur de Bours,' began Arthur.

'Please, call me Gabriel,' interrupted that young man.

'Very well, Gabriel,' Arthur said the name stiffly, 'you must realise that relations between England and France are far from good at the moment. A marriage between the two of you at this time is impossible. In fact, what I really ought to do is detain you as a prisoner of war.'

The young man's face fell. We saw then through all the fine clothes and courtly manners and beheld only a lovesick boy, smitten with desire for my beautiful and frivolous daughter. We were only too aware of the power of such feelings and I knew Arthur felt as I did, caught between what he knew was his duty and the forlorn wish not to thwart their happiness. Arthur was opening his mouth to say more when the door opened softly, and Mary stood on the threshold. She had changed into her best day-gown. Of a pastel cream shade, it fell in gentle folds from the tightly fitting low-cut bodice. She had dressed her hair and covered it with an attractive matching hood, the folds of which hung attractively over her bare, white shoulders and neck. She looked like an angel and Montmorency's face changed as he looked at her, from despondency to wondrous adulation.

He stood slowly as if entranced and crossed the room to take her hands in his own and kiss them long and lovingly.

'Mary, my dearest angel,' he murmured as he gazed into her eyes, 'you are even more beautiful than I remember.'

She giggled and preened herself, confident now and able to relax in his company. Hand in hand they came back into the room and sat down beside each other, both looking at us, he in desperation and she in naive joy.

There was another long silence, during which Mary's face gradually changed as she began to realise that all was not well.

'Why does someone not say something?' she asked with a little catch in her voice.

There was another silence before Montmorency, himself, spoke.

'Your father has said that we may not marry, Mary,' he said simply.

She looked incredulously at Arthur and then at me.

'But Mother,' she selected me as the easiest target, 'you have known for years that Gabriel and I have plighted our troth. If our marriage was to be prevented, how could you be so cruel as not to tell me?' She began to cry softly.

I desperately sought for the right words.

'Mary, Arthur has just told Gabriel that it is because of the political situation between England and France. It is not because we bear Gabriel any ill-will. Indeed, the opposite is true, we have been glad for your happiness, both of you. But events have taken such a turn now that it would be seen as consorting with the enemy if you two were to marry.'

'Then we must part?' Mary asked tragically, in a voice designed to wring the hardest heart.

'No, no Mary, I will never leave you,' answered her swain, in tones reminiscent of my own lover all those years ago.

Arthur and I looked helplessly at each other. Who were we to deny these young people their chance of happiness, just as ours had been so cruelly snatched from us at one time? Arthur was the one to speak what was in both our minds.

'We would not wish to cause you to part, my children,' he said gently, 'only to wait for a while. These troubles inevitably pass given time.'

Montmorency saw the sense in that but had one more suggestion to make.

'Then if we cannot marry, would you agree to us pre-contracting a marriage, which will be binding to us but which no-one need know about until it is safe for us to marry formally?' He looked so beseechingly at us that we capitulated. Arthur's notary was called in and a pre-contract of marriage was made. Mary was now legally bound to marry Gabriel de Montmorency, a Frenchman and an enemy of the realm of England.

To the utter astonishment of the guardsman, Arthur granted Montmorency safe passage and ordered him to escort the young man back to the Lantern Gate and to his retinue. We did not miss the look of accusation and the glint of suspicion in the eye of the guard, as he sullenly did as Arthur bade him.

Meanwhile trouble had been brewing again regarding Arthur's management at Calais. Before we really knew what was happening another Commission of Enquiry was set up by Cromwell to examine what was termed 'the state of unrest in Calais'. As before, we were not informed of exactly what Arthur's misdemeanours were supposed to have been but were kept in ignorance whilst the Commission took place. Fortunately for us, even though Stephen Gardiner was not present, John Wallop was a member of the bench and was sure to put in a good word for us.

As on the previous occasion, Arthur was completely exonerated from all blame. Any unrest in Calais, it was decided, was due to religious troublemakers and was in no way a result of my husband's management. Strategies were put into place for the punishing of offenders and no more was said. Once again, we breathed more easily.

'Well, that was not too bad,' Wallop said to us after it was all over.

'No, John,' replied Arthur, 'and I thank you for it. But I wonder how often they can have these enquiries without eventually deciding that I must be to blame.'

Trouble also appeared from another direction at that time. Earlier in the year, in February, Gregory Botolf and his eager accomplice Clement Philpot had requested Arthur's permission to go to England. This, Arthur readily gave, asking no questions and being given no reason. We were still very fond of both young men and as far as we were concerned neither of them had given us any cause to mistrust their motives.

As we learned later, they gave everyone the impression that England was their destination, lingering at waterfront taverns until late into the evening, as if they intended to cross by the boat, which was catching the night tide at 2am. But what really happened was that only Philpot actually caught the boat, with Botolf disappearing into the night. Of course, we knew nothing of this at the time, innocently believing both men to be safely in England going about some private business of their own. We forgot about them.

Shortly after the enquiry Gregory Botolf and Clement Philpot returned to Calais. Yes, they had been in England we were told and yes, their business had been satisfactorily conducted. No more details were forthcoming and no more were requested. We had no reason to be suspicious as we were led like lambs to the slaughter.

Only Botolf's old adversary, Oliver Browne, still mistrusted him and was not averse to tackling him as to his whereabouts. They were both present at supper on the night Botolf returned from his travels.

'So, Master Botolf, you have returned, I see,' said Browne.

'Indeed, Sir, you find me back amongst you safe and well,' answered Gregory.

'And how, may I ask, did you enjoy your time in France?' Browne asked sweetly, placing emphasis on the word 'France', at which everyone within earshot looked up in surprise.

'You are mistaken, Sir, I was never in France.' Botolf looked shaken.

'Then how, Sir, do you explain meeting my servant, Hugh Middleton, on the road between Amiens and Boulogne only yesterday?' Browne looked triumphantly at Botolf who quailed visibly, small beads of perspiration breaking out on his forehead.

'If you must know all my business, Master Browne,' Gregory collected himself masterfully, 'my ship was wind-driven off course and forced to seek shelter on the French

Chapter Twenty Five

coast. That explains my arrival in Calais from that direction. And now,' he stood up and spoke directly to Arthur, 'if you will excuse me, My Lord, I am tired from my journey and have no wish to be interrogated further by knaves such as this. With your permission, I will retire to my chamber.'

Arthur nodded assent and Botolf left the room. Incredibly as it seems in hindsight, both Arthur and I still chose to trust him over the honest Oliver Browne, who, we feared was becoming old and overly suspicious.

The next morning as I was on my way to the Chapel, Gregory Botolf waylaid me in the hall and pressed my hand earnestly.

'If you please, my good Lady, I have an urgent request to make of you.'

Since he was blocking my path, I had no choice but to hear him out.

'Make it quick, Master Botolf. I have no wish to shorten my prayers this morning.' Even though I still trusted him I was feeling cross over the scene at supper the previous evening. I deplore such shows of unpleasantness at the meal table.

'My Lady, I seek permission to take leave from my post here and to further my studies in Louvain,' he begged and with my mind already on the Mass, which was shortly to begin, I agreed to speak to Arthur on his behalf.

'Very well Master Botolf, I will see what can be arranged,' I said carelessly as I brushed past him and entered the Chapel.

After the service I spoke to Arthur, who also agreed readily.

'I see no reason to keep Botolf here,' he said without interest. 'One Priest more or less will make no difference to me.'

And thus Gregory Botolf departed from Calais with our full knowledge and consent. Whether or not he went to Louvain no-one knows, as he was never seen nor heard of again. Clement Philpot went about his normal duties as if nothing had happened and, indeed, to the best of our knowledge, nothing had.

It was the second of April when we learned the terrible truth of what had taken place. I remember the day well. It was the hour after the midday meal, when we habitually engaged in quiet pursuits of our own. Mary, Philippa and I were sitting in the garden, busy with our needlework and chatting idly. Mary was sewing silk flowers as a present for Gabriel and her talk was all of him and how wonderful he was and of her desire for the hostilities to be soon over, so that they could be married properly. It was a warm morning with a freshness in the air that was not often felt in the stifled atmosphere of Calais. For at least the hundredth time since we had gone to that city, I was feeling a glimmer of hope that our luck might at last be changing for the better. A servant came over to us as my daughters and I worked thus peacefully together in the sun.

'My Lady, Lord Lisle requests your presence in the parlour,' was all he said.

Hastily gathering up my work, I left the girls still sitting contentedly in the garden and went indoors, wondering as I did so what could be of such importance that Arthur desired my presence at that hour of the day, when he was normally resting.

Chapter Twenty Five

I found Clement Philpot and Oliver Browne in the parlour with my husband. Clement Philpot looked terrified, Oliver Browne had a smug look on his face and poor Arthur appeared totally confused.

'My dear,' began Arthur, motioning me to sit down, 'Master Browne has told me such a strange tale that I would have him relate it to you himself.'

I looked enquiringly at Browne. 'My Lady, after I began to have my suspicions as to what Master Botolf was doing in France when he was supposed to have been in England, I made some enquiries in the waterfront taverns. I have found several witnesses who will swear to it that Master Philpot boarded the ship for Dover alone that night. Gregory Botolf did not go with him.'

Feeling a great weight of foreboding descending upon me, I turned from Oliver Browne and spoke directly to Philpot. 'Master Philpot tell us the truth of what happened that night – and why. Master Browne, you may leave us now.' I said imperiously.

Oliver Browne did as I bade him, with one backward, gloating glance at Philpot as he went. Clement Philpot tearfully and with a shaking voice told us the awful truth of what had happened.

'My Lord, My Lady, I know not how I got myself involved in all this but the night I went to England I was only covering for Botolf, who did not accompany me but went instead to - to Rome.' He paused for breath whilst I looked aghast at Arthur.

Then he continued, as if by telling all he could in some way purge himself of guilt.

'He wished to speak with the Pope and Cardinal Pole and offer himself to their service. He had a plan whereby Calais could be gained for Rome.'

My sharp intake of breath stopped his confession briefly, but I could say nothing, only look helplessly at Arthur, then back at Philpot to continue.

'The plan was,' he went on, 'that I would enlist the help of a dozen men and overwhelm the night-watch at the Lantern Gate whilst Botolf and his company would scale the walls. He was hoping,' he said lamely, 'to get five or six hundred men from the Pope's armies to help him.'

Arthur groaned, as much I felt sure from the absurdity of such an idea, as from the duplicity of the man Botolf.

Philpot went on. 'They would then break open the door and enter the town by the stairs which I and my troupe would, by that time, be holding.'

'And the Pope, I gather, was unimpressed by this plan?' Arthur's voice was edged, not only with sarcasm but with anger.

'Botolf told me nothing of what transpired after he left Calais. I know not whether he actually got as far as Rome or had an audience with the Pope at all.' Philpot's voice was laden with misery.

'Oh, what a surprise!' Arthur shouted at him. 'How could you have taken such a plot seriously? How could you have been duped by such a hare-brained scheme? How could you have allowed yourself to be so taken in by that scoundrel? Did it never occur to you to question just what the Pope would want with this little town? Did you not just once question what he might do with it once you and your fellow idiots had captured it for him?'

Chapter Twenty Five

'No,' said Philpot in a small voice, 'I just followed Gregory.'

'And now Gregory is gone, leaving you to take full responsibility,' I found my voice at last. I spoke quietly, not wanting to shout as Arthur had done but understanding fully his need to do so. We were implicated in this. Botolf was our Priest and he had come to Calais at our invitation. It was with our permission that he had left on his failed mission to Rome and with our permission that he had now disappeared. That we had no prior knowledge of his real activities was yet to be proved, if indeed, it could be.

But first we had to deal with Philpot. If it was mercy he was hoping for, it was not within our power to grant it. Arthur called the guards and had him arrested immediately. After he had been taken away, we sat down together and wrote a letter to the King, outlining what had just been told to us and emphasising that knowledge of the plot had only that minute reached our ears. We dispatched the prisoner and the letter with the next tide.

Then we could do no more but wait for a reply.

Our wait was not to be for long. On the eighth of April a group of Commissioners arrived to commence rounding up suspects and witnesses. All suspects were confined in a different part of the town to prevent their colluding amongst each other. Half a dozen young men in our household were arrested, along with another of our domestic chaplains.

But a letter from the King assured us that we had done no wrong and thanked us for our prompt actions in the arresting of Philpot and notification of the conspiracy. The King urged Arthur to report immediately to London for the chapter meeting of the Order of the Garter at Westminster, which was due to take place on April the twenty-third. It was hinted that he may even be in line for an Earldom.

Once again, we prepared for Arthur's departure, for what was to be another short trip to London. Our minds had been set at rest by the King's letter and the night before his departure he was relaxed and confident.

'Who knows, some good might come out of all this after all,' he said hopefully as we prepared for bed that night, the sixteenth of April 1540.

The next morning dawned dark and chill. I had not slept well and was feeling irritable and out of temper with a throbbing headache and a painfully sore throat. We were still dressing when a servant entered our chamber and announced that the boat was ready to depart and as the tide was about to turn, Arthur would need to make haste. We had hardly spoken since arising, so ill I felt, and for once I made no attempt to accompany him to the shore.

He came over to where I sat in front of my mirror and leaning over me, planted a kiss on top of my head.

'I will write as soon as I reach London, my dear,' he said as he left, 'and I will return very soon.'

And with that he was gone.

Chapter Twenty Six

How can I write of the events to follow? How, without screaming and shouting my despair to the four winds, can I force myself to dwell on the calamity which befell us? But this is my story and somehow, I must force myself to tell the whole of it.

At first all went well for my husband in London. I rapidly recovered from my chill and regretted our casual and hasty parting, but my regret was tempered by the belief that we would soon be together again. He wrote to me one week after arriving, that he had been cordially received at the meeting of the Knights of the Garter. The proposed Earldom had not yet eventuated, but he felt himself to be in high favour with the King. Three more weeks went by and I was becoming uneasy that no more letters had arrived from him and wondering what the reason could be when my world fell apart.

Mary, Philippa and I were coming out of morning Mass on the twentieth of May 1540 when there was a loud knocking at the solid front doors of the Staple Inn followed by the shouted words: 'Open, in the name of the King!'

We stood as if rooted to the spot, instinctively grabbing each other's hands for support as the porter hastened to open the door. As he pulled back the heavy oaken panel, a group of soldiers came charging in. Once over our threshold, they made straight for us, seven stout officers of our own Calais guard and we were each grabbed roughly by the arms, a soldier on each side. The seventh, a heavily built man with a leering and depraved face, stated in a loud voice so that the servants, now clustered all about us, could hear.

'Honora Lisle, Philippa Basset and Mary Basset, by order of Thomas Cromwell Lord Great Chamberlain of England, you are under arrest for treason.'

I turned frantically towards my daughters but was powerless to help them. Then I saw the ugly brutish fellow who had hold of my beautiful Mary let go of her arm momentarily and run his hand over the front of her bodice in a grossly obscene gesture of power. The walls about me were closing in and I could not breathe. I was engulfed by blackness and the last thing I remember is the foul smell of the soldier's uniform as I slumped against him.

When I came to, I found myself lying on my own bed in my chamber at the Staple Inn. Relief flooded over me; it had all been a dream, a terrible, terrible dream. Stumbling to my feet I made my way shakily towards the door and went to open it, but it was stuck fast and would not budge. I tried again, using every ounce of force I could muster but again it refused to open. Then I began to shout.

'Let me out, someone please, my door is stuck. Let me out.'

My shouting fell on deaf ears and I sank in despair to the floor as the realisation dawned on me that it had not been a dream at all, and I was now a prisoner in my own home. Then my fear for myself turned to terror for the fate of my virgin daughters as I remembered the revolting way the arresting officer had handled Mary. Once again panic gripped me and with the extra strength engendered by my rapidly rising hysteria I managed to stand up and run to the window. Leaning out as far as I could, I shouted to the deserted courtyard.

'Help me, oh please, is there not someone to take pity on an innocent woman?'

A soldier appeared from where he had been lounging against the wall of the yard and glared up at me.

'Be silent! It is not for you to ask for pity, traitor.'

Again, I tried.

'But I am not a traitor, and neither are my daughters. Where are they, oh, please tell me? Are they still here?' But he turned away with a deliberately insulting indifference and resumed his stance by the wall.

Leaving the window, I returned to my bed and lay down. What was there to do? Nothing, nothing at all but wait. Soon this misunderstanding would be cleared up. Arthur was due back shortly from London. And then the fear and panic gripped me once more. If the girls and I had been arrested, what had become of Arthur? He must be a prisoner as well. Cromwell had closed the trap about us, and we were all at his mercy. It was then that I began to cry. My tears were not for myself but for the man I loved and for what unknown terrors he was facing.

'Arthur, Arthur, my sweet love,' I sobbed. 'Whatever happens, treasure our love and let it be your strength in the days to come.'

How long I lay there in my misery I know not but the room was darkening when at last I heard the sounds of the barricade at the door being moved and I hastily stood and straightened my gown to present at least some semblance of dignity to my jailor.

To my partial relief the door was opened, not by the filthy thug who had overseen my arrest but by Robert Radcliffe the Earl of Sussex, husband to my own niece Mary Arundel. He greeted me civilly.

'Lady Lisle, I have come to lay the terms of your imprisonment before you.' He sounded almost apologetic.

'Please,' I begged, 'what of my husband? How fares he?'

'I am not at liberty to give you any reports of what occurs outside this house, Madam,' he answered.

'But Lord Sussex, Robert, please,' I entreated, 'in the name of pity, I cannot live unless I know what has become of Arthur.' I fell to my knees before him and lifted my hands in supplication.

He was not a bad man and after one more hesitation he said softly: 'Your husband, Madam, is confined in the Tower of London on a charge of treason against His Majesty.'

'Oh, Dear God,' I thought, 'at his age to be imprisoned in that dreadful place. How will he stand it?' I looked frantically to Lord Sussex for some words of reassurance.

'But how, treason? In what way have we erred? What is it we are supposed to have done? Oh, this matter will soon be remedied, will it not? We are innocent and our innocence will be proved in no time at all.'

Radcliffe became official again. 'The charges will all be laid before you at your questioning but for now Lady Lisle I suggest you get some rest. The servants here are now no longer under your employ. You may have one gentlewoman only, to see to your needs. I will have food and water sent to your chamber.'

He began to turn away and I flung myself at his feet, tugging frantically at his clothing.

Chapter Twenty Six

'What of my daughters? What have you done with Mary and Philippa?'

'You are to have no communication with them,' he answered wearily, anxious to be away. 'They have been removed to separate prisons in Calais. And that is all you are to know.' He detached my fingers from their hold on his cloak and left me, locking the door behind him.

Once he had gone, I lay where I was for some time, overwhelmed with despair but after a while I became determined to collect my thoughts again. I stood up, straightened my dishevelled clothing and began pacing the floor of my prison. Our situation seemed hopeless but there must soon be an end to it. We were innocent and after questioning we would all be released. It only remained for us to tell the truth and soon we would be together again as free people. Perhaps then we could leave Calais and our lives could return to normal.

After a short while the door opened again and my gentlewoman, Elizabeth Husee, appeared. She is a kinswoman to our good servant John and had only recently joined my service. As my only contact with the outside world at that time she was to become invaluable to me.

'Good evening, My Lady,' she greeted me respectfully, her voice laden with sorrow. 'I have brought you some food.'

'Thank you, Elizabeth,' I replied as if nothing was wrong and I was still the Lady of the Manor taking refreshment willingly in my chamber. 'Would you be so kind as to place it on the table by the window? I will be needing some water for washing as well, if you please.'

'Yes, certainly My Lady. Oh, it grieves me to see you brought to this My Lady, it does indeed.'

I endeavoured to maintain my dignity and poise. 'We all have bad times in our lives, Elizabeth and by the Grace of God this episode will soon be over, and all will be set to rights again. But if you hear anything of my daughters you will let me know will you not?' I grabbed her arm in desperation, my brief show of bravery was over.

'Oh, yes, certainly My Lady,' she said earnestly. 'You can rely on me, I will find out whatever I can.'

But when she had cleared away my dishes and helped me to bed and I was left alone with only my thoughts for company the dread set in again. I put out my hand and felt the empty space beside me where my beloved ought to have been lying and stroked the sheet as if his body were there still. Then I rolled across and lay there, burying my face in his pillow which still bore the scent of his presence.

The next morning, having fallen asleep only with the coming of the dawn, I was woken by loud sounds of banging and scraping from downstairs. Having no idea what might be happening, I had no choice but to await Elizabeth's arrival with my breakfast. She soon appeared with a small serving of rye bread.

'Good morning, My Lady, I hope you spent a tolerable night.'

At least she had the good sense not to ask if I had slept well.

'Elizabeth, what is all the noise?' I was abrupt with her in my anxiety to know.

'Oh, Lady Honora, there are men downstairs, soldiers and clerks both. The soldiers are removing all your lovely furniture and the clerks are taking your papers. All your letters and household accounts are being taken away, even

Lady Mary's pretty drawings are being rudely stuffed into their pouches.'

So, it had already come to this. We were indeed lost, guilty until proven innocent, if indeed our innocence could be proven at all. Our household was being dismantled systematically and our lives seemed already forfeit. With an effort I snapped out of the lethargy which I felt descending upon my spirit. I would not accept defeat so easily.

I spoke urgently. 'Elizabeth, please send one of the men upstairs to speak to me. Lord Sussex if he is there, otherwise whoever seems to be in charge of this rabble.'

She obediently went to attend to the errand, and I waited for her return. Soon she was back, but she was alone.

'My Lady, I was told that you must await your summons,' she said.

And so, I waited. Day after day dragged by and there was no relief from the boredom or the fear. My chamber was invaded by the searchers and all our personal belongings were rifled and strewn about. They were like a hoard of locusts and after they had gone, nothing remained but the bare necessities of life. I still had my bed, closet and table but everything else was removed, even the hangings from the walls. All my fine gowns were taken away and I was left with only two plain day gowns, the oldest and most frayed which I possessed. They even went through my underwear, taking the finest silk garments and leaving only some coarse linen in its place. All Arthur's clothes were taken. They were leaving me nothing to remember him by.

'Are you taking those to him?' I asked one who was stuffing my husband's fine clothes into a hessian sack, knowing full well I would receive no reply. They went about their work methodically and silently, speaking neither to me nor to each other. I was totally ignored.

At last after two weeks, the summons came. Elizabeth bustled into my chamber one hot morning in early June with the news.

'You are to be interrogated today, Lady Honora,' she said excitedly, as if imparting good tidings.

It is a reflection on my state of mind at the time that I could take such news almost gladly. At last something was happening, at last I would have my chance to clear up the misunderstandings and our lives could return to normal. As Elizabeth helped me to dress in the least worn of my two gowns I tried to focus on what answers I should give to my questioners but having no idea of what I was accused or what the questions might be I soon gave up and forced my mind to numbness.

As I was led downstairs by a member of the guard later that morning, I had difficulty focusing on the enormity of what was happening. It was the first time I had been allowed out of my room in two weeks and my legs were weak from lack of exercise and sleep. I found that I had to concentrate so as not to fall headlong down the stairs. The guard stood at the doorway of the parlour, our parlour, and gestured for me to enter. I felt a rush of anger as I walked through the door and saw that it had also been stripped and only a few chairs and Arthur's desk remained.

But it was no longer Arthur's desk. It had been moved so that it was placed in front of the large bay window and there was someone sitting behind it. Because of the strong sunlight streaming through the window behind the chair I

Chapter Twenty Six

could not see who was there but as soon as he spoke, I felt the blood turn to ice in my veins, and I knew.

'So, Lady Lisle, you are not laughing now,' he said, his voice heavy with malevolence.

I was unable to answer. The last time I had seen Thomas Wriothesley was when he was fleeing for his life from the Netherlands and in my stupidity, I had not hidden my mirth at his predicament.

'Well,' he rasped, 'have you lost your tongue? You had plenty to say for yourself when last we met, I seem to remember.'

Still I remained silent, accepting my fate. If Wriothesley was to be my inquisitor, then all was lost. I had not yet seen his face, so hidden was it by his deliberate placement of the chair in front of the window but I could hear in his voice the glee and gloating triumph.

'And how is your terrible affliction which so caused you to choke and hold your mouth on that occasion?' He sneered. 'Do you think I am so foolish that I knew not what you were about, you and your bastard aristocrat of a husband?' His voice rose almost to a rasping screech as he said these words and I wondered for a moment if his burning hatred for us had unhinged his mind. If that was the case, then we were certainly doomed.

He stood up and moved menacingly around the desk towards me.

He leaned close to me and as he spoke, I could feel his spittle hitting my face. 'Well, Lady Lisle, you are in my power now and if there is any laughing to be done, I very much doubt it will be done by you.'

He had not removed his riding cloak and it hung darkly about his shoulders so that he looked like a monstrous bird of prey. His cold eyes glinted like steel, sharpened to a killing point.

Mustering what little strength I could, I spoke at last.

'Sir Thomas, am I to know of what I am charged?'

He returned to his chair by the window so that I was forced to squint my eyes in order to look at him. Before sitting down, he slowly removed his cloak and hung it carefully on the back of the chair, Arthur's chair. Then he suddenly rapped three times on the desk with his cane, making me jump nervously and at this signal a clerk entered from a side door carrying a large bundle of papers. The clerk ignored me completely and placed the parcel in front of his master, then he sat down at the end of the desk with his writing quill at the ready to take down all that was said.

Wriothesley waited until all was in readiness before he began the formal part of the proceedings. It became clear to me that the first, unwitnessed interview, had been for his enjoyment only. Now the questioning was to start.

'You are charged with treason on two counts. Firstly, that you carried on an illegal correspondence with Rome via your Priest Gregory Botolf and secondly, that you contracted an illegal marriage contract between your daughter and a French squire.'

So that was it. My thoughts raced. As for the first charge, that should hopefully be easy to disprove since we had had no knowledge of what Botolf was up to and had already written as much to the King but as for Mary's pre-contract of marriage - we obviously knew of that and would be forced to admit it. The net, it seemed, had already closed about us. There was no point in saying more, so I composed myself to simply answering his questions.

On and on he went, probing, seeking answers that would incriminate and condemn us. I remember at one stage hearing the clerk give a little sigh of exasperation or weariness as he wrote, no doubt wondering as I was when it would end. I have no idea of how long I was in that room. It must have been well over an hour for the sun moved around during the interrogation and gradually I found that I could see more of the details on my tormentor's face. I could see out the window too and remember watching the inhabitants of the Staple Inn going about their daily business outside, either unknowing or simply uncaring as to the dreadful events taking place inside its doors.

I had to force myself to concentrate on Wriothesley's voice as he spent most of the time looking down at the desk and speaking in a monotone, only to suddenly lift his head and screech at me, causing my nerves to jangle. I tried to give honest answers, there was nothing else to be done. I repeated over and over again that we had been innocent of any knowledge of, or complicity in, the Botolf conspiracy and then quite suddenly he moved on Mary's marriage contract with Montmorency. He shuffled the papers in front of him until he came to one which I recognised as the document signed by Mary and Gabriel in our presence on March 13th.

'During your beautiful daughter's interrogation she contradicted herself several times, which only helped to prove her guilt.' He licked his lips lasciviously and I felt the cold droplets of fear running down my spine as I contemplated the fate which may have befallen Mary. My belly knotted and I felt physically sick as dreadful images sprang unbidden into my mind.

I realised when it was too late that this was the real accusation. He had known all along that we were innocent of the Botolf conspiracy. All that had gone before had been to wear me out so that I would more easily condemn myself when the real point of the interrogation was reached. I fell neatly into the trap.

In an agonized outpouring of maternal love and concern, I lost all sense of caution and sprang to her defence. 'Mary is guilty of nothing but of falling in love!' I shouted shrilly. 'When she first met Montmorency, we were at peace with France. How was she to change the feelings of her heart just because our countries became hostile to each other? And how could we as loving parents forbid her to marry him?'

I realised my mistake as soon as the words were out of my mouth.

'Lay Lisle, that is exactly what you would have done had you wished to avoid treachery to your King,' Wriothesley said with menace in his voice and nodded to the clerk to make sure he had written down my words.

That was it then. By admitting that Mary had indeed pre-contracted a marriage with Montmorency and with our knowledge, I had implicated us all. Wriothesley had known the facts already, all he had needed was my confession, and now he had it. Mary's, they presumably had already, and even Philippa, by her knowledge of and failure to report a treasonable offense, was guilty by association.

Wriothesley began packing up the papers and motioned to the clerk to do likewise. Then, with another rapping on

Chapter Twenty Six

the desk with his cane, Wriothesley summoned the guard who entered and took my arm roughly. My questioning was over.

I was returned immediately to my chamber where Elizabeth was waiting with refreshments for me. She hurried to my side.

'My Lady how was it?' she enquired with concern.

I shook my head despondently. 'Elizabeth, if there was ever any doubt in their minds that we were guilty, I have succeeded in abolishing it,' I replied. 'Our fate is sealed.'

She turned away quickly but not before I saw tears spring to her eyes.

'My Lady, I have news of your daughters.' She spoke reluctantly and her voice was muffled.

'What have you heard?' I grabbed her arm and turned her to face me.

'I am friendly with one of the guards,' she began. 'He moves from place to place and sees all that goes on.' I knew instinctively that this was a new friendship and one deliberately cultivated to help me.

Gratefully, I released her arm and apologised for handling her so roughly.

'I am afraid the news is not good,' she continued. 'Philippa has not yet been questioned but Mary has succumbed to fits of hysteria and collapsed at her last interrogation. It is said that she has lost her wits.'

I was completely powerless. My lovely, fragile daughter could never take the kind of treatment that I imagined she had received. Even if she had not met with rape at the hands of her jailors, which I feared she may have, she would never cope with the pressures of interrogation and imprisonment.

In fury and frustration, I almost shouted at Elizabeth.

'Elizabeth, I want you to go straight away downstairs and demand that I see Lord Sussex immediately. Say that I am ill if necessary but somehow, I must see him. I must save my daughters,' I sobbed as I turned away from her.

She left to do my bidding and soon afterwards I heard heavy footsteps approaching my door. However, it was not Sussex who entered but one of the guards. 'Move yourself Honora Lisle,' he said rudely. 'You are to leave this place.'

And with that he marched me out of my chamber and away from the bed I had shared with my husband. I had no time think or to pick up anything, even his pillow upon which I had cried my tears nightly since my arrest. My last link with him was gone.

I was taken to the home of a man called Francis Hall, a soldier in the Calais regiment. Elizabeth was allowed to come with me, but I was still not allowed anywhere near my daughters who continued to be detained at unknown prisons elsewhere in the town. I found out that Lord Sussex had been recalled to London, so any hope I had harboured of kinder treatment out of familial duty was gone.

Still, Hall's house was comfortable and situated in a fresher part of the town than the Staple Inn, so I tried to be positive about the move. There was also a small garden and as the summer was already becoming stiflingly hot, I was grateful to be allowed access to that area.

Apart from being allowed to walk in the garden, I was confined to one chamber in which I slept and ate. I was allowed no letters and was able to send none. What news my children may have had of me, I knew not. I saw no-one apart from Elizabeth. She was my only link with the outside world, and I will be grateful to her until the day I die.

A few days after our arrival, Elizabeth bustled in looking a little happier than before. I enquired as to the reason.

'Master Cromwell has been arrested,' she told me breathlessly. 'He has been accused of heresy and of secretly working against the King's purposes in religious matters.'

This was news indeed. I had felt all along that our troubles stemmed from Cromwell and his hatred of us. If he was now disgraced, might not our luck change for the better?

'Well, thank Heaven for small mercies,' I said, 'and may he rot in his dungeon a good long time before he meets his final reward in Hell.'

What I did not know at the time was that King Henry was already having second thoughts about our arrest. He was still very fond of my daughter Anne and she had no doubt been assiduous in pleading for our release. In fact, we heard later from Stephen Gardiner that the King had said quite early on in our imprisonment that he did not believe Arthur had erred out of malice but rather out of poor judgement and was seriously considering releasing us. But, as usual for us, events moved too fast and we suffered as a result of it.

Thomas Howard Duke of Norfolk was created Chancellor in place of Cromwell and quickly found places at Court for several members of his family. One of these was the youthful and pretty Catherine, daughter of our old friend Edmund Howard, he of the kidney stones. On first setting eyes upon Catherine the ageing King Henry's mind was rapidly emptied of everything but of courting and winning her. Our distress faded into the vast recesses of his memory.

In July, as the weather became ever hotter and more oppressive, Henry FitzAlan Lord Maltravers arrived in Calais to take over the position of Deputy. Whatever happened from now on, Arthur's position at Calais was no more. Maltravers moved into the Staple Inn, recently vacated so unceremoniously by me.

A few days later, Elizabeth brought me more insight from the world outside my four walls.

'The King has divorced Queen Anne,' she told me. 'He is set to marry Norfolk's niece and it is said she is already his mistress. They say he has eyes for no other and follows her about like a puppy.' She whispered this last to me and capped it with a wink.

I managed a wan smile. My enjoyment for such gossip was a thing of the past, a memory of Arthur's and my life together. I could no longer take any pleasure in such discussions.

A few days later I received a visitor, the first since my imprisonment and a truly welcome sight he made.

'Dear John, how did you manage to get here?' I dismissed with all formality and hugged John Wallop tightly.

'No trouble at all,' he replied. 'It seems that now Cromwell is out of action and your friend Wriothesley has bigger fish to fry, the conditions of your imprisonment are to be relaxed.'

'Do you mean we are shortly to be released?' I asked, clinging to the hope.

'Perhaps,' he said, 'but I have heard nothing as to that. I have been a guest of His Majesty in the Tower myself, you know.'

I gasped. 'Why?'

Chapter Twenty Six

'It was at the time of Cromwell's fall. For some reason I was accused along with the limping pig. But it took me only a short while to talk myself out of that,' he laughed light-heartedly.

'Have you seen Arthur?' I was desperate for news of my love and am ashamed to say it took precedence over my friend's trials.

'No, I have not,' he sounded sorry. 'I tried to get a message to him when I was imprisoned but without success, then after my release I tried again. There was no way I am afraid, but I do have news of your daughter Catherine. She has left the Court and is now lady in waiting to Anne of Cleves at Richmond Palace.'

I was relieved for Catherine. Her future was settled and secure, whoever she served, now that she was experienced in her field but the lack of knowledge of Arthur's plight and the constant worrying about him was sapping the life from my veins.

Wallop left me with a promise to return as soon as he could. I was grateful to him. After all, I was a convicted traitor and he was running a risk by openly showing me friendship. How on earth he had evaded my guards to reach me at all was a mystery to me.

That summer had turned into the hottest in living memory. The stifling heat seared the plants in the little garden and added to the discomfort of my imprisonment. I thought daily of Arthur in his airless cell and prayed for his safety. Early in August I was sitting outside in the shade of a tree fanning myself to get whatever relief I could from the scant breeze when Elizabeth brought me more news.

'I have overheard Master Hall talking with a messenger,' she whispered. 'Cromwell was executed last month.'

I drew breath sharply. I could hardly believe it, Cromwell dead. After all the trouble he had caused us with his delaying tactics and his accusations, now he was gone. It seemed somehow unreal. Here we were imprisoned largely as a result of his troublemaking, or so I still believed, and the source of all our troubles was dead himself. Surely our release could not be far off now.

But Elizabeth had more to say. 'On the same day that Cromwell met his maker, the King married Catherine Howard at Oatlands Palace. We have a new Queen.'

How like Henry, I thought bitterly. It was history repeating itself. I remembered how soon after the fall of Anne Boleyn he had married Jane Seymour. And now he had contracted this new marriage on the very day of Cromwell's execution. Henry had excelled himself. I had no love for either Anne Boleyn or Thomas Cromwell, but it still gave me a sick feeling in the pit of my stomach that the King could so dishonour the deaths of those he had once held dear.

My gentlewoman had one more piece of news to impart.

'Just yesterday, My Lady, Clement Philpot was hanged, drawn and quartered at Tyburn.'

Poor Clement, I mourned him only long enough to thank God for giving Philippa the sense to avoid marriage with him before my thoughts turned once more to Arthur. Try as I might I could not dispel the images which kept forming in my mind of my beloved's beautiful body being tortured and maimed by the traitor's death.

Chapter Twenty Six

The summer burned on well into October and no relief came either from the cruel heat or for my troubled mind. When the weather finally broke it was only to turn into a miserable, depressing autumn, followed by a long and dismal winter. I received no visitors and no news. Elizabeth tried to keep me bright, but the despair ate into my soul.

The small hope for our release which had flared in me after John Wallop's visit faded and died.

'Why, oh why are we still prisoners?' I asked myself over and over as I paced back and forth in the confines of my prison. Of my jailer, Francis Hall, I saw nothing. The guards were forever changing and made a point of not speaking to me or even making eye contact. If it were not for Elizabeth I would have effectively been in solitary confinement. My food was plain and basic and of a quantity only just enough to maintain life. I was given only water to drink.

By the time the thaw came in early 1541, I was in such a state of despondency that my sanity was threatened. My hair had turned white and the flesh had shrivelled on my body. I was barely a skeleton, covered in withered skin. At the age of fifty years I looked like an old woman.

I awoke each day expecting to hear of Arthur's death and bracing myself for the news.

Chapter Twenty Seven

'Master Wallop to see you, My Lady,' said Elizabeth as she ushered that good gentleman into the small chamber in which I was permitted to spend my days.

I sprang up as quickly as my poor aching bones and feeble legs would allow and flung myself at him, my need for human contact being so great. I buried my face in his clothing. 'Oh John, it seems so long.'

As I stood there, held tightly against him, I became aware that he had not yet spoken. I looked up at him. I had never seen John Wallop looking so grave and uncertain of what to say. He moved away from me a little, avoiding my eyes and removed his cap, twirling it around and around in his hands.

This is it, I thought, as the leaden fear settled on my heart. This is the day I have been preparing for and I am to hear of my cruel widowhood at the hands of the executioners.

I sat down stiffly and spoke with all the composure I could muster.

'You may as well tell me, John. I am prepared, you know.'

Still he seemed not to know how to begin, then, steeling himself he sat down beside me, took my hands in his own and commenced to speak.

'Honora, dear friend, the news I have to tell you is not that which you have been fearing. Your husband is, to the best of my knowledge, still alive and well in the Tower.' Again, he hesitated, and with my heart beating heavily and unevenly I waited for him to continue.

Chapter Twenty Seven

'Oh, my dear, the news which I have for you distresses me more than any I have ever had to impart.' He stopped for a second and looked desperately into my eyes. 'Honora, your son John died last week.' He spoke as if the words were acid burning his throat and when he had completed the sentence his shoulders sagged, and he buried his face in his hands.

I sat stunned, unable to comprehend. John, my angel, my first-born son, dead?

'No! No!' Someone was screaming, who was it? Then I realised it was me. John Wallop was holding my arms by my side as I tried to hit and scratch his face, to hurt the mouth that had uttered those vile words. Then as my screams turned to sobs, he released his grip on my arms and held me tenderly to his chest as I continued to whimper my futile denial.

'No, no, no,' my voice grew quieter until it stopped, and the numbness took over.

A long time later when I was at last able to talk about it, he told me that the end had come gradually much as his own father, John Basset's, had. He had simply faded week by week until, his loving wife by his side, he had departed this life for a better one. Whether he had suffered, I was afraid to ask, and John Wallop did not say but a part of me died that day. That piece of my heart which had been unlocked at his birth closed again with his death.

After Wallop's departure I went about in a state of stupefied shock. My beautiful son was dead, leaving only a wife and daughter. I was distressed for Frances and at our inability to comfort each other. At times I ranted and raved and shouted at Elizabeth, but she understood and went about her duties efficiently and kindly, never berating me for my behaviour.

About a month after Wallop's visit and his terrible news, Elizabeth's manner changed towards me. She still did her work well and thoroughly but kept her eyes averted and said little. So absorbed was I in my own troubles that it took me a while to notice but one day when she failed to answer a simple question even after I repeated had it a second time, I took her to task.

'Elizabeth, what is the matter with you these days?' I asked. 'You go about like a ghost.'

'It is nothing, My Lady,' she answered hurriedly, not meeting my eyes.

'Elizabeth, I can see that is far from 'nothing'. Something is wrong, and I wish you to tell me what it is.'

'Please Lady Honora, there is nothing amiss. I must go now, I have washing to do,' she tried to edge past me, but I was quite angry by now and would not allow her to leave.

'Tell me, Elizabeth,' I shook her roughly by the arm.

She yielded then and reluctantly told me what she had heard from her soldier friend.

'Oh, My Lady, there has been terrible news from Court. It all started with the King becoming unwell and bad-tempered. He has a badly ulcerated leg which causes him constant suffering and his moods have become unpredictable. It is reported that what he says in the morning he contradicts by nightfall. He has grown more and more suspicious of treason even amongst his most trusted servants and everyone at court goes in daily fear for their lives. His new wife is bringing him little joy either, naturally preferring the company of younger, more handsome courtiers than that of her ill-tempered spouse.' She stopped there, and I waited for more.

'Well,' I said at last, 'go on.'

She knew I would not let it go at that, so she reluctantly continued. 'The King has ordered the executions of many of the prisoners in the Tower.'

Once again, I prepared to hear of Arthur's death and took a deep breath to steady myself.

'Oh, no, My Lady, Lord Lisle was not one of those executed.'

'Oh, thank God, thank God. Tell me, Elizabeth, who is it this time?'

She took courage from my obvious relief. 'It was his cousin, the Countess of Salisbury.'

As I recoiled in horror, she told me the details of the barbaric execution of Arthur's seventy-year-old cousin, Margaret Pole. The usual executioner being absent, the killing was carried out by an unskilled youth who literally hacked her head and shoulders to pieces in his attempt to behead her. Her head, or what was left of it, was then stuck on a pike on London Bridge to act as a reminder to all of the fate of traitors.

As I sat shuddering and shaking from the vivid pictures in my mind, Elizabeth said softly.

'My Lady, the worst of it is that more executions are expected.'

I nodded, accepting the inevitable. I almost wished by that time that our suffering would end quickly in the only way I thought possible. If we are to die, then please God, let it be soon, I prayed.

But the summer wore on, not as hot as the previous one but wet and steamy. The flowers in the little garden, starved of moisture the previous year almost strangled each other in the profusion of their growth. Day after day when the weather allowed, I sat out there and willed myself to think of as little as possible. I would force myself to concentrate on an ant or a spider crawling up a leaf or on a cloud in the sky, on anything but the reality of my miserable existence.

That we were still prisoners after all this time made no sense. If we were not to be executed, then why were we not released? It seemed that we had been entirely forgotten.

Summer turned to autumn with gentle grace, cooling down gradually day by day. It was early November and the leaves had hardly changed colour when the next news came from London.

Elizabeth had heard the story as usual from her soldier friends and this time had no compunction in telling me about it.

'The Queen has been arrested, My Lady. She has been carrying on a love affair right under the King's nose with Thomas Culpepper, a gentleman of the King's Privy Chamber.' She bristled with excitement and righteous indignation.

I really could not have cared less about this latest in the long line of the King's matrimonial difficulties, but she was determined to talk so I allowed her to continue.

'They say the King was so overcome by the discovery that he called for a sword to kill her himself. But he had to be satisfied with having her entire household arrested, all of whom had known about the affair and concealed their knowledge.'

Chapter Twenty Seven

These troubles in the King's life were of no consequence to me. They inhabited another world, a world that I had been unwillingly plunged into years ago and then so rudely removed from a few years later. In my world, the world of these four walls of my prison, autumn turned to winter, Christmas came and went and soon 1542 was upon us. In the middle of February John Wallop again visited me.

'I have better news for you this time, Honora,' he said cheerfully. 'Arthur's Coat of Arms has again been set up in the Chapel of the Garter Knights at Windsor. That means that he has been pardoned and must soon be free. Nothing has been said as yet, but I saw the Arms with my own eyes.'

I was afraid to share his optimism but could not help but feel a little relaxing of my tension.

'The King has greatly recovered his spirits,' said John. 'Catherine Howard has been executed, you know?'

I replied that I did not know but took the news calmly, as it had been inevitable once the truth about her adultery was known.

He continued. 'King Henry has been entertaining large parties of ladies and gentlemen since his wife's death, and before it. He still has a fancy for your daughter Anne. Although he has dismissed all Queen Catherine's other ladies from the Court, he has kept her on and he always seats her near to him at the banquets.'

I did not know whether to be glad for this news or not, given the shortened lifespan of most of the King's wives but John thought it very good news indeed.

'Anne has been emboldened by this renewal of the King's interest in her and has been earnestly pleading for her stepfather's life and freedom. I think the time is near,

Honora. Take heart, my dear.' He gave me some money to purchase items I would need upon my release. Dear, good friend, what would I have done without him?

Against my better judgement I was infected by his optimism and began to look forward to the future. I even began to worry about my appearance again and started to force more of the unappetising prison food down my neck. Arthur would not want to find a skinny, shapeless wife waiting for him when he emerged from his prison. I sent Elizabeth looking for material to sew some new garments. Together we spent many happy hours sewing and planning for the future, which I was allowing myself to believe might be bright after all. So little notice was taken of me these days that it seemed quite an easy task for Elizabeth to ease the conditions of my imprisonment without discovery.

Then, on the fourth of March the news was announced. Wallop arrived back with great ceremony and threw open the doors of Francis Hall's house with a flourish.

'Lady Honora!' he shouted at the top of his voice. 'Come forth! You are now a free woman.'

Dazed, I left my chamber and walked out of the front door of the house for the first time in almost two years. There, waiting to greet me were my two daughters Mary and Philippa. Philippa had not changed so much but Mary was almost unrecognisable. Gone was the sparkling beauty and rounded shapeliness which had won the heart that cost her so dear. Gone was the twinkle of her eye and the spring in her step. She trembled and shook as she stood there, and her hands fidgeted constantly with the girdle at her waist. When I approached her to hold her close, she started violently and moved away as if afraid of me. My joy turned to dismay as I realised that she knew not who I was.

John Wallop gently touched my elbow. 'Give her time. With nurturing, some part of her may return to you.'

Philippa embraced me tightly and we stayed that way for many minutes, unable to speak and barely believing that our time of imprisonment was at an end. While we stood there clinging to each other, it began to rain and with the rain came thunder.

John spoke to us through the torrents.

'We must go now, Honora. I hurried over on a small fishing vessel as soon as your release was announced but your ship will be arriving any minute from Dover and we must catch the tide to return with it.'

We had few belongings to collect, Elizabeth and I, and so together with she who had been my sole consolation and confidante throughout my imprisonment, I mounted the horse which stood saddled and waiting and rode with John Wallop and my daughters to the docks.

It was still pouring with rain when we arrived, and the ship had just anchored. We waited for the disembarking passengers to alight and were preparing to board when I spotted our old servant John Husee amongst the arrivals. Waving joyfully to him, I missed for a moment seeing the agonised expression on his face.

He hurried over to where we waited under the shelter of a loading tent and stood silently before us, drowning not only in the torrential rain but under the weight of his oppressive misery.

'John,' I said, failing to understand what could be troubling him, 'we are free, we are to return to England. Did not you know?'

'Oh, My Lady, my dear Lady Lisle, my heart grieves me, but I have evil news for you,' he said with a terrible expression on his face. He turned with a helpless expression to John Wallop as if pleading with him for assistance, but Wallop was just as ignorant of what was troubling him as I was. And so, taking a deep breath and looking steadily into my eyes, Husee told me.

'Honora, My Lady, please forgive me for being the bearer of these tidings but your husband, Lord Lisle, died last evening only hours after receiving his pardon,' said Husee, his voice laden with sympathy and unhappiness.

'No, that is not possible,' I replied. I think I even laughed a little, as if this was some kind of foolish jest. 'We are just at this moment travelling to be reunited with him.'

Husee went on, explaining to me as if I was a child.

'He had been so weakened by his years of imprisonment that when the news of his release was given to him his excitement was too great and he suffered a seizure from which he failed to recover.'

The next events are clear to me even though those about me thought I had lost my wits. I know I walked out into the rain and screamed loud and long, venting my anguish and rage to the storm, shouting my despair aloud to the God who had cheated me so cruelly just when happiness was within reach.

Then I ran over to where the horses were tethered and clumsily mounted the one I had ridden earlier, wheeling it about before the others knew what I was doing and

Chapter Twenty Seven

whipping it to a gallop up the hill and away from the docks. In the distance I heard frantic shouts as my friends began their pursuit of me, a woman gone mad with grief.

I did not stop when I reached the town but continued on past the houses and out into the countryside, never pausing until I reached Landretun. The wind and rain still lashed violently, and the trees were swaying fearfully about me as I dismounted clumsily, almost falling from the terrified horse which shied and bolted away. Slipping and tripping over my sodden skirts I ran through the gaping hole where the door had been and into the ruins of the cottage, which had been stripped bare just as our home in Calais had been. So vandalised and ravaged was it that nothing remained of our last refuge of love but a few broken shards of glass and the splintered timbers of broken furniture. I grabbed a stout piece of wood and ran out to the garden, just as Wallop and Husee arrived, shouting desperately at me to stop.

Still I ran, down to the bottom of the tangled wreck of our garden as far as the fence. Quickly locating the marking stone, I threw myself to the ground and using the piece of wood as a lever, began frantically digging like one possessed. I soon struck something hard and plunging my hands into the muddy ground retrieved the jar in which I had buried my love's letter, all that was left of our lives together. Triumphantly I drew it forth from the mire and held it aloft, screaming in despair and fury: 'They thought they had taken everything, but they were wrong!'

I began to sob and clutched the bottle to my chest covering myself with mud and grime as I did so. My friends approached and gently lifted me to my feet. The rain had stopped now, and the afternoon was bathed in a soft golden light. Steam was rising in clouds as the puddles evaporated in the warmth. My horse had long since beaten a terrified retreat, so Wallop mounted me before him on his saddle and slowly we returned to the waiting ship which was to take us back to England.

There was a dismal little group awaiting us at the water's edge. Poor Elizabeth was trying to console Philippa whose composure had finally deserted her. They sat together on a rough bench while Mary still stood wringing her hands and biting her fingernails, engulfed in a terrible misery of her own.

Gathering some inner strength which I never knew I had, I resolved to put my own tragedy behind me at least for the moment. My duty lay in supporting my daughters. Dismounting with as much dignity as I could muster and still clutching my precious jar, I walked straight and tall over to where they waited and spoke with a firm voice.

'Come, my dears, the ship awaits. Let us return to England.'

5. RETURN TO UMBERLEIGH

Chapter Twenty Eight

The crossing from Calais back to the land of my birth was mercifully smooth on a glassy sea, the calm after the storm. Once we were on board, Elizabeth Husee, Philippa and I settled Mary in a cabin and she soon fell into a fitful sleep. We took turns sitting with her and soothing her with small sounds of reassurance. When not with Mary I walked on the deck. The evening was clear and moonlit, its beam reflected off the silky water and leading us like a beacon back to our homeland.

It all felt unreal as if the last years had never happened, almost as if I hardly knew who I was. I was in a vacuum there on the empty sea, surrounded by darkness with only a moonbeam showing me the way. Somehow, I found it comforting although I knew even then that the feeling was transient and that very soon the realities of life would crowd about me again.

'How goes it, my dear?' It was John Wallop who spoke.

I did not answer, but stood pensively, looking out over the still, dark water.

'Will you be all right, Honora?' He spoke again. 'What will you do now?'

'Oh yes, I will be all right John,' and I knew I spoke truth. 'I am a Grenville, you know.'

'Will you remain in London?' He sounded as if he hoped I would.

Again, I stared out over the water. 'No John, I will return to Umberleigh.'

After a slow but smooth crossing we arrived in Dover in the early hours of the morning. Husee quickly found us lodgings where we spent the remainder of the night. We made a late start the next day and moved in gradual stages towards London. Mary was not strong enough to ride for more than a few hours each day and we were in no hurry.

On our third day back on English soil we were staying at lodgings in Rochester when we had a visitor. Stephen Gardiner had got wind of our arrival and hurried down to meet us. Next to him was a tall, handsome young man who smiled at me with bright eyes.

'James!' I stood stiffly from my chair in order to embrace him. 'Oh James, how tall you have grown.'

What trivial things we say on such momentous occasions. When so much needed to be said, the first words that dribbled from my mouth were inanities. But soon we were at our ease and able to talk properly.

'Dearest Mother, I have been so worried about you,' said my darling boy. 'If it were not for Stephen's kindness, I know not how I would have coped.' He smiled gratefully at his benefactor.

'It has been a terrible time, Honora, mostly for you of course, but also for your friends and family. Not being able to see you or to have news of you was torture for all of us,' said Stephen.

Chapter Twenty Eight

'If it were not for John Wallop, I would have seen no-one and had no information passed on to me at all,' I replied.

'Wallop acted very bravely, Honora,' said Stephen. 'He risked arrest himself, you know, for visiting you. It is good that your jailor Francis Hall was rarely at home and that Wallop was able to line your guards' pockets handsomely for their silence. Not being made of martyr material myself,' he continued in a lighter tone, 'I chose to further your interests in less a less heroic manner by taking good care of your boy here.'

We both looked indulgently at James, who blushed and smiled. He was now sixteen and growing up fast but for me he would forever be my baby. Stephen now broached the subject which neither of us had so far mentioned.

'Honora, I am so sorry for your loss. I know how much Arthur meant to you and my heart grieves for your pain.'

I felt my chest swelling as if it would burst, as great wells of misery rose within me. Since leaving Calais I had tried to think of anything else but not of Arthur, not that. I had spent my time mostly with Mary, my poor broken daughter. I had concentrated on making plans for our future and had been sending messengers to Devon to have Umberleigh prepared for our arrival. I had discussed with Husee what he would do now that I no longer needed his services. With all this and more I had filled my days, until exhaustion claimed me, and I was able to sleep a few hours of troubled, restless sleep at night. But now Stephen was forcing me to remember, to grieve.

'Oh Stephen,' I moaned as the feelings of loss and wretchedness flooded back, 'I loved him so.'

'I know, I know,' he said and gently rocked me in his arms as I sobbed against his chest.

James, showing a maturity beyond his years, came over and embraced me too. Resting his head on mine he held me close providing such comfort that the pain was eased a little and I could face the day again.

It came as a relief to me when Stephen told me that none of my family in England had been questioned. Their lives had continued uninterrupted, save for the nightmare of worrying about us and their inability to get any news of our welfare.

At Stephen's suggestion we decided to remain a few days at Rochester. He advised against travelling through London, instead he said we should skirt the south side of the river and head west that way.

'But I would like to see my other children,' I protested.

'I can try and arrange for them to visit you here,' said Stephen. 'I was wondering about George. Now that he is eighteen, perhaps he should leave Bryan's household and travel back to Devon with you.'

The idea had occurred to me already.

'Do you think Bryan would mind?' I asked. 'I do not wish to create animosity at Court so soon after everything that has passed.'

Gardiner obviously had little time for Bryan.

'I think it would be in George's best interest to remove him from Bryan now,' he said firmly. 'The man is a dissolute wastrel.'

It was quickly arranged and soon George joined us at Rochester for the journey west. He had hardly changed and his years in the household of a 'dissolute wastrel' seemed not to have affected him at all. He greeted me dutifully. He was eighteen now and since John's death, was my oldest son and the head of the family. It was obvious that the responsibility would be taken seriously by him and he would not fail in his duties.

Bridget also visited us at Rochester. She was a bright and endearing seventeen years old and apart from a dutiful expression of sorrow at her father's death, the events of the past years seemed not to have touched her at all. That was understandable, for she had been cared for and protected by Sir Anthony Windsor and had no doubt been told little of the truth about what had happened. She told me that she was shortly to marry William Carden of Kent. Sir Anthony had arranged the marriage and it was to her liking. Thus, we parted, never to meet again. It was another cruel twist of fate that if we had been allowed a normal family life Bridget could have remained as close to me as my own daughters, but we parted as strangers. James was not present for her visit and she did not mention him.

To my disappointment I was unable to see Anne or Catherine. Anne was too involved at Court and was now, according to the rumours, being seriously courted by the King. I trembled for her safety and hoped that some other young lady would catch Henry's eye before Anne became wife number six. I had no ambitions to become the mother of the next Queen of England, especially given the extremely temporary status of the other recent holders of that title. I was unable to see Catherine as she was busy at Richmond, serving Anne of Cleves.

We left Rochester late in March 1542 and continued our slow progress west. As we drew near to London, I tried to avert my eyes but, in the end, could not stop myself from looking across the river to the Tower where my beloved husband had spent his last unhappy years. We stopped at the bridge and my sorrow was compounded by having to bid farewell to three of the best friends I had known. Husee and Wallop were to return to London where Wallop was to resume his duties as a soldier in the King's army. Husee had been granted a secretarial position at Court.

How was I to thank John Husee, the man who cared for and watched over our children when we first went to Calais, who had organised everything for us and kept us informed? He had been a good and faithful servant for almost ten years.

I gripped his hand tightly in mine. 'I wish our parting could be under more prosperous circumstances, John. But my heartfelt thanks go to you for everything you did for Lord Lisle and myself.'

'It was a pleasure, My Lady,' he answered, hastily wiping a tear from his eye. 'I was more than happy to serve you both, and I wish you well for the future. May God be with you. Farewell, cousin,' he shouted to Elizabeth who waved at him from her constant place by Mary's side.

He turned from us and mounted his horse, riding away over the bridge towards his new life.

Then I turned to John Wallop who stood silently by.

'What can I say, John?' I asked him after we had stood mutely for a while.

'Very little, Honora,' he replied. 'I think it has all been said between us over the years.'

Chapter Twenty Eight

'John,' I struggled for words, 'Stephen told me about the dangers you faced in showing me friendship during my imprisonment.'

'That was nothing,' he said firmly. 'I would do it again if it were necessary, which I pray God it will not!' he added with a tense laugh.

'But I still want you to know that you have my undying gratitude,' I told him. 'I think I would have lost my sanity without your visits.'

We stood again for a while, not knowing what to say but wishing to prolong the parting.

'Well,' he said at last, stiffening his shoulders, 'I must be off.' He began to turn away then came back and took my hands between his own.

'Honora, if you ever need anything, anything at all, send me a message. I am always at your service.' He looked deeply into my eyes then he, too, rode away.

Then came the saddest parting of all. As Stephen and James prepared to return to their busy lives in London, I could barely contain my sorrow. No, that is wrong, I made no effort to contain it. Hugging my youngest son closely I sobbed loud and long, huge, gut-wrenching howls, until I felt a gentle hand on my shoulder as Stephen spoke lovingly to me.

'It is not forever, Honora. For now, your place is at Umberleigh with your daughters and George. We will, the three of us, see each other again as soon as it is possible to do so. In the meantime, you can be sure that your son is developing into one of the finest young men I have had the privilege to know.'

With that, my sobbing eased, and I regained some semblance of composure. With one, last loving look in my direction, James mounted his horse and rode away with his friend and mentor, back to his life in London.

I watched them ride over the bridge towards the city and then re-joined my travelling party. And so, I set out with George, Philippa, Mary, Elizabeth Husee, a few servants and a small group of armed men to guard us on our long journey. Those were not dangerous times in which to travel but with so many women in our group it was a sensible precaution.

Mary had not improved at all from that first day of her release and due to her extreme frailty of mind and body we continued to travel very slowly, frequently with her lying on a litter. She had not spoken a word since Calais and continued to remain locked away in her own silent agony. None of us knew what terrors she had experienced, and no-one was able to reach her to offer consolation. Philippa rarely left her side.

'I think I can help her by just being there, Mother,' she said. 'I only wish she would speak to me.'

'Philippa, it is possible Mary has been mistreated badly by her jailors,' I chose my words carefully.

'Yes, I know what you mean,' she replied sadly. 'She was such a beautiful girl.'

At this we both looked sorrowfully at the wreckage of Mary's beauty. We had stopped at a ford for the horses to have a drink. Mary remained in her litter where she lay staring up at the leaves and the clouds, but to all appearances seeing nothing. Her eyes were empty of expression and her haggard face was a blank mask.

Chapter Twenty Eight

'Perhaps it is not such a good thing at all to be a beauty,' Philippa said pensively. 'I was always just a little jealous of Mary in Calais, you know.'

This took me completely by surprise.

'Oh Philippa, you had no need!' I exclaimed.

'Yes, I did really,' she insisted. 'People always exclaimed and marvelled at her beauty and charm and ignored me completely. And then she had Gabriel de Montmorency begging for her favours. No-one ever noticed me and when I was in prison, I was questioned a few times then left alone. No-one bothered with me there either.'

My heart filled with love for my dear, plain daughter. 'Well, as you say, poor Mary's beauty has done her little service in the end.'

We took a full ten days to cover the miles, not arriving at Umberleigh until April was well advanced. Some days we carried Mary in her litter and on others she rode a little, but it was with a profound feeling of home-coming that we at last saw the comforting white-washed walls of Umberleigh welcoming us in the distance.

A great sense of relief and safety flooded over me as we entered the enclosure of the stable yard and the family and servants crowded around us. Mary was taken carefully out of her litter by gentle hands amidst cries of horror at her changed appearance. She had been only six years old when last seen by the servants at Umberleigh, a bright, precocious and beautiful child, loved by all.

'Oh, for shame', and 'Poor lamb', were repeated over and over as she was taken straight away into the house accompanied by Elizabeth and Philippa.

Then it was my turn to be greeted by those who remained. I had not been back to Umberleigh since my second marriage in 1528 and although only fourteen years had passed, I knew my appearance had also changed markedly for the worse. But no surprise showed in the faces of the servants as they greeted me one by one with encouraging words.

'Welcome home, My Lady,' or 'Welcome, Mistress Basset, sorry Madam, I mean Lady Lisle,' as they each spoke their few words.

After the servants, it was the turn of the family. Jane hovered in the background, still looking disapproving but somehow even her frowns were a source of reassurance to me.

I took her outstretched hand. 'Umberleigh looks wonderful, Jane. You have kept it beautifully.'

She managed a smile and said that she was glad I was not disappointed.

Thomasine and Margery were there, together with Margery's husband, the rustic William Marres. How my heart swelled when my hand was grasped firmly in his huge calloused paw.

Then I felt a tug on my skirts and looked down to see a plump, pretty little girl with curly red-gold hair. She was, I judged, three years or more and was smiling guilelessly up at me. I bent down.

'Are you by any chance Mistress Honora Basset?' I enquired.

'Yes, My Lady,' she answered pertly. 'Are you my Grandmother?'

'Yes, oh yes, I am,' I replied, kneeling down and embracing her tightly. She wriggled uncomfortably so I released her, but she showed no fear of me and placed her hand in mine after I stood up again.

With tears of both sadness and joy coursing freely down my cheeks, I was just about to ask where Frances was, since her daughter was here at Umberleigh, when I heard soft steps on the gravel and, looking up, saw her walking towards us. In her arms was a baby of about ten months of age.

'Mother,' she greeted me serenely, 'I would like to introduce you to Master Arthur Basset.' And into my arms she placed her baby boy.

Time stood still as I held my grandson in my arms for the first time. How long I stared into his serious brown eyes, so like my first husband's and beheld the sun shining on his soft golden hair, so like that of his namesake I know not. Both my husbands were grandfathers to this little boy. All the love I had felt for the two men I had married had born fruit in this boy-child named Arthur.

After a time, I looked enquiringly at Frances.

'Did John know of this child before he ...'

'I was large with child when John died, Mother. He felt certain he was leaving a son and it was his request that he be named Arthur.'

Still carrying my grandson and loathe to be parted from him I entered the house in the company of my family. Calais was history, the terror was over, and the next phase of my life had begun.

Chapter Twenty Nine

Life at Umberleigh soon settled into a daily pattern of activity in which everyone had a place and a job to do. There was something to keep us all occupied in the busy process of rebuilding our lives.

The most important task of all was the healing of Mary. Philippa wanted to remain with her night and day, but I needed to keep reminding myself that Philippa had also suffered and needed some comforting herself. Between the three of us, Philippa, Elizabeth Husee and myself, we gave Mary round the clock care and ever so gradually she began to change for the better. She would never be like her former self but, with God's grace, we hoped that she might one day be able to live a normal life.

Jane continued on as housekeeper, a position which she still carefully guards as her own to this day. I was content to let that be, she had done a good job in my years of absence.

Thomasine stayed living with her sister Margery. She had lived contentedly with Margery and William ever since the stresses of living at Umberleigh under the misrule of John Bonde had become too much for her tender spirit to bear. Umberleigh was a place of peace now, made more so by the urgent need of those of us who had suffered to find refuge and healing. Even Jane managed to curb her acid tongue when faced with such necessity.

George took on the responsibilities of running the estate with an assurance which belied his years. He had not enjoyed his time with Francis Bryan in London, so it seemed. In fact, he confided as much to me one day.

Chapter Twenty Nine

'But George, why did you not tell me?' I asked, exasperated.

'Because, Mother, you did not ask,' he replied, 'and then you were imprisoned so my troubles were as nothing.'

I was moved by a sudden guilt but covered it by an attack on him.

'You were in London for a good two years before I was imprisoned,' I pointed out acidly. 'You should have told me. James would have.'

'Yes, Mother, I know James would have,' he said quietly, 'but I am not James. Perhaps you would prefer that I was.'

I felt a sudden rush of love and affection for my second son.

'George, I am so sorry,' I said with sincerity. 'I have always supposed that because you said little you felt just as little. And no, I do not wish you were James, I am more than happy that you are who you are. And I am very confident knowing that you are responsible for Umberleigh and the family.'

And I meant that. He is capable and sensible, and I knew that we were in good hands.

Frances remained with us at Umberleigh. She had moved there as soon as she heard that we were free and on our way home. I felt that I could not let her return to Tehidy even if she had wished to, so fond was I of her children. Honora was a delight to me, and I fancied that she may have been quite like I was as a child, surrounded by family yet self-possessed and quite her own person. And as for Arthur, I hated to let him out of my sight for a second. He was also good for Mary and often when I sat with her, I would bring him along. She responded more to his cooing and babbling than to any of the rest of us. Often, I would see her reach out and touch his cheek or let him hold her hand, whereas she still recoiled at the touch of an adult hand. When we dressed her or helped her with the cleansing of her body she shivered and trembled so violently with fear that we detested what we had to do.

Even so, life went on and each little improvement in Mary's condition was greeted by celebrations of joy from all of us and noted as a milestone in her recovery. I think at that time she did not remember any of us from before her ordeal but accepted that we were her family and grew to trust us. Her fidgeting and nail-biting ceased and as the weeks went by, she began to learn how to take care of herself again. As she improved, she began to share the joy with us as she learned to do something and gained in confidence and would give a little laugh vaguely reminiscent of her old self. But still she did not speak. We never heard from her old lover Gabriel de Montmorency and assumed that he had not tried to get in touch with us following our disgrace.

Meanwhile, Frances was making plans of her own. The heir to the wealthy estate of Potheridge near Torrington, had approached her with an offer of marriage.

'What do you think, Mother?' she asked me after telling me of the offer.

'Do you like him?' I asked.

'I am glad you have not changed,' she said laughing. 'So many people would have left that question until last, but not you! Yes, I suppose I like him. He is no John,' she added sadly, 'but there is no point in looking back, is there?'

'No point at all,' I agreed, forcing myself not to do just that. 'Of course, Frances I would far prefer to keep you and my grandchildren here by my side but that is a selfish wish and I must put it away.'

'I must remarry,' she said sensibly. 'There is no life for me now unless I do, you know that. My children and I need the protection of a husband and father.'

I knew how true that was. A world where a young woman with small children could live alone and fend for herself was nothing but fantasy, certainly not a reality and never would be. Once George married and had a wife of his own there would be no place at Umberleigh for Frances.

'You and your Thomas Monk have my blessing,' I said to her, 'but do not make it too soon. I need little Arthur and Honora about me for a while longer yet.'

In November of that year my niece Mary's husband, Robert Radcliffe Earl of Sussex, died. He it was who had been my first jailor in Calais. I suppose he had been as kind to me as he was permitted to be but my memories of him were still very unhappy ones. When Mary remarried a few years later, I hoped her new husband was a gentler man than her first.

Our first Christmas at Umberleigh was bitter-sweet. It was difficult to be entirely cheerful when the brightest light in my life had been extinguished but, surrounded as I was by loved ones and far removed from the perils and fears of the last years, it was impossible not to feel some measure of happiness.

The following year, 1543, was a peaceful and contented one for us in Devon. Back in London we heard of the persecution of Papists and the burning of heretics. There was still no easy middle ground, it seemed. How grateful I was that we were away from the danger and how I shuddered when I remembered the terror of being caught up in the net as we were.

My granddaughter was now known as Nora. This was what her little brother, Arthur, called her when he began to speak. It stuck, and she was known by the name from that moment on. She became my devoted follower and we spent many happy hours walking in the garden and exploring the woods and hedgerows together. I taught her the names of several of the plants and told her that many of them could be used to heal us when we became ill. I was not sure whether she would remember any of it, but I enjoyed her company and the feel of her soft warm hand in mine. Her red curls bobbed about her face in undisciplined profusion as she ran on ahead of me and bent over a new plant.

'What is the name of this one, Grandmother?' Her bright, bubbly voice had the power to distract me from morbid thoughts then as the memory of it still does to this day.

That summer Frances married Thomas Monk at Atherington Church. Frances had prepared for her wedding with the calm serenity with which she did all things and during the ceremony maintained a dignified, tranquil demeanour. Arthur, who was then two years old, toddled into the church, taking everything in with huge, wondrous eyes. Little Nora was self-possessed and prim in her new gown, reminding me of myself many years ago at my sister's wedding. She kept a tight hold of Arthur's hand and at one stage I observed her admonishing him to be quiet. Frances had insisted on her children being in the Church although usually small children were not present at such events. She had even ordered matching gowns to be made for herself and her daughter. They were both dressed in lemon brocade

Chapter Twenty Nine

with green velvet overskirts. I had a new gown as well but kept frills to a minimum. The days when I longed for fine clothes were long past.

The wedding banquet was held at Umberleigh and was a lavish affair by Devonshire standards. As I sat there, surrounded by my family, I thought of all the grand banquets I had attended at Court and at Calais before the terror. Apart from the absence of Arthur from my side, I far preferred this one. There was a large amount of food but only enough to feed all the guests. I knew that what little was left over would be used, if not by our own household, then given to the village poor. The wanton wastage at Henry's Court had always sickened me.

As I observed Frances and her new husband at the head of the table, my heart went out to her. I could see that what she had said was true, he was no John. He looked like a very stern man as he sat there. He hardly looked at his new bride and when he did, I detected no softness in his glance. Oh, how I hoped that my dear Frances would be happy in her new home.

After the banquet was over, I went out to the stable yard with the other guests as the newly married couple prepared to leave with their servants, taking my grandchildren with them. A large crowd of villagers had gathered for the spectacle. I had no opportunity to speak with the little ones again, for Nora was already seated upon her mount and Arthur was being passed up to sit in front of his new stepfather as I arrived. That was when I heard a gasp behind me, and Mary rushed forward.

She ran over to where Arthur was propped in front of Thomas Monk and frantically grabbed at him as if she would pull him off the horse.

'Do not take him! Please do not take him!' she cried out in anguish. These were the first words Mary had spoken since Calais and we were all dumbfounded.

As Monk wheeled his horse about, he pushed at Mary with his other arm and the child in front of him started screaming in fear. Mary was still trying to grab at the bridle and in doing so her skirts became entangled in the legs of the horse which reared violently threatening to dislodge both the rider and his small charge. Just when all seemed lost, a stranger emerged from the crowd which was rapidly forming about us and, placing one strong arm about Mary to restrain her, he used the other to calm the frightened horse, uttering soothing sounds which settled them both.

In no time at all the situation was over, calm was restored, and the riding party set off on their journey. When their dust had settled and the crowd was dispersing, the stranger turned to where Philippa and I were still comforting Mary, doffed his cap and introduced himself.

'James Pitts at your service, My Lady,' he said.

We began to see quite a lot of James Pitts after that. He was a prosperous farmer from Atherington who soon became a firm favourite with all of us, especially Philippa. He was always on hand to provide extra help when a roof needed mending, or a field needed ploughing and also added some much-needed male company for social occasions. Apart from George, we remained a firmly female-dominated household.

Chapter Twenty Nine

There was a second marriage later that summer - that of the King and his sixth wife, Catherine Parr, which took place at Hampton Court Palace. Fortunately, in my opinion, he had opted for a more mature-aged woman to fill the role this time and my daughter Anne escaped once again. Anne was, however, kept on at Court as lady-in-waiting to the new Queen.

She wrote to me once she was settled in her position. She was careful not to mention more than the bare facts of the marriage and of her own employment in Queen Catherine's retinue, but I was able to detect from the light-hearted manner of her writing that she was very happy with the changes. A more worrying note was a postscript to her letter describing the effects of the plague which had once again struck in the city.

> *'We are fortunate that the Court is not at present in London for the city is sorely affected by plague. Every afflicted house has the cross painted on the door and infected people must remain indoors for at least 40 days or until they die. All dogs except hunting dogs are destroyed and all straw and bedding must be burned. Beggars are not allowed in the Churches and the streets are cleaned daily.'*

I prayed every day for Anne and for my other children whose lives were spent in the midst of such dangers. For once God heeded my prayers and none of them were affected.

The months went by for us in Devon with no momentous happenings apart from the many small joys and tribulations which make up peaceful rural life. After the commotion on the day of Frances' wedding, Mary had retreated back into her silent, tormented world but we had a new weapon in the fight for her recovery and that was James Pitts.

Of the many services he rendered us, by far the greatest was the way in which he helped Mary. For some reason unknown to us she trusted him immediately and with him she was able to achieve many things which previously she had been unable to do, such as speaking again. James explained to us that Mary had not forgotten how to speak, indeed she still understood exactly what was being said to her, but it was his opinion that at some stage during her ordeal in prison she had decided that not speaking was the only way she could remain safe from her inquisitors. As her state of mind deteriorated, her power of speech finally deserted her altogether. James felt that, rather than be taught how to speak, Mary had to be coaxed into using her voice.

Together with Philippa, James spent hour after hour with Mary encouraging her and teasing her, until gradually and almost reluctantly, the words began to come. It was no sudden process but once her voice was unlocked Mary was on the way to recovery.

One day when I was sitting with her in the garden, she looked directly into my eyes, something else which she had avoided doing until very recently. 'Mother,' she said, 'I do remember now. I remember you all – from before. I think I always remembered but it was safer to try not to. I even remember Gabriel …' Here her voice gave a little catch and tears sprang to her eyes.

Chapter Twenty Nine

I was careful not to prompt her with questions about how much else she remembered. I did not want to reawaken any of the dreadful memories of her years of imprisonment. James Pitts 'the wise' as I came to call him, advised us to let the memories come of their own accord and to deal with them as they came, good and bad.

I held out my hand to her and she took it in hers.

The year 1544 came and went and our lives continued peacefully, the serenity and solitude of Devon broken only by one visitor, who arrived in early May.

'John! John Wallop!' I could hardly believe my eyes when he rode into the yard. I had just returned from the fields where I had been watching the fallow being ploughed, a past-time of which I was inordinately fond. My plain gown was torn from the fence I had climbed and stained by clover. Burrs adhered to the hem.

'Well, well, my fine Lady was a country lass at heart after all!' He alighted lithely from his horse, belying his age which was the same as mine.

'What are you doing here, John?' I expect I was somewhat abrupt and must have seemed unwelcoming but my amazement at seeing him so far from his usual haunts made me forget myself.

'I can see your manners have become quite as rustic as your dress, Honora,' he feigned hurt feelings. 'However, in answer to your question, I am here to visit my old friend Lady Lisle. Pray, Madam, do you know where I can find her, for I fail to see anybody resembling her about me here?' He looked about him in an exaggerated manner.

'Oh John,' I laughed, the first really good laugh I had had in years. 'Do stop teasing. Come inside, and if you can bear to sit with such a bumpkin as myself you can tell me all about what you have been up to since we parted.'

It was so good to see him again. He stayed with us for three days, during which time we talked and laughed until late into the night and all the day as well. George, always an early riser, showed his disapproval of my guest's and my late hours and continued to retire early, leaving us to ourselves. On one occasion I asked John a question which I had never asked before.

'John, you never mention your wife and I have never met her. Is there anything amiss between you two?'

'Nothing amiss, Honora, nothing at all,' he answered blithely. 'Provided that we never have to be in the same house at the same time as each other we get on famously.' He laughed uproariously, and I was saddened that this wonderful, kind, funny, brave man had not managed to find marital happiness.

Choosing not to ask anything more about that subject I selected a more general topic.

'What is the news of the Court, John? And what of the King's marriage?'

'We have a new Chancellor now,' he said, and then, matter-of-factly, as if the name was a new one to both of us, he added, 'his name is Thomas Wriothesley.'

'What!' I spluttered. 'How horrible, oh, how absolutely awful that is! The man is a sadist, he is not natural, he is, oh he is ... oh, even Cromwell was better than that,' I finished in confusion.

'I thought you would be well pleased,' John sounded amused. 'Better steer clear of London for a while, eh, Honora?'

Chapter Twenty Nine

'You can be sure of that,' I said firmly. 'I will never set foot in the place while he is in a position of power, or ever if I can help it.'

'And as regards the King's marriage, all is not smooth sailing there either,' his mirth dissipated suddenly. 'The Queen is a fine and intelligent lady, far better than Henry deserves.'

He stopped suddenly and looked furtively about him.

'Any spies hereabouts, Honora? I fear I have just spoken treason.'

'No John, to the best of my knowledge there are no spies at Umberleigh,' I laughed again. 'Oh, do go on, John, and stop larking about.'

'Well, Queen Catherine is a very well-read lady who likes to think deeply about all matters especially those of a religious nature. There is a fear amongst her friends that she may be sliding too deeply into a Reformist frame of mind.' He said the word 'Reformist' as if it were a very bad word indeed and hastily crossed himself and lifted his eyes to Heaven in an exaggerated manner.

'John, you know better than to joke with me about such matters,' I said sternly. 'You know I have no time for the Reformists.'

'Yes, but even you, Honora, with your narrow-minded Popishness, must see that to think about these matters should not be a crime.' For once he spoke with all sincerity and I was forced to examine my conscience. Perhaps I was just a little narrow-minded, but more than content to remain that way since I knew I was right.

'Anyway,' he continued, 'the Queen naturally has enemies - who at Court does not? And these enemies are busy already plotting her downfall.'

I admitted that, whatever her religious beliefs, it was a sad reflection on our times that the Queen's position should be so uncertain, and I thanked God once more that Anne had escaped from a similar fate.

I missed John sorely after he left. It had been a wonderful visit which had added a different colour to my life at Umberleigh for a few days, but it also served to remind me that never again did I want to have anything to do with the dangerous and duplicitous life of the Court.

Chapter Thirty

The year 1545 began with a joyful event. My plain and homely daughter Philippa was married to James Pitts in Atherington Church. It was no grand marriage for her, and her life would never be luxurious, but she had the security of knowing that she had gained for herself the trust and love of a good and steadfast man. Mary was by now almost fully recovered, thanks to James' patient and persistent attentions and she looked smilingly on as the newly married couple left to begin their life together. I had feared that she may resent James' love for Philippa but to my relief she had seemed, in the weeks leading up to the marriage, to bear no jealousy.

'How are you feeling now, Mary?' I stood by her side as they rode away.

'Well enough, thank you, Mother.' Her words still came slowly as if drawn from some well deep within her. 'You and I and Jane can now settle down to a life of peaceful spinsterhood together.'

She turned away then and walked inside, her head bent. I wondered sadly if she did indeed bear some resentment that she, who had been the beautiful one, should be left at home while plain Philippa rode away with her lover.

But settle into peaceful domesticity we did, and life went gradually from tranquil to dull as the months went by. Mary no longer needed me as she had before and since I had more time to myself, I began to think and remember, and my thoughts and memories were rarely pleasant. Day after day, night after night I pined for my briefly known and cruelly lost happiness.

Each morning when I arose my pillow would be wet with tears from a night of crying for the love I had known. So often I would dream that Arthur was by my side and I would reach out to hold him, hugging him close against my body, loving him, feeling him loving me, then I would awaken to find the bed in disarray and only a crumpled pillow in my arms. At those times I would contemplate death and wish for the peace it could provide. I could not bear to go on living day after day without him. I was sinking further and further into a despondency of spirit similar to that which I had experienced years before when I had lost him for the first time.

My melancholy was interrupted in July by the arrival of a messenger. He came from Cornwall and bore a message from my nephew Richard's wife, Maud.

'Dear Honora,' it read, 'please come as soon as you can to Stowe. Our dearly beloved son Roger has been drowned in a tragic accident on one of the King's ships. Richard is bringing his body back to Cornwall for burial. Your loving niece, Maud Grenville.'

Once again history was repeating itself. Whereas years ago, my own misery had been overtaken by John Arundel's illness and death, again I was forced out of my personal sadness by another's suffering. My heart went out to Maud, I also knew how it was to lose a son. I hurried to prepare myself for the journey to Stowe.

I set out early the next morning accompanied only by Elizabeth Husee and two grooms. The morning was fine and sunny, and it promised to be a pleasant day for the trip

Chapter Thirty

to my childhood home. We passed through Torrington a few hours later and I had been so wrapped in my own thoughts that I had quite forgotten what lay just to the west of that town.

But suddenly there it was, the ruined shell of Frithelstock Priory. I took a great gasp and reined my horse to a standstill as the enormity of what had happened there dawned on me. This was my monastery now and even if I had not personally torn apart the Holy Relics and pulled down the walls, I remained the guilty party here. Gone were the monks toiling patiently in their fields, gone were the orchards and the herb gardens. All that remained were the burnt out shell and crumbling walls of the priory, overgrown now with brambles, cloaked in deathly silence. And the plundering had been done in my name.

Elizabeth looked at me with a worried expression on her face. 'Are you all right, My Lady? You look very pale.'

I collected myself as best I could. 'Oh, yes, thank you, Elizabeth, I am well. What's done is done,' I added softly as we moved off again.

She must have wondered what I meant, having no knowledge of my ownership of the priory, but as a good servant should, she kept her curiosity to herself. The remainder of the journey passed in almost total silence, as I was in no mood for talking and we reached Stowe towards evening.

Maud came out immediately to meet us. The grooms moved off with the horses and Elizabeth saw to the baggage. I was left alone with Richard's wife in the gathering twilight. She said nothing but her face was lined with grief. We had not seen each other since she and Richard had left Calais just before the troubles and there was so much to say but none of it needed to be said. We simply stood there holding each other and crying softly together, two women each consumed by their own grief, helping each other to bear it.

We were joined by a young woman who approached silently with a small boy by her side. Maud moved away from me at her approach and introduced us.

'Honora, this is Roger's widow, Thomasine.' She reached out to the woman and gently drew her closer. The boy looked shyly towards us, chewing violently on his thumb as he did so. 'And this is Richard,' Maud added as she lovingly picked up her grandson in her arms

So, this was Roger's only living child, the heir to Stowe and to the entire Grenville fortune.

Together we moved towards the house. As we did so I looked about me and was once again assailed by the unchanging solidity of it. This was Stowe, my childhood home, the rock upon which my life would forever be anchored. How I wished then that I had been born male; that I, like this unknowing child could have inherited and remained here, never needing to leave. How unfair this life was to women, forever forced to move and change, to go wherever the tide of marriage and fortune took us.

Richard was not due back until the following day with his son's body and I retired early, exhausted by the journey and the overwhelming sadness of the day. I slept in my old chamber, the same one I had slept in as a child. As I drifted off to sleep my last thought was of the first Mistress Basset and of how I had thwarted her plan to spend a night there.

The next morning, soon after breakfast, I had a visitor. It was my brother John, now twenty years settled into his post

Chapter Thirty

as Rector of Kilkhampton. We had not seen each other since that day when he had first taken up his living but the loving bond which we had formed as children still remained.

'Honora, dear sister, it is so good to see you.' He kissed me fondly. 'You can have no idea how we worried for you during your imprisonment. I fear God must have wearied of my constant prayers for your safety.'

'Enough of that!' I did not wish to spoil our time together by dissolving into tears again. 'Tell me of yourself.'

He obligingly related for me a brief description of his life since we had last met, which was, of course, not nearly as tumultuous as my own. He finished his story by saying, 'I am currently taking care of the Parish of Morwenstowe whilst the incumbent, Reverend Fisher, is unwell. It is a wonderful place, Honora, right near the cliffs. I need to travel there today to visit a dying parishioner. Would you care to ride there with me?'

I agreed readily and so we set out. It was only a three-mile ride from Stowe to Morwenstowe and the journey took us first through the Coombe Valley. As we descended deeper into the leafy depths, I could feel John growing tense beside me.

'I have not ridden this way since we were children Honora,' he said quietly. 'I always take the high road from Kilkhampton to Morwenstowe.'

'It does no damage to visit the past,' I replied softly, 'even if it hurts a little.'

Soon we detoured from the track which led over the ford and up the other side of the valley and found the way to our special spot. It remained unchanged and we dismounted silently. So much had happened in my life since I was last here. I had reached the pinnacle of happiness and the depth of despair, my handsome Prince had come and transported me to far-off places where I had lived the life of a fine Lady. Then my Prince was taken away and I had fallen headlong into imprisonment and disgrace. And through it all this little place in the Coombe Valley had remained the same. The same birds still hopped about happily in the branches of the trees, the same rivulet still trickled merrily along the valley floor, and the same rocks still stood solidly in the clearing.

What John's thoughts were, I do not know. Perhaps he thought of Richard and of how he had spoilt this place for us and if he did so then he must have sorrowed for Richard and for the tragedy which had now visited him. After a while we moved off again, leaving our little spot which, for me at least, had regained its lost magic.

Morwenstowe was as lovely as John had told me. The solid stone Church was built in a sheltered spot only a few hundred yards inland from the sea. It would have been protected there from the fierce gales of the North Cornish coast and had stood defiantly since Norman times. Indeed, the ancient doorway through which we passed was the same through which our ancestors had walked for almost five hundred years and the Baptismal font just inside the door had been carved by a Saxon stonemason even before that.

John left me for an hour, during which I prayed in the Church, while he went to the village to visit the sick parishioner and when he returned, he suggested we walk out to the cliff top. After checking that my horse was still securely tethered, I followed his suggestion. The day was fine and warm but out on the cliff a stiff breeze blew from the

Chapter Thirty

sea whipping up large waves which crashed rhythmically against the cliffs far below us.

'I love to come out here,' John said after we had sat a while in silence. 'I feel just as close to God here as I do in a Church.'

I must have answered something, but my attention was elsewhere. A group of young pigeons was flying out over the water. They had left their nests which were situated in small cavities in the rocks beneath us and were fluttering happily about, supported by the strong breezes which blew up the cliff face. They were gorged and contented from feasting on the plentiful seeds and fruits from the headland plants. It was almost as if they flew for the sheer joy of it and for no other reason at all. Then, as I watched, a peregrine falcon which must have been watching from high in the air above came hurtling down like an arrow and plucked a pigeon out of the air, flying effortlessly away with it still flapping helplessly between its talons.

'Oh, no!' I shouted and jumped up impotently waving my arms about as if I could somehow induce the falcon to drop its prey.

'What is it, Honora?' John had apparently not seen what I had.

'A peregrine John, it took one of the pigeons!' And suddenly the grief, which I had been so carefully suppressing, overwhelmed me again. 'It was just like they did to us!' I exclaimed. 'We were not harming anyone. We had done no wrong and wished no evil on the King. John, we committed no crime and yet we were taken just as cruelly and without warning as that pigeon was. And Arthur never came back to me.' My voice rose to a high-pitched wail as I broke down again at the memory of the terrible injustice which had been done to us.

I wept again, as I had so often, great storms of tears which seemed as if they would never stop. So painful was the wound in my heart that it burned like a fire within me, threatening never to stop.

John spoke to me then, both as a brother and a priest, telling me all the things which I knew to be truth but found so hard to accept.

'Honora, you can never go back. I know you suffer, and God sees it too, but you must accept what has happened. Arthur is dead and that part of your life is over,' he said gently.

'And how I wish that I was dead too, John. I cannot go on like this,' I sobbed.

'I agree Honora that you cannot go on like this,' he said, 'but wishing for death is a sin. Only God decides when our time is to come. Sister dear, look about you and take heart from that which is good in your life. You still have two of your sons, your daughters and grandchildren. You have returned to your peaceful life here in the West. Everybody has sadness, Honora. Tomorrow is Roger's funeral. Richard and Maud have no other son to ease their grief, but they will recover, as you also must recover.'

'Yes, John, I know you speak truth and sense,' I said bitterly, 'but Arthur was my soul and without him I have nothing.'

'Then I know not what to say to you except to counsel you to pray, for only by prayer can you achieve your salvation both now and for eternity,' he sounded disappointed in me.

Chapter Thirty

'I really thought that you were made of sterner stuff than this, Honora.'

'But John,' I cried, 'you have never loved as I have! You have never possessed and been possessed as totally as I have by another person!'

'No,' he replied more harshly than I had ever heard him speak, 'and from what you are saying it is perhaps fortunate for me that I have not.'

I said no more. He could never understand that even in all my anguish and despair I would not regret the love I had known with Arthur.

Richard returned that afternoon with his son's body. He brought the coffin back to Stowe in preparation for the funeral procession to Kilkhampton the following day. He looked so gaunt and haggard that for the first time in my life I felt some affection for my nephew, so great had been his loss.

Later that evening he told Maud, Thomasine and me what he had heard of the tragedy which had befallen the King's flagship, 'Mary Rose', as she had passed out of Portsmouth harbour.

'Apparently some fool of a gunner had failed to chain the cannons and had left the gun-holes open. When the ship turned to exit the harbour the guns all slid to one side and the ship listed heavily bringing the open gun-holes under the level of the water. Within a few minutes the ship filled with water and sank, drowning all on board.' He related the story matter-of-factly, but his voice was edged with grief.

'Did none survive?' Maud asked in a small, self-controlled voice.

'Not one,' answered Richard. 'In the full sight of King Henry, his most beautiful and valuable ship sank out of sight taking her entire crew with her.'

Thomasine gave a little gasp, as she pictured her husband's sudden and violent death in the cold waters of Portsmouth harbour. Maud moved closer to her daughter-in-law and placed her arm about her, drawing Thomasine's head down to rest on her shoulder. Richard still sat stony-faced in his chair, alone with his grief. But a short time later when Thomasine was helped away to bed by her gentlewoman, I observed Maud approach her husband and tenderly help him to his feet. How she managed to love Richard I never knew but love him she did, and together they would face their tragedy.

The funeral took place the following morning at Kilkhampton. John led a beautiful service for his young kinsman and Roger was laid to rest with dignity amongst his ancestors.

After the funeral I stayed on at Stowe for several weeks. There was nothing particular for me to do but Maud seemed to want me to stay. Richard was soon off and about his business leaving the women to attend to theirs so perhaps it was just my company she craved. It took a great effort for me to fight the desire to wallow in my own misery but, taking heed from John's strong words and still smarting under the weight of his disapproval, I did my best.

Just before my departure in early September, John paid me one last visit.

'I know I spoke harshly to you, Honora,' he said, 'but sometimes it is necessary to speak thus.'

Chapter Thirty

'Were you speaking as a brother or as a Priest, John?' I asked.

'More as a Priest, I think,' he replied after consideration. 'Did my words help you, do you think?'

I was silent for a long time.

'John,' I said at last, 'nothing has changed for me. Yes, I have heeded all you have said and understood the correctness of it, but I am not like you and never have been. Do you remember when we were young together?'

He took my hand and squeezed it tightly.

'Yes, dear sister, I do. You were the comfort of my childhood,' he said warmly.

'Even back then, John, we were so very different. You were always the spiritual one and took your strength from God, and God has not failed you. It was I who protected you from Richard and gave you some comfort, but God was always your mainstay, was he not?'

He looked shocked.

'Yes, of course He was. And so He is for all of us.'

'Not for me, John, not anymore, not ever perhaps.' I looked away from his dismayed expression, not wanting to meet his eyes. 'Even when we were young, and I was pious and devoted it was not your kind of devotion. My love for Jesus was more because of the kind eyes in his statue than for any other reason. And now, even though I stick to the old ways and do not wish for changes to the Mass, it is only because I love the ritual and the mystery of the way we worship.' I forced myself to look him full in the face. 'Sometimes, John, I wonder if God cares for us at all.'

'Oh Honora, sister dear, you cannot mean that. God sees everything and takes all into account. Pray, sister, pray for guidance and forgiveness.' He looked so terribly upset and I realised then that this was one battle I needed to fight alone. John would never be able to understand how I felt, and I was being heartless to express my doubts to him at all.

'I am sorry, John,' I told him sincerely. 'Please forgive me for saying such foolish things. Perhaps my mind has not yet recovered from my troubles and is still clouded. My words meant nothing. Let us part as friends.'

'Always friends, Honora,' he said, relief flooding his voice. 'I will always be your friend and loving brother. Go with God, dearly beloved sister.'

My travelling companions and I left Stowe the next day, taking a more southerly route which not only avoided Frithelstock but took us towards Potheridge where Frances lived with her new husband. We arrived there in the late afternoon, having sent one of the grooms on ahead to notify Frances of our impending arrival.

As we rode into the stable yard, we were first greeted by two small children who ran out of the house excitedly.

'Grandmother, Grandmother!' Nora and Arthur aged six and fours years old almost knocked each other over in their hurry to reach me first.

I did not know who to cuddle first, so I took one in each arm and held them both until Arthur began to wriggle. I let him go then but Nora continued to cling on to me. 'I have missed you, Grandmother,' she whispered into my ear.

I felt such a surge of love for that child. 'When you are rested, Grandmother, can we go and look at the plants in the garden?' Bless her, she remembered all I had told her two years earlier and now she wanted to learn about how they could cure us when we had 'bodily ailments'. I had no

Chapter Thirty

recollection of using that phrase to her previously, but I must have, for she would not have heard it from anybody else.

So, over the next few days, I began instructing her about the plants but warned her not to try any of them unless I was with her because the wrong plant could do her much harm.

'Could the wrong plant cause me to die, Grandmother? Mother told me that Grandfather died. Did he eat the wrong plant?"

I had to control my tears then as I explained to her that her grandfather had died because his body was old and tired. I watched her face as she absorbed this information and was steeling myself for more questions when Frances approached with Arthur running by her side, one-year old Margaret in her arms and baby Marie in the arms of the nurse.

Nora and Arthur went off to play whilst Frances and I spoke together.

'Are you happy with Thomas?' I asked her.

'I am happy with my children, Mother,' was her guarded response, 'and Thomas is frequently away on business.'

My heart went out to this most gentle of creatures at that moment, for the answer to my question was held in what remained unsaid.

Even so, I spent three happy days with the little family at Potheridge before completing my journey back to Umberleigh. I was determined to keep pleasant thoughts in my mind and not to sink back into depression, but such determination is difficult to maintain.

Chapter Thirty One

Another year went by and life at Umberleigh continued unchanged. Jane and Mary between them managed the running of the house and there was little for me to do. Philippa and James Pitts were our most frequent visitors. They called often, and we spent pleasant, if unexciting evenings together. George was rapidly becoming one of the best businessmen in the district and was gaining the same kind of respect that his father had known. He was now a strong and upstanding young man of twenty-two years of age and had recently decided that the time was right to commence looking for a wife. He was methodically examining the prospects of all the major landholders in Devon who had daughters of a marriageable age. George would never be carried away foolishly by the torrents of unbridled passion and make an unwise choice!

Just when I was beginning to think that I would go mad from boredom John Wallop arrived in late July 1546 to save me from myself. He was as completely unchanged as ever and blew into my life like a fresh breeze, reviving and refreshing me.

'Honora, my dear, too long a time has passed without the pleasure of speaking to you,' he said, as he took my outstretched hands in his own. 'Oh, life is dull without your company.'

'John Wallop, happy as I am to see you, I must beg you not to complain to me about your life being dull,' I said, half laughing and half serious. 'If you really want to know about boredom, just stay here with me for a few weeks. I am nearly dying of it.'

'And to think when I last saw you, you were the perfect picture of rural contentment,' he said. 'In fact, I seem to remember you saying that the last thing you wished for was stimulation and excitement.'

I sighed. 'That was then, but I find that I am stifled here with nothing to do and now that everything has quietened down in London I am seriously considering travelling back for a while. I do, so wish to see my family there.'

'That might not be such a good idea, Honora,' John said at length.

'Why not, John, is there more trouble? I hear so very little from London.'

'There is always trouble,' he said. 'The King is sick and irascible. He is heavily under the influence of his ministers, Wriothesley for one.'

I shuddered at the mention of that name.

'Oh, yes, I remember now that I vowed never to return while he was about,' I said.

'There has recently been a spate of martyrdoms,' continued John. 'Your friend Wriothesley has personally turned the screws of the rack during his questioning of a young lady by the name of Anne Askew. Her crime was that she was too keen on debating matters of a religious nature and leaned too strongly to a Reformist frame of mind. Her folly was that she pig-headedly refused to recant any of her views when faced with death.'

'And what happened to her?' I asked quietly.

'Oh, she burned,' John replied, feigning carelessness. 'She was too weak from the torture to walk to her execution so was carried in a chair to Smithfield and tied to the stake by a chain around the waist. Wriothesley had a bench brought close so that he could sit in comfort and have a better view of the entertainment.'

He gave a harsh little laugh then. 'His foul curiosity almost got the better of him,' he said bitterly. 'Gunpowder had been placed among the faggots to shorten the victim's suffering and if he had been just a little closer, he would have got more than he bargained for. As the flames caught hold the explosions almost reached him but not quite, unfortunately.'

'Did she suffer for long?' I remained subdued and pensive.

"Mercifully not,' he replied. 'The gunpowder did its work well. She was only twenty-five years old, Honora,' he added, bitterness heavy in his voice.

'But John,' I said, 'I would hardly meet with Anne Askew's fate. I am, after all, not a Reformist.'

'It matters not what you are, Honora,' he said. 'Take my advice and bide your time here in Devon. Do you really think Wriothesley cared a fig for Anne Askew's religious beliefs? Come now, think clearly. All he cares about is maintaining his position of power and satisfying his sadistic desires. Any victim will do, and you would be a prime target, having escaped his clutches once already.'

I saw the sense in that and put away any idea of returning to London. Over the next few days John remained at Umberleigh and no further mention was made of troubles of any kind. Together we walked over the fields and along the banks of the River Taw. In his company I regained my ability to appreciate the pleasures of country living and to take joy in small things.

Chapter Thirty One

One hot afternoon we were sitting on the riverbank engaging in our usual easy banter when he suddenly stopped talking and placed a finger to his lips.

'Sshh!' He tensed and leaned forward. 'There,' he whispered and pointed across to the other bank.

I craned forward but could see nothing for a while, then became aware of gentle ripples disturbing the smooth inkiness of the water.

'What is it?' I whispered.

'Just wait,' he answered in hushed tones, 'but do not move or speak.'

I did as I was bidden and after several minutes something broke the surface of the water in the shelter of some overhanging willow branches. It was difficult to see more due to the shade formed by the dense growth and I turned to John for explanation.

'It is an otter,' he said quietly. 'If it knows we are here we will never see it.'

We waited in silence and after a time the otter surfaced again, this time climbing right out of the water and onto the far bank. It lay there for a while, preening itself in the dappled sunlight then, with a lazy stretch which elongated its body so that it shone like a sleek arrow, it slid languorously, headfirst back into the water.

'Oh John, that was wonderful!' I gasped, taking a deep breath. I realised I had been holding my breath for fear of startling the creature away.

'Yes,' he answered, 'they are very shy of humans. We have been privileged.'

So once again, this soldier who spent his life travelling from country to country in the service of his King, was able to force me to stop and take stock of myself. Perhaps that was a trick he had learned through sheer necessity, the ability to take pleasure in the small things and to gain the most from each day, whatever the circumstances.

We parted, as always, with regret, he to resume his duties in Guisnes, where he now commanded the King's forces and I to continue with my peaceful life at Umberleigh. I often revisited the riverbank after that day. Usually the peace was unbroken but from time to time I would be blessed with the sight of an otter. From that time on I made sure that I tried to be more like my friend John Wallop and to appreciate the small beauties around me.

There was no further news from London until the following year. Then in early February a messenger arrived from the Court. My daughter Anne sent him, and her news was momentous indeed. The King had died on the twenty-eighth of January at Whitehall Palace. We now had a new King, a nine-year-old boy, Edward V. Anne assured me that she would be remaining at Court. Her position there was secure, that much had already been made clear by the new 'Protector', Edward Seymour, recently proclaimed Duke of Somerset. Thomas Wriothesley had been removed from power and had faded into obscurity.

It is difficult to describe my feelings on hearing of the King's death. Henry Tudor had been a powerful and terrifying King and a vain and selfish man, but he had also had his moments of kindliness and gentleness. If Arthur and I could have remained in relative obscurity at the fringes of the Court we may have continued to enjoy the King's good favour and not seen that frightening and ruthless side of him, which ended our happiness and ultimately, Arthur's

Chapter Thirty One

life. But having suffered as I did because of Henry VIII, I was not about to mourn his death

With a young boy on the throne, the chance of men such as Seymour to become King in all but name was there for the taking. Seymour had never been a friend of ours. Ever since his attempted trickery of us failed back in 1535 he had an axe to grind. I was surprised Anne was being allowed to remain at Court. Still, there was nothing to do but to wait and see what happened.

The first real change was that the Reformist movement became stronger under the new regime. There were no more martyrdoms such as that of Anne Askew; indeed, it was now more dangerous for those such as I who still practiced the old ways.

'Mother dearest,' George would frequently beg me, 'surely it cannot matter what outward form your worship takes. Please, just follow the stipulated practices, it is not much to ask of you.'

But stubbornly I refused. The only way I could bring myself to worship at all was to maintain the rites and rituals of my childhood. Beyond that there was nothing.

In the spring we had a letter from my daughter Catherine. She still held her position in attendance on the divorced Queen Anne of Cleves but was to be married during the summer to Henry Ashley. She would very much like George and me to attend her wedding and hoped that George would give her away. Despite some misgivings about travelling back to a troubled London, I agreed. Wriothesley was, after all, no longer a threat.

We set out in early June in fine warm weather. I was no longer young, and the trip was to be taken slowly. George had schooled me sternly about my actions once we reached the Capital, especially about quietly attending Church services and not voicing any opinions about doctrinal matters. He was obviously very concerned that I would not behave, which I found quite amusing.

After a week spent travelling, we reached our destination just as the weather was turning and were grateful to settle into our lodgings at Richmond. George had business to attend to in the city, so he said, and was not present the following day when Catherine came to visit. She looked radiant and had obviously been happy with her kindly mistress.

'Mother, oh my dear Mother, it has been so long!' I could feel her trembling as she embraced me.

I stood back and took a good long look at her. My second eldest daughter was nearly thirty years of age now, but her relatively easy life with Anne of Cleves had kept her looking youthful.

'Mother, I cannot believe it has been ten years since I last saw you. Oh, what terrors you must have experienced in that time whilst I have been cossetted here in London.' Tears brimmed in her eyes and fell softly down her unlined cheeks.

We talked for hours, she wanted to know about Calais and what had happened there after she left. She had heard very little about our imprisonment and what had happened in the lead up to it. So, much as it caused me pain, I had to relive those years again in the telling. As the story unfolded it became easier for me, almost as if it was someone else's life I was relating and not my own. At last it was over, and

Chapter Thirty One

she wept for me and for her ignorance of what I had been through.

'Oh, Mother, if only I had known,' she said sadly.

'Catherine dear, it is as well that you did not know. It would only have caused you distress and you could have done nothing to help us,' I reassured her. 'We had powerful men like John Wallop and Stephen Gardiner on our side, but even they were unable to save us,' I said.

And then, almost as if on cue, Stephen Gardiner was announced. James was with him, my baby, now twenty-one years old.

I was unsure who to embrace first. But James solved that for me by collecting me up in his strong arms and lifting me off the floor.

'Little Mother, it is good to see you again,' he said as he settled me gently back to my feet.

Once I had regained my composure, I turned to Stephen. It was five years since we had last met but he had not changed so very much. He still retained his plump healthy visage and benign good looks. However, on closer inspection I detected a tautness about his features which had not been present before.

He greeted me with his old warmth. 'Honora, dear friend, how have you been since returning to England?' His genuine concern was apparent in his voice.

'It has taken some time, Stephen,' I replied honestly, 'but I am recovering. I have had two visits from John Wallop which have provided a tonic on each occasion.'

He laughed merrily, 'Yes, John is good medicine to be sure.'

'And now to be united with two of my dear children and with you, my friend, it is impossible to feel anything but joy.'

The four of us went out to the garden for a private talk. Even with King Henry dead, it was not advisable to speak openly within earshot of the servants. We had so much to talk about and before long we had turned to the subject of the new regime ruling the country.

Stephen began by speaking of our new King. 'Edward is a good boy,' he said. 'There is no doubt about that, but he is only very young and completely under the domination of his uncle Seymour. That fellow, under the mantle of his self-styled title of 'Protector' has taken to referring to himself as 'We'. His airs and graces are preposterous.'

'I have no reason to be fond of Seymour either. He and his friend John Dudley almost succeeded in robbing Arthur and me of a large amount of money twelve years ago,' I said.

'Then you will be happy to hear that his friendship with Dudley is tenuous in the extreme,' continued Stephen. 'They have an uneasy truce at present and are to all outward appearances working together to rule the country but there is only room at the top for one of them and John Dudley is very keen for that one to be himself. Seymour had better keep a sharp watch behind him because Dudley's knives are being sharpened.'

'What of Wriothesley?' I asked, hating to even speak the name.

'Perhaps the only good thing to come from the exchange of power has been that Wriothesley has had the Great Seal taken away from him and is confined to his house in Ely Place. He will trouble you no longer, Honora,' he replied.

Chapter Thirty One

'And how do you fare in all this Stephen?' I asked. 'Do you take a part in public affairs now?'

'Very little,' he answered. 'I spend as much time as I can at Winchester. There is enough to occupy my time there and I stay away from Court as much as possible.'

'Have you lost your taste for the Court then?'

'Honora, you know that I never had a great fondness for the Court. But the truth is that the Court has lost its taste for me. You see, my dear, after a lifetime of remaining silent and treading the middle ground, I have at last begun to speak out. I like not the new direction our faith is taking.'

'Oh, Stephen!' I gasped, feeling both pleased and frightened by my friend's decision to take a stand. 'Is that not a dangerous path to take now after all this time?'

'Yes, Honora, it is,' he said truthfully, 'but now the changes are not only to do with who leads the Church. They are real doctrinal changes. I can no longer ignore my conscience but must go wherever it leads me.'

'Even to martyrdom?' I asked.

'If necessary, then I suppose so,' he replied. 'But still definitely not being made of martyr material I sincerely hope it does not come to that!' He laughed at this and I was obliged to laugh too but I almost wished he had not changed. At that moment I preferred my living, laughing, fallible friend to the prospect of a dead and saintly one.

Catherine and James had been conversing quietly between themselves whilst Stephen and I had been speaking. We left the subject of politics then and for the remainder of the afternoon the four of us engaged in far more light-hearted conversation.

A few days later, Catherine's wedding was celebrated at Richmond. Anne joined us for the event, so for the first time in many years Catherine, George, Anne, James and I were united, even if only briefly. With Anne was her best friend, a young lady by the name of Mary Roper. I spoke to the two of them after the ceremony.

'Mary's grandfather was a very famous man,' said Anne smiling at her friend proudly.

'Oh Anne, do not brag about that,' said Mary blushing.

'But I must,' continued my daughter. 'Mother will be well pleased when I tell her.' She turned, smiling broadly, to me. 'Mary's grandfather was Sir Thomas More, Mother.'

'Well, now I know who it is, I must say it is something of which to be proud,' I said to Mary. 'You have a saint for a grandsire, my dear.'

At this stage we were joined by James.

'A saint, how so? Whose grandsire is a saint?' As usual James was not bothered by formalities.

'James,' said Anne, her sense of propriety offended by such a breach of protocol, 'allow me to introduce you. This is my friend Mary Roper. Her mother was Sir Thomas More's daughter Margaret.'

'I am very pleased to meet you, Mistress Saint,' said James, bowing low over her hand. And he did indeed seem pleased. His eyes glowed with an appreciative light as they met hers.

The remainder of the afternoon was spent in agreeable conversation. Whenever I glanced in his direction James was still to be seen in the company of Mary Roper. Judging from the gentle sounds of her frequent laughter she did not mind his attentions in the least.

Chapter Thirty One

Sir Henry Ashley, Catherine's new husband, had land at Hever in Kent and Catherine left the service of Anne of Cleves and moved there after her wedding. It had been a happy sojourn for me in the city and had rejuvenated me greatly to be once more in the company of my friend Stephen Gardiner and my family, but my home was at Umberleigh and at the end of June George announced that he had been away too long already, so we set out for home.

Back at Umberleigh I was far better equipped now to face each day and enjoy life as far as possible. I was living together with George, Jane and Mary and a fair degree of contentment when the next blow fell.

I received a letter from James in late September telling of the arrest of Stephen Gardiner for speaking out against the religious reforms. It was not known at this stage when, if ever, he would be brought to trial but in the meantime, James was running Gardiner's household. There was hope of a quick release and I was not to worry.

I did indeed worry very much and very often until, as hoped, the release came in December of that same year, but it was understood that Stephen was now to be closely watched. Cranmer, the Archbishop of Canterbury, who was instrumental in designing and pushing the reforms, personally warned our friend that his days were numbered if he continued not to conform to the new doctrines.

Chapter Thirty Two

Early in the following year, 1548, I was blessed with another grandson. My dear daughter Philippa and her husband, James Pitts, had a son whom they christened Arthur. Because they lived so close to Umberleigh I was able to spend a great deal of time with little Arthur Pitts and he filled a space in my heart which had been empty since Frances had taken her children away to Potheridge.

In early March I received a sudden and surprise visitor. It was my daughter Anne. She had travelled from London, where she was still employed at Court and was one of the gentlewomen in the service of Lady Anne Stanhope, the Protector's wife. Poor Anne had suffered a recurrence of the illness that had so weakened her years before and which had necessitated her leaving Court for a time. On this occasion she had felt the need to recover with her family in the comfort of her old home.

'Oh Mother, I never thought I would see Umberleigh again,' she sighed. She was lying on a cushioned bench in the solar chamber, gazing happily out over the green Devonshire fields. Her hair had been freed from the restrictive coils and formal head-dress of Court attire and was loosely tied under a plain lettice bonnet. The gown she wore was one of my own, a simple kirtle of plain cotton fabric. I believed her illness to be more to do with an exhaustion of the mind than a malady of the body. Rest was what she needed and Umberleigh was the best place for that, so I did not trouble her with questions although I was almost bursting with curiosity to hear the latest news from London.

Chapter Thirty Two

Gradually her spirits lifted and after the first week had passed, we began to have long talks. I had very little to tell her, so it was mostly Anne who did the talking.

'The trouble began two months ago when the Protector's brother, Thomas Seymour, married Catherine Parr, the King's widow,' she said. 'It is all very humorous really, but I can only see the funny side now I am far removed from it all.'

'That is often the case with such matters,' I agreed. 'Tell me more.'

'I do not know if you have ever met Thomas Seymour, have you Mother?' She asked.

I laughed at that. 'Oh yes, I have met him.' I told her what I remembered of that gentleman. 'He was one of those in Calais in 1539 who met Anne of Cleves on her way to England. My memory of him is of a vain and foolish fellow with a much higher opinion of himself than his abilities warranted.'

'You show yourself an admirable judge of character,' laughed Anne. 'He is also blessed with the worst sense of timing and judgement of anyone I know. Shortly after Catherine Howard's execution he began to court Catherine Parr but was forced to take a step backwards when King Henry himself chose that lady. As if that was not enough, he has, since the King's death sought the hands of Princess Elizabeth, Princess Mary and Anne of Cleves, being naturally turned down by each of those ladies in rapid succession! He turned to his old flame, Catherine Parr, as a balm for his wounded pride I think,' she concluded.

'What a foolish man to seek the hands of the Princesses,' I said. 'The Seymours do indeed have an inflated opinion of themselves these days.'

'My trouble began in earnest after his marriage,' continued Anne. 'The Protector's wife, Lady Anne Stanhope, is a proud and haughty lady. I had difficulty enough pleasing her before but now she is impossible. The trouble lies in deciding which lady has the highest rank. You are familiar with Court protocol, Mother, and know that rank is of the utmost importance at all Court functions.'

I agreed I had some experience of that.

'Lady Anne feels that as the wife of the Protector, who is also a Duke and an Earl, she ought to take precedence. But Thomas Seymour thinks that his wife, Catherine Parr, as the Queen Dowager is entitled to highest precedence. I really think Lady Catherine herself, as a lady of high intelligence, could not care less but her husband is determined to see it through.' She sighed in exasperation. 'So, you can see how difficult it is to live and work in such an environment,' she said.

'Such frustrations would indeed make for a great wear and tear on the mind and spirit,' I acknowledged sympathetically.

'But that is not all,' she continued. 'Thomas Seymour is making trouble in other ways, too. He tries to poison the young King's mind against his brother, the Protector, and bribes him with gifts and money. It is all very unpleasant and unseemly. Frankly, Mother, I have had enough of it,' her voice started to falter.

'Now, my dear,' I said firmly, 'you will think no more of Thomas Seymour and you will rest. You are home now and far away from such unpleasantness. Oh look!' I had glanced out of the solar window and seen horses arriving. 'I do believe young Arthur Pitts has brought his parents to visit us! You wait here, and I will bring them in to you.'

As the days passed, Anne told me all her troubles. Once she was able to see them in perspective, they were revealed more as petty annoyances than as grievous calamities.

'After all, Anne,' I said to her on one occasion, 'none of these difficulties places you in any danger. They are, after all, other peoples' problems. If Thomas Seymour cannot see where his follies are leading him then he is even more of a fool than we already know him to be. Bide your time, my dear, everything passes given time.'

Who better to know that for truth than I?

After several weeks at Umberleigh, Anne felt herself ready to return to Court and duly made her arrangements. The evening before her departure we were speaking of everything and nothing. I think I mentioned John Husee and what a good servant he had been. With a gasp Anne clapped her hand to her mouth.

'Oh, what a selfish fool I have been, so wrapped up in my own troubles. I have not thought to tell you!' she exclaimed.

'To tell me what?' I asked.

'Mother, Husee died just before I came here to you. He was still employed by the Court as a general letter-writer and messenger. His death was sudden and unexpected.'

I felt a pang of sadness. One more link with the past was gone. I had not seen or heard from Husee since returning to Umberleigh, but we had known each other well and parted as friends. My gentlewoman Elizabeth, who was kin to Husee, would need to be told. His death was one more in a long line of deaths and I was so used to grieving that I could not grieve for long.

Far more disturbing news arrived two months after Anne's return to London. James sent another messenger with the news that Stephen Gardiner had again been arrested. He was imprisoned in the Fleet Prison and this time his release was not expected. How I worried and fretted in my impotence. What could I do? Nothing at all. Just as Stephen himself had been unable to help Arthur and me years earlier so was I even more completely powerless to help him now.

James wrote regularly to keep me informed about Gardiner's situation, but it remained unchanged. He languished in prison and no date had yet been set for his trial. The summer came and went. Life in Devon remained unaffected by events in London. In September, James wrote of the death of Catherine Parr at Sudely Castle after giving birth to a daughter. I wondered what new follies Thomas Seymour would dream up now that he was widowed.

James also wrote of the ardent hope of the Protector that King Edward could be married to Mary of Scotland.

'However, his manner of conducting the courtship negotiations leaves much to be desired,' wrote James showing characteristic rashness by trusting his thoughts to writing. *'He has pressed the young King's suit by savagely routing the Scots in battle at a place called Pinkie. A strange way of seeking to seal a marriage alliance, if you ask me.'* I quickly burned this letter, having had prior experience of the dangers of the written word.

Chapter Thirty Two

Early the following year, Anne wrote to me and told of Thomas Seymour's arrest. This was so completely expected that the only feeling I had was one of amazement that he could have been so foolish. Apparently, having treated Princess Elizabeth with indelicate familiarity even during his wife's lifetime, he had immediately upon Catherine's death, renewed his suit for her hand. He had been warned by his brother that he must desist from this behaviour but had chosen to take no notice. Even on the day of his execution he wrote to both the Princesses urging them to conspire against the Protector. Princess Elizabeth summed up his character perfectly in a fitting obituary: 'A man of much wit and very little judgement,' was how she described him.

That year, 1549, saw an acceleration in the so-called religious reforms. These included permitting the marriage of Priests, the suppression of the Latin Mass and the abolition of most of the holy days. A new service was introduced together with a prayer book called The Book of Common Prayer. I was not alone amongst West-country folk who deplored these sacrilegious changes. Indeed, to the peasant population, so much of the colour and variety of their lives was bound up in religious symbolism that by taking it away, the reformists had denied a vast number of people of the whole meaning of their lives and had reduced them to the bare bones of the daily grind. Margery's husband, William Marres, was a close sympathiser with the gathering forces of protest.

'They've taken away our feast days and our saints' days, see,' he said by way of explaining his worries to George. 'How are we to know when to sow or reap or plough the fallow if we have not got those days to point the way? If I have not got the winter corn in by Hallowmass I might as well forget it.'

'William,' George explained patiently, 'Hallowmass is the first of November. That has not changed.'

'First of November, first of November,' muttered William. 'And what is that supposed to mean, I ask you?'

'George,' I interjected, 'most of the families about here have no notion of the secular calendar. Their year is measured by the holy days.'

'Well, they will have to learn,' said George doggedly.

'It is not only a loss in the practical sense,' I tried to explain to George, 'but the colour and variety has gone out of the working peoples' lives. God knows, they have little enough to celebrate apart from their Saints' days.'

'They are removing all the ornaments,' went on William. 'People have precious little beauty of their own, only the holy images in the churches. Now they are destroying even those, and for what reason?'

I reminded George of the beautiful gilded shrine which used to hold pride of place in Atherington Church.

'And do you know where that is now?' William retorted angrily. 'Trodden on and broken all to pieces under the boots of the commissioners, that is where.'

The Rebellion began in Devon. In village after village the parishioners compelled the Priests to don their vestments and celebrate the Mass in the old fashion. It soon spread to Cornwall and by the end of June large areas of both shires were in open rebellion. George was incensed.

'What do they think to gain?' He paced backwards and forwards in his fury. 'The only result of all this will be more hangings and more commissioners. Our Churches will most likely end up worse off than those in other shires.'

I had to agree that the rebellion was doomed to failure, but I still admired those who risked their lives in defence of Catholic ways. The rebels came closest to some kind of success at Exeter, which they encircled. A priest called Walsh, who was a leader of the group of rebels surrounding Exeter, only narrowly prevented his followers from setting fire to the town. His reward was to be hanged by John Russell, the leader of the government forces, dressed in his vestments with a bucket of holy water and a pair of Rosary beads hung around his neck in mockery.

By the end of August, it was all over. Thousands of peasant households mourned their menfolk, either killed on the battlefield or hung on the gallows. They had achieved nothing. Fortunately, the violence had not got as far north as Umberleigh.

Another indirect casualty of the rebellion was the Protector himself. His power struggle with John Dudley had continued unabated ever since King Henry's death. Dudley used the Scottish campaign and the Rebellions to mount an attack on Seymour's position. For there had been another rebellion at the same time as ours. In Norfolk a man called Robert Kett had led another more serious revolt which was ruthlessly put down by Dudley's forces. Dudley had also covered himself in glory at the Battle of Pinkie. He began gathering together a band of adherents, those who had been left out of the exclusive group currently governing the country. He was aided by the Protector's own unpopularity. Seymour's despotic arrogance was a sore point with everybody, even his cronies. The common people hated him with a vengeance, so it was with no difficulty at all that, on the fourteenth of October, Dudley and his cohorts had Seymour arrested and sent to the Tower, stripped of his title of 'Protector'.

'There is no mercy given when thieves fall out,' was my only comment when news of the deposition reached Umberleigh. I cared not which of those two ruled as long as I could be left in peace. My daughter Anne wrote to me soon after.

'Mother dear, as you so wisely told me, everything passes given time and in so short a space of time my life has once again turned serene. I am now employed as gentlewoman to cousin Dudley's wife, Jane Guildford, and a kinder, gentler mistress I have never known.'

So at least my daughter was happy and with that I was content. The year 1549 ended and my only real worry was for my good friend Stephen Gardiner, to whom the exchange of power had meant little. He was still a prisoner with no hope of release.

But for one prisoner release came quickly. John Dudley, in an act of beneficent kindness designed to win over the last few nobles who still adhered to Seymour, freed him from the Tower in February 1550. He was not given anything like his former power and his title 'Protector' was not given back to him, but he was pardoned, and to cement their renewed friendship one of Dudley's sons was married to Seymour's daughter Anne.

Chapter Thirty Two

'So, the thieves have been reunited,' I observed, at this latest development. I think we all felt that the honeymoon would not last long.

It was only a few weeks later that a messenger arrived from Stowe. My nephew Richard had died from an illness he had contracted during the uprising. The rebels (who I quietly regarded as loyalists) had attacked and occupied Trematon castle. Richard had gone with a troupe of soldiers to try and regain it and had been captured and imprisoned in Launceston Castle. It was there that he contracted the illness from which he failed to recover. Whilst my sympathies lay with the rebels, who had in any case been defeated soon after, I was sad for Maud and immediately prepared for another journey to Stowe.

I travelled there on a chilly, overcast day in March. Together with Elizabeth and George and a few menservants, I again crossed the hills and valleys which separated Umberleigh from Stowe, which had a hushed, dismal air about it when we arrived just on dusk. Gone were the old sights and sounds which had so characterised Stowe, the tangible proofs of the throngs of ever-present children. What a change from the Stowe of my time and from that of my brother Roger and his wife Margaret, both long gone.

Maud came out to meet me. I gasped in shock at her appearance, she looked near death herself, so pale and haggard had she become.

'Maud dear, I came as soon as I heard the news.' I embraced her gently, fearing she would break to pieces in my arms, so small and frail and lonely she looked.

'Honora, it is good you came,' she replied with a tired, almost uncaring voice. I wondered if she had lost the will to live herself, now that Richard was gone. If that was the case then I could well understand how she felt, having been just that way myself so short a time ago.

'It is so quiet, Maud,' I said to her as we walked towards the house. 'Are Thomasine and young Richard not here?'

'Thomasine has remarried, Honora. She is now the wife of Thomas Arundel and lives at Clifton. It is so far away, I rarely see them at all.'

My heart went out to Maud. It seemed ironic that with so many Grenvilles being born to previous generations and so many families in Devon and Cornwall having Grenville blood that she should be entirely alone in this, her hour of need.

'I expect Thomasine and her husband to be here for Richard's funeral,' she said and at the mention of her husband's name she broke down in tears.

I consoled her as best I could, still unable to imagine what hidden virtues my nephew had possessed which had so endeared him to his wife. But perhaps others had been equally puzzled by my own devotion to Arthur. Who had ever understood the secret workings of a woman's heart?

The funeral took place on the twenty-fourth of March and Richard was buried at Kilkhampton beside his son. Maud was inconsolable during the service, which I blamed partly on the fact that the prayers were all in English as was stipulated in the new Prayer Book. I spoke to my brother John about it later.

'I do believe that when Latin was used, and no-one understood the words, they had a mystic and soothing effect,' I argued. 'Now there is a bluntness and coldness about them. To my mind they are not fitting prayers for a funeral at all.'

But John would not allow himself to be drawn into such an argument. He had held his parishes together during the Rebellion by the use of tact and diplomacy. He was not about to waste those efforts now.

'There is good and bad to be found in all things, Honora,' was all he said. 'What matters in the end is what is in our hearts. You know what Maud is feeling now, more than anyone else here. Go to her and comfort her.'

I tried every day during the week I stayed at Stowe to help Maud but each day she sank deeper and deeper into depression and her mind clouded, so that she became unable to speak or respond when we spoke to her. Even Thomasine and young Richard were unable to reach her.

It was with a heavy heart that I left my childhood home after that visit and I knew that I would not be seeing Maud again. George had returned to Umberleigh, but I needed some comforting, so journeyed on to Potheridge.

I was greeted on arrival there by my small darlings, Nora and Arthur. Oh, with what gladness did I hold them both to me! They had both grown so much since I had last seen them. Nora was eleven now and Arthur was nine. They were both bright, wonderful children. Frances had produced two more babies since my previous visit, a daughter, Katherine and a son Anthony. She told me with some bitterness of Thomas' gleeful reaction when his son was born.

'It was as if I had failed him up until then by having the gall to produce three daughters before his precious son.'

'Try not to be too upset, my dear, John Basset was just the same when I produced my first son after the birth of two daughters. Men must have their heirs, you know.' But all the same, I suspected that Thomas had been far crueller in expressing himself than my John would ever have been.

'Is all well between you two?' I asked with concern.

'No, not really,' she admitted, 'and before I forget, Mother, Thomas has said that you are not to voice any opinion you might hold regarding the uprising.' There was a catch in her voice, as if she was on the verge of tears. 'He says that if you do you will no longer be welcome in this house. Please, Mother, I could not bear it if I were never to see you here again.' She did cry then, and I reassured her that I would keep my opinions to myself for her sake.

My darling Nora piped up at that moment. She had been listening in to our conversation quite openly and I gained the impression that she frequently heard more than a child of eleven ought to. She demanded to know why I could not express my opinion if I chose to and took issue with her mother's explanation that it was because her stepfather disagreed with it. I could see her little brain working feverishly over this matter and did not miss the determined look in her eyes.

'That one will never be reluctant to express her opinions, methinks,' I whispered to Frances.

'Oh, no, Mother, she certainly will not. In fact, she has already begun.' We shared an indulgent laugh at this. But Nora was not finished with her questions yet.

'Why can girls not be heirs?' She demanded to know.

What could Frances and I say but that it was a fact that they could not and that was that? 'Our little Miss Nora is going to have a hard road ahead of her if she continues to question everything,' I said to her mother when the child had gone off to play.

It was such a pleasant sojourn with Frances and her growing brood at Potheridge. Thomas Monk was away for the entire time I was there, which meant that we were able to relax. It was with mixed feelings that I left them after a week and returned to Umberleigh.

It came as no surprise to me when, exactly one month after Richard's death, I received the news that Maud had been buried alongside her husband.

Stowe was to be a sad and empty place now, with young Richard, the heir, living so far away with his new stepfather. I hoped it would be well cared for until such a time as Richard returned to take up his inheritance.

Chapter Thirty Three

The months seem to go by so much faster the older I get, and the years follow each other so quickly it is difficult for me at times to remember just when certain events took place. It is often only by recalling other happenings of the same time that I can work it out at all. This is the method I have used to fix the year 1550 in my mind as the year of Thomas Wriothesley's death. I know for certain that it occurred shortly after Maud's death and just prior to George's wedding.

For George had, after a thorough and careful examination of the merits and suitability of every eligible young woman in Devon, selected Jaquet Coffin of Portledge as his bride. The only preparations we carried out at Umberleigh were a thorough cleaning and tidying of the house and surrounds as a welcome for the new Mistress Basset. The actual wedding was to take place at Portledge. I was to remain at home with Jane, as George chose to take only Mary with him. It was the first time Mary had left Umberleigh in eight years and she was both nervous and excited at the prospect.

'Do you think it is a good idea, Mother?' she asked. I had gone to her chamber in search of her and found her together with Elizabeth Husee packing gowns for the journey. Mary's voice still came hesitantly and had a deeper, hollow tone so unlike her voice of old which had been full of music and lightness.

'Only if you wish to go, Mary,' I replied. 'The matter is entirely your choice. George would very much like his sister to be by his side, but he is not such an ogre that he would force you to accompany him against your will.'

'I wish to go,' she continued, 'but I feel so safe and strong here at Umberleigh and I do not know how I will be once I am amongst a crowd of strangers. I am afraid I may do something foolish and draw attention to myself.'

'I am sure you will do no such thing Mary,' I said soothingly. 'If you feel afraid at any time simply go outside for a while, or into a room by yourself. You will be all right I am certain of it.'

I was in fact by no means certain of anything, but Mary was nearly thirty years of age now and unless she soon began to mix with people again, she would end up an old maid like Jane and Thomasine. Whatever happened I was very anxious that she go to George's wedding.

The marriage took place in early August and soon afterwards the travelling party returned, this time with an extra member, George's new wife, Jaquet. I had not met my daughter-in-law prior to the wedding, trusting to George's good sense in selecting his bride. I knew as soon as I saw Jaquet that my trust had not been misplaced. As she alighted from her mount and came towards me, I observed a tallish woman of moderately good looks and sensible attire. Her dark hair was tucked away neatly under her headdress and her riding gown was of good quality though of a sober and practical material. She gripped my outstretched hand firmly and looked straight into my eyes as she greeted me, showing just the correct amount of humility and decorum but not overdoing it. George had chosen well.

After spending a few minutes with Jaquet and then leaving it to George to introduce her to her new home, I looked towards Mary. How had the trip away affected her? To my surprise and joy, she approached me with a bouncing step such as I had not seen her use for over ten years. Her face was radiant with a hint of her youthful beauty.

'Well, Mary, how did you enjoy your trip away?' I asked, although the answer was shining from her face.

'Oh, Mother it was wonderful!' Even her voice was lighter. 'At first I was nervous and thought I may not be able to enjoy it at all but then I met someone who stayed by my side constantly and after that I had no trouble at all.' She suddenly looked sheepish and blushed to the roots of her hair.

I was almost too afraid to ask but the question was hanging in the air.

'Mary, was this someone a male person, by any chance?'

'Yes, Mother, it was,' she replied with a dreamy sigh. 'His name is John Wollacombe.'

The name was familiar to me as belonging to a good, sound, west-country family. I dreaded asking too much or raising Mary's hopes too high but at the same time I promised myself to investigate this possibility and to encourage a match if it was at all suitable.

Later that evening we sat in the parlour. George was telling us about his wedding and Jaquet joined in showing no nervousness or embarrassment. She was already proving herself to be a woman of practical good sense with no feigned coyness or superficial manners - an admirable wife for George. Philippa and James Pitts had joined us to welcome the new bride to Umberleigh and we were a happy and contented family together.

Chapter Thirty Three

'I have one piece of news which ought to please you, Mother,' George said during the course of the conversation.

'And what might that be?' I asked, sipping contentedly on my wine.

'Thomas Wriothesley has recently gone to meet his maker,' George replied.

I sat very still. I should have been happy, overjoyed even, but I was beset by a strange feeling of numbness. All that I had suffered, all that Arthur and Mary had suffered had already shown itself to have been such a cruel twist of fate, such an impossibly diabolical turn of events that I was hardened now to any strong feelings where it was concerned. Arthur was dead, Cromwell was dead, King Henry was dead and now Wriothesley was also dead. So much suffering and all for nothing. Only Mary and I were left to bear the burden and now she seemed at last to have her chance to break away from the chains of her suffering. My joy for her was tainted by an increasing sense of aloneness.

'Mother are you all right?' Mary was stroking my hand, begging me with her eyes not to dwell in the past.

I brought myself out of my reverie with an effort and smiled at her.

'Yes, my dear I am all right,' I assured her. I would bear it, there was nothing else to do.

Another winter came and went. John Wollacombe was quietly and patiently courting Mary. I told him of Mary's troubles in Calais and of the unknown suffering she had endured. He needed to know of those things if he was to understand her. It would have been unfair to both of them for him not to be told. The only facts I left out were the story of her love affair with Gabriel de Montmorency. There was no need for him to know about that. He seemed an understanding man, quite capable of giving Mary the time she needed. She was certainly not yet ready for marriage. I only hoped she would be ready before his patience gave out.

The following May George and Jaquet had their first child, a son, whom they christened George. Jaquet's pregnancy had been trouble-free and she gave birth with the same sensible steadfastness with which she did all things. George showed no excessive joy at this, the birth of his son and heir only nine months after his marriage. I thought of his own father, denied such happiness until he was an old man and wished my son would at least celebrate just a little, but that was not in his nature. He accepted it as no more than his due, just as he accepted everything. I could have kicked him!

That summer there was an outbreak of Sweating Sickness. We had almost forgotten about this curse as it had been many years since it had last struck. I worried constantly about my children in and near the capital, but they came through it unscathed. In late July, when the worst of the sickness was over and I was beginning to relax again, I received a letter from James.

> 'Dearest Mother, it pains me sorely to be the bearer of bad tidings but this time my tidings are unfortunately very bad indeed. Our dear friend Stephen Gardiner has been more closely confined than before. He has refused to recant and may now be under threat of a far more severe penalty. The conditions of his imprisonment are more rigorous. I beg you Mother, as Stephen's friend, come to London before it is too late.'

Chapter Thirty Three

I leaned back in my chair before continuing to read the missive so that I could digest the information. What could I do by going to London? Would I even be able to see Stephen? If he was so closely confined as James indicated, then probably not. But if I did not go and Stephen died it would be just one more cross for me to bear, to know that I abandoned my good and true friend in his hour of need. I read on.

> 'Secondly, dear Mother, and I know this news will pain you more than any other, I must inform you that John Wallop has become a victim of the Sweat. He died at Guisnes on the thirteenth day of July.'

The writing blurred, and I could read no further. Large teardrops fell onto the page, smudging the ink and running into each other, collecting in dirty black pools which smeared the words into illegibility. John Wallop, my dear, irreverent, cynical friend. He who had brightened even the bleakest day with his wit and humour, who had been the instrument of my healing after Arthur's death, who had taught me to laugh and smile at small things when the big things were too much to bear. I felt yet another part of my heart wither and die as I slowly accepted that he, also, was gone.

I made a hasty decision. I would make the long trip to London. I was no longer young, and my years of suffering had taken their toll, but Stephen was now the only one left of Arthur's and my small circle of friends. I had to see him if I could and if I was unable to see him, at least to get a message to him that I was close by. George tried desperately to dissuade me.

'Mother, will you never learn sense?' He fumed at me and punched his fist into his open palm. This was the closest to a show of passion I had ever seen from George.

'George dear, please do not shout so,' I chided him. 'You know I deplore such exhibitions.'

'You know very well that 'such exhibitions' as you describe them are not something in which I indulge as a rule,' he said in a wounded tone, 'but I cannot believe that you would be foolish enough to place yourself in danger having once experienced imprisonment already. By openly showing friendship to Gardiner at this time you are courting disaster not only for yourself but for your whole family.' His voice began to rise again.

'Oh, hush, George!' I dismissed his fears with a wave of my hand. 'That is nonsense and you know it. No harm came to you before when I was accused of treason, so why do you worry now? I am mistress of my own destiny, George and am not beholden to you or to anyone else. I choose to stand by my friend now and nothing you can say or do will stop me.'

The fact was that I cared not what happened to me. If I was to be imprisoned again then so be it. All the old fears for myself had gone, I had only my conscience to assuage. And so, in early September, taking only Elizabeth Husee and two grooms, I set out for London. It was a long and arduous journey for me to undertake but determination and, I suspect, a degree of stubbornness enabled me to overcome physical frailty and tiredness. We arrived in London a week after leaving Umberleigh.

Chapter Thirty Three

Upon arrival we were met by James, who took us immediately to our lodgings in one of Stephen's own houses. James was also living there and managing Stephen's business affairs for him.

'It does not look good,' James told me. 'He still nominally holds the Bishopric of Winchester but receives none of the benefits. The Council has sequestrated them.'

'Is he not to have a trial?' I asked.

'That has been mentioned and cannot, I think, be far off,' he said, 'although, Stephen has acquired an unexpected supporter.'

'And who is that?' I enquired.

'Edward Seymour,' said James, raising his eyebrows, and after my gasp of astonishment he continued. 'Yes, you may be surprised to learn that Seymour is not by far the most ardent of the Reformists. Indeed, besides endeavouring to have Stephen released he has also been trying to prevent the withdrawal of Princess Mary's license to practice the Catholic Faith.'

My surprise lasted only a short while. I had become so used to the unexpected twists and turns of political life that nothing really shocked me anymore.

'I do wonder,' mused James, 'if Seymour is not gambling on the young King's poor health becoming worse. Indeed, if King Edward were to die, Princess Mary would become Queen. To have been openly supporting her and Gardiner would stand him in good stead if that were to occur.'

'And is the King's health as bad as that?' I enquired.

'It is difficult to get a truthful opinion,' said James, 'but rumour has it that he will not live to attain his majority.'

But for the moment the King lived, and John Dudley held the reins of power. As I had feared, there was no chance for me to see Stephen, but James was still allowed limited access and was able to pass letters to him from me. I cared not whether I was found out.

The relationship between Seymour and Dudley, always one of suspicion, worsened during this time as Seymour openly opposed more reforms. He managed to gather some support in high places and already had popular support from the general population, as they had never supported the Reformist movement anyway. But fate again played its part and for the whole of September, just when Seymour was beginning to build a strong alliance to support him, he was laid low by illness. Dudley seized his chance. On the sixteenth of October Seymour was arrested and sent to the Tower. Dudley now had himself created Duke of Northumberland and was the undisputed ruler of England. He had achieved the pinnacle of his power.

I had a visit from my daughter Anne shortly after this. She was still happy in the service of Dudley's wife, Jane, but abhorred Dudley himself.

'Mother, he is the most ruthless man I have ever known,' she confided softly to me, looking hastily about her.

Having known many ruthless men in my time, I failed to be impressed but listened sympathetically.

'And I think he really feels he is the King. Now that Seymour is safely locked away there is no end to his arrogance,' she whispered. 'I really like Lady Jane, the Duchess. If it were not for devotion to her, I would not stay.'

'Hush now Anne,' I admonished her. 'Do you remember only a short while ago when it was the Seymours who

Chapter Thirty Three

troubled you so? And look how that changed. Bide your time, my dear, bide your time. Dudley's reign will be a brief one, I feel it in my bones.'

She agreed to do as I advised and then described for me the household of the newly created Duke of Northumberland.

'We are 166 persons in the household,' she said. 'Can you imagine that? All those people to minister to one man and his family! His retinue is grander and more populous than that of King Edward by far.'

I thought a lot during the next few weeks about Anne and her situation in Northumberland's household, but I did not worry for her. She was by now highly trained and qualified as a Lady-in-Waiting and had served several of the highest ranked ladies in the Kingdom. Her security would be assured whatever happened to the Dudley's.

Then in December, the blow for which we had been waiting in dread finally fell. Stephen Gardiner was sent to Lambeth for trial.

James and I hastened to be present at the hearing. There was a small public gallery in which we were allowed to sit. After half an hour, during which Cranmer and the other members of the bench talked mysteriously amongst themselves and shuffled papers, a silence ensued, and Stephen was brought in. He was not manacled; indeed, he wore his Bishop's robes and from his manner of dress might have been one of the presiding officers. But he was much changed. He was thinner and where the flesh of his face had been round and plump it now hung in saggy pouches, the skin grey and pallid from lack of good food and fresh air. His eyes alone, were unchanged and twinkled with good humour as he looked from one to the other of his judges, as if in challenge.

'Please be seated Bishop Gardiner,' said Archbishop Cranmer and immediately began to read out the charges.

As the indictments were laid before Stephen, one by one he vigorously denied each of them using solid and true arguments. As the afternoon wore on, I felt that he was doing very well and that the bench would have no other recourse than to set him free. He had certainly proved himself no traitor during his spirited defence. When all the accusations had been made and Stephen's arguments had been politely listened to, the bench retired to consider their verdict. After what I felt to be a very short time indeed, they reappeared.

'Stephen Gardiner,' Cranmer began, ominously omitting his title from the greeting, 'you are found guilty of plotting against the King in that you continue to oppose His authority in matters of religion. I therefore deprive you of your Bishopric and sentence you to imprisonment in the Tower of London until such time as you recant your treasonous opinions.'

The whole bench then stood and began to file out of the chamber. I was suddenly filled with the knowledge that this had been nothing more than a show trial. Stephen's fate had been sealed long before he entered the court room.

'Shame! Shame on all of you!' The outburst came from next to me. It was James who stood shaking his fist and shouting his condemnation, halting the departing councillors in their tracks. I stared in horror as he continued his tirade. 'You are all a bunch of petty tyrants and ignorant fools!' I tugged at his sleeve, begging him to be silent but there was

Chapter Thirty Three

no stopping him. 'How dare you imprison the finest mind and most noble spirit this country possesses? How dare you lock away the only one among you who has any goodness and integrity?' He was still shouting and struggling as the guards took him away. 'Shame! Shame on you!' His words echoed back into the stillness of the chamber long after he had gone.

As the ghastly reality of what had happened began to sink in, I sat as if frozen, for how long I knew not but I was aroused at last by a gentle touch on my shoulder.

'My Lady, Lady Lisle,' a soft voice spoke behind me.

'Yes, that is I,' I replied, still dazed and uncomprehending.

'Lady Lisle, it is Mary Roper,' the voice said. I turned around and recognised the young lady with whom James had been so friendly at Catherine's wedding, Thomas More's granddaughter. 'I also came to witness Bishop Gardiner's trial and have, since then, been downstairs to see what has become of James,' she said.

'James, James, what has become of James?' I repeated parrot-like, still unable to formulate any thoughts of my own.

'I am afraid he has been put in prison as well,' she told me.

At these words I was jolted out of my stupor and recoiled in horror.

'Oh no! Prison! What will they do to him? Which prison? Where have they sent him?'

Gently she told me, trying to soothe me by the kindly tone of her voice but nothing could soften the blow of the words she spoke.

'He has been sent to the Tower, along with his Master,' she replied.

'Then all is lost,' I said. Already I had one son gone from me through death and now James, the most gifted and dearly beloved of the three was taken from me. My heart, though hardened and scarred from being broken so many times, tore open and bled again.

Chapter Thirty Four

Mary Roper took me home with her. She sent a messenger to my previous lodgings for Elizabeth and the grooms that they should bring my belongings and horses to her family's house and then proceeded to care for me as though she were my own daughter. Daily she either went herself or sent a servant to the Tower for news of James but the answer was always the same.

'Master Basset is allowed no visitors and no messages.'

Christmas came and went. I was entertained by the Roper family as if I was one of them and a more remarkable group of people would be hard to find. They were at once devout and fun-loving, combining the religious observances and merry making of the season with ease. Whether they always were that way or whether they tried harder because of their enforced houseguest I know not for certain, but I suspect that there was no pretence and that I was merely a privileged on-looker into this family's normal way of life. Being surrounded by such people renewed my faith in humanity and took the edge off my agonised fears for James' safety.

'A letter has arrived for you, Lady Lisle.' Mary entered the solar one bitterly cold grey day in early January.

It was from George. All was well at Umberleigh. He was distraught on receiving my letter which described the trial and James' subsequent imprisonment. I really ought to leave London immediately and return to Devon. How could James be so foolish? My sister Jane Chamond had died. All this he told me, and more, with no more tact and sensitivity than a sledgehammer. The letter was as formal and impersonal as a Court edict.

I put the letter down heavily. My sister Jane was dead. She, who had given me such sound and good advice in my youth and who had taught me how to love again, was no more. She had lived over eighty years, a good long life. I had not seen her for the last thirty of those years and had seen her son but once, that child she had late in life after her second marriage to John Chamond, but I treasure her memory still and honour her wisdom and gentleness.

As I looked out over the freezing roof-tops and filthy streets of London I had a sudden yearning to return to the West. I did not belong here but was now a prisoner just as James was, unable to return until his fate was decided.

The so-called religious reforms continued and on the twenty-second day of January in that year 1552, Edward Seymour was beheaded for treason on Tower Hill. He had been hated during his days as 'Protector' but now, in death, he was mourned by a populace who hated Dudley with an even greater fervour and laboured under the yoke of the enforced changes. But it seems men never learn from others' misfortunes and Dudley persisted blindly, deluded by his momentary power and unable to see what I saw all too clearly. His days were numbered.

For the duration of that year I stayed with the Roper family. James and Stephen Gardiner remained in the Tower and we knew nothing except that they still lived.

'I have something to say to you, Lady Lisle,' confided Mary one day. It was a warm morning in spring and London was not as dreadful a place as usual. It was not yet so hot that the stench from the filth in the streets had become unbearable and we were able to sit in moderate comfort in the garden of her house.

'When I first met James at your daughter Catherine's wedding, I admit that I fell completely and madly in love with him,' she said with a sad little laugh. 'And for months after that he courted me with a persistence which I found very difficult to resist.'

'And what reason did you have for wishing to resist?' I asked.

'This is hard for me to say to you as James' mother,' she struggled for words. 'I do not wish to sound pompous or self-righteous, but I was never sure of James' true strength of character. Certainly, he was charming and intelligent and seemed sincere. Bishop Gardiner obviously had a high opinion of him. All that told in his favour.' She paused and sought for the right words to express whatever it was she wanted to say.

I came to her aid. 'But you felt that so many apparently good qualities might conceal an underlying weakness in his character?' I asked gently.

'Yes,' she seemed reluctant to admit it, 'he had acquired so well the courtly manners and bearing, and I have seen so many who use such manners to conceal a flawed nature that I was afraid.'

'James has suffered all his life from being misjudged, my dear,' I said sadly. 'At times it has seemed that I was the only one who could see what lay behind his facile exterior and that has been frequently dismissed as a mother's foolish fondness for her youngest son, I am afraid.' I reflected on all those who had accused me of favouring James, even my beloved Arthur. Only Stephen had long shared my faith in

James and had been rewarded for this faith by selfless, even reckless devotion.

'I feel so guilty now,' said Mary, 'now that I have seen the truth about him and am unable to tell him how dearly I love him.' She started to cry.

'Hush now, my dear, hush,' I took on the role of comforter. 'All will be well. The present situation cannot last forever. The King's health is in constant decline and Dudley's fall will come. Let us pray now that Stephen and James can be strong enough to survive just a little longer.'

Daily, we prayed together. All through that year and into the next, we waited and prayed and still nothing happened to ease our minds.

George wrote regularly, each letter a stern missive condemning James' foolishness and my own. In one brief line early in the year 1553 he wrote of the birth of his second son. This child had been christened James. I found that both wryly amusing and touching. Perhaps George had a sentimental streak in his nature after all!

In the spring of that year Dudley had his son Guildford married to Lady Jane Grey. This young lady was of the blood Royal, being the granddaughter of Henry VIII's sister Mary. King Edward's poor health was now talked of openly and his death seemed imminent. Dudley's plan was for the dying King to bequeath his crown to Jane Grey, thus ensuring that a Reformist would continue on the throne and more importantly, that he, John Dudley would remain in power.

In July Edward V died at Greenwich Palace and Lady Jane Grey was proclaimed Queen. For thirteen days Dudley was King in all but name, but the rightful Queen's supporters

Chapter Thirty Four

were too numerous and rapidly his own supporters deserted him. On the nineteenth of July, Jane Grey was deposed, Dudley was arrested at Cambridge and Princess Mary was declared Queen. The Roper household was just one of thousands to celebrate this joyous event. People danced in the streets and banners flew from the rooftops. Church bells rang from every belfry in the city. Mary and I hastened towards the Tower but were hindered by the crowds which seemed to become thicker as we made our way towards the river.

'Why are all these people here?' Mary asked a woman who, like us, was fighting her way through the throngs.

'Our blessed Queen Mary is said to be returning this way,' said the woman. 'She has been to the Tower and has freed the prisoners there.'

Then, as she spoke, a deafening shout went up. 'Long live the Queen! God save the Queen!' I was almost being crushed by the press of the crowd, but Mary grabbed my hand and helped me to step on to a cart, which was already packed with people and threatening to collapse under the weight.

'Long live the Queen! Long live Queen Mary!' As her entourage rode by, I had a glimpse of a stately, dark-haired woman in sombre clothes. Her face, smiling and regal, had yet the look of one who had suffered and who even now, seemed wary that this moment of triumph might pass.

Once she had gone by, the crowds dissipated, and we were able to continue on our way unhindered towards the Tower. Once there we were greeted by a scene of complete turmoil. The guards seemed not to know what to do or where to go. We approached one who seemed to carry some authority.

Mary spoke for us as I was at the point of collapse from the long walk, the heat and the jostling crowds.

'If you please, kind sir, my name is Mary Roper, and this is Lady Honora Lisle. We have come to seek news of Bishop Gardiner and his gentleman servant, James Basset.'

'Madam,' he inclined his head to Mary, 'My Lady,' he made a humble obeisance to me, 'Bishop Gardiner and Mister Basset have both been pardoned by the Queen and are even now on their way to the outer portal. If you care to come this way, I can take you to meet them there.' He seemed confused and unsure but was so careful to show us respect that I felt sorry for him. He, like so many, was to be caught on the wrong side now that the tide of events was to be reversed.

We reached the door just as James and Stephen had passed through. They were making their way shakily towards a barge moored a little way downstream. They were both squinting as their eyes were stung by the bright sunshine after so many months of incarceration. Their poor bodies were gaunt and weak from deprivation.

'James! Stephen!' I dispensed with decorum and, lifting my skirts, moved towards them as quickly as age and exhaustion would allow me.

'Honora! Mother! Mary!' They turned in unison and cried out in joy.

Oh, what a day that was! It took me weeks to recover, and indeed, for several days afterwards I was so ill and fatigued that James told me later he had feared that happiness at his release was to be replaced by sadness at my death.

As I was unable to stand or even to sit upright for more than a short time, Mary and James' wedding was celebrated in the chapel of the Ropers' house in order that I should be able to attend. A settle was brought into the chapel and placed along the side wall where I lay propped up in stately splendour as the two young people were married by Stephen Gardiner.

Thus, it was, that after twenty years of fear and misery, years which had seen the unjust and cruel suffering of so many good people, justice and rectitude at last prevailed. It came too late for Arthur, long since departed to his untimely grave. It came too late for me, hardened and embittered as I was. But for the young and optimistic the new era promised much, a new life patterned on the old ways, so long repressed and outlawed.

In August, Dudley was executed on Tower Hill. Showing extraordinary mercy, the Queen chose to let most of his supporters go with a fine and a warning. Those who did not meet with such clemency included that arch-reformist Archbishop Cranmer, the would-be Queen Jane Grey and her husband Guildford Dudley. They were all confined in the Tower.

That same month, Stephen was made Lord Chancellor. He was kept busy reversing all the reformist laws and bringing England back into the fold of the Pope. James was just as busy. He was still in Stephen's employ and had, as well, his new responsibilities as a husband. I remained in the Roper home as a guest but as I was no longer needed in London, once my strength had returned, I began to make plans to return to Umberleigh.

'Do not return until after the Coronation, Honora,' begged Stephen. 'It will be the culmination of all we have hoped for.'

I agreed to wait until October and wrote to George informing him that I would be back then.

'The Queen is planning her marriage,' James told me one day soon after his own. 'She is to marry King Philip of Spain as soon as it can be arranged.'

I was happy for that. England would have a Catholic King and after that the hope of an heir to quickly secure Queen Mary's tenure on the throne. What could be better?

'That is good,' I said, 'and what has my friend Stephen been working on? I never see him.'

'He has written a Statute of Repeal,' answered James. 'The Books of Common Prayer have been renounced, the Mass is to be restored and married clergy are to be disallowed.'

'Thank God,' I heaved a sigh of relief. 'Of course, I have never abandoned the Mass anyway, but it is nice to know I am no longer a law-breaker. What of those Priests who have taken wives?' I asked.

'They will have a choice,' said James. 'They can either quit their positions or to leave their wives. It is up to them.'

I laughed. 'A merry dilemma, to be sure!' Oh, we all felt so light-hearted in those early days of Queen Mary's reign. I was happier than I had been since Arthur's death and only wished he could have been sharing the triumph with me.

On the last day of September, attended by seventy ladies including my daughter Anne, the Queen entered Westminster. The following morning, I attended her Coronation in the Abbey. It was almost a family affair for me. Her train was carried by my daughter who had been given a prominent position in the retinue. Stephen placed the crown on her head and James stood close by his side during the entire ceremony.

Chapter Thirty Four

I had a grand view of the proceedings from my place of honour at the very front of the congregation. The Queen was resplendent in crimson velvet, minever fur, ribbons of Venetian gold, silk and gold lace. Princess Elizabeth and Anne of Cleves were also in attendance upon the Queen and at the coronation banquet in Westminster Hall they sat on her left hand while Stephen Gardiner sat on her right. It was a day of supreme jubilation for me and a fitting end to my time in London.

It was with very mixed feelings that I prepared to leave a few days after the coronation. We were still in high spirits from the ceremony and the heady joys of that day, but the leave-taking wrung my heart. I was over sixty years of age, too old to ever think of planning another such journey. Anne's and James' lives were busy and full in London, as was Stephen's. I tried not to think of when, if ever, we should meet again.

'Mother,' urged James as the day of departure drew near, 'I beg of you to take up Stephen's offer and accept the escort he has provided for you. I do not wish you to return to Devon in the same way you arrived, with barely more than the horse you rode upon for company. You are now a prominent lady again with powerful connections at Court. Please agree to travel in a manner befitting your station.'

I agreed to this. After all, I had been in this position before, playing at being a grand lady. There would be no harm in doing it again, even if it was only to be for one journey. A few days later, on the day of my departure, James and I faced each other for the last time. Anne and Stephen were unable to be present. We had said our farewells the day before. As I stood in the parlour with my son, I could see through the window the retinue Stephen had provided. There were two dozen liveried horsemen, armed for my protection and standing to attention, patiently awaiting my emergence from the house.

'How the worm turns,' I thought bitterly.

'This is goodbye then,' James said. 'Take care, Mother. God speed you on your journey and give you long life and happiness.'

I was barely able to respond, so great was the lump in my throat.

'James,' I pleaded with him, 'if you can get away please come to Devon soon? Please visit me there if you can?'

'I will do what I can, Mother,' he soothed.

'And say goodbye to Anne and Stephen for me will you not? And also pass on my love to Catherine if you ever see her. I am so sorry I have been unable to meet my grandson.'

For my daughter Catherine Ashley in Kent had been delivered of a son, called Henry after his father. But due to Ashley's firm adherence to the previous regime they had considered it wise to remain quietly in the country for a while until old allegiances faded into memory.

The Roper family were waiting in the vestibule when James and I came out. I parted from them fondly and gratefully. They had been like a family to me ever since the trial. Then with one last embrace for Mary and James, which tore my heart asunder yet again, I walked over to my splendidly decorated mount. A groom rushed forward to assist me, placing a little footstool for me to step upon. With great pomp and some assistance, I was seated, and the journey began.

Chapter Thirty Four

Oh, with what renewed vigour did I set out on that triumphant journey out of London! I headed west with my splendid retinue, feeling for all the world like royalty. As we passed through villages on the way people came out to stare and doff their caps and when we stopped for the night nothing was too much trouble for the innkeepers. I thought with cynicism of that day in Calais when I had been shut in my room and called 'traitor' and of how my own servants, many of whom had been with me for years, had turned from me. Much as I enjoyed myself on that journey, I never imagined for a moment that these folk would behave any differently.

Acting on a self-indulgent impulse, instead of heading straight for Umberleigh, I directed my escort towards Potheridge. The furore I caused when I rode up the drive to the house will remain in my memory to this day. The day was fine, and all the children were playing outside. Upon seeing my grand party approaching, they began running about in excitement. Nora, who was fourteen by then, gathered the little ones up in alarm. I expect, not recognising me from that distance, she was not sure if we boded well or ill. She was heading towards the house with her charges before she spotted me in the group. Almost dropping the babies in her surprise, she ran towards me, reaching me just as I was alighting on to the embroidered footstool which one of the grooms had brought with him all the way from London. Such ridiculous luxury!

Frances and Nora listened with rapt attention as I related all that had befallen me in the city.

'Thomas is away from home again, Mother,' said Frances with obvious relief in her voice. 'These are very uncertain times for him, as he has been such a vocal supporter of the reformists.'

'That is why we were alarmed when we saw your retinue arriving, Grandmother,' interspersed Nora.

'I am sure that Thomas need have no fear,' said I with naïve certainty. 'Queen Mary is a gentle and tolerant soul. I am quite certain she will be only too happy to leave people alone as long as they do not openly oppose her.'

I met Frances' two new sons, James who was two and baby Francis. When I commented that Thomas must be well-pleased now that he had three sons, I once again gained the impression that all was not well between husband and wife. Ever loyal, Frances said little, but the sadness was in her eyes when his name was mentioned.

I remained with my dear family at Potheridge for several days and, as on the previous occasion, when the time came for me to depart I did so with an uneasy mind. I dearly loved to see Frances and her family. Nora was a curly-haired delight and Arthur was becoming a studious, serious boy, much as his father had been. All the little Monks were nice enough children, but I did fear for Frances. She sometimes looked almost afraid when she mentioned her husband. I had not seen him on any of my visits so could only be glad for her that he seemed to be rarely at home.

Chapter Thirty Five

The year 1554 began with an unforeseen state of unrest throughout the country. It seemed that whilst Mary herself remained popular as Queen, the populace did not wish for a Spanish King. In the West there was little trouble but in the Eastern counties unrest rapidly turned to open rebellion. George, who was rising in importance in local affairs, was always among the first to receive the latest news from London. Never a supporter of Queen Mary, he spoke quite savagely when he brought the news of the rebellion to me.

'It seems your angelic and merciful Queen is to be no more reticent in the shedding of blood than her predecessors,' he said with an uncharacteristic show of feeling. He was still angry at me for going to London and for my prolonged stay there. The fact that my journey had turned out well and that I had arrived home in triumph with my armed and liveried escort had done nothing to appease him.

'What has happened?' I was alarmed by his outburst.

'Thomas Wyatt, a wild and impulsive man of Kent, has led a rebellion against Her Majesty,' George said briefly.

The name was familiar to me. 'Where have I heard that name before?' I asked.

'His father was that Thomas Wyatt who was too familiar with Anne Boleyn and almost lost his head because of it,' answered George. 'It seems the son has inherited his father's tendency to dice with death.'

'Tell me about the rebellion, George?'

'There is much opposition to this Spanish fellow marrying the Queen,' he said. 'Wyatt had no difficulty in collecting four thousand followers at Rochester, all of whom were prepared to express their displeasure along with him. They marched towards London and were defeated at Temple Bar. Wyatt and his fellow ring-leaders were arrested and placed in the Tower.'

'Is he there still?' I asked.

'Yes, he is,' answered George, 'but dozens of his followers have gone to the gallows.'

George then went on to tell me of the execution of Jane Grey and her husband as a direct consequence of the rebellion.

'That poor young girl, she was no more than a pawn in Dudley's game.' George really did sound upset. Perhaps marriage had softened him.

In the ensuing weeks Wyatt was questioned, probably with the use of torture, and his evidence implicated Princess Elizabeth in the uprising. In March she was also sent to the Tower. Wyatt was executed in April and that was the end of the open protests against the Queen's marriage plans.

In April I received some tidings in a letter from my daughter Anne, which ought to have cheered me.

'Mother dearest,' she began, 'I am writing to tell you of my marriage. In the presence of the Queen and in her own private Chapel at Richmond Palace, I have been married to Sir Walter Hungerford. He has been restored to his estate of Farleigh by the Queen, his father having lost it when he was executed with Thomas Cromwell.'

She wrote that she would not be leaving Court but would be staying on in her position as Maid of Honour to the

Chapter Thirty Five

Queen. I knew not whether to be happy or otherwise. I had heard of the late Sir Walter, father to Anne's husband and crony of Cromwell. He had been accused of several offences at his trial, among them of 'unnatural practices' and his wife had accused him of cruelty and of trying to poison her. I prayed that the son had inherited none of his father's unpleasant traits.

The following month Princess Elizabeth was released from prison and sent to Woodstock. The Queen was disposed to show her clemency as long as Elizabeth remained at Woodstock and made no further attempts to plot against her Majesty.

In early August I received a letter from James.

'*Good news, Mother,*' he wrote with his usual informality and spontaneity. '*Her Majesty has been married to Philip of Spain. They were wedded at Winchester Cathedral with Stephen officiating. I was there, of course, and only just made it back to London in time for the birth of my son. Yes, I am a father! Oh, I wish you could see the baby. He is so beautiful and perfect. We have named him Philip in honour of our new King.*'

Much as I would have dearly loved to see the child, I felt too old and tired to undertake another journey of such length.

James wrote again in December.

'*Mother dear, I write to keep you abreast of the latest happenings in the Capital. In my little home all is well. My darling Mary and our little Philip prosper. Mary*

sends her love to you. You will be pleased to hear that Cardinal Pole has returned to England. He arrived in great state as Papal Legate and was conducted to Lambeth Palace by Bishop Gardiner. The Cardinal seemed much tired from his journey but managed to speak for some time before granting absolution to England for the transgressions of the past twenty years. The other good news from here is that Her Majesty is expecting a child. We are all anxiously awaiting this event with joy and anticipation. No more for now, Mother dear. Long life and happiness be yours.
Your loving son, James.'

For the hundredth time I wished Arthur could have been present. On this occasion it would be to see his cousin returned from exile and in such triumph. My pleasure at each happy event was halved by not having my beloved to enjoy it with me.

George continued to be half-hearted in his enthusiasm for the new regime.

'It seems we are to be back under the thumb of Rome, then,' he said on reading my letter from James. 'I thought it more suitable when Englishmen were their own masters, I must admit.'

'Oh George,' I admonished, 'it is only in matters of religion that we look to Rome. Do not make a meal out of this.'

'And now the Heresy Law has been revived. Mark my words, there will be persecutions to follow and burnings a-plenty. But we need not worry overmuch I suppose,' he

Chapter Thirty Five

said, 'we are hardly likely to see you burnt for a heretic are we Mother?'

'George do not tease your mother!' ordered Jaquet. 'After all that she has suffered I am glad for her that she can at last worship peacefully in the way she pleases.' She looked kindly at me and I suppose I was grateful for her words, although they had a somewhat patronising tone. She and George are in no way religious and would be content to worship in any way, or not at all, whichever suited the dogma of the time.

George continued speaking, still educating us on the latest Statute from the Queen's Parliament.

'Every Act passed against Rome since 1528 has been repealed except one.'

'And what might that be?' I was tired of this discussion.

'Do not sound so impatient, Mother, this affects you,' George said. 'The Dissolution Acts remain in force. Otherwise you would have had to give back Frithelstock.'

'You know as well as I do George, that there are two reasons why that law has not been repealed. Firstly, the Queen has to leave the monastic lands with the present owners to buy their loyalty and secondly, there are no monks left now to give them back to anyway!' Although used to George's insensitivity, I was very upset by this discussion and left the room, all the guilt and shame I felt over my acquisition of Frithelstock returning in full force.

Thus, ended the year 1554. The following year began with another birth at Umberleigh. A daughter, whom they named Blanche was born to Jaquet. The house was filling with children, and with the familiar sounds of their play. Jane, carping old spinster that she was, continued to act as housekeeper. Jaquet managed her beautifully, allowing her just enough authority to keep her happy but taking the more important responsibilities upon herself. Mary helped with the babies and continued to be courted by the patient and understanding John Wollacombe. Philippa and James Pitts still visited quite often, though not as often as before. I think they both found Jaquet somewhat formidable.

'The burnings have begun,' George announced in a voice of gloom one cold February afternoon. He had just returned from a trip to Tehidy to check on the tin works and had travelled back through Launceston where the latest news had reached him. 'A fellow called John Rogers has been burnt at Smithfield for heresy. Do not look at me that way Mother,' he said as he caught the look in my eye.

'I will look at you any way I choose, George,' I said testily. 'If the man was burnt as a heretic then a heretic he undoubtedly was. I see no reason to feel sorrow for him. He made his choice.'

George was about to say more but I saw Jaquet flash him a look of warning and he fell silent. They had obviously decided between them that I was too old to argue with and may as well be humoured.

'Oh, a pox on both of you!' I said angrily and left the room. I knew I was old and irritable, and I cared not.

I continued to receive letters from James, but they told me little. I think the shine was beginning to wear off and he was now able to see past the gloss of the Queen's marriage which was being revealed as a sham.

In April he wrote briefly that the Queen's supposed pregnancy had been proved false. How I sympathised with her then, knowing full well how she felt to be so sorely

Chapter Thirty Five

disappointed. What James did not say but I heard from George, was that the King was being constantly unfaithful to his wife and was treating her most shamefully, showing her scant respect even when they were in public. Indeed, he was hardly ever together with her at all. In August he and his retinue left England, to the joy of the populace but to the sorrow of his despairing wife.

The persecution of heretics seemed to grow in intensity at this time and I began to wonder whether the Queen was not taking her grief and sorrow out on them.

'She has gone too far this time!' George returned from a trip to London in late October 1555 and stormed into the parlour where we women were quietly sitting with our needlework.

'Husband, that is no way to greet your womenfolk,' admonished Jaquet. 'Pray, calm yourself, and come to the dining room for some refreshment.'

George meekly did as he was bidden, and I exchanged a conspiratorial wink with Mary at the firm manner of Jaquet's dealing with the supposed head of our household. After he had been soothed and nourished and not before, Jaquet allowed her husband to re-enter the parlour and tell us the latest news from London.

'At risk of wounding the sensitive ears of you women,' George began, determined not to be entirely defeated and showing fighting spirit still, 'I have an unsavoury tale to tell. Anyone who would rather not hear it had best leave the room now.'

Naturally, we all stayed.

'Two of the finest minds of our century have been extinguished this last week in an act of such barbarity as numbs the mind,' he said. 'Hugh Latimer, Bishop of Worcester and Nicholas Ridley, Bishop of London have both been cruelly and unjustly burned at the stake for heresy.'

'George, dear, please mind what you say?' Jaquet jumped up and checked that the door was firmly closed. 'You have always in the past urged your mother to discretion, now do show some yourself.'

'My apologies, my dear,' George collected himself at last. 'I suppose I was so profoundly affected because I was there at Smithfield when the tragedy occurred. I not only witnessed the burnings but heard the comments of the crowds around me. Queen Mary has gained herself no friends by this act. I rather think Bishop Latimer gained some converts to the reformist movement by his last words as the flames were lit.'

'And what were they?' I asked quietly.

'He said,' began George, "... we shall this day light such a candle, by God's grace, in England as I trust shall never be put out."

The room was thrust into silence and as the daylight faded and the evening chill settled, we were at length roused by a housemaid who entered to light the fire.

'Well,' I said brusquely as we were stirred into activity once more, 'I can tell you of one whom he has not gained as a convert, and that is me.'

But my words were only greeted by more silence and I went to my bedchamber to prepare myself for supper.

In November we had a visitor. To my joy and surprise, it was James who came. I had begged him to visit us but had not dared to expect that he would. He arrived late one cold, wet day, shivering from hunger and exposure. I also saw

Chapter Thirty Five

lines of grief etched into his face. I ordered food to be sent to us in the parlour and had the fire built up. Whilst this was being attended to, he handed me a document.

'I have brought you a letter, Mother,' he said. 'Stephen wrote it to you as he lay dying.'

'Dying?' I asked. 'Do you tell me that Stephen is dead?'

'Yes, I do,' James replied. 'Please, just read the letter. I will talk to you after you have read it.'

With shaking hands, I broke the seal.

'My dear friend, this is by way of saying farewell to you. I am not sad to be leaving and I hope we will meet again in a more perfect place than this world has shown itself to be. These last months have not been happy ones for me. Since Pole came back to England, I have lost much of the sway I had previously held over the Queen, most notably my ability to curb her tendency towards fanaticism and since her husband left her, she has been like a woman possessed. We are seeing a return to the days of terror and this is not what I had hoped for when I so gladly placed the crown on her head. Long before the deaths of Latimer and Ridley I had sickened of the whole business but now I am more than ever glad to be shortly out of it. Goodbye my dear. May God be with you and keep you. Your Friend, Stephen.'

'Now we are to burn it,' said James as I put it down. 'That was his instruction when he gave it to me. We agreed that he should not write in the letter who was to be its recipient. Only I as the courier would run any risk.'

Obediently, I placed the document reverently in the flames and together we watched it burn and turn to ashes, just as Stephen's own dreams had done. Although I grieved for my friend, I understood that for him, the time had come. He was not one to rejoice in the martyrdoms any more than he had ever wished to become a martyr himself. He was safely out of it all now.

'James, is it really so bad?' I asked him. 'Has this reign which promised so much really turned so sour?'

'The Queen is not a bad woman, Mother,' he said evasively. 'It is her unhappiness which has blinded her, but none of us imagined that the return to Rome would usher in a new era of persecutions. All I and my friends ever wanted was to be allowed to worship true to our beliefs. We would wish that for men such as Latimer and Ridley also.'

James did not remain long in Devon. He had to return to his wife and son. He had also the huge task ahead of administering Stephen's estate but delivering Stephen's letter to me had been his first priority and for that I was grateful. He left after only two days, promising to return as soon as his business matters had been finalised.

The following month Reginald Pole was made Archbishop of Canterbury in place of Thomas Cranmer who had been confined in the Tower.

The next year, 1556, saw few changes. The Queen spent most of the year in retirement at Greenwich. I heard twice from Anne, but her letters were brief and unsatisfactory. I felt that she was unhappy but not a word did she write as to the cause. The heady excitement of Queen Mary's coronation day and the glorious visions we had all entertained at that time for a future of freedom and peace were now a fading dream, receding into the past just as all my other hopes and dreams had done.

By the time Thomas Cranmer followed Latimer and Ridley to the stake I, like Stephen Gardiner, was heartily sick of the whole business.

Chapter Thirty Six

In March 1557, Mary married her patient suitor, John Wollacombe. She looked beautiful again in her pale blue gown with a white lace head dress. We all felt a great sense of achievement at Mary's recovery and I stole a look at James Pitts as she made her vows. He was the one who had led us during those difficult early days with his wisdom and kindness. I felt a huge lump in my throat as she rode off to her new home at Roborough with her husband. This was the day we had all feared might never come, back in those dark days after our return from Calais.

The summer passed pleasantly enough, and autumn set in gently with no warning of what was to come. In late October, my life, which I had begun to almost enjoy once more, collapsed in pieces around me yet again. I can still see the messenger arriving, dressed in the Queen's livery and can remember the flurry of excitement and curiosity as he was admitted to the house. I can recall my not unpleasant surprise when he asked to see Lady Lisle.

'I am Honora Lisle,' I said.

He bowed low. 'My Lady, I have been entrusted to deliver this letter into your hands and no other's,' he said and handed me a rolled parchment bearing the Queen's seal. 'With your leave My Lady,' he said, bowed again and was gone.

Surprised, but still with no foreboding, I sat down and broke the seal. It was not from the Queen but from Reginald Pole, writing on the Queen's behalf.

Chapter Thirty Six

'My singular good Lady, I write to you both as messenger and kinsman. The former duty entails the imparting of dread news. The latter ensures that you have my sincere sympathy at your loss. On Tuesday last your daughter Anne Basset Lady Hungerford died in childbed at Richmond Palace. Much as it pains me to write what I next must tell you, Lady Lisle, write it I must. Your daughter was not happy in her marriage, and was, I believe, sorely mistreated by her husband. It is my opinion that, tragic though it must seem to you at this moment, her death came as a blessed relief to her. May she rest for eternity in the light of God's love.
Your assured friend, Reginald Pole.'

'No!' My scream of denial rang out through the corridors. The echo of it mocked me as it rebounded off the walls. 'No, no, no!'

I had no tears. The time for shedding tears was past. Jaquet entered the room furtively.

'What is it Mother? What have you been told this day?'

I looked coldly at her, the ice in my heart forming the words I spoke.

'I am not your mother,' I said coldly and walked past her and out the door. Somehow, I found my way through the clouds of misery which enveloped me and down to the riverbank. There I sat, on the spot where John Wallop had sat with me and tried to find some measure of comfort from his memory.

'Honora my darling, do not despair,' he said. 'I am with you my one and only love, with you forever. It is our destiny.' Then I saw him, not John Wallop but Arthur, my Arthur.

He was sitting just along the riverbank from me, the sun reflected off his golden hair. His skin was glowing as if he were lit from inside by a hundred candles and his eyes looked straight at me, loving me tenderly.

'Arthur?' I asked. 'Is it really you?'

'Yes, my love it is I. I told you I would come for you,' he said.

'Now, my love, have you come for me now?' I reached out to him, begging him to take me, wanting desperately to leave with him, but as I tried to touch him, he faded, and his voice faded also.

'Not yet, my dearest,' he said faintly, 'but I will come for you.' And he was gone.

'Arthur!' I screamed, tearing at my clothes and pulling at my hair, casting my headdress into the river in anguish. 'Arthur, come for me, come back, oh please come back and take me now!'

I felt myself pinioned by strong arms as George hurried to silence me and fight as I may I was no match for him. Still calling to my husband, I was half led, and half carried back to the house.

I could hear their voices through the door as I lay on my bed, whispering among themselves. I knew they discussed me and what to do with me now that I had lost my wits. Let them talk, I cared not. I cared for nothing but death. This life could deal me no worse blows than I had already received. I slept, awakened, and ate then slept again. How many hours, days or weeks passed I knew not. And still the voices whispered outside my door. The fog was lifting from my brain and I gradually realised that time had passed. The

Chapter Thirty Six

voices could not be the same as before! Stealthily I tip-toed across the room and placed my ear to the door.

'We must keep it from her at all costs.' It was George's voice. 'She must never know.'

'But George,' Jaquet spoke, 'she is bound to hear it somehow, from a servant or casual visitor. I know your mother only too well, she is not going to stay grieving in her room forever. This illness of her mind is already passing.'

'Then what do you suggest we do?' George asked, 'simply walk in there and tell her now? For pity's sake Jaquet, I cannot do it. Can you?'

'No,' she admitted, 'I cannot. I do believe it would kill her.'

I threw open the door.

'What would kill me?' I asked with blazing eyes. 'What merciful tale do you have to tell which would end this miserable existence for me?'

Their faces were aghast as they looked one to the other, daring each other to be the first to speak. But they remained silent.

'Speak!' I shouted. 'Do you imagine you can keep your silence now? I command you to speak!'

'Oh Mother,' George's voice was heavy with sadness, 'come back into your chamber and I will tell you.'

Jaquet took the opportunity to disappear as George followed me reluctantly into my room. He sat next to me on my bed and more gently than I had ever heard him speak he told me the only news which had the power to further increase my suffering.

'Mother, James is dead.'

Oh God, God, why did you do this to me? Why did you take my James? Is it something I did, some punishment I have merited for my sins that you needed to take my boy?

My groans of anguish rent the air and I felt myself rocking backwards and forwards on the bed, my arms holding tightly to my knees. Back and forth, back and forth I swayed ever more violently until George took hold of me and lay me down. There I continued to rock, curling myself ever more tightly into a ball and groaning still.

How long I lay there I know not. I ate nothing and drank only enough to wet my tortured throat. My brother John came from Kilkhampton and tried to help in the only way he knew how.

'Honora, dear sister, can we not pray together?'

I ignored him.

'Please, Honora, it pains me to see you like this. You must eat something, or you will die.'

I said nothing and remained quite still, curled in my ball facing away from him. He tried again.

'If you die as a result of refusing to eat, it is a mortal sin, Sister.'

Again, I responded not.

'Honora, dear love, I am unable to grant you the last rites if you persist in this behaviour.'

Faced with my continued silence he left me then. I felt myself getting weaker and weaker as the days came and went. I discovered that once the initial pangs of hunger have passed, the body becomes quite used to no food and as the mind clouds a state of peace descends. This is the condition I was in when I heard the door softly open and one by one all the curtains were pushed wide. I buttoned

Chapter Thirty Six

up my eyes against the glare, so long had I lain in darkness. Then I heard a chair being dragged to my bedside and felt a soft, gentle hand smoothing the hair away from my brow. The stroking continued until, curiosity getting the better of me, I turned my head to see who it was.

The person I beheld sitting by me was the only one who had the power to restore me to life. 'Oh, Nora, my darling, darling Nora.'

Over the next hours using some gentle persuasion and quite a bit of bullying, she drew me out of my depression and had me eating and drinking again. I had to take only small amounts at first as my throat and stomach rebelled at every mouthful but patiently and determinedly, she persisted. Once I had consumed all I was able to, she bathed and changed me and remained by my side while I drifted off to the best sleep I had had since hearing of James' death.

She has a power, that girl. I am not sure from whence it comes as she makes no bones about the fact of her lack of religious faith; a dangerous position which I have advised her frequently to only speak of in private.

The following morning John visited me prior to returning to his Parish. He was overjoyed at my recovery and praised George for his enlightened idea to send for Nora. I was still very weak but was able to apologise for my bad treatment of him. 'It was unforgiveable, John.'

'Oh no, Honora, not unforgiveable. Everything is forgivable except that which you were attempting to do before Nora arrived. To do away with your own life is the one and only unforgivable sin, which is why I was so distraught on your behalf, my dear.'

Nora entered the chamber then, accompanied by Elizabeth Husee. I could see that they were on good terms. This pleased me, since the faithful Elizabeth had failed in her many attempts to help me. Nora must have used all her tact and charm to win her over.

With my granddaughter by my side I began to recover much faster than anyone thought I would. Of course, I remained broken-hearted at the loss of two more of my children but with every word she spoke she was able to make me see that whatever happened there was always something to look forward to in this life.

'You have overcome so much, Grandmother. You have the strength to overcome this as well.'

'With your help, darling Nora, I can overcome anything but, my dear, this is proving a hard battle to win.'

'I know, Grandmother, I know,' and I think she did know. For even though she has never experienced tragedy in her own life, she has the ability to see inside my soul.

After a few weeks she began to speak of returning to her family at Potheridge. 'You have no need of me now, Grandmother, and I know my mother will be missing me sorely.'

I understood that but selfishly I begged her to stay with me and so she did. She was with me when George returned from one of his trips to London with some startling news.

'The French have laid siege to Calais and have defeated our troops there. Calais has now been reclaimed and is French territory once more.'

I felt the black gloom, which was never too far away, descend once more. 'So, it was all for nothing,' was all I said. All the suffering, all the deaths, our miserable existence in that hellhole, imprisonment, Arthur's death, all for nothing. It took all of Nora's skill to bring me out of my black despair on that occasion.

When I was feeling more like myself again, I thanked her. 'You see, Nora, I do still need you for who knows when a piece of news such as that will not tip me back into despondency once again?'

'Oh Grandmother, you are made of sterner stuff than that. You must gain your strength from inside yourself, not from me all the time. After all, I will not be able to remain by your side forever, will I?'

'And why not?' Selfish woman that I was, I wanted her all to myself.

As has happened before in my life, I was spurred into action by the need of a loved one. Poor Mary gave birth to a daughter, and almost immediately lost the baby to death. This is a frequent enough occurrence but due to Mary's own fragility of mind, Nora and I made the journey to her home at Roborough to be by her side. It is a short journey of only a few miles so took no time at all.

Mary's husband, that good, kind man, John Wollacombe was in a sad state since Mary had sunk back into her silent world. He, of course, had not known her in those days after Calais but was terrified as we had all told him about how she was at that time. Once again Nora worked her magic and within no time at all we had the old Mary back. Well, not quite the old Mary, but a very adequate, more mature version.

After two weeks we made the short journey back to Umberleigh. On the way I told Nora about the Mary of old, of her light-heartedness and beauty, of her love for Gabriel de Montmorency and of how it was that love affair which was to be the cause of our downfall when England went to war with France. How she bristled with indignation at the injustice of it!

The following year, I was still selfishly keeping Nora with me, but I could sense her homesickness, so we went to Potheridge for a month in the summer. Frances looked much better than when I had last seen her. Somehow or other she had managed to put a stop to having babies. Perhaps now that Thomas Monk had his three sons, he was leaving her alone. I did not ask. I saw Monk briefly on that visit but only for a day or so. Apparently, he had important business in Exeter which kept him from home most of the time. Frances seemed incurious as to the nature of his business, so I took my cue from her. Taking Nora with me, I returned to Umberleigh feeling a little lighter in my mind than after my previous visits.

In November of that year the Queen died. That poor, sad lady had never regained the popularity which had greeted her when she first acceded to the throne. Her reign had sunk into unpopularity and tragedy. Childless and abandoned by her husband she had become a figure of pity and her reign had turned into one of cruelty and martyrdoms. Although I have remained true to the Pope in my own life, I could not condone the hideous penalties she meted out to the Reformists. I think my own sufferings have made me a kinder person, more inclined to forgiveness. Meeting people such as Thirlby, a Reformist and one of the loveliest people I ever knew, has served to broaden my mind.

We now have another Queen, Anne Boleyn's daughter, Elizabeth. It says much about how my disposition has

Chapter Thirty Six

changed that I can even contemplate this without rancour. It is, after all, no fault of hers that she is her mother's daughter. Once Queen Elizabeth recovered from the pox, she set about ruling England with wisdom and common sense. I even have to admit that under her rule this country is prospering, and the fear has gone.

My grandson Arthur now lives at Umberleigh and George, together with his family has moved to Tehidy, taking me with them. It was painful to part from my Nora for we both know that we shall never meet again in this life. She is destined for greatness, that one. Oh, not the kind of greatness which I achieved, which is not greatness at all, but barren frippery, devoid of substance. Her greatness lies within herself and in her ability to improve the lives of those around her. I wish her well.

Elizabeth Husee is still with me and has shown no resentment over all the time I spent with Nora these last years. Elizabeth has been my steadfast and loyal companion since the darkest Calais days and was most understanding when I apologised for my neglect of her. 'Blood is thicker than water, My Lady.'

And so, I come to the end of my story and it finds me back in Cornwall, the land of my birth. It has proved a healing time for me, writing this narrative. I am not the same person as when I started out.

EPILOGUE

I have this day attended the funeral of my dearly beloved sister Honora Lisle which took place at Illogan Church. She was interred with all the ceremony and ritual of the old religion which is the way she would have wished it. She never could see that such trappings are not necessary. Perhaps they were to her, because she was unable to feel close to God without them. The tragedies which befell her had so undermined her faith.

The Priest who had given her the Last Rights spoke to me as her body was being lowered into the tomb. He described her face in the last moments of life, as the breath left her body.

'It was filled with the most unimaginable joy,' he said, 'and her eyes were fixed at a point close by and yet beyond. I do believe she saw God at that moment,' he said reverently.

'Did she speak at all?' I asked.

'Yes,' he answered with awe in his voice, 'her final words were, 'I knew you would come for me."

I did not reply as it would have been a pity to disappoint him.

They say she lost her wits and perhaps she did for a time, just after the twin shocks of Anne and James' deaths. But I saw her in 1562 when she was on her way to Tehidy to

EPILOGUE

spend her final years and she was as clear in her mind then as at any time in her life.

'What will I do?' she asked me. 'How will I spend my days?'

'Why not write about your life?' I suggested.

She snorted at such a preposterous idea and I put the thought out of my mind, but after the funeral George placed this manuscript in my hands. I have only glanced at it so far but can see that she has, indeed, written it all down.

My sister lived through one of the most turbulent and disturbing episodes in this country's history and she lived right at the centre of it, so who better to tell the tale? In my remote and secluded outpost at Kilkhampton I have managed to live unscathed by the events which tore her life asunder. But she would never have been content to remain so. Her dreams were always so very different to mine.

Rest in peace, dear sister, and may God be with you.

John Grenville 30th April 1566

AUTHOR'S NOTE

The story of Honora and Arthur first presented itself to me many years ago when I was studying my family history. I had traced my mother's lineage back to Arthur Plantagenet and Honora Grenville and went to the local library to find out more about them. This was back in the dark ages before the internet.

Perusing the history section, I came across a book entitled *The Lisle Letters* by Muriel St Clare Byrne. Feeling both excited and curious, I peeked inside and found an absolute treasure trove of information.

As I have written in the story, every document and scrap of paper was confiscated at the time of their arrest and these were intended to be used at Arthur's trial. They included personal papers, notes to and from the children, even shopping lists, as well as important documents and letters. As Arthur never came to trial the documents were never used and were kept locked away in the Tower of London.

There had been attempts to study them prior to Muriel St Clare Byrne's mammoth undertaking but in 1930, when she was a young student of Tudor England, she set herself the task of transcribing, annotating and arranging the documents. This took her several decades and the work was not published until 1981.

Thank you, Muriel.

BV - #0020 - 100120 - C0 - 216/140/28 - PB - 9781912419838